THE
UNTOUCHABLES

Ruthless People #2

J.J. McAvoy

The Untouchables

J.J. McAvoy

This ebook is licensed to you for your personal enjoyment only.
This ebook may not be sold, shared, or given away.

This is a work of fiction. Names, characters, places, and incidents are either products of the writer's imagination or are used fictitiously and are not to be construed as real. Any resemblance to actual events, locales, organizations, or persons, living or dead, is entirely coincidental.

The Untouchables
Copyright © 2014 by Judy Onyegbado
Ebook ISBN: 9781625177001

ALL RIGHTS RESERVED.

No part of this work may be used, reproduced, or transmitted in any form or by any means, electronic or mechanical, without prior permission in writing from the publisher, except in the case of brief quotations embodied in critical articles or reviews.

NYLA Publishing
350 7th Avenue, Suite 2003, NY 10001, New York.
http://www.nyliterary.com

ISBN-13: 9781507526743

DEDICATION

*Dedicated to those who aren't so polite in their minds.
I understand.*

Prologue

"If only these walls could talk...the world would know just how hard it is to tell the truth in a story in which everyone's a liar."
—Gregg Olsen

Melody

"You will all be queued in the moment we come back from commercial break. All you have to do is yell, 'Good Morning, Chicago!' You all look prefect," the producer for Good Morning Chicago said to all of us, as she and the rest of the camera crew moved to their places.

"Whose bloody idea was this again?" Liam muttered right beside me, placing his hand on my back and working downward.

"Liam."

He sighed, his hand stopping on my ass, as we all stood, waiting like one big happy family in the middle of the newly renovated park we had spent millions on for the "community."

To mark the grand opening, we were having a large neighborhood picnic. I found myself eyeing the crowd, as more and more people gathered with their stupid fanny packs and grubby hands all reaching for something free to stick in their mouths. The worst were the clowns who were walking around us handing out balloon hats.

"Don't you dare," I muttered to myself, as I watched the freak march its fat feet towards me. He pulled out a white balloon, twisting it until it was some sort of hat. Bowing comically, he handed it to me.

"A crown fit for a queen," he said.

Liam snickered beside me, and I fought the urge to snap at them both. Taking it, I smiled and placed it on my head.

"Thank you." *You stupid fuck.*

"And we're on in ten..." The producer pointed to us, pulling us back into focus.

We squashed up beside each other, as if we all loved each other so much that we were glued together. Normally Liam and I would be in the center of the family for these things, but not today. Instead, Olivia and her family stood in the center, while we were pushed off to the side.

It was Senator Colemen who was running for President after all, and since today was the day of the primary elections, good press couldn't hurt. Elections are just popularity contests. How much do you give? How much do you take? How put together is your family? Can you throw a football? Do you like The Beatles? That's all that mattered to them—no matter how much they pretended to care about the "issues." And all of that could be faked. We were all fakers; lying to people who were lying to themselves.

Three.

Two.

One.

"Good morning, Chicago!"

One

*"Every unpunished murder takes away
something from the security of every man's life."*
—*Daniel Webster*

Liam

I simply wanted to close my eyes. We had spent all damn day at that goddamned park, and now we had to spend the evening smiling for more political cameras. But that wasn't even the least of my problems. I wasn't sure what was coming, but I knew it was coming straight from hell.

I didn't want to deal with this. I didn't want spend my days and nights trying to uncover the mystery of Mel's mother. I didn't want this photo I held in my hands to be real, because now I would have to tell my wife why I'd been hiding the truth from her. She had searched for answers only to come up empty handed. This was another thing that I'd have to apologize for; I had Declan delete everything he'd found so that she couldn't get her hands on it. She thought she was working with him, but instead, he was doing everything he could to hide information from her.

She's going to fucking kill me. I sighed.

Eventually, she came to the conclusion that Vance had been lying to her. Sadly, he wasn't. I hated when liars started telling the truth; it was bad for business. Mel's mother was alive, very much so, in fact. We'd discovered that she was in the South of France right before she entered the US.

"So, I have to tell her," I said, as I pinched the bridge of my nose. The question was *how*. She was going to kill my sorry ass.

"Remind her that I was simply following orders. I'd prefer not to die tonight," Declan said as he frowned and adjusted his tie for this night's gala.

"Even that won't save you." Not that I let him around Melody alone anyway. She could take him, and he wouldn't try anything, but I enjoyed threatening him whenever he came too close to my wife. The only feelings he should have had for her were fear and respect.

We both stood silently in the security room. This was the calm before the storm, the break before the final wave.

"Have Anna meet me at the gala," I told him walking out of the room and into the study.

Fixing my cufflinks as I walked, I made sure to nod at the help as I walked past. *Rule Thirty-Three: Respect the help, they know more than they let on.*

None of them would say anything, but it was still a rule to live by. Entering the living room, I found my beautiful wife, her dark hair in perfectly curled waves, and brown eyes glued to the letter she finished up writing before handing it to Fedel, who stood in the corner of the room, almost as her shadow.

The rest of the family sat around the television like figures waiting to be painted. The only ones who looked out of place were Olivia's parents, and our new political strategist, Mina Sung. She and the Senator remained standing, as if they were afraid our furniture would eat them alive, while Mrs. Colemen sat by her daughter and squeezed her hand.

Why were they so worried? We would win by a landslide.

Melody nodded to Fedel as she rose gracefully from her chair and moved over to me. Declan, with his shady brown hair brushed, and black suit pressed, entered and made his way to Cora. He kissed her brown cheek before leaning on the arm of the couch beside her.

My eyes focused on Melody and the way her sliver dress clung to every inch of her body. Her olive skin begged for me to kiss it, and I longed to slowly peel her dress off of her...before she cut off my hands.

"You look beyond the realm of beautiful."

"Thank you," she said. "Now, what are you hiding from me, Liam? You've been acting odd for weeks. I've done the wife thing and I've given you time, but you're starting to piss me off," she finished fixing the bracelets on her arm.

"What do you think I'm hiding, *wife?*"

"Now you're avoiding my question." She frowned as she looked me over. Then she reached out and adjusted my bowtie. She was either going to try to strangle me with it, or she was simply annoyed at how I had tied it...it was more likely the former.

"Whatever you think I'm hiding, you're wrong."

"But you are hiding *something*."

Lucky for me, my mother turned up the volume on the screen.

"There you have it, America! It is official. Senator Daniel Colemen is this year's Republican Candidate and our contender for future president. As the primary favorite, this news shouldn't come to as a surprise to anyone. Tonight, he will be giving his victory speech at a Charity Gala hosted by the Callahans. His only child, Olivia-Ann, married Neal Callahan five years ago. Tonight, they celebrate, tomorrow, he has his work cut for him if he wants to defeat current president, Franklin Monroe."

"Your work cut out for you indeed," Mina said, as she muted the television, and turned back to face us.

"What? They all love me," Senator Colemen responded, grinning at the television from his seat, "I won by a landslide."

Told you.

My father shook his head as he poured himself a glass of brandy. "That's because every other candidate was an idiot."

"Or not rich enough to out-campaign you," Declan added.

"All of that is true, yes," Mina, said as she walked around the couch, and stopped right behind Olivia's chair. "The people do love you, the problem is her royal highness here."

"I haven't done anything." Olivia glared at her.

Melody and I had been trying our best to stay out of this. The less we were involved during the election, the less likely people would question any favors that came our way. Sadly, the Colemens were a bunch of political morons who had no idea how to work the system. I would have been surprised if they even knew where the goddamn White House was. It was the reason why I had personally hired Mina Sung; a second generation Korean-American, with an IQ almost as high as mine. I fought her for the top of the class while at Dartmouth. She was a political animal who would do anything to win. She was short, with thick-rimmed glasses, and silky black hair that was always pulled into a bun. I couldn't dismiss anyone who knew how to get their job done. For the last six months, she had all but sold her soul to destroy any candidate that stood in her way. Melody and I called her our little pit bull.

"That's the problem." I sighed. I did not have time for this stupidity. "The people think you're cold and heartless, with a rich husband, and a powerful daddy. They dislike you and will continue to dislike you until you stop showing them who you really are and start being who they want you to be."

"I couldn't have said it any better myself," Mina said as she adjusted her glasses, "The people aren't just picking a President, they're picking a first family. They like your father, they like your mother, but you're the black sheep who needs to be dyed white."

"Fine," Melody said, speaking up. "I will handle Olivia. Just keep working on everyone else."

"You?" Neal questioned worriedly, but with a hint of amusement.

"Yes, me," she snapped as she sat up. "The woman the public loves. The woman who bats her eyelashes at the cameras, who accepts stupid balloon crowns from annoying-ass clowns, and donates shitloads of money to so many kids that they want to name a fucking school library after me. I know how to act in public. Your wife, on the other hand, needs a few lessons. You should be glad I haven't thrown her off the bridge for the pity vote."

"You wouldn't." Mrs. Colemen's blue eyes widened as she stood up quickly. Standing next to her daughter they looked eerie similar, the only difference being Mrs. Colemen's wrinkled skin and shoulder length gray-blonde hair.

"She would," my mother replied. She hated when we fought. But you'd think she would be used to it by now. When *didn't* we fight?

"She would enjoy it too." Coraline grinned. Melody had "fixed" Cora, as she liked to say. In other words, Coraline now lived on the dark side of the moon with us.

Mrs. Colemen stood. "We're all family here…"

"No, *we're* family." I pointed at myself and my immediate family. "You are a chess piece, a stepping stone to our goals, Mrs. Colemen. Harsh, I know. But it's the truth, and it's better you hear it now just so we don't have a misunderstanding in the future. You hold no value other than arm candy to your husband. I thought we made that clear when we asked you to get remarried for the sake of this campaign. That's the deal *you* made. So save your life and sit back down, before you don't have legs to stand on. There are plenty of pretty blondes in the sea to replace you."

Shocked, she sat back down.

Welcome to the family.

Maybe now what she signed up for was finally hitting her. She wanted to be the first lady so that she could be the face for environmental and educational change. That was the deal. Melody and I were the hands that fed her, and if she bit us, we would pull out every one of her teeth.

"Well then, Senator, we should go over your speech once more," Mina told Mr. Colemen as she typed away on her tablet.

"I think I will follow along as well," Mrs. Colemen said. She smiled nervously before walking out.

"They are my parents, could you please refrain from threatening them?" Olivia hissed through her teeth, causing Neal to grab her hand.

"Why? We threaten you, and you're married to the family," Melody said, and I smiled.

Olivia looked over to Evelyn and Sedric, who seemed to be having their own private conversation, and stomped her foot like the brat she was. My parents couldn't do shit, nor would they. Evelyn…well, my mother was happy when my father was happy, and as long as she could throw as many parties as she wanted, she was fine as well. My father was out of this "business;" he was keeping his hands clean and instead focused on our more legitimate affairs. The Callahan family didn't just control the drug trade. Hotels, restaurants, spas, clubs…we owned so many of them that I've honestly lost count. Not to mention the amount of shares we now owned in some of the world's biggest corporations due to the Giovanni family, which now really consisted of just Mel. The Callahans hid our secret behind small business ventures over the generations, but since Melody had all but rebuilt the Giovanni by herself, she needed a quicker way to hide her blood money. Between us both, we truly did own this city…this state, and Olivia, after all this time, still didn't seem to understand that.

"This family is fucked in the head and so dysfunctional," Olivia snapped, walking towards the door, "We're supposed to have each other's backs and protect one another. Yet all you ever do is remind us that you wouldn't hesitate to kill any of us."

"Apparently we don't remind you enough." My eyes narrowed while I moved towards her. Her eyes widened, and Neal immediately stood between us.

"Step aside, brother," I said softly. "I won't hurt her."

Neal's jaw clenched, and he only took a slight step to the right, allowing me to step in front of Olivia.

"Every day, you bitch and whine at us, and everyday, you manage to wake up. That isn't luck, it isn't even the will of God; it's because you're family. That is the only reason your tongue hasn't been ripped from your throat. You're alive because my brother, whom I've come to care for, was stupid enough to fall in love with you. Over the years, you've been given the freedom of speech, but now I'm revoking that right." I cupped the side of her face and could feel Neal flinch beside me. "Never again will you ever tell me what this family is supposed to be like. For if you do, Olivia Callahan, there won't be enough love in the world to protect you from me."

When I pulled back, she was paler than the blue dress she wore.

"Maybe we should all rest privately for the remainder of the evening before the gala," my mother said as she walked over to me and wrapped her hand around my own. She pulled me back, giving Neal a moment with Olivia.

"Brilliant idea, Mother." I kissed her on the cheek before turning to Melody. Seeing the look of lust in her eyes made me forget everything else.

I reached out for her hand. "Wife."

She shook her head. "Olivia and I are going to work on fixing her public appearance before this gala."

"I think Olivia has had enough lessons for one night," my father said, looking over at the still pale woman in Neal's arms. It made me sick; she looked like one of those stupid girls on the cover of those romance novels.

"There's still some time before the gala," Melody said. "Hopefully this won't take long."

"Should I come along as well?" Neal asked, which was code for, *you're not going anywhere with my wife unless I follow.*

Melody didn't back down, nor did I think she would. "Olivia doesn't want you to come along. Or at least that's what she told Adriana when she was told of our plans this evening."

Only God knew what that meant.

"I'll be fine, Neal," Olivia declared, letting go of him.

"Am I coming along?" Coraline asked cheerfully, almost knocking over her chair. Declan leered at her, wrapping his arm around her waist. She glared at him, but didn't push him away. Therapy was helping them...slowly, but it was helping.

"Sorry, Cora, it's a private meeting," she replied.

Before she could leave, I pulled her back, ignoring the excitement that ran through me just by touching her.

"What are you up to, love?" I questioned, kissing her deeply when she opened her lips to reply.

"You will find out soon enough," she declared. "We'll be back within the hour."

I had a bad feeling about this, but Mel killing Olivia was the least of my worries right now.

MELODY

I left him and the rest of the family behind, knowing full well that Olivia would follow. The whole night had gone so perfectly, you would have thought I could see the future. However, with each passing day, Olivia was becoming a bigger problem. She didn't seem to understand the world around her. She couldn't see the bigger picture, and the longer she stayed blind to the reality of our lives, the bigger liability we faced. Family, for us, was everything, but it was also the one thing that could destroy us.

Cops didn't bring down the greatest bosses in history, they brought down their families, the people they provided for and protected. It was the idiots who were lucky enough to either share DNA or have a ring on their finger. They enjoyed all the rewards—the money, the fame, and the respect. But none of them really understood how fragile it all was, especially the wives. Our weakest link was Olivia, and I would be damned if I let her continue on the way she was.

It had taken Liam and I weeks of planning to figure out exactly what we wanted. It wasn't like we just woke up one morning and said, 'let's own the White House.' We went back and forth over whether or not to use Senator Colemen, since he was already so close to the family. But it was because of that reason that he was perfect.

"Where are we going?" Olivia asked, once we stepped into the garage. Fedel handed me the keys to my white Aston Martin before handing me a gun.

"Get in the car, Olivia," was all I said to her, but she was frozen with her blue eyes glued to the weapon in my hand.

"Fedel." I sighed, taking a seat behind the wheel.

"Let go of me!" Olivia yelled, as he grabbed her and forced her into the car.

Holding her down, he buckled her in before slamming the door shut and I stomped on the gas.

"What the hell do you want with me, Melody?" she screamed.

"I want you to be a Callahan, not a Colemen," I replied, relaxing into my seat.

"What the fuck does that mean? I *am* a Callahan. I was one before you were, remember?" She huffed, glaring out the window.

I laughed; she so badly wanted something to trump me with. "No, you are a Colemen hiding in Callahan's clothing. You bitch like a Colemen, hide like a Colemen, and have no balls like a Colemen. Which means you look like your mother, but act like your father. So scared of what you could actually be if you put forth the effort. Seems like Liam and I have to teach your entire family how to grow balls."

"Thank you, Obi Wan Kenobi, but I don't need, nor do I want, your help. Take me home or I will walk!" she snapped, as she twirled her blonde hair between her fingers.

It bothered me.

"In a pair of seven hundred dollar Jimmy Choos? That will be the day." I was sort of impressed she knew who Obi Wan Kenobi was though. Must have been due to Neal.

"Whatever game..."

"I don't play games, Olivia. Games are for children. I work. Every moment of every damn day, I am working. I work so that this family—*our* family—can move mountains. I work so that I never want for anything, so that I can obtain anything I wish. Right now, I'm working on you, so shut the fuck up." I wanted to bash her fucking skull in.

Luckily, she didn't say anything else, and we soon reached our destination; a cliff that overlooked the beautiful Lake Michigan.

"Sorry, my gate doesn't swing that way," she joked, but it wasn't at all funny. "It's a pretty spot for a date though."

"Get out, Olivia."

She glared like always, but did as she was told.

Stepping around to the back of the car, I opened the trunk. "It's time you grow up, Olivia."

"You know what, Melody—" She stopped the moment she looked down and saw the naked man curled up in a ball in the trunk.

Backing away slowly, she covered her mouth, and her eyes shined with tears. The man struggled against his chains and screamed against the gag in his mouth. Every sound he made, Olivia shook. Finally, she threw up everything she had just eaten and sobbed.

"We'll be right back. Family meeting," I told him before closing the trunk again. Hopping up on top of it, I watched her as she tried her best to calm down.

"What did you do?" she screamed.

I thought it was obvious.

"He's one of the men who raped you, isn't he? Matt, Harvey's best friend? I brought him here to help you."

"You aren't helping me! I don't need your help! I never asked for your fucking help!" she roared, causing her whole body to shake.

Sighing, I sat forward. "You told no one but me. Not Neal, not Evelyn, not even your parents. I personally tracked your records. Searched the entire cyber universe and found a rape kit, simply logged in as Courtney A. O'Brien, height: 5'8, blood type: AB, hair color: Blonde, eye color: Blue... She's you. CAO, your initials backwards? You were scared and couldn't come up with a lie fast enough. Your parents were nobodies who were on the verge of being somebodies. You went to the hospital and even filed a police report. All of which were so easily found once I had that name. Every year, on the anniversary, you end up in the hospital for violent vomiting and weight loss..."

"Shut up, Melody!" She clamped her hands over her ears as if that would help.

"Every year, you've been waiting for someone to connect the dots. To give you justice, to help you. That's why you came to me...."

"I came to you because you wouldn't get out of fucking bed!" she cried.

"You came to me because Adriana spoke to you. Deep down, you wanted this. You were crying out for this. You wanted me to find your rapists and deep down, you didn't want them to go jail. You wanted them dead. You wanted them to suffer as you've suffered. You came to me so I could make you a Callahan." I jumped off the trunk and grabbed hold of her, forcing her hands from her ears.

"You're waiting for someone to save you, but no one can do that. You need to save yourself. I can help you. But I can't save you, Olivia. You're a motherfucking Callahan. We are never victims; we are the victimizers. The penalty for coming after us is, and will always be, death. It's time for your retribution."

She looked so lost as I handed her the gun. "I'm not like you, Mel. I can't kill another person. I'm not a murderer.

This isn't the justice I wanted," she declared, once again lying to herself.

I hated liars. Walking back to the trunk, I opened it and the stupid pig squealed again.

"Looks like you get to go back to Cancun," I said to him. "Don't worry about the girl you raped and murdered there, we made sure to clean it up. Her *grieving* parents will be burying her this weekend…"

"What are you doing? You can't let him go!" Olivia screamed, but couldn't bring herself to come any closer to the car.

"You wanted justice, well, according to the law, this is justice. There is a statue of limitations on rape. Courtney A. O'Brien isn't even your real name; your case would be thrown out. I'm not going to kill him. He isn't my demon. So my hands are tied," I said, pulling the pig out of trunk. I smirked at his bound wrists. "Poor word choice, huh?"

Olivia said nothing, so I pushed more. "I'm hoping this will serve as a lesson. But I doubt it. Pigs like you can't help but roll in the mud. Where will Harvey hide you now once you tell him? He's the one who sent you to Mexico after Olivia here became a Callahan, wasn't he?"

Pulling the gag from his mouth, he tried to speak, but Olivia held the gun to his skull.

"Don't speak, just run far away," was all she said to him. *Really? Kill him!*

The pig didn't even wait for me to unbind his legs before he tried to run. He fell to his knees, but still tried to run.

"Remember, no means no." I frowned, and just when I had given up on her, Olivia pulled the trigger. Not once, not twice, but she emptied the magazine into his body.

"NO means no! I said no! I said no!" she screamed at his body before collapsing onto me. I wasn't a hugger;

truthfully, I hated all forms of touch except Liam's. However, she needed something, so I let her hug my waist as I petted her head.

"A Callahan, through and through."

Progress.

Liam

"Mr. Callahan!" The vultures with cameras called out once I exited the car. Adjusting my jacket, I waved at them, smiling my pretty boy smile...they ate it up like cake.

"Who is this handsome fella?" A hand ran across my back and I spun Melody around, dipping her down.

"Liam Callahan, and you are?" I smiled as she rolled her eyes.

"Melody Callahan. Can you bring me up now please?" she asked sweetly, causing the vultures to laugh.

"Well if it isn't my lucky day." I grinned, pulling her closer to me and whispering, "Where have you been, love, and why did you change?"

She was now dressed in a blood red dress that hugged her every curve.

"Not now, Liam," she said through her smile before turning back to the cameras.

"Mr. and Mrs. Callahan," a reporter called out." Many say that your support for Senator Colemen was what has gotten him to this point. Are you only voting for him because of your sister-in-law?"

"Of course not," Mel replied kindly. "We support Senator Colemen because we think he is the best man for the job. He is kind, outgoing, and hardworking. But above even that, his politics are what I support."

"Last year, your father was reportedly killed by a bombing in Turkey, of which no one was convicted. If Senator Colemen becomes president, he will be one of the first Republican presidents staunchly against the death penalty and against war. Victims of terrorism, like your father, will get no justice," he stated, and I felt the urge to put a bullet between his eyes.

"Can't speak much on war, but as a Catholic, I don't believe in the death penalty. But let's save all the political questions for the candidate. I'm a voter, just like you." She winked at him and he looked like he wanted to cum in his pants.

"I wholeheartedly agree with my wife," I said like I was reading a cue card, causing them to laugh.

We only stood for a second longer before making our way in, and I spotted Anna's wavy long blonde hair right away; she couldn't have been here long—technically she shouldn't be here at all, but she was family no matter what. When I called, she answered, even when she didn't want to.

"I'll be right back, love," I whispered to Melody as I kissed her cheek.

She looked over to the woman in the back dressed in green, and I took pleasure in the way her eyebrow twitched. "Who is she? You had a thing for blondes, didn't you?"

"She isn't..." I sighed. "I'll explain later."

I loved when she was jealous.

Kissing her again, my tongue brushed against hers and I enjoyed how sweet she tasted when she moaned in my mouth. I had to force myself to pull away.

"When you moan like that baby, I want nothing more than to hike up that dress, spread your thighs, and fuck you until your legs go weak," I whispered in her ear.

"Then do it," she dared me, a devious smile on her red lips. "Fuck me so hard that I slide to the ground when you're done. Make me scream your name until my voice is gone, *please,* Liam. Please fuck me."

Jesus Christ. I couldn't speak, I was so turned on. My cock throbbed in my now-too-tight pants, and I longed to give her exactly what she wanted, exactly the way she wanted it.

"Your friend is waiting." She winked at me before wiping the lipstick from my lips, and moving away from me.

I watched her go, and I longed to follow.

Later. Right now I had business.

Turning back, I made my way through the crowd towards Anna. I nodded for her to follow me up the stairs, leaving the poor bastard she was flirting with where he stood. I understood how he felt. Anna did her best to remain unseen as she walked the top balcony that overlooked the ballroom.

"Speak quickly," I said to her as I looked down at my wife.

"Nice to see you too, cousin. Did you cut your hair? It's nice…."

"Anna."

She laughed. "I ran the photo through the Interpol database and yes, everything you've found out about her is true. She goes by Aviela, Aviela DeRosa, of the DeRosa crime family. My contacts say she's the best hired gun on the western side of the globe. Her father, Ivan DeRosa, hasn't been seen above ground in seventeen years. We still have no idea what he looks like."

"The DeRosas." *Goddamn it.* The moment we took down one family, another rose in its place.

"The DeRosas," she confirmed. "They've never been big in the states, but they're one of the most ruthless crime families in Europe and Brazil. From what I can see, this

Ivan was using the Valero as his face in order to remain hidden. There have been all kinds of reports and charges filed against him, but the man is fucking untouchable. Aviela takes out the biggest competition or anyone on the rise."

"I know." It was the reason why we stayed out of Brazil for the most part. The rest of South America we had our hands in, but Brazil…it wasn't worth losing men over. As long as the DeRosas stayed down there we didn't have a problem…but if Aviela was a DeRosa, it meant that Melody was from not one, but *two* criminal families. This shit was getting foul quickly.

Anna handed me a USB drive.

"What is this?"

"Her kill list. Nothing is confirmed, but I'm willing to bet she was the one that killed every last person on that list. She leaves a calling card somewhere at the scene. White gloves. I have no idea what it means but…"

"That is all, Anna," I cut her off.

"Liam, if they're coming for you, you might want to back down from this one. You're all insane, but the things the DeRosas do…I've been doing my best to cover up, and pin almost everything you all have asked me to on other families. But even I have bosses Liam, I don't run Interpol. There are hundreds of people working on this shit, and there's only so much I can do to keep you clean. Slow down, batten down the hatches, before this gets out of control—"

"You see that woman down there?" I asked, looking at Melody.

"Your wife?" She frowned.

"She has a right to know who her mother really is." *Even if it may drive her off the deep end and crashing into flames.*

"Shit," Anna said. "She's a DeRosa? Shit."

My thoughts exactly.

"I don't know what they want, Anna, but this isn't going to just go away. For now just stay and keep watch…besides, out of the hundreds of people working on this, you never know who's on our side." I winked at her. It was funny how she thought she was the only spy working in the government.

"Liam—"

"Enjoy the gala Anna," I said as I left her.

For now, I would have to lock away the monster within me that wanted nothing more than to burn my mother-in-law alive. I had to pretend to be an honorable member of society who didn't believe in the death penalty, and went to church on Sundays. For tonight, I would be Dr. Jekyll, and come tomorrow, I would become Mr. Hyde.

When Mel's eyes met mine, I could only imagine the monster that would be unleashed once she knew.

Two

"Murder is like potato chips: you can't stop with just one."
—*Stephen King*

Olivia

"Are you okay?" Neal whispered into my ear as we danced for the tenth time.

I couldn't answer. I could only hold onto him. I gripped him so tightly, you would think this was the last time we would be together.

I had to tell him, but I was so scared. I was scared of what he would think, which was stupid, really. Neal was a murderer, and now, I was too. But he liked the fact that my hands were clean. He always said he wasn't good enough for me, but it was the other way around. The one thing that I had—my bloodless slate—was gone. What bothered me was how happy I was to pull that trigger. I wanted to kill that animal. It replayed over and over again in my mind.

Matt and the rest were like targets, and I had taken one down and was ready to move on to the next.

I was ready to kill again.

I *wanted* to kill again.

It was wrong, but it was justice, *my* justice, just like Melody had said. I felt like I had been in the dark for so long, locked away from the rest of the world, and now I was a step closer to being free; to running wild with the other monsters.

"I killed a man tonight, Neal," I whispered as we danced, and I felt him freeze.

He pulled back and his hazel eyes stared into mine, as if he would be able to tell from just looking at me. He frowned before pulling me away from the dance floor. He didn't speak, yet somehow, everyone knew to get out his way. He didn't stop until we were outside with the driver.

"Mr. Callahan…"

"Keys," he snapped at the man. "NOW!"

The man checked all over himself before grabbing the keys and handing them to Neal. Opening the door for me, he slammed it shut before sitting in the driver's seat. When they said zero to sixty in three seconds, they weren't kidding. He slammed down on the gas so hard you would think we were drag racing.

"Say something Neal, please," I begged him.

He didn't. He just sat, rubbing his lip with the back of his thumb as he drove further and further down the road.

Déjà vu, I thought as I looked out into the night sky.

He only stopped when we were in front of the mansion. Sighing, he leaned back against the seat. "I'm going to figure a way to get you out," he whispered, taking my hand.

"What?"

He kissed my hand. "I thought if we just laid low, if we did what they asked, then eventually we would all learn to live with one another. But they keep crossing the line! Melody had no right to force you to do anything involving the business. She's morphed Coraline into this bloodthirsty kitten over the last few months, and now she's trying to fuck with you. I may not be able to kill her, but I will protect you. I will not have her corrupt you any more than I already do on a daily basis. She's crossed the fucking line!"

I don't deserve him.

"She was helping me," I whispered, trying my best fight back the tears that were forming, but it was in vain; it burned as they blinded me.

"Helping you?" he snapped. "This is how she helps you? She makes everyone into a monster so she can feel better about herself. She's sick! She is…"

"Helping!" I yelled back, wiping my eyes.

Just rip off the bandage.

"I was…" I stammered, "I killed one of the men who raped me. I shot him, until there were no bullets left. I got a tire iron and smashed his head, over and over again. Then Melody helped me throw his body off the cliff and change my clothes. I'd do it again. I *will* do it again! She was helping me! She's helped me get rid of one of my demons, Neal."

It all came out as he stared at me, as if he didn't know what to say or where to start.

"You were…" He couldn't even it say it.

"Raped. R-A-P-E-D. I was forced into a room by a group of assholes in college and raped again and again and again before they got tired of me and left. I think about it daily, and I hate myself. I was raped. No one knew. Not you, not Evelyn. Not my even my parents."

"But you told Melody?" He was trying to stay calm, but he was shaking as much as I was.

"She makes you talk!" I said. "You look into her eyes and you know she can walk into the darkest part of your mind and still manage to smile for a photo. I don't know why I told her. I was trying to bow to the fucking queen like you said. I wanted her to understand! She did. She understood better than anyone else. She found one of them."

"I could have done that!" he roared at me. "I would have gladly done worse than that five years ago when I married you! I don't understand why you didn't tell me!"

"Because I was ashamed, because I wanted to deny it, because you would have killed them." I stopped, thinking about the last part. "I...I...needed to kill them myself."

That was what I needed.

We sat there, tense, for what seemed like hours, just staring at the house.

"Next time, bash their heads in while they're alive and then shoot them," Neal whispered. "The longer they suffer, the better." He took my hand again.

The stupid tears wouldn't go away.

"Okay," was all I could think to say.

"And I will be there when we find the others."

"Okay."

"I'm staying. I love you, and you can tell me anything, always. I'm going to be there, and Melody can go screw herself."

"I love you too. And I'm going to tell her you said that."

He paled, and I wanted to have that effect on men one day...even my husband.

Three

"You should have died when I killed you."
~ John le Carré

Melody

"What are you hiding from me, Liam?" I asked, as we danced in the middle of the ballroom.

He pulled me closer to him. "I could say the same for you, love."

"True, but I'm discussing those secrets with family, not outsiders." I searched around for the blonde he had spoken to, but she had disappeared and no one else seemed to notice or even care. She wasn't somebody with title or fame, but either *had* or *knew* something of worth to be able to speak with Liam privately.

"Are you jealous, love?" He squeezed my ass. "Because you shouldn't be. I love you and you alone."

"That's the fifth 'I love you' you've said tonight. I'm really going to kill you once I find out what you did, aren't I?" I said calmly. I would remain so until he gave me a reason not to be. I truly wanted to beat the shit out of him until he told me, but the sick fuck would more than likely enjoy it.

He sighed. "You, love, may just kill me when I tell you."

"Liam…"

He kissed me so hard and passionately, he all but lifted me from the ground.

"After the gala," he whispered as his eyes begged me to drop it, "okay? After the gala?"

I didn't like this. I didn't like this at all. Whatever he was hiding, that made him act like this—like I was a time bomb waiting to explode—was probably going to make me do just that.

"Do you ever wish you could be like them?" he asked, nodding at the political interns helping with Senators Colemen's campaign. They were all around the same age, if not older, than us.

"You mean do I wish my life was filled with nothing but exams and school, getting a degree I won't use for a job I hate, and student loans I can't pay off? A life of binge drinking, and horrible sex that I think is good because of the binge drinking?" I looked them over. "No, I don't wish I could be them. It sucks to be them. That's why they're here, hoping that if they stand close enough, and say the right things, they have a chance to escape their shitty lives."

"Don't hold back, love, it's not in your nature." He laughed, spinning me around before bringing me back to him. "You've never wished your life was simple?"

"It is. I get what I want and if you stand in my way, I will wipe you off the face of the earth, then go after everyone who shares your DNA. Simple." I smiled.

He smirked as well. "Now you're just trying to turn me on."

"You're always waiting to be turned on." Proving my point, I pushed my breasts up against him and I could feel him hardening against my stomach.

"Did you get a smaller gun?" I asked, trying to feel around for it.

He moaned as I grabbed him through his pants, squeezing tightly before pulling away. I was having so much fun toying with him tonight. His green eyes glared at me as I turned to Sedric and Evelyn cutting into their dance.

"Evelyn, do you mind if I cut in? Liam wishes to dance with you."

Evelyn eyed me carefully, as if she could read my damn mind. The woman had her own set of superpowers, I swore.

Shaking her head at me, she kissed Sedric before turning to Liam who glared at me evilly.

"Watch out, Sedric has two left feet. It's taken me years to work around it." She winked before taking her son's hands.

"She exaggerates." Sedric huffed, offering me his hand.

"I'm sure, just don't step on my toes." If he did, I would ram my heel into his knee.

"I will do my best, your highness." He laughed, looking around the room. "I must say, your plan for this country is worrying me."

"Why, because it's possible?" I asked.

He nodded. "Exactly. I would have settled for a Supreme Court judge. But, then again, I no longer have that type of power."

"No, you do not." He always seemed to forget. "My father gave up power because he was dying. Why did you? You're young…enough, and you don't seem to be dying."

"You know the answer to that." He sighed, looking over to Evelyn. "This was never supposed to be my life. I saw what my father did for a living and he enjoyed it. He enjoyed it like you and Liam enjoy it. He saw that and only forced me to work harder. I never understood why my older brother was going to take over."

I already knew this but let him speak anyway.

"He died young," he whispered sadly. "We all die young. He was around your age then. I had just turned eighteen and met Evelyn. We fell hard for each other. Any moment I could find, I was with her, which in turn led to her getting pregnant with Neal. My plan was for us to take my inheritance and live on some remote island somewhere. But, when my brother died, I had to step forward. I hated the life with a passion."

"And now you can't let go."

He was good at what he did. The stories of young Sedric were the things that nightmares were made of.

"It's like a possession," he whispered. "It crawls into your soul and takes root. You have no control over it. You allow it to grow, because it helps. It's the reason you can let blood flow across the floor like fine wine and not flinch. It helps you become the monster you need to be. The only side effect is that it's always there. No amount of holy water can wash it off. So there's no letting go. I will forever be who I allowed myself to be, and the person I allowed myself to be enjoys the chaos."

Truer words were never spoken.

"Evelyn must love hearing about that."

"She understands. There are two halves of me, always at odds with each other, but she always wins out." He chuckled glancing back at her.

"True love conquers all," I mocked, rolling my eyes before glaring at Liam.

"So, why are you torturing my son?" he asked as we danced much slower than everyone else.

"Because he's keeping things from me. Important things you wouldn't happen to know anything about, would you, my dear father-in-law?" I looked into his eyes and he raised an eyebrow at me.

"So now I see that my thoughts are worth something?" he questioned.

"Yes, now they are. So again, what do you know?" I hated when people made me repeat myself, why waste words?

"Nothing, dear daughter-in-law," he replied, spinning me around a little awkwardly, but I adjusted. "Which bothers me, seeing as how Liam was speaking to Interpol."

I stopped. "Repeat that last part again."

He froze, realizing that he did in fact know something that I didn't.

"Sedric, now is the time to use more words, not less." I dug my nails into his arm.

"Anna, the blonde woman he spoke with upon entering, she's family—or ex-family. Liam's second cousin, her parents planned to betray the family, my father killed them. Anna was given money, but no connections and went into…"

"I don't give a shit about who she is or how she came into being. I want to know why the fuck Liam is speaking to Interpol." Now I was pissed, pulling myself away from him, I turned towards Liam and his mother.

They were speaking causally, but after tonight, they wouldn't be speaking at all if he didn't tell me what I wanted to know.

"Once again, Evelyn, I'm so sorry," I cut in, glaring into Liam's eyes. "But it seems your son and I need to have a little chat."

Evelyn rolled her eyes. "Please don't make a scene, dear. The press."

"Of course, there are private rooms here, correct?" I didn't even wait for her to answer. Instead, I brushed past Liam and towards the grand staircase.

I could feel him, his warmth, and the heat rolling off him as he followed me. Opening one of the doors, I let him in first.

He looked me in the eyes before stepping inside. Sadly, the sight of Coraline riding Declan with her head thrown back and his face buried in her chest kissing her breasts, greeted us.

"OUT!" I yelled, causing them both to jump.

Coraline shot off him and pulled the sheet around herself quickly, her brown eyes wide and shocked.

Declan on the other and was livid. "Are you fucking kidding me? This is the first time we've been this close to each other in months!"

"This is me giving a fuck. Get out, or I swear, Declan, I will feed you your own dick."

"You should go." Liam sighed, looking for a mini bar.

Declan grumbled.

"Now."

"I'm going! For the love of Christ, Liam, did you tell her already?" he yelled, grabbing his boxers.

Liam groaned loudly. "Why is it that you and Neal can't seem to keep your goddamn mouths shut! What is she made of, Kryptonite? The moment she comes by the both of you can't hold water? When I say shut the fuck up, that means shut your bitch-ass up!"

He told his cousin…before me?

"Declan, sit back down, you too, Coraline. Both of us may be widows at the end of the evening."

Declan stood up, but I pulled a gun on him and he sat back down.

"Somebody better start explaining before I start shooting." I waited and neither of them spoke. "Have you people been setting me up?"

"What the hell, Melody, seriously?" Liam said.

"Well you see, things aren't adding up for me, Liam. You're talking to people; you're talking to the police. Tell me to my face, you bastards. Have you been playing me for a fool? You're setting me up, aren't you?"

He just stared at me dumbfounded...and hurt. "You really think after everything we've been through that I would betray you? You're my wife."

"Think of it as a compliment. I know how much you like power, Liam. With me out of the way, you could take—"

"We found your mother," he snapped at me, as his nostrils flared. "I had Declan back-hack you, he was deleting and rewriting codes as you searched because I wanted to be sure what we were dealing with before sending you down the goddamn rabbit hole. I was trying to protect you because I was worried about what this would do to you; how this would hurt you. Everything I do is for *you*, and you think I would sell out? For what? Power I already have?"

I looked back to Declan who now stood with Coraline behind him, neither moving, nor daring to speak.

Slowly, my hand lowered as I tried to think.

"My mother was killed in a plane crash by the Valero."

"You mother, goes by the name Aviela DeRosa, and she controlled the Valero, or at least your grandfather did as part of the DeRosa Family. She's a pit bull for him, a hired gun. Here," he pulled out a flash drive, "It's a list of every last person she's killed. Your mother, is a cold-blooded killer. You grandfather, is a Mafia Boss, and they knew about you, yet still they had the Valero come after us. Most likely, he sent them after us. Now that the Valero is gone, who knows who will come next?" He snapped.

My mind was spinning.

"You should have told me," I whispered, trying to think, but I was drawing a blank. "You were fucking out of line! How dare you Liam! Who the hell do you think you are?"

"YOUR HUSBAND!" he roared back, "You want an apology? Ask your mother, better yet, ask your bloody father. They were the ones lying to you for *years*, not me! I did what

I had to do. You would have emotionally compromised everything. Not because you're weak, but because you're human. Everything you are is a product of what happened to you. You are who you are because your mother was supposedly murdered. But she wasn't. Finding that out—"

"You think you know me! What, after only a year? Screw you, Liam Callahan. I am who I am because I *made myself* this way. I had a right to know! But instead, you went behind my back like a two bit crack-headed bitch." My whole body shook, all I could see was red.

"I went behind your back because I wanted to come to you with all of the information, not half of it. Why? Because I knew you would overact!"

He thought I was overreacting?

"This is me overreacting," I hissed, pointing my gun at him.

"Mel—"

I fired.

Fuck him! Fuck them all.

Four

*"Honestly, I don't understand why people get
so worked up about a little murder!"*
—Patricia Highsmith,
RIPLEY UNDER GROUND

Liam

"**B**ITCH!" I yelled, as I grabbed my thigh. This was the second time this woman—this goddamn cursed wife of mine—had shot me. The bullet grazed my inner thigh, but it still hurt like a motherfucker...damn her. If it weren't for her damn silencer, the whole goddamn hotel would have heard. I had noticed both Declan and Coraline make their escape.

"Now you have a matching set." She glared, and without thinking, I lunged for her legs like a damned linebacker, forcing her to the ground and pinning her arms down.

"You're getting on my last damn nerve woman!" I hollered as she clawed at me.

"I could say the same about you!"

"I swear to God almighty, if you do not calm the fuck down, I will beat the shit out of you." *Great now I sounded like a wife beater*. However, she wasn't any woman, she was Melody. Even the devil pitied me.

She glared up at me with a rage so deep, her brown eyes looked pure black. She struggled, trying to push me away, but despite her skills, she was still much smaller than I was.

Finally, I thought, when it looked like she had given up, but like a damn piranha, the bitch bit my bottom lip so hard I could taste blood. In that moment, I released her hands, and she took the opportunity to punch me in the throat before kicking me off of her.

"Swear to whatever God you want," she hissed, right before stretching out her legs to kick me.

I grabbed one and slammed her into a wall. She reached for the lamp and threw it at my head. Reacting quickly, I ducked only to come back up to have her foot collide with my jaw.

Wiping the blood from my chin, I was done. When she tried to kick me again, I grabbed onto her arm and pulled her into me before ramming her body right into the mirror. It shattered on impact. Liked a damned snake, she wrapped her body around mine, squeezing tightly, making it almost impossible for me to shake her loose.

Spinning to another wall, I again rammed her back against it and her hold on me slipped just enough for me to push her back. Gripping onto her neck, I held my gun to her skull.

The look in her eyes haunted me; they were no longer dark, but full of a pain that was killing her anger, and chipping away at mine.

"Do it," she demanded. "Pull the trigger, Liam."

"You're insane," I told her before kissing her hard. She had to be insane to think I would ever want to kill her; that I would even consider pulling the trigger…that I would ever betray her. I wanted nothing more than to make her calm down, to let her know I loved her. She was just too damn hard-headed and emotional…just like I knew she would be.

Her dress at this point was all but ripped on both sides. However, I pulled from the top, ripping it open like a jacket. Snapping her bra off, I threw it right next to the dress. It looked better on the ground anyway.

"You really have a problem with my clothing," she said, breaking our kiss as she wrapped her legs around me.

"I do." There was no point in lying. "So stop wearing it around me."

Before she could speak, I thrust myself inside of her and her back arched up against the wall as she pulled on my hair.

"Ahh—" Her mouth opened while her body shook in shock and pleasure.

As much as I loved her, I was still pissed that she shot me...again. I still wanted to beat the shit out of her, but I would've gladly fuck her senseless instead.

"Liam..."

"Remember what you asked me to do to you?" I squeezed her thighs, as I thrust forward again and again, so hard, in fact, anything still hanging on the wall fell to the ground. Her nails dug into my shoulders. "Fuck you until your legs go weak you said."

Again, I slammed myself into her, enjoying how tightly her walls clenched on to me.

"Fuck you until you scream my name...you *begged*." The faster I went, the louder her moans became.

"Liam...I...Ohh..." Her breasts bounced uncontrollably as she squeezed her eyes shut.

"If you could see the face you're making baby," I whispered as I licked her bottom lip and she opened her mouth for me. But I didn't kiss her, instead, I bit her earlobe as I buried myself between her thighs.

"Liam I can't—"

"You want to come baby?" I slowed down and she almost whimpered. My Melody whimpering. It was a sight. "Why should you get to get off after what you did to me tonight."

Kissing her. I slowed down, until it was almost too painful to bear, pulling her out of the high she was reaching.

"No, Liam, I'm so close…" she moaned as my cock slowly slid in and out of her. She became wetter each time, dripping down her thighs and even onto my hands.

I pulled her hair back, forcing her to look me in the eyes. "You don't control this. I do. And you've pissed me off, wife."

She, of course, slapped me, and I smiled to myself as I pulled out completely and rubbed myself against her slick, wet folds. She shook with need, she was so close.

"Say it, Melody. I'm getting off just by watching you squirm."

Just fucking say it, Jesus Christ this was killing me.

"I can't, because I hate you right now," she said through gritted teeth, just to piss me off.

I flipped her around and without a care in the world, I took hold of her ass. As I spread her cheeks apart, she braced herself against the wall and I smirked. "Don't you dare move," I commanded.

I gripped on to her breasts, her nipples hard in my palms I slid into pressing us both against the wall.

"This is all for me. My pleasure." I grunted as I took her hard and rough, thrusting deeper and deeper into her ass.

One of my hand grabbed hers above her head holding on to it as I kissed the back of her neck.

"Melody!" I came inside her.

When I released her, her legs gave out, forcing her to rest against the wall. "Damn it, LIAM!"

She sat there, naked, frustrated and covered in sweat, blood and my seed…I'd never been prouder.

Adjusting myself, I took a few deep breaths before I glared down at her. "I have a bullet wound I need to attend to, along with a cousin I need to kill. You're pissed, I understand, but all your anger isn't for me. If I could do it all over again, I still wouldn't tell you. If this is how you reacted because of me withholding information, imagine what you would have done before. We have too much riding on our public image right now for you to become a homicidal bitch."

I was so infuriated with her, damn it! The pain in my thigh was only starting to sink in now, now that the adrenaline was wearing off from the haze of our fight and sex. When she was pissed, she should use her motherfucking words and not her gun, at least for me. Here we were, ten steps back, when we didn't have the time to back pedal.

"Don't go," she said when I opened the door to leave.

"Maybe you forgot, but you shot me, I have a wound—"

"Liam—"

She looked to me and I could see she was finally calm… hurt and calm.

"I'm going to need stitches." I muttered, as I moved back over to where she was and took a seat on the ground again. Pain flared up my body and I winced.

"I'll call Coraline for a med kit and clothes," she whispered as she took off my pants and used the torn part of her dress to wrap the wound.

She didn't look up at me and I didn't push her. I closed my eyes.

"The first time I kissed you, I was shot in the thigh. The first time we had sex, I was shot in arm. You seem to like me bloody, Mrs. Callahan."

"I just like you," she stated, and I opened my eyes to find her kneeling between my legs, still naked, her hair tousled, eyes wild, and she was covered in cuts and scrapes from our fight. She was beautifully savage in this moment. "I still think you were wrong for keeping this from me."

"And I do not. So we're at an impasse then. I do believe you and I have a special system for dealing with our issues."

"We've already fucked it out, Liam."

"Just because I'm sitting here doesn't mean I'm not still annoyed with you, wife…believe me, there is plenty left for us to fuck out." I winked at her.

With both of us naked in each other's arms, there was nothing we couldn't get through.

Melody

The moment I got out of the hotel bathroom, I came face to face with a very ticked off Coraline in the ruins of the room. I sighed, closing the door for Liam to finish up.

"I brought you a change of clothes and there's a car in the back, waiting to take you home to avoid the press. The gala is winding down, but some people are still lingering." She pointed to the bag hanging on what was left of the mirror fame.

I didn't say a word, I simply stepped over the shards of glass.

"One more thing," she said.

When I turned back to her, she slapped me right across the face. My head snapped back, and the side of my face burned like hell, but I said not a word as I regarded her.

"You've messed with my husband long enough. You could have killed him, but you were so blinded…"

Grabbing hold of her neck, I pulled her to my face.

"I'm going to let the slap go, because I was a *little* temperamental. Remember, Coraline, I made you. I gave you the balls you're so willing to put on display, try to lecture me again, and I will rip them right out from under you, and then I'll go after Declan. Are we clear?" I asked, squeezing just a little bit tighter before letting go.

So, I flipped out. I didn't want a lecture from Liam, and I sure as hell didn't want one from Coraline.

She coughed holding onto her neck before speaking again. "I'm sorry. I'm sorry your mother is a…"

"You're pushing me, Coraline," I said as I dropped the towel.

"So be it then. I'm still going to speak my mind, balls or no balls. We are family; you are my sister, okay? I'm on your side, Melody, I promise. Just please, be on mine." With that, she left me alone to finish getting dressed.

Those who got high occasionally should know that the come down was horrible, especially if you aren't ready for it. Life was fine for Liam and I; everything we wanted was slowly falling into our laps, and then this.

My mother…was dead. She died when I was young… she was murdered when I was little…but that was a lie. It was like my brain didn't—couldn't—wrap itself around that thought.

When I was younger, I had come to terms with the fact that I was motherless. The first Mother's Day after her death, I cried until Orlando sat me down and told me we don't cry. No matter how bad our lives got, Giovannis did not cry. I was a child, crying was one of the things children did, but after that moment, the tears went away. I found the deepest part of my soul and buried my sorrow there.

The only time I truly remember giving in to the tears and the pain was last year, right after I lost our child. That was the first time in years I had truly felt pain like that. When Liam was hurt, from what I now know was his own plan, I felt fear. That's why I needed my revenge and killed Saige. It still gave me satisfaction to think about her and the twelve mile drive before her screams stopped.

That night, I made Liam scream in a different sort of way. I wasn't a huge fan of bondage, but tying him up as I sexually tortured him for hours was fun. At the end, he all but begged to be free. When he was, the room looked sort of like the hotel room looked now...like two wild animals had been set loose.

In one year, I had felt fear and pain. Now, it seemed I'd moved on to hurt and anger. All the reasons I tired to come up with to explain Aviela DeRosa's existence didn't hold any water. Nothing could explain how she could be alive... how she could have just left. How she could be nothing like I thought she would be. The white shoes were a lie...the white gloves were a lie. She didn't have clean hands; they were dipped in as much blood as mine were. She'd literally left me in the middle of the ocean as a child, clinging to life. The chances of anyone living through that were slim to none, and yet she took that chance and I was her child.

Kneeling down, I reached for the flash drive that Liam must have dropped during our fight; I knew that if I opened its contents, there would be more questions than answers. The biggest ones being—why did my own mother hate me so much that she had people trying to kill me and my family? If I saw her today, would I be able to kill her as well? From the very day you are born, you're told family is everything. Even if you had to hurt them every once in a while, family still came first. Would I be able to kill her? I hoped so. I hoped I would be able to show her why we didn't let anyone live.

When I turned around, I found Liam leaning against the bathroom door looking like Satan himself, his dark brown hair dripping wet and disheveled, and his green eyes focused only on me.

"Coraline is still following in your footsteps it seems." He dried his hair. "What happened to there being only one Bloody Melody?"

I snorted. "Coraline still has a ways to go. Either way, she's family right?"

He looked to me and a soft smile grew on his face, as he wrapped his arms around me. "Let's go home. I have something for you."

I knew that look.

"Liam, once we get back, we have work to do. No sex of any kind," I stated. But he didn't seem to be listening.

LIAM

I drank from her, my tongue licking up everything she gave me as she rode my face. She bounced and rocked against my tongue, bracing herself against the bed, as I braced myself between her thighs.

"LIAM!" she screamed, as she came all over my face.

I reveled in her juices, enjoying each drop of her. Spent, she rolled herself off of me and came to rest beside me. I watched her chest rising and falling as she tried to catch her breath, and as I licked my fingers clean of her, she turned to watch me.

"No love making of any kind?" I mocked, sitting up against the headboard. "I guess that went out window the moment you sat on my face. You taste divine by the way."

"Fuck you," she said, as she pulled the sheets around her and reached for her laptop beside the bed.

"You already did, three times, and quite nicely I may add." I laughed when she glared at me.

Neither of us had spoken on the car ride over. We didn't even look at each other, yet there was still sexual tension between us, because there was always sexual tension between us. By the time we got home, both of us were horny and annoyed with one another. Sex seemed to be the only thing we could agree on.

I knew she was using me as a distraction. She didn't want to focus on the shit in front of her. Neither of us did really, so instead we'd had our fill of brandy, wine, and sex.

All of the sex had calmed her down, and now she was ready…or at least I hoped she was ready. Two bullets from her were enough for a lifetime.

She sat next to me and placed the flash drive in as I leaned back to see the list. Hundreds of names, some of them I knew, some were before my time, others I had never even known existed. Each person had a name, photo, date of birth, and the day that they were murdered going back at least twenty-five years… Aviela DeRosa had been killing for a long time.

"Orlando," Mel whispered softly, as she looked at the name and photo. It didn't say Orlando but Iron Hands.

"She didn't kill him," I stated the obvious.

I tried to grab the laptop, but she slapped my hands away and did it herself.

"Iron Hands. Arsenic," she read before freezing. Inside the file was a photo of what happened to be another list with dates and doses.

"She poisoned him," Mel whispered. "For six years straight. She poisoned him slowly. Orlando never knew because he always figured he would get cancer. He had done everything to prevent it, but when it came, he just thought there was no fighting it. That it was too deep in our family line. She gave him cancer. She poisoned him and just waited."

When I grabbed the mouse from her, she didn't fight me; she was in too much shock to fight.

"What's your grandfather's name on your father's side?" I asked her trying to sort through.

"Ignazio Giovanni, the second," she said, still dazed.

When I hit enter, there he was. He died at sixty-one after being diagnosed with stage four colon cancer; he died in four months, his dosage of Arsenic were ten times higher than Orlando's. They wanted him dead, fast, but without raising suspicion.

"Orlando had an older brother, Francesco Angelo Giovanni. He died at twenty-six." She searched and he came up as well. He died a year before his father. Two months she spent killing him. It seemed the only person she tortured for so long was Orlando.

One by one, Melody typed up names of who I guessed were her family, and one by one they popped up.

"She's been killing off your family for years," I whispered. But why?

"And now she's coming after the last Giovanni." Mel tensed.

"You're a Callahan, not a Giovanni," I said. "And she isn't coming near you, or anyone in this family, unless it's in a body bag."

She looked back at me, her eyes blazing with fire.

"Everything I know is a lie. She's the only one that knows the truth. When we get our hands on her, we can break her, but we're not going to kill her until I know the truth," She said before looking back at the screen.

But, as I went through the list, looking for any of my past family and finding none, I wondered if a woman like Aviela, who had killed the father of her child, and left that same child for dead, could be broken.

How could you break something that was obviously never whole to begin with?

Five

"All the motives for murder are covered by four Ls: Love, Lust, Lucre and Loathing."
~ P.D. James

Melody

"Bless me Father, for I have sinned. It has been seven days since my last Confession, in that time I have…"

"You have lied," Father Antony interrupted me.

"Yes, father and I…"

"You have killed, stolen, and much worse," he cut me off again. Only a man of God could do that and still have his tongue.

"You're going off script, father," I whispered, leaning against my seat. He could neither see me, nor I him, but I felt more comfortable. Not because I felt ashamed, more because I liked the darkness here; it was the only place I wasn't afraid of it. I liked the peace it gave me within the church.

"Yes, well I cannot offer you forgiveness." He sighed. "You've come in here once a week for the last year asking for the same thing. Yet neither I, nor God, can forgive you for something you do not truly wish forgiveness for. It doesn't work that way."

"May I continue, Father?" I asked him.

"Very well," he said.

"Since you have confessed my past sins for me, I shall confess my future ones." I felt the rage and hate crawl up inside me as I thought about it. "I will kill my mother. I swear it."

He was silent. We were both silent for what seemed like forever.

"Honor thy father and thy mother, Melody. Of all sins to break among man, the one you speak of is…"

"Honor thy father and thy mother?" I snapped; it was my turn to cut him off. "Where is honor thy child? Why is that not written in stone somewhere for us to hold above our heads? Some fathers and mothers should not be honored! Some should not even be given the title."

"What was done to you, my child?" he whispered, but I didn't answer. Instead I stared out at the stained glass.

It made me think of my childhood.

"When I was a child, the church was the only place I felt at peace. I would lie in the pews and stare up at the paintings on the ceiling. Sometimes I would speak to God, sometimes I would dream, but often times I would think about my mom. Wishing she would come find me, worried because she couldn't find me in the house. I even prayed about it and God never answered. I knew that wasn't how it worked. But, I was angry. In my mind, he was Santa Claus, and the one thing I wanted, he wouldn't give me." I sighed at my own stupidity, "Here I am, years later, and my mother is alive and well."

"Is that not something to be thankful for?" he asked, slightly confused.

I looked to the screen blocking our faces. "Not when she is worse than I am…far worse, and sadly, I'm not being sarcastic."

"I see." I could feel his worry even though I couldn't see it. "Is there a sin I can ask the father to forgive, one in which you regret?"

I thought for a moment.

"I shot my husband." I said.

"Is he still alive?" he asked with amusement.

"Yes." For now. "He's still alive. I shot him out of anger, and I'm sorry for it. I abuse him often, actually."

"You don't seem regretful," he added.

"I am." That wasn't a lie. " I lov…I love him. But, I'm not good with caring for anyone but myself, my own needs. With each passing day, I notice more and more sex won't distract him."

"Distract him from what?"

I knew I set myself up for this, but I didn't want to think about it.

"Distract him from getting even closer to you," he answered his own question. "You love him, but you live a life of constant loss. You do not want to hurt him. You do not want to love him. You'd rather push him away because you want to have control over how you lose him…if you lose him."

I didn't want to say anything. I didn't want to admit to it. But he was right. It was one of the reasons why I came back every week. He was the only one outside of the family that did not judge and could never speak about our conversations, even with a gun to his head.

"Yes, Father," I whispered finally.

"Pray to our mother for guidance and loving heart. Ask our father for the strength to forgive. Go and do these things, for you are forgiven, my child. Give thanks to the Lord, for he is good."

"His mercy endures forever, Amen." I blessed myself before leaving my peaceful confessional at the back of the church.

I mentally sighed at the sight of Coraline and Olivia, both sitting up front in the pews. Taking care of the family was trying—all their issues, their problems, hopes and fears. I wanted to go back into the confessional and just rest. But it was my job, mine and Liam's, to take care of the family, to keep things going, to keep each other safe.

Despite all the killing we'd done, that really wasn't our role. We weren't hired killers. We were business people who sometimes had to bash a few heads in to make sure things got done.

That was part one.

Part two was to make sure the family was happy and safe. That meant listening and handling problems in their lives. Yes, there were times when we had to knock some sense into them, but that was the life.

My red heels echoed throughout the church as I walked right past them and towards the altar to light a candle before kneeling to pray. I believed in God, but talking to him was difficult. I was a conversation starter. I listened and reacted. Liam was the talker.

I wasn't sure how long I had been kneeling there before I heard Coraline or Olivia's cell phone vibrate for what had to be the ninth time. Rising, I turned to them; I wanted to chuck a motherfucking candle in one of their faces.

Do not kill in the lord's house. Do not kill in the lord's house.

"I'm sorry, it's Evelyn," Coraline whispered. "We're late for the charity brunch."

"We're Callahans, we're never late. Everyone else is early and impatient," I stated as I grabbed the phone from her and turned it off before taking my kneeling stance back at the altar.

But no sooner had my knees touched the pillow did Olivia's phone go off. I turned towards her again, and the fear that crossed her face meant that she saw the hell I would unleash on her if she didn't shut her phone off immediately. She did, which only made my private phone go off.

Looking up at the cross, I sighed. "You see what I go through?"

LIAM

"When did you get so good at hand-to-hand combat?" Declan snickered as I dodged Neal's fist.

"I'll do my best not to take that as an insult." I grunted, blocking my face before jumping back and landing one to the side of Neal's face.

He and I danced around the ring, staring down each other like hungry lions.

Over the last year, this had been my and Neal's thing. After years of not speaking to each other, except when needed, we were working ourselves back to brotherly status. I wasn't sure how long that would take, but every Saturday, while my beautiful wife was at confession and her charity, we boxed. When Neal was in his fighting mode, there was no speaking, just calculated attacks. He was almost like a robot. But in the moments in between our attempts at killing each other, there was a look or a smirk that passed between us. That smirk said far more than any words. We were in a much better place than we were a year ago.

"Isn't it obvious?" I asked, ducking down slightly as Neal's fist came towards my jaw. "My wife tries to murder me every other week. A few of those times, have in fact led to combat...amongst other things."

"One day your dick is going to fall off. I'm just not sure what will castrate you first; the sex, or the fighting before the sex." Declan laughed.

"The sex," my father said from the sideline. "You do know the walls are thin enough that every sound carries, right? We all can hear you."

"I know, I just don't give a fuck." I tried to punch Neal once more, but he blocked. "It's my damn house, if we want to make love in the center of the dining table at dinner, we shall."

"Please don't," he said.

"She puts a bullet in your thigh and you make love? I still don't understand your relationship. After a year, she still hasn't warmed up to you," Declan said as Neal kicked into my side.

Of course he would think that. My Mel didn't show much emotion other than anger or fake kindness in public. However, it was different when we were alone. We had gone from murderous fuck buddies, to husband and wife. She let me hold her, which often led to more sex. But even after that, we'd fall asleep in each other's arms. She didn't say 'I love you' as often as I did, but when she did, it made me want to stay in bed with her forever. Love wasn't her thing. She struggled with it. How could they expect someone who never really received love to express it to others? I wasn't going to push her any more than I already had.

"How can you understand my relationship when you're just beginning to understand your own?" I grunted out as Neal bore down on me. The damn giant.

"Prick," he yelled. "We're in therapy."

"Something I still do not agree with," Sedric snapped. "I don't understand why you allowed such a thing, Liam.

Matters within the family should be handled by the family or a priest, if you insist."

"It has been helping. We're finally talking and not yelling anymore. There was so much I didn't see or simply overlooked. I've learned loving someone isn't enough," Declan said, and I could see Neal smirk for a split second before I knocked it off his face.

"I allowed it. That wife of his destroyed a million dollars worth of equipment, with a baseball bat...*my* baseball bat. I almost preferred it when she gave all our money away to charities," I answered just before Neal took me down.

"She gives because of her parents—it's the only way she feels needed. She likes being there for others because at least then they see her. If I told you how her parents treated her..." He sounded worse than me, and I was the one who was getting my face pounded in.

"Couldn't you have spoken to me and your aunt? We would have helped."

"Both of us would have felt like you were being judgmental. We know you wouldn't, but we wanted to speak to someone on the same playing field as us..."

"We're Callahans, no one is on the same damn playing field as us!" I yelled out, flipping over and returning the favor to Neal.

"Fine, someone under us then." He rolled his eyes. "Either way, it's working. We were even going to have sex for the first time in months, before your wife came in like the fucking Terminator!"

"Please, file your complaint with the office of 'I Don't Give a Fuck' and I'll be sure not to get back to you!"

It wasn't my fault their sexual needs came at the wrong time.

"Well, your highness, I was wondering if we could *handle* her parents as retribution," he said, forcing me to look up at him. Sure enough, he was as serious as ever.

Neal took the opportunity to punch me in the jaw and put me in a chokehold. I tried to fight my way out, but he had the upper hand. Sadly, I was going to lose this round.

Thank you, homicidal Declan.

I tapped out and Neal released his hold on me.

Sitting up, I took a few deep breaths before I rose and walked over to the edge of the ring. "We aren't killing her parents," I said before squirting the water into my mouth then pouring some over my head.

Declan glared at me. "I said *handle,* not kill. Besides, they fucked with her…"

"They fucked—past tense. The wounds Coraline has from that will heal. Have you even asked her if she wanted them dead?" I glared back and he shook his head. "And this is why you're in therapy. Stop acting for your wife and act *with* her you idiot. Coraline isn't the same mouse of a wife you had before. You can thank my wife for that, for whatever good and bad that causes. Nevertheless, if Coraline wants something, she will ask you."

"She would want to handle them." His eyes darkened.

"They're her parents," Neal finally spoke out. "Regardless of what they've done, they're still her parents. Yes, she remembers the bad, but she will always remember the good as well, however short it was. It's not as easy to kill family as everyone makes it seem."

"This moment of wisdom was brought to you by—" I was cut off as a water bottle came flying at my head. I caught it and laughed.

"He's right though," our father replied. "We can't just keep killing everyone…especially our in-laws."

True, we were running out of places to hide the bodies. I snickered at the thought.

"Speaking of killing, Fedel has informed me that they found another one of the men who raped Olivia," I said bluntly, and I felt them stiffen. Neal however, looked like stone. I wasn't going to sugarcoat it because Mel and Olivia weren't.

Mel had informed me of the finding during our shower together, which effectively killed my hard on. By the time we went downstairs, my mother was crying; Declan was already on the phone, and my father and Neal were all ready to go to war. It was the first time my mother demanded to me that I kill someone immediately. When Olivia told her she was going to do it herself, she froze. I stared into her eyes then nodded.

The next morning, breakfast was a silent affair, and I knew that everyone was lost in thought. Well, not everyone. It was a little twisted, maybe a bit sick of me, but my wife had made me horny and I couldn't help but reach under the table to finger her. Not one of them noticed, but watching my wife fight back a moan was damn sexy.

"So, how is she going to do this?" Declan asked pulling me out of my sweet thoughts.

"She's murdered one already," I answered, grabbing a towel as we headed to the sauna room. I dropped my pants right there before entering without a care.

"From what I understand, Mel pulled it out of her," Declan hissed at the steam, stretching slightly.

Sedric poured the water over the stones before leaning back. "Now that she's done it, I doubt the second time will be as hard as the first. I say she should cut the motherfucker's balls off and make him eat them."

That was a disgusting thought, but it fit the crime.

"Whatever she chooses, it's up to her," Neal tried to end the conversation.

He hated thinking about it and I didn't blame him. I looked at Olivia differently now; her past explained many of her actions over the past few years, and I wondered how Neal felt. I could never know or want to know. I doubted it could happen to a woman like Mel, but I didn't want to ever tempt fate with such a thing.

"We aren't going after Aviela DeRosa," I told them, shifting the heat from Neal.

"Neal, I think you hit him too hard," my father said, causing them to snicker. "She killed your wife's father, uncle and grandfather. Not to mention, she left said wife to die as a child."

"Really, Father? I didn't know." *Of course I fucking knew.* I told him, "There are too many pieces to the puzzle. Like, why the hell would she have a child with a man she hated and planned to kill?"

"Or why did she choose that method in killing them? She poisoned Orlando for six bloody years, that takes dedication and patience," Neal said.

Patience wasn't one of our strong suits. Well, maybe with the exception of Declan.

"Maybe she likes it? Maybe that's how she gets off," Declan wondered, but my father shook his head.

Closing his eyes, he took a deep breath. "It doesn't match the profile of a hired killer. Their job is to kill and leave no trails and move on. Aviela's way does that, but it means investing more time than she would want."

"Like I said, too many missing pieces. Monte will be looking into it. Mel and I have too much to do to get wrapped up in the mysteries of her family's past right now," I said. "We're still trying to fix all the damage that Valero did last year. Most of our heroin stock in Mexico was destroyed. However, we're now smuggling it in from Afghanistan... their shit is better anyway." I sighed, rubbing my shoulder.

"It's better, but its costs us more," Declan added. "If we raise the prices, we lose our lower end druggies. Sadly, there aren't enough rock stars to live off of."

He had a point.

"Things were much easier in your day, right, Pop? The whole free love and shit? You could just hide the smack in your bellbottoms? Or were you all still wearing the Larry King suspenders?" Neal snorted and my father glared at him.

"Yes, Neal, when the dinosaurs ran the across the earth, shit was easier," he snapped, causing Declan and I to laugh.

"It won't cost us so much anymore," I replied, pouring more water over the stones.

"Care to share?" my father asked. The nosy prick.

They all waited and I rolled my eyes. "We just donated to a few cemeteries."

"This helps how?" Declan pushed.

"Soldiers die. What better way to bring our product into the country but with the help of Uncle Sam?" They all just stared, as the possibilities sank in.

"That's fucking brilliant," Neal said. "It will become even easier when Colemen becomes President." He grinned.

"Mel's idea?" My father looked at me.

I glared. My inner brat wanted to say it was teamwork, but it really was Mel's idea.

"We'll also be smuggling in marijuana seeds as well. All of which will be growing in Colorado," I added, changing the subject.

Neal looked confused. "Why Colorado?"

I sighed, feeling the urge to throw a hot rock at his face.

"Don't you ever watch the news?" Declan snapped.

"No, it's too depressing," he said. "They start the night off with a 'good evening', and then they go on to tell you all the reasons why it's a shitty night all across the country."

My father sighed like he did when we were kids, when we did, or said, something he couldn't understand.

"They legalized weed, dipshit," he said, and I couldn't help but laugh. It was just a regular Saturday morning with the family.

"I wonder if the girls' conversations are like this." Declan laughed.

"It's not and it's probably killing my poor wife." I could see her now, thinking of clawing her eyes out with a fork. "One wrong move, you may want to watch the news tonight, Neal."

MELODY

"Kill me..." I uttered out loud as they brought another painting for us to bid on. The money they raised would go towards the building of some stupid elementary school.

"Now come on, ladies, get out those checkbooks, call your husbands if you must. This school is just too important not to!" the peppy woman up front yelled.

In my fingers was a small fork. I knew I could throw it with just enough force to shut her up. However, Evelyn placed her hand on my wrist—again—and took the fork from me.

I sighed and sat back in my seat, watching the women pay anywhere from five to nine hundred dollars for any given artwork.

"Thank you all so much, we're doing so well, we only have nineteen paintings left! Come on, ladies, I know you want them," the stupid woman called out again.

Nineteen more? Nineteen motherfucking paintings more? I can't do it. I can't. I will claw my own damn eyes out with a spoon if I have to sit through one more painting.

Standing up caused them all to turn and look at me, and I put my Stepford wife smile on. "Will $250,000 cover them all?"

There were gasps, followed by a round of applause as the woman stared at me flabbergasted.

"Mrs. Callahan, you truly are a Godsend. Thank you so much!" she said, starting the applause all over again. I smiled and waved like a broken doll before taking my seat again.

"Now we're going to have to sit through art shows every damn month." Olivia sighed.

Then I would buy the paintings every damn month to get it over with.

"This concludes our afternoon. Your artwork will be shipped to you this evening!" the woman said. I wrote a check, waving it for one of her art-boys to come snatch it up like a wild animal.

We all but ran out of there, and it wasn't until we were in the car that Coraline broke out into laughter.

"Thank God. We came late and it still felt like we had been in there forever."

"Now you all know how I feel. How dare you leave me all alone with those people?" Evelyn scoffed, pulling out her phone.

"I'm sorry, but God comes first, what can I say?" I added, finally able to relax into my seat.

"I can't believe you bought all those paintings. Where're you going to put them?" Olivia asked, trying her best to be "nice" to me.

"I don't know, and I don't care. I just had to get out of that place." I was starting to get a headache from that woman's voice.

Coraline looked out the window and frowned. "This isn't the direction of the house."

"That's because Olivia and I are making a pit stop," I answered, causing Evelyn and Coraline to pause, and Olivia to freeze.

I didn't mind the silence, I enjoyed the ride. I didn't tell Olivia earlier because I didn't want her over thinking it. It was so cliché: a warehouse. That was because Liam didn't want the prick in our house. I didn't care either way. Declan, Neal, and Sedric would all be present, and normally, that would be stupid. Outside of the house and public functions, we were never all in the same place at once. However, Neal insisted, Sedric wouldn't budge, and Declan was the one double-checking all the cameras. Another reason why we hated having everyone together was the amount of time we spent on security. It was just plain annoying.

When we pulled up, the driver opened the door for Olivia and I, and I noticed Antonio, along with four other snipers, on the rooftops.

"I'm coming." Evelyn stepped out along with Coraline.

"This is not a field trip, and even if it were, I would be the person who signs the damn permission slip. Neither of you are coming," I told them both.

However, Evelyn stepped up and looked me dead in the eyes, something very few people could do.

"I'm coming. Try and stop me, *sweetheart*." She glared, and I wanted to show her that I could do more than try.

"Mel, you don't want to add to your rap sheet, you spent more than an hour in confession," Coraline said quickly, trying to get in between Evelyn and me.

"You people keep pushing me and then act all surprised when I snap." I took a deep breath before turning around.

This was bad. Olivia did not need the whole family for this. She may have killed once, but I pushed her...I pulled the baby ruthless murderer right out of her. But she was still a baby. Babies got scared and nervous. Some even had performance issues.

When we stepped in, the first thing I had to get used to was the smell of weed from all the plants in the room. The second were the screams as Neal cut the fingers off of the pig.

"What the fuck?" Liam said to me, as he looked over at his mother and Coraline. Evelyn walked over to Sedric, who looked just as surprised as Liam, and kissed his cheek.

"They wanted to come along. I said no, but they didn't want to listen," I said as Coraline and Declan held hands.

"Since when do people not listening to you stop you from getting your way?" he asked, amused and running his hand up my side softly. I pulled away slightly; PDA was never my thing. He frowned, but dropped his hand to pull out his phone.

"Since I married you, I didn't think you would like me using a sniper on your mother," I replied, standing closer to him.

"Thanks, you're too kind."

"Been told that all day…"

"Neal, stop!" Olivia screamed, reminding me why I was here.

Neal, however, didn't stop. He kept snipping away with the cutting pliers.

"You think this is bad?" he hissed, gripping the man's thumb. "Wait until I get farther south, you stupid, motherfucking, cock-sucking piece of shit."

The man looked dazed, but spoke anyway. "Believe me, that bitch had no cock when I sucked on her."

That did it.

I thought the term 'ape shit' was generally overused, however in this case, Neal really did go 'ape shit.' The pliers fell from his hands as he started to beat into the pig's face.

"NEAL STOP!" Olivia screamed.

But he didn't. I wasn't even sure if he could hear anything at this point. He wanted blood.

"Take him outside," Liam said. It took two of our men and Declan to pull him back.

"I will motherfucking end you!" he yelled, trying his best to break free of their grasp. "You hear me? I will make sure every last person in your fucking family burns!"

"And this is why I wanted to tell everyone after she'd killed them all," I whispered once he was finally out the door.

"'They wanted to come along,'" Liam mocked me. "'I said no, but they didn't want to listen.'"

I cupped his ass.

"Love, if you wanted me, all you had to do was say so." He smirked before winking.

Olivia stood still for a moment, looking back at the door before turning back to the half-dead pig. He spit out his teeth, trying his best to open his eyes and breathe.

"I remember you. Harvey's girl." He coughed. "Is this revenge? Aren't you a little late? It's been years. I doubt any of them remember like I do. Harvey was always a watcher. I could never get that sound out of my head. That cry when I became your first…you never forget your first they say."

Evelyn moved forward, but Sedric held her back so all she could do was spit on him and unleash a few colorful words that I'd never thought I'd hear Evelyn say.

Even Liam's hand twitched towards his gun.

"They're wrong," was all Olivia said before stabbing the pliers right in his head. She pulled it out only to stab him once more and dropped the pliers. Her hands shook as she stepped back.

That's one way to do it.

He trembled violently before his body just gave out. Dropping it, she left to go find Neal.

"I don't care how you take out the trash, just make sure it's done," Liam told the men, before leading me to our private car outside, and for a moment, my eyes connected with Olivia's outside as Neal hugged her.

"You're welcome," I mouthed to her before getting in.

When Liam took his seat, I crawled onto his lap and straddled his waist. His stare travelled up my leg, stopping at my breasts before looking at my face.

"Hello, wife," he whispered, gripping onto my thigh. Kissing him deeply, I felt him harden under me while he pulled me closer to him.

"I love you, you know that, right? I don't say it often, I'm not good at saying it or showing…"

He cut me off again, flipping me onto the back seat.

"Take the long way home, Sal," he told the driver as he looked down at me.

"Yes, sir," he said as he rolled up the partition.

Slowly, Liam unbuttoned my dress, not speaking, just breathing heavily. I tried to get his belt buckle off, but he pushed my hands away.

"Yes, I know you love me," he whispered, kissing down my chest. "I know you don't say it often, but I don't forget that you do, nor do I not feel it, ever. Even when you shoot me."

I tried to speak, but he flipped me over and smacked my ass. I hated how much I liked it and how wet it made me. Pulling off the rest of my dress, he kissed up my back, rubbing my ass softly before smacking me harder. This time a moan did escape my lips.

I loved it when he got like this.

"My only question is, what brought this on?" he whispered, as he kissed the back of my neck.

"A revelation at confession." I shivered when he reached under to pinch my nipples.

"Really now?" he kissed my shoulder. "What did the good father tell you?"

The moment I opened my mouth, he smacked my ass again and I bit my lip in order to control myself… it didn't work.

"Jesus, Liam…" I moaned.

"Yes, I know about Jesus. I'm asking about your revelation." He kissed my ass cheek.

Licking my lips, I took a deep breath. "I fear losing you."

His kisses stopped only briefly before they were back at my ear.

"My silly wife, you can't lose me. Nothing is going to keep me from having your mind, soul and body." He said the last part as he slapped my ass cheek again.

"I…"

"Shh, love. I'm going to give you something you're going to need to confess about later. Maybe more than once," he said, smacking my ass over and over again until I was squirming with pleasure under him.

"Does it hurt, love?" he asked, rubbing my skin.

I moaned out something, but I wasn't sure what. He snickered, smacking me a few more times before putting three of his beautiful fingers inside my wet pussy.

"Goddamn, you're wet. You like it when it when I punish you?" he asked before pulling his fingers out and bringing me up to straddle his lap once more.

"Only in bed, and even then, it depends." I kissed him, reaching inside his pants for his cock.

"When we're in a car, like right now, I want you on your knees with those beautiful lips of yours on my dick, " he said as I stroked him.

"And if I say no?" I smirked, kissing his nose.

"You really must love it when I take you from behind." He grinned.

"Don't pretend like you don't like it either. It's more of a reward than a punishment, isn't it?" I asked. Before he could answer, I slid down to his knees and took him into my mouth.

"Fuck!" he moaned loudly, grabbing hold of my hair.

I was proud that I could take most of him into my mouth, that was something that was far from easy.

He thrust forward once before letting go of my hair, and pulling me back up to him. He didn't even wait before thrusting forward and pushing me up against the window.

Liam

I loved my wife. There was no doubt in my mind that she was God's personal gift to me, but...

"I can't believe you bought all this fucking shit," I said, picking up the bottle of wine before joining her on our bedroom floor. There had to be at least fifteen to twenty paintings spread throughout the room.

"What would you have done if you had to sit through that shit?" she asked, biting into her strawberry. I watched the juice run down the side of lips before leaning forward and licking it.

"A napkin would have worked as well." She rolled her eyes, as she wiped the corner of her mouth.

"Yes, but then I wouldn't have been able to taste you." I grinned as I grabbed, a strawberry. "Plus, you love me, remember?"

"That car ride was such a bad idea," she said as she tried to stretch out the knot in her neck.

"Blasphemy. Car sex is never a bad idea." I would swear by it. "Besides, you enjoyed it as much as I did."

"What do you think that is anyway?" she asked, changing the subject to point to the painting closest to us.

I looked closely and smiled. "I see two people having sex in the shower."

"It's abstract." She laughed.

"I abstractly see two people having sex in the shower," I whispered, pulling her to me.

"Maybe you're having a vision of the future. However, I see a hot bubble bath." She smiled.

I loved to see her smile.

"I can work with that," I replied, picking her up.

I really loved my wife.

Six

*"It is not enough to stare up the steps,
we must step up the stairs."*
~Vaclav Havel

Declan

"Have you had sex yet?" Dr. Bell, our therapist, asked bluntly. I looked over at Coraline, who just stared down at her nails.

"No, we haven't," I answered. "I mean, we were going to but…"

"You weren't able to get…"

"No!" I snapped. I knew where he was going, and I didn't like it. "My dick works fine, thank you."

"Then what happened?" he asked.

"Our sister-in law cut in. *That* killed the mood," Coraline replied.

"How long ago was that?"

"Five days ago," I said.

"And in those five days you weren't able to get into the mood again?"

Neither of us answered.

"How long has it been since either of you have had sex?"

"I don't…"

"Seven months, two weeks, five days and three hours," I said, causing Coraline to stare at me wide-eyed. Even Dr. Bell stared at me oddly.

"I'm good with numbers," I said, sitting back in my chair.

"I see," he said. "The reason why I worry about it is because a healthy sex life is highly important in a marriage.

It brings you closer together and allows you to see each other in the most intimate way. The longer you both stay away from each other, the harder it is to find your way back. Declan, what was it that set the mood last time?"

I shrugged. "She looked beautiful in her dress and I couldn't take her my eyes off her as we danced. Plus, it was the longest I'd gotten to hold her in some time."

"Coraline?"

"He looked at me like he used to…" She sighed, finally looking at me. "Like I mattered."

"You do matter. You matter a lot, more than anything." I took her hand.

"It's one thing to say it, but it's another to show it," she whispered, pulling her hand away.

"See, that's our problem." I groaned as I sat forward. "I'm trying all the time. I am fucking trying, but she always goes back a step and blames me for everything in the past. I know I screwed up, but I feel like we're never going to get past that point."

"Maybe we shouldn't!" she yelled at me, and I felt the sudden urge to strangle her.

"Is that what you really want, Coraline? Do you want a divorce?" Dr. Bell asked her and I felt my heart slowly sink. I couldn't even bring myself to look at her. It was worse when she didn't answer.

"Divorce, means something *completely* different in this family, Doc." She replied, with a hint of sarcasm he didn't get.

"What do you mean?" He asked.

She didn't say anything.

"Either way I don't think you want to get a divorce," the doctor answered for her. "I think you want to make him suffer because you suffered. You want him to feel everything you felt. You know he loves you and you love him, but you're still angry."

That got my attention.

"Maybe." She frowned and we all fell silent.

He was good at letting us be silent. The motherfucker got paid by the hour anyway.

"Fine, I'm still angry and hurt. He doesn't just get to come in with his charm and make it all better. He just wants to wipe the slate clean and pretend he never did anything!" She pointed at me.

"No, I don't! I want to wipe the slate clean so I can stop sleeping in the fucking guest bedroom and hold my wife again. I want to wipe the slate clean so we can move on! That doesn't mean I want to forget. I don't think I could ever forget the seven months of blue balls and short jabs you've taken at me. You want me to suffer, Coraline? Well I'm suffering! I have a beautiful, amazing wife who won't let me hold her, who won't even speak to me! I'm suffering!" I yelled.

I stood up.

"I'm done for the day, Doc." And with that, I left.

Coraline

"I know you're hurt, Coraline. But you have to let go of it or let go of your husband, because it's not fair to you or him," Doctor Bell said to me and I just stared at my wedding ring.

I didn't know he was suffering. He seemed fine, always happy to see me when I stepped out in the hall. I was tired of this too…

"Thanks, Doc. See you next week," I said as I walked out.

The moment I got down to the car, the driver opened the door for me. Declan sat with his head up and eyes closed.

"Clean slate," I said, taking his hand.

He looked to me. "What?"

"It's time for a clean slate, and starting from now, there is one," I whispered.

"Clean slate," he repeated in shock as I sat on to his lap to kiss him.

"God, I've missed you," he muttered, as he wrapped his arms around me.

It was going to take baby steps, but it was time.

Seven

*"All good things are difficult to achieve; and
bad things are very easy to get."*
~ Confucius

LIAM

"Please, tell me I heard you wrong." I was doing my best to stay calm, but it seemed the world was on piss-the-fuck-out-of-Liam mode.

Sedric sighed, pouring himself a glass of brandy. "I'm afraid not, son. Apparently your grandfather will be making a stop in the States."

"But grandfather hates America," Declan stated the obvious, making me want to throw my glass at his face.

Mel leaned against the desk, forcing me to calm down with her eyes. She could do that now. Her own little superpower; where she could control what I was feeling with just her beautiful brown eyes. But she couldn't understand how much I hated my grandfather and how much he hated me. I didn't even want to give him the satisfaction of talking about him.

"When will he be here?" Neal asked, not bothered at all. Out of all of he was the only one our grandfather "liked". If he had it his way, our grandfather would have killed me a long time ago.

"I don't give a fuck, he isn't staying here! He can take his old motherfucking cane and shov—"

"Shove it where, grandson?" The devil himself said, dressed in a ten thousand dollar suit, as my mother opened the door for him and his three bodyguards.

My father, Neal, Declan and even my own mother stood up straighter, each one of them gave my grandfather the respect his title commanded. I may be the one who ran the Callahan clan now, but my grandfather was the one who built it. He was the original. Before him, we were a bunch of street thugs. He created our empire after being a drug runner for a boss much older and wiser than himself. One day, he snapped and took an ax to the motherfucker. War broke out. My grandfather had three very simple skills: killing, thinking and stealing. If he wanted something, he could have it.

"I think he was going to say, 'shove it up your old ass.'" Mel stated with ease, causing the whole family to pause. Even I couldn't speak to the asshole like that.

No matter how high up I was, no matter how powerful, custom made it impossible. When our grandfather passed down the family business, he had my father sign a contract—the same one I had to sign—stating that he'd get five percent of everything, and that he was always treated with respect deserved. Everything was put into writing like this was some civilized business deal. It used to be based on honor, but everyone wised up to that real quick. Families had to sign their souls away in ink to make sure people knew their place.

His wrinkled old hand tightly gripped his wooden cane as he took a step forward. If you were to age my father thirty years and give him silver hair, he and my grandfather would look exactly the same.

As children, Declan and I used to joke that the reason he had so few wrinkles was the fact that he would scare them away when he looked in the mirror. Though now he did look rather worn out.

"You must be the Italian cow now sharing my last name." He looked her up and down with disgust. As I stood, Mel glared, telling me to back the down or else.

She moved from behind the desk and stood directly in front of his face, causing his bodyguards to step forward as well.

"Old man, you're in my house. That makes you a fucking guest. I don't owe you shit and you will respect me if you want my respect. My name is Melody. Mrs. Callahan if it suits you, but..." She leaned in until their noses were almost touching. She was shorter, but the black heels helped. "If you ever call me a cow again, I will kill you painfully slow. I don't care how many motherfucking body guards you have."

Two of his bodyguards drew their guns and the last had a knife hidden in his sleeve.

Shit. I thought as she pulled her gun. Declan and Neal were already backing her up. My father just rolled his eyes and took my mother into the corner, all while drinking his brandy. This was ridiculous.

"Lower your weapons," Grandfather said as he glared into her eyes. "The Italian *cow...*"

The moment he said it, three bullets went flying into them. One in the chest, one in the wrist and the other the knee; they all went down like cards. You don't out gun Mel.

"What the fuck? Where did she pull the gun out from?" Neal whispered. "I swear, she's a motherfucking ninja."

"M-E-L-O-D-Y. Me-lo-dy. I will let the second time slide due to your old age. I've heard hearing loss is common." She stepped back, looking to the guards as she took off the silencer on her gun. "Please stop bleeding all over our rug, it's quite rude."

My grandfather looked down and smirked. "Shame. It was their first day too, I warned them that you could be as ruthless as your repetition called for, Giovanni."

"Better...who says you can't teach an old dog new tricks?" Mel replied, and my blood began to boil.

"You came across the fucking ocean just to test my wife?" I snapped, stepping forward as well.

"Adriana!" I roared, causing the ex-ugly duckling to come in, "Have a doctor see to these idiots, and then have a new rug brought up."

She nodded, opening the door for the men to crawl out like the pieces of shit they were.

My grandfather simply stepped around them, pulled out a pipe, cleaned the handle of the chair and sat down like he fucking owned it.

"I heard about the Bloody Melody that was now part of my family and I figured a trip to this godforsaken country was worth it, so we could speak face to face," he said as he blew out smoke.

"Try using Skype next time." I glared at him.

He glared in return before turning to my parents. "You should have taken my advice and beat the wit out of him as a child."

"You can't beat out personality, Shamus," Evelyn said respectfully. "I kind of enjoy it actually."

"Of course you do." He sighed, turning to my father. "Son, do I not get a welcoming?"

"Welcome, Shamus," was all Sedric said.

"Grandfather..."

"Speak when spoken to, child, or did all those seizures distort your brain as a youth?" he asked, reminding me once again why I hated him.

"They helped me become head of this fucking family, so, with respect, I'm asking you to get out of my chair," I hissed through my teeth.

"And what a man you are. Allowing your home to burn down, your wife to lose her child, and losing millions in the process, I applaud you. I bow down to your greatness, *child.*" He snickered and Melody stood forward, but it was my turn to glare at her.

This was not her fight.

"Mr. and Mrs. Callahan," Mina burst in. "We need to leave for the rally. Senator…" She froze at the sight of the blood on the carpet.

"We were just leaving, Mina. You're dismissed." I didn't even bother to turn towards her.

When the door closed, I stepped forward, leaning across my desk. "My family and I will be leaving. I suggest…"

"Beautiful, I will come along." Shamus smirked, cutting me off once again. "What is the point of being so done up if no one can see me?" He rose to his feet, blowing the smoke from his pipe in my face.

He walked forward only to stop right next to Mel to present his arm.

"I'd rather hang myself while on fire," Mel told him, but he took her arm anyway.

"I wasn't asking, my dear. There is no need to be so hostile, we're family," he said as he led her to the door. He, like all Callahan men, had charm, and it disgusted me.

"You called me a cow. Twice," she said with no emotion.

"I'm sure you've been called worse." He winked and the look on Mel's face worried me. She didn't hate him.

Sedric stood in front of me as he tried to figure out the words to say. But, like always, when it came to Shamus

Callahan, there were no words. My mother kissed my cheek as I leaned against the desk. One by one, they all left as the clean up crew came in.

"There better not be a fucking spot left behind." I finished off the rest of my brandy before leaving.

Melody

"Where is Liam?" I asked, stepping out of the car. I had been waiting for half an hour and that prick still hadn't come into the car.

The maids, who I didn't even bother to get to know, stood outside waiting. They weren't supposed to leave the driveway until we left. None of them looked uncomfortable, but that was years of training at work.

"Ma'am," one of them said. "He went to change in his room and never came back out."

"You're dismissed," I told them, as I walked in. I had no idea what the hell his problem was, but he needed to put on his big boy pants and deal with it.

The moment Sedric brought up Shamus, Liam went ridged. I knew of Shamus; he had killed, stolen and bribed his way into the history books...but then again, we all had. The things he had done were things that I myself had studied and copied. He impressed me, and I was not an easy person to impress. Shamus was deadly, cocky, and an asshole. He demanded respect, which he earned, but I would never give him that satisfaction. He was in my house.

The moment I stepped into our room, I followed the music drifting through the air from Liam's closet. His closet had to be as big as mine, if not bigger; the ass loved his suits.

On the far center wall was a black upright piano.

Walking up behind him, I grabbed his hair and pulled it back, bringing my face to the side of his cheek. "I hate being stood up, Liam."

"Ask my grandfather to take you," he snapped like a child.

Letting go of his hair, I sat on his lap. "That was passive-aggressive. What the hell is wrong with you?"

He sighed, pulling me closer to him as he kissed me. I kissed him back before biting his bottom lip.

"You aren't going to use sex as a way out of this. As much as I enjoyed putting your grandfather in his place, I need to know what level of bitch to be," I told him truthfully.

"I loathe Shamus with a burning passion," he whispered as he held me tighter.

"I see that. Why?" There had to be some reason he held such hatred.

I found it sexy. However, he was in pain, and he was growing on me. I wasn't sure when we had changed into this lovely couple, but with each passing day, he was becoming a bigger part of my soul. Part of me was still worried about it.

"Shamus has always believed in survival of the fittest. My father thought the city was one of the reasons I was so sick. He took us all to Ireland and the very first time I met him, he looked me up and down and said, 'In the wild, animals eat their young if they're sick.' He and my father got in a fight…though it was more like my father yelling and Shamus smoking in his chair. He told my father that if he were too weak to put me down, he would do the honors. That a man in his position couldn't have a child like me; that he should be happy he was given another son and could raise Declan to replace me if he wanted to." His grip on my thigh tightened, but I let him squeeze as hard as he needed.

"But you did survive, and you are the fittest," I whispered, holding onto the side of his face.

He kissed my palm. "Shamus likes things done his way. He wanted the company to go to Neal and my father actually refused. My father has gotten quite good at refusing my grandfather. He was never supposed to marry my mother. She, after all, wasn't a pure breed. Being half-Irish is as good as being Italian." He leered at me, leaving me torn between kissing him and breaking his face open.

"My full blood Italian can kick any Irish—"

"Yes, I know, love. You're a badass." He grinned as he squeezed my ass.

"Didn't Evelyn have Neal when she was young?" She had to have been sixteen or seventeen at the time.

"She had us all when she was young. My grandfather swears Sedric got her pregnant on purpose. He knew Shamus wouldn't approve of his only living son marrying anyone other than his choosing. However, after Evelyn became pregnant, there was nothing he could do," he explained. "We are good Catholic folk, you know," he said in his accent.

"Tá tú ar leathcheann," (*You're an idiot.*) I said, as I got off of him.

"You love me, you hate me, make up your damn mind, wife. I'm getting whiplash." He smirked, rising as well.

"You're getting a whip? What kind of kinky shit are you into, Callahan?" I asked, causing him to push me up against his mirror.

His expression darkened and his lips hovered over mine. "Let's find out. God only knows what I have in this closet."

I pushed up against him. "You mean the cheerleading uniform for the Chicago Bulls you have hidden behind your gray suits? Or the very whorish nun outfit you have in the hidden compartment under your socks?"

His eyes widened and I could only grin.

"Keep your cock on lock, we're late for the rally," I said, pushing him away before leaving the closet.

"At least I get to look at your ass," he yelled behind me and I held my middle finger up.

Liam

"I know a lot of you don't know me," Olivia said to the crowd. "I know a lot of you don't think you can relate to me, or the life I have been so blessed to live. However, I want to tell you a story. About a young college student, who was fresh faced and naïve to the world around her. Her father, the man who always checked under the bed for monsters, and who read to her in animated voices, wanted to do everything in his power to keep his daughter safe. Sadly, sometimes the world is a dark place. Sometimes, a young college student with everything going for her is given a new title: rape victim. It's a title I have tried so hard to hide because I didn't have the voice to stand up. I didn't have the courage to tell my father until last night. He pulled me into a hug and said, 'when I become President, there will no longer be a statute of limitations for rape.'"

The crowd cheered and screamed, blinding us with flashes as they ate up her words like candy.

"When people ask why do I think my father is the best man for the job, I think about moments like last night. When he held me and promised to always fight for justice. He will fight for me—he will fight for men and women all across this country. My father is a good man, and with your support, he will be a great president." Senator Colemen hugged his daughter once more before taking his place behind the podium to give his own scripted political bullshit.

Neal held on tightly to Olivia, which I'm sure would have made a great cover photo for the *New York Times*.

"She's good," I whispered to my wife as we stood like dolls on stage.

"She is. They will love her, and those who don't will get backlash for not supporting a rape victim," she replied, waving into the crowd.

That was my wife, always planning and trying to figure out how to get a leg up on all those around her.

I felt like we'd been on display for hours, waving and smiling as Senator Colemen talked about how he was going to save the environment, bring down the unemployment rate, and make sure borders were secure; the same bullshit all presidents say.

By the time we were free to go to the private screening rooms up stairs, I had almost forgotten all about Shamus… until I saw the asshole already eating his lamb, in the head chair of the dinner table. Behind him stood two much stronger looking guards, who eyed my wife with both lust and fear.

A misguided fear.

Taking Mel's hand, I pulled out her chair for her before taking a seat on the opposite side. The moment I sat down, the rest of the family took their seats as well.

"So, this is your big plan? Have the fool and his family as president?" he asked, but I didn't answer. Instead I took a sip of my brandy.

"We do not discuss business at the dinner table," Mel said kindly, throwing me off. I looked into her eyes and for a second I thought maybe the bodyguards were right in fearing her.

This seemed to be our new thing; the ability to look into each other's eyes and just read them.

"Don't be sweet, Giovanni. It doesn't suit you." He snickered like an old pig before turning to Olivia. "Did some men violate ya' or was them some lies you told to the public?"

Olivia glared, but nodded. "Yes, sir…"

"Neal, I hope you've corrected this situation," he cut her off to give his attention to his favorite.

"Actually, grandpa, Olivia has been handling things just fine on her own," he hissed out. But that anger had more to do with Olivia's rape, and the fact that we couldn't find Harvey yet, than grandfather's words.

"Huh." He frowned, looking over at Coraline. "Nice hair, when did you become a lesbian?"

"Never," Declan and Coraline said at the same time. They didn't speak much when Shamus was around.

"How far you all have strayed from tradition," he said, cutting his lamb.

For a decrepit old man he had a strong grip.

"How long do you plan on staying, Shamus?" Evelyn asked softly as she ate.

"As long as I please," he snapped, causing my father to grab his knife. However, my mother held his arm. I wished she hadn't.

"For someone who says he came so far to see me, you and I haven't spoken much. I don't care how long you stay, my question is: why are you here?" Mel glared.

Shamus chuckled at her, taking his time to chew. "It's a shame you aren't male. I could respect you more."

"It's a shame you don't have manners. Now answer my question, old man, or I will pull it out of you," was her reply, causing Shamus to just laugh, allowing us to see all the food in his mouth.

"You try so very hard to be something you can never be. A woman will never be a boss. No matter how many people you kill, no matter how much you threaten. You will always be a cunt. All women are cunts, I wish my grandson would have found one with even a drop Irish blood in her veins to make up for it." I expected Mel to flip out, but instead, she regarded him carefully.

"You've lowered your standards. I've heard even being half Irish wasn't good enough for you," Mel stated, much calmer than I was.

He had come into my home uninvited and insulted us all. He spoke as if we were nothing but gum under his shoe. As if we weren't even family. Shamus was a pig. Every time he spoke, the pressure from keeping my mouth shut built up behind my eyes.

"I was not unreasonable. After all, if my son had chosen the woman I'd gotten for him, I'm sure he wouldn't have a dumbass, a mouse, and a cripple as sons. But apparently, my words fall on deaf ears." The pig snickered.

A dumbass…Neal

A mouse…Declan

A cripple…Me

We all knew our titles, he had made it clear to all of us when we were children, but he always said he'd rather have a dumbass than a mouse or a cripple.

"I would have sooner killed myself than marry Catharine Briar," my father snapped, and again my mother held him back.

"Maybe you should have and saved me so much trouble!" Shamus yelled. I prayed the man would have a stroke.

"So you're here due to the Briar's," Mel stated, eyeing him carefully. "Let me guess, you wanted Liam to marry her daughter."

"Look at you, using that pretty little brain of yours. I wish you would have done the same when you locked Natasha Briar away."

I tried to figure out where the dots connected. As far as I knew, the Briar family didn't have anything worth taking, and yet he seemed adamant we marry the trash.

"That was your grandson's idea. I wanted to kill her. I came close one time in church," Mel confessed.

How she could manage to stay composed was beyond me.

Shamus turned to me as I watched him, biting my tongue once again. He looked me over, held his nose up high, as if *I* were filth.

"How did you two, of all people, become the Boss? You, Liam, will never be great," he said. "You will always be the crippled boy trying so hard to be a man. I guess that was why you can handle being married to someone with bigger balls."

I grabbed the table knife just like my father, wanting to ram it into his goddamn throat, but Melody squeezed my leg.

"I do believe I will take that as my queue to leave. These old bones of mine need to be rested," Shamus said as he rose with the help of his cane. "You all enjoy your evening."

"*Father*," Sedric called out to him, stretching out the word to the point where he grimaced just by saying it.

Shamus stopped, turning back to him and looked just as surprised as I was.

"Do not spend the night in our house," he said.

"That's where you are wrong, son. It's *my* house. All of this—everything you have, everything you have accomplished—is because of the deals I made."

With that, he left.

Melody

No one said anything. With each passing moment, Shamus disgusted me. I was tempted to kill him the second I saw where he was sitting. But it wasn't my place. I had enough issues with my family line.

Liam grabbed his plate and threw the damn thing at the door after Shamus left.

"I want him GONE!" he yelled. "I don't care how, duct tape him to the bottom of a goddamn plane and send him back to Ireland for all I care. He'd better not be back at our fucking house!"

"Liam," I whispered, but he didn't say anything, just backed away from the table trying to breathe as he reached for the closet bottle.

"Mr. and Mrs. Callahan, I would like to remind you that this isn't your home." Mina snapped. "There are cameras everywhere and not to mention, I don't know, a political candidate! Can you people stop going Rambo on whoever walks through the door?"

"Can't we just buy the building?" Coraline asked. Mina took a deep breath before dragging Senator Colemen out of the room. Walking over to Liam, I placed my hand on his shoulder.

"I thought we were quite civilized, didn't you?" I asked Liam.

He looked around the building. "Honestly, if people would stop testing us, the world would be a better place."

"You both are so…" Olivia started, but stopped, perhaps remembering she too had blood on her hands and she wanted more. When you are part of this family you then you can't judge anyone…We all made the choice to be here.

"Well then, my wife and I will be calling it a night," Liam said, taking my hand.

Neither of us said anything as we left through the back, where all of our cars were now parked and waiting for us. Monte and Fedel had two cars up front while Dylan, Liam's new right hand since Eric's death, manned the cars behind ours.

It was only when we took our seats that Liam pulled off his tie and leaned back, pinching the bridge of his nose.

"I need to kill my grandfather," he said to himself. "But if I do, it will be all-out war. We have a shit load of product coming in tomorrow, and I can't take out Ireland's superman. He knows it. He's been pumping money into the country for so long I'm surprised they haven't made him king yet. He's untouchable."

"If you can see him, he's touchable. Being untouchable is just an illusion people like us create to intimidate others. Everyone has a weakness. We will deal with him, he won't get away with talking to you like that, I swear," I said, staring out the window.

"When did you become so sweet?" He kissed into the back of my hand.

I hated how much I enjoyed that and how I couldn't admit it. "I don't know what you mean. Him calling you a cripple was insult to me. As if I would marry someone with less balls than me."

He smiled so wide it made me uncomfortable. Like he knew something I didn't.

"What?"

"Nothing. Anyway do you find it odd that my father, a former rival of your family, came into town around the same time your mother suddenly popped up?" he asked, staring out into the city.

"You don't think—"

"I don't know what I think. But if I were my grandfather, after everything that happened last year, maybe he wants to take back the business."

"Over my dead body," I muttered, pulling out my phone. "We're going into lock down until we can talk to father crime himself."

Eight

*"Children aren't coloring books. You don't get
to fill them with your favorite colors."*
—*K Colemend Hosseini*

Evelyn

I wasn't sure what to say to him. No, that was a lie. I knew what I *wanted* to say. I knew *how* I wanted to say it. Sadly, I couldn't. It wouldn't be right. I never once flinched at Liam or Melody's actions. My moral compass was shattered beyond repair, but that didn't bother me either. When I first married Sedric, knowing what his life was going to be, I thought I could keep my head up above it all. But this life has away of sucking the good out of you…how can it not when you are surrounded by the worst of people. I've never physically killed a man, but twice in my life I've asked for retribution, and twice Sedric had ensured that it was done it for me.

"What are you going to do?" I whispered as he lay on our bed. He stared up at the ceiling, not bothering to move like a fat cat after a feast. I knew this Sedric. He was about to do something…something evil.

"I have no idea what you're talking about," he said, as I took off my heels.

They were originally Melody's and the damned girl wanted to burn nine hundred dollar Jimmy Choos, just because they were white.

We were the same size, and like the shoe hoarder I was, I took them with pleasure. However, it seemed like they were molded for her feet alone and were going to kill me.

"You're a bad liar. Thank God I keep you locked away." I laughed, crawling on top of him.

"I'm a great liar. We're just born with a strong pair of bullshit detectors."

"Raising three boys—four if I count you—it was a required skill."

He chuckled, but didn't reply.

"Sedric, what are you about to do?"

"Shh…" he whispered, just holding me.

I stopped struggling, allowing him to just hold me. It was what he did, what he always did. He held onto me as if he were worried I would never forgive him for whatever he was about to do, but I always did. No matter what, I always would.

We sat there, wrapped in each other's arms, and I felt sixteen again. I felt like that same loud mouth, know it all, rash, love-struck teenager who saw her prince charming and went weak at the knees the moment he looked my way.

"What?" he asked, as I smiled to myself.

"Nothing," I said, and in one swift motion, he flipped me onto my back and pinned me under him.

He glared into my eyes with a smirk on his lips. "Woman, what is so damn funny?"

"Man," I lifted my head up to him, "I said nothing."

"The hard way then…"

"Sedric, don't…" before I could stop him, he ripped my shirt open. "Damn it all to hell, Sedric, that shirt was a gift."

"My gift will be so much better." He kissed my neck and with one hand, he ripped my bra from my chest.

"Really?" I dared him, crossing my arms over my chest, but the moment they covered my breasts, he pried them away.

"Isn't it obvious?" he whispered, one of his hands wandering down the side of my arm, which were pinned over my head, until he reached my nipples. He played with them as he stared into my eyes.

"Sedric..."

"What better way can I show my wife I care, than to give her pleasure?" he whispered again, kissing my lips before trailing the side of my jaw. "Give us both pleasure."

"Father, Liam wants..." Neal burst through the door before I could speak. "Jesus, mother fucking Christ of Nazareth, my eyes!"

I grabbed for a pillow, and Sedric reached for his gun in a fit of rage.

"What have I told you about knocking?" he roared, before firing a round at Neal's head.

Neal ducked but it took off piece of the door. "SORRY..."

"Neal, I swear, if you don't leave, I will skin you!" Sedric shouted, getting off the bed once I was covered.

Neal's head dropped, and I tried really hard not to laugh. He looked like he did when he was a child and caught us doing the same thing.

"Liam said..."

"I don't care what your brother said. I don't care if the goddamn moon is falling out of the sky. Get out, boy!" he roared.

His throat was going to be sore in the morning.

"Father, I'd rather die at your hands than at Liam's...or worse, Mel's. Give me one second to tell you and then I will run faster than Forrest Gump."

That did it, I couldn't hold back from laughing, and Sedric glared at me, forcing me to place my hand over my mouth.

He stood in front of Neal, not that he could see since he was forcing his eyelids shut, and put a gun to his skull.

"Sedric…"

"You rather I kill you than Liam or Mel?" he asked, and I wanted to smack him over the head.

Neal smirked. "You would kill me quickly, and then mom will kick your ass. Liam and Mel would take a page out of George Bugs Morgan's book, and hang me by my testicles with piano wire from a ceiling. Then burn my eyes out with cigarettes. Then maybe go after Olivia too, just for the heck off it. So yes, I fear them much more than I fear you, because they are bat shit crazy."

Sedric's jaw clenched.

"Neal, what is it?" I asked, before Sedric really did pull the trigger.

"Aviela DeRosa is in Chicago, and Liam thinks she's related to gramps somehow. Gramps isn't home yet, but we're on lockdown. Which means…"

"I taught you the damn rules, I know what it fucking means, you dumbass!" Sedric snapped, pulling Neal by the ear just as he used to. "Out." He pushed him out the door.

"Liam wants a family meeting…"

"Tell your brother that your mother and I are having our own meeting. With the grace of God, maybe we can have another child to replace you three knuckleheads!" he said, slamming the door in his face.

Another child? Who were we, Abraham and Sarah?

"Urgh! Really? As if I haven't been scarred enough for one lifetime!" Neal's muffled voice rang through the door.

"Pull up a chair at Declan's therapy lessons and cry to them," Sedric yelled back before falling onto our bed. "I knew that boy would forever cock-block me. I knew it from the first month he was home."

Laughing, I kissed his back before lying next to him. He was right. Between all of our children, Neal was the only one who had ever caught us in the act. The others might have heard, but only Neal ever came in and killed our moment. He did it as an infant, he did it as a young boy, and even as a teen. And now, he did it as an adult.

"Remember, he is also the one who makes you laugh harder than the rest. Neal is the laugher. Declan, the quiet observer. Liam is…"

"A smart ass, controlling prick, with a God complex to rival my father's," he added, turning to look up at me and pushing the pillow away in order to see me.

I shook my head. "No, Liam is the thinker, the master chess player. It's why you love him so much. It's always a back and forth between you. But each one of them is like you. Neal radiates joy, the way you used to before this life; Declan reads like you, studies like you, listens like you. He enjoys the peace…"

"And then Liam, oh wise mother?" He smirked, kissing my hand.

I smacked his arm. "Liam is the tiny part of you that wishes to achieve greatness at all costs. Yes, he is a smart-ass, and yes, he is controlling. He may even have a God complex. But you see him and you see what you could never have become and you respect him for it. You and I both know if Liam were first born and never ill, Shamus would have tried to adopt him."

"I knew it even when he was sick," he whispered. For some reason, his voice was stuck at this level with me tonight. "He had so much fight. He used to tell me while in bed that once he was better, he was going to buy the damn hospital, just so they could stock it with better food. When I asked why he didn't just suggest it to them, he said, 'that's too much talking and I want it done.' He was seven. I took him and the boys fishing when he was thirteen. Neal caught five fish, Declan three, and I seven."

"Liam didn't catch anything? Are you sure?" I frowned, trying my best to remember those days, but he and I both knew that time for me was like the dark ages.

"He caught one. He was just getting over his trip from the hospital and still a bit weak. I was surprised he caught anything. I just wanted him to get fresh air and relax. We camped out by the lake, but when I woke up in the morning, Liam was gone…"

"Sedric!" I slapped his arm.

"Ouch. Damn it, woman!" he yelled, holding onto me tighter. "I found him, didn't I? The little brat took the boat, went out on the water and fished until he caught eighteen fish. Kid was half frozen, his fingers were cut from the wires. I never wanted to kick his ass so much!"

I could see how now, years later, he couldn't stop himself from smiling at the memory of it.

"He was so determined to out-do us all. He could have stopped at ten, but no, the damn kid had to double it. He was so proud of himself, even though he reeked to high heaven," he added.

"That sounds like our Liam. He has to be number one, and everyone has to know it." I laughed.

"Yeah." He kissed my head. "It's how I knew he was the one who was going to take over. Liam could barely stand to bow down to me. If it were Neal or Declan, I know he would have broken away or killed them. Never in my life was I more grateful to Neal than when he accepted it without question."

"That's because he's like you and never wanted to be in charge. He hates working under pressure." I would never admit it, but Neal's fun craziness came from me.

"Your biggest success was finding Mel, you know that, right? Liam would not be half the man he is now if it weren't for her," I added.

"Both a good and bad thing. Good for the family and the company. The world may just hate me for it. Liam feeds off of her, and she him. They both like to out-do the other and it's scary. Liam would have killed Shamus, but Melody pulled him back."

I could see it in his eyes. Pride. They were finally growing.

"What are you going to do?" I asked for the third and final time.

He kissed me before sitting up. "I'm going to have a talk with my father."

Sedric

There comes a time in every child's life where they have to look their parents in the eye and say enough.

I always wondered when that time would come. Or how I could look my demon of a father in the eye, whilst standing with my head held high with no fear. We are all afraid of something or someone. Shamus had always been that person. Yet, as we walked through the back woods behind our home, I felt nothing…and nothing was a familiar feeling.

It was how I spent almost thirty years running the family. There were brief moments of relief; the moment I met Evelyn, the moment each of my children were born, and the moment Evelyn came back to me. But that nothingness was always there eating away at me.

"I didn't seek company," Shamus spoke in the darkness, as the wind blew the leaves above us.

"I didn't seek your presence," I said to him, moving to stand beside the tree. I hated coming this far back in our property, but I still made the trip once a year with Evelyn, just to see the tombstones that rested right under the tress. One for my mother and one for the daughter we never got to raise.

"I told you that boy of yours was going to cock-up everything I've built."

I didn't reply for a moment, enjoying the chill of the wind as we stood.

"Why are you back here, Shamus?"

"Because death is coming," he replied. Turning to me, I noticed for the first time he held a gun in his hand. "You have no idea what you did when you arranged for their marriage. There are rules even we have to follow."

"Any rules I broke was because you failed to teach," I replied. "Are you truly going to kill me out here, in the woods, in front of my own mother and daughter?"

"Not you," he said before turning the gun onto himself.

Before I could blink, the shot echoed through the night. His body fell onto the leaves, and I couldn't bring myself to care. Not even a little bit.

Kneeling down, I stared at him. "You should have done that a long time go."

Sighing, I pulled out my phone. Liam was going to be pissed.

Nine

"Older men declare war. But it is youth that must fight and die."
—*Herbert Hoover*

Liam

"I'm sorry, what the fuck did you just say?" Neal asked our father as he poured himself a drink.

"Your grandfather shot himself in the head with a nine millimeter while we were talking in the woods," he repeated before downing the entire glass.

I opened my mouth, but for the first time in my life, I wasn't sure what the hell to say. How he could just stand there all calm and collected as if he'd just told us about the weather and not a man's suicide. Melody, Declan, Neal and I sat there, and I allowed them a moment for the news to sink in.

"Shamus just shot himself?" Melody asked, eyeing him. "In the woods?"

"I feel as though you are implying something. Which is odd because you've always been so direct." He glared at her.

Melody crossed her legs, folding her hands in her lap. "Fine, then let me be direct; did you kill Shamus?"

"No, but I planned on it. Just like the bastard to go and ruin that for me as well." He frowned, still colder than ice.

This was the father that taught me everything I needed to know growing up.

"The Shamus I knew loved himself way too much to take his own life," Declan added.

"We all fear something no matter how much we try to deny it," he replied, moving to look out the window. "I can only guess it has something to do with Melody's mother."

"I do not have a mother," Melody said quickly.

"Either way, Shamus' last words were 'You have no idea what you did when you arranged for their marriage. There are rules even we have to follow.' So whoever that woman is, he was afraid enough to take his own life because of her."

"None of this makes any fucking sense," Neal groaned, rubbing his temple. "I mean I can't be the only one totally confused."

He wasn't, and the fact that I was now as clueless as my brother pissed me off to no end.

"Enough is enough," I snapped. "We've been behind this for far too long. I want answers. I want them *yesterday*. Who the hell is this woman? What does she want with our family?"

Melody sat up and turned to my father. "Shamus did two things when he got here: he insulted us, and he said you should have married Catherine Briar."

"I've checked over that Briar family," Declan replied. "They're nothing but a small bunch of Irish thugs. They have a few dealings with ecstasy and other second rate drugs, but they can't even hold a flame to us."

"That doesn't matter," I said, looking Melody in the eye. *Was she thinking what I was thinking?* "If Shamus wasted his breath on it, then it has to be important. We need to get to the Briars so that we can piece together whatever the hell is going on."

"Only problem is, after you threw Natasha into the nut house, her family went into hiding. No one has seen them," Neal said.

"Then do your fucking job and find them!" Melody and I yelled together.

Declan shook his head but rose along with Neal, heading to the door. It was only after they'd left that I turned to my father. "Were you really going to kill him?" I asked, already knowing the answer.

He didn't reply, he just looked out the window. "You both have a mystery to solve and I have a parent to bury."

"You're really going bury that bastard?"

"Rule forty-four," he replied before walking out the door.

Melody looked to me, eyebrow raised and questioning me.

"Rule forty-four: Family is family, even when you wish they weren't," I explained.

She laughed as she moved beside me. "If this has anything to do with my family as well, I'm going to look into it."

"Everyone in your family is dead."

"Rule 171." She smirked, and I stared at her in confusion. "Care to share?"

She grinned, kissing my cheek. "Rule 171: even the men are family."

I smiled. "You just made that up."

"That doesn't make it any less of a great rule."

True.

"I have a bad feeling about this. All of this," I told her.

"So do I."

Just as I had suspected, something was coming out of Hell and straight towards us. And it was coming fast.

Ten

"I used to murder people for money, but these days it's more of a survival technique."
Jennifer Estep

Fedel

Some people think you'd have to be a real messed up son of a bitch to live the life I do. I see them walking around with their heads held up high, talking on their cell phones, pretending to be good people. But the truth is, they're not. Truly good people, which are very hard to find, don't *think* they're good people. They believe that they're doing what anyone else would do. The truth is, ninety percent of us are hiding from the world and our true selves. We force ourselves to do the "right" thing because we're afraid of the consequences of doing what we really want to do.

I used to be one of those people. I used to lie to myself too. I knew what my father—Gino the One-Eye—did for a living. I only saw him on holidays, and on my birthday, but I knew I didn't want to be like him. Every time my mother washed the blood out of his shirts, I felt my disgust build. I didn't want to be like him, I didn't want his life, and I didn't want to spend my time kissing people's shoes.

And then he came back in a wheelchair and told me I was going to go work for the devil himself. Gino's loyalty to Orlando knew no bounds, and I guess Orlando liked the old man. So when Gino lost his legs, Orlando allowed him a way out of the life and to prove his gratitude, and Gino gave me up; I would work in his place, that way no one would ever think he would become a rat. A man could rat on his boss, but a true man could never rat out his only son.

I hated him for it. I tried to run. I packed all my shit in a bag, jumped out the window and ran down the street, only to find Orlando's daughter leaning against a beat up old Chevy.

"I told my dad you were going to run." She said, as the wall of muscle I grew to know as Antonio opened the door for her and myself. The look in his eyes as he held the door open, and his visible gun, told me I didn't have any choice in the matter.

Melody didn't speak to me. Instead she sat back, flipping through an Irish-to-English dictionary. I tried getting them to talk, I called them every name in the book, but Melody's only response was to take out a knife and drive its blade deep into the dashboard. That shut me up quick.

As we pulled up to their mansion, she laid down the law. "Your loyalty is to my father and me for the rest of your life," she said. "You will kill for us, you will fight for us, and you will lie for us. In return, you will not only be a very wealthy man, but you will be much safer than you would be without us. Your father has pissed off a lot of people, all of whom would kill you just to get back at him. Run again, and Antonio will put a bullet in the back of your skull. Goodnight." And with that, she got out of the car and walked into her house, leaving me completely stumped.

"How old is she?" I asked Antonio.

"Fourteen," he said, as he shook his head, a thin smile playing on his lips. "The boss wanted to put her in high school, but was afraid she would eat the other students." He laughed. "Come on, time to show the new dog his cage. Wouldn't want to kill you so soon. She ain't joking about the rules."

No, she wasn't. Over the years I spent there, I grew to understand my place. I grew more loyal to her. I wasn't sure why. She just had a way of getting into your head and staying there. She worked ten times harder than the rest of us, and never asked for anything in return. She just worked…more than any girl her age should. You wanted to make her life easier. You wanted to do anything she needed. And by doing almost nothing but being cold, calculating and murderous, she had gained our loyalty. She was the reason I was making this call now.

"Gino," I said into the phone.

"Fedel? Why…"

"I don't have time, Pop. I have one question and I need you to answer it as honestly as possible." I could feel her gaze on the back of my neck.

"I cannot lie," he lied into the phone.

I fought the urge to roll my eyes. "What do you know about Aviela, Orlando's ex-wife?"

"Aviela? Why are you asking? That woman has been dead for years," he replied, lying to me again.

Damn it, Pop.

"Do you know anything?" I asked again.

"No son, I don't."

With that, I hung up.

I was going to have to do this the hard way.

"Well?" she asked, seated behind me as Antonio pulled up at the looney bin. She never spoke unless she had to.

I met her brown eyes in the rear-view mirror.

"He's lying, ma'am. He knows something," I told her honestly, and I watched her as she stared at me.

"Can I trust you to do what's needed?" she asked.

"Yes." Because I was loyal; the ranking of my life was Melody, Liam, God, then family. It was fucked up, but that was just part of life.

Melody

Was my request of Fedel too much? Would he really do everything he needed to do to get the job done? Time would only tell, and right now, I had bigger fish to fry. As I walked up the stairs and into the stone structure—which looked like it belonged in a Stephen King novel—rats ran freely into building.

"Mrs. Callahan, I was so happ…"

"I want Natasha Briar, you can kiss my ass later," I told the short doctor, who looked like he needed to be a patient himself.

"You can wait out here."

"Take me to her." I leaned into his face. "Now."

He jumped, and the nurses behind him stood back as he opened the door for me. I could feel Antonio walking beside me. The moment the doors opened, all I could hear was gibberish mixed in with different levels of screaming. It was madhouse, that was for sure. The women were all frizzy-haired and pale faced, and they seemed to be in their own worlds. Some sat in the corner shaking, while others played with their hands or talked to themselves.

"Shoes!" A woman yelled suddenly, trying to reach for me. Antonio grabbed her, though I doubt she noticed. "Shoes! Me want shoes! Red Shoes! Me want red shoes!"

"What good are shoes with no feet?" I warned her, just as the doctor told the two nurses to take her away.

"I dated a chick like her once." Antonio stated. "Actually, I think that may very well have been her."

"I'm sorry about that, Mrs. Callahan," said the doctor. "I try to let them out of their rooms so they can socialize and so they don't feel like caged animals. Believe me, you are perfectly…"

"Are you trying to sell me something, Doctor?" I asked.

"No ma'am…"

"Then stop wasting my time," I hissed through my teeth, causing him to drop his keys. He grabbed them quickly before rushing down the hall.

Her "room," which looked more like a cell, was the last door on the left. Through the small window, I could see that her blonde hair was all over the floor as she sat in the corner. Every time she brushed a lock back, it seemed to fall off, making her sob… it kind of reminded me of Orlando.

"Ms. Briar, Mrs. Callahan is here to see you." The moment he said it was me, she was up and pushing herself further into the wall.

"No. No. No. Please, no. NO!" she screamed before she started crying.

The doctor turned for the nurses, but that wouldn't help.

"Open the door," I demanded. Before he could argue, Antonio took the keys and opened the door himself.

"NO! PLEASE NO!" Natasha begged, curling into a ball.

"'No. No. No.' Oh shut up," I snapped, pulling her from the ground. Her eyes were wide, and she was covered in dirt and dried blood—from only God knows what or where. She looked like a complete savage, and she sure as hell smelled like one.

"It's your lucky day. I've come to save you."

"No," she said again. "You don't know how to save. God saves. The devil destroys."

"Good thing I'm neither. But I can do both. Now, do you want to leave or would you rather stay here with the good doctor?" I didn't give her time to think before pushing her to Antonio.

"You can't just take her!" The doctor yelled as we walked out.

"Who's going to stop me?" I called out as I walked away. "Watch out, doctor. I like destroying things way more than I do saving them."

The moment we stepped out, Neal and Monte pulled up in the car behind Fedel. Walking up to her, Monte pressed the needle into her arm.

"What are you doing? Stop, please stop," Natasha cried, forcing me to take a deep breath.

"We're clearing your system of any drugs you may have been given. So stop struggling," I replied, waiting for Monte to finish as Fedel held open the door for us.

Neal handed me the burger and milkshake before helping Natasha into the car. It was only when she was seated that I stepped inside and handed her the food. She eyed it before glaring up at me.

"I wouldn't have gone through all that trouble just to poison you." I leaned against the seat, texting Liam to let him know we were on our way back. With Antonio driving, we would be there in two hours.

She didn't speak. Instead, she stuffed her face as quickly and savagely as possible. Licking her hands and lips, Fedel turned to her, which caused her to slow down and freeze.

"Do you need something, Fedel?" I glared at him, forcing him to meet my gaze.

"No, ma'am," he said, turning around once more.

I handed her a tissue and she slowed down, but she still continued eating at a steady pace, all while watching me carefully.

"If you don't want to kill me, what do you want?" she asked. She sounded so tired, as though she hadn't slept in years.

At least she hasn't lost her mind yet.

"Just eat and rest. We can talk about that later. I promise I won't hurt you." She was the only piece of the puzzle we had.

She glared and it almost made her look like the old Natasha...almost.

"I've already hurt myself. So whatever it is—"

"Natasha," I cut her off. "I don't care about your pain. I don't care about your suffering. I warned you and you didn't make the right choice. You chose your fate and lost. But now you've become useful again, and you have a second chance. Don't fuck it up, Natasha. Be smart."

She stared at me again, making her look like a deer caught in headlights, before she dropped her head and finished her meal.

Placing my sunglasses back on, I tried to calm the raging headache that had been on and off for the last week. My head felt as though it was going to explode. No matter how much either Liam or I tried to piece together the mystery of our lives, we both came up empty handed. All of Shamus' records had been whipped clean. There were no traces that he even had records to begin with. Every last cent of his wealth was gone as well. There was no way that that much money could be just wiped from the system without any trace. Even if it were in a private offshore account, there would still be a trace.

Someone had all but erased Shamus from history. Most things that included his name were either gone or unimportant. I didn't like this. I felt like we were in the middle of some sort of spy novel. This was the mafia. I didn't have time to be chasing down secrets or trying to find the key to the past. We had a drug shipment coming in this morning and instead of checking it out with Liam, I was here, in a car with Natasha.

"Ma'am, your phone," Fedel called, pulling me away from my train of thought.

My phone was ringing.

"Well?" I asked into the receiver.

"Hello, love. How are you today? Did you miss me? Those are the questions I would like hear when you answer the phone." Liam said.

"Liam, I don't…" I stopped, not because I wanted to, but because the phone was no longer in my hand, and I was no longer in my seat…and the car was no longer on the road… In that moment, everything was in the air.

The glass shattered. Metal sheared against metal, ripping part of the car off as we rolled. Natasha screamed, or it looked like she was screaming, but I was deaf to it all. It felt like hours—years, maybe—when the car finally stopped. I was too dazed to move for a moment. I just sat there, hanging upside down, staring at the blood that dripped down Fedel's arm.

Was he dead?

"What happened?" Antonio yelled, trying to pull on his seat belt. "What the…what just happened?"

It was then that I noticed the large piece of glass in his arm. He was losing blood—a lot of blood—and he was panicking.

"Antonio, breathe." He wasn't listening to me. "Antonio! Listen to me right now."

Pulling off my seatbelt, I fell straight to the top of the car. Natasha lay there, knocked out, but still breathing. Crawling forward, I pulled my knife from my thigh, and reached up to cut his seat belt.

"Are you alive in there, sweetheart?" Someone called, and I froze. Antonio looked me in the eye before taking the knife from my hands.

"Mel bear? I'm going to be really disappointed if you're dead."

Aviela.

I fought back the memories; ones of me in her arms as she called me Mel bear. Grabbing a spear gun that had fallen, I tucked it into the back of my pants before I made a move to the window.

"Don't go," Fedel whispered. "Trap."

"Help him when you're stable, Antonio," was all I could bring myself to say as I crawled on my stomach and hands, ignoring the shards of glass that cut into my skin.

I pulled myself out through the window, and onto the grass, only to find six guns pointed in my face, and my mother, white gloves and all, smiling down at me. She, unlike the rest of her men, looked as though she was going for lunch with the queen and not out for blood.

She looked so much like me. Her dark hair cropped at her shoulders with bright brown eyes staring back. Grabbing onto my arm, one of her men pulled me up, and out of the corner of my eye, I saw Neal crawling out of his mangled car, but I couldn't see Monte anywhere.

"Despite the blood and mud, I have to say, I made one attractive kid." Aviela smirked.

I spat at her feet and was slapped by one of her men. I felt the blood pool at the side of my mouth.

"So rude. Is this what your father taught you?" she asked, walking toward me.

"He taught me a lot of things before you killed him." With my only free hand, I was able to reach my gun and shoot the man who'd slapped me in his back.

He screamed and a bullet went through my shoulder, sending me onto my back.

"Rude and rash," Aviela said, kneeling next to me as I gripped my shoulder and fought the urge to scream.

"You'd better kill me now, Aviela," I hissed up at her. "Or I swear to God, I will not rest until I take your head from your shoulders."

She pulled a gun and pressed it into my wound.

"You are a cub. I'm a lioness, sweetheart. Count your lucky stars you're not on my list today." With that, she shot me once more before rising.

The sun was in my eyes and all I could see was her shadow as she pulled off her white gloves.

"I'm your daughter..." I whispered as I started to fade.

"I never wanted you. I had orders. I followed them, and you were a side effect. No hard feelings." Another gunshot went off, but I didn't feel it. Everything went dark and all I could think of was...*Liam.*

Liam

"Where is my wife?" I roared to the hospital nurse behind the desk.

"Liam, son, breathe." Sedric pulled me back as I tried to keep calm. But that was hopeless at this point. I could barely see straight.

"I *am* breathing, where the fuck is my wife?" I screamed again, pulling the very first nurse who came out.

She stared at me, wide eyed, buckling under my grip.

"My wife," I hissed into her face.

"I…I you're hurting me." She sobbed, trying to pull away.

"Liam, they just took her to room 228," Declan called out and I ran. I ran like a man without his head.

I was going mad.

I knew it.

I could feel it.

One moment she was there, on the phone and the next, all I could hear were the windows shattering, the grating sounds of metal, and finally a chorus of screams.

Over and over again I called into the phone.

Over and over again I tried to get a message out to any of them, but nothing. For over two hours, we had nothing but radio silence. The GPS on all of our cars had been stripped.

I demanded Jinx to take me to their last signal location, but she wasn't there.

It wasn't until my mother called, saying someone had leaked to the press about a car accident, that we were we able to find her. She was in some small rundown hospital on the edge of the city, and I didn't even know if she was alive, or…I didn't know anything. She wasn't answering my calls. Neither was my brother. But I knew this wasn't just a car accident. The bullet shells and Natasha's skull had proven that.

They had killed her. Two shots to the back of the head. That was now Natasha Briar. Her body was found only two miles from the "accident" and the moment we found it, I feared what had happened to Mel… my Mel.

The moment I opened—more liked kicked down—the door, I came face to face with Neal, who sat at her side; busted eye, broken ribs and arm. He looked like hell.

But Mel, who lay as pale as the sheet on top of her body, looked far worse.

"They fucked us, brother…" Neal whispered. "Aviela DeRosa and her men. They waited until we got Natasha and ran us off the road. It happened so fast. She shot Mel three times…I tried. I tried to get her, but Aviela's men. She had the power to kill us. She *could have* killed us. She wanted us to know she could fuck with us. *Us*. We Callahans, she could bring us to our knees."

I grabbed his face, grabbing on to his hand before walking over to my wife. Sitting on the side of her bed, I brushed her hair back, trying my best not to imagine her being shot three times.

"Rest, brother," I said. "Rest long. Rest well. Because they will pay for this. I will make her suffer. I swear it. She thinks she can bring us to our knees, but she can't. No one can." I kissed Mel's lips before lying next to her and I felt myself calm at the sound of her heart.

Neal looked as though he didn't believe me. Like he had seen the devil, and suddenly I didn't seem as scary anymore.

But this wasn't over.

This was far from over.

He shook his head before leaving, and I saw a flash of blonde hair that had to be his wife's.

"She was toying with me," Mel whispered, gripping onto my chest.

Pulling her closer, I kissed the top of her head. "I didn't know you were up."

"She played me like a child. She outdid me with ease, and left me on the ground powerless to stop her, Liam. She…"

"Shh, love. Rest. Just rest. This isn't the end," I told her.

"It's not the end because she let me live."

The thought of her being "allowed" to live angered me like nothing else.

"Mel, rest," I hissed, holding her tighter.

Aviela would pay. She would pay dearly. Nothing, not even God himself could stop me from getting revenge. But right now I needed to keep my wife calm. I need the family calm. We would come out on top. We were Callahans, no matter what, we came out better and stronger. We couldn't ignore this anymore. We couldn't ignore her.

You did not fuck with my business. You did not fuck with my brother, and you sure as hell did not fucking mess with my wife. There would be blood. It would rain blood until justice was met.

We were going to Ireland.

"Liam," Mel whispered into my ear as I stroked her arm.

"Yes, love."

"...I'm pregnant again."

God had a twisted sense of humor.

Eleven

"The business of murder took time, patience, skill, and a tolerance for the monotonous."
~J.D. Robb

LIAM

Neither of us spoke. Neither of us really knew what to say, nor where to even begin. A lot had happened in the last forty-eight hours. Too much in fact, and I was still trying to sort through it all in my mind. I tried focusing on her breathing, the beating of her heart as it beeped on the machines around us. I tried to calm myself down and just clear my mind, but then it hit me. It hit me like the car that hit her. I almost lost her… *them*. Everything would have been over.

"Ahh…" Mel groaned, forcing me to sit up quickly.

"What's wrong?" I scanned her body, but other than the obvious, I couldn't find anything wrong.

"Nothing," she lied, making herself comfortable once again on the hospital bed.

Ignoring her, I went to look at her chart, Neal had already been moved to another room.

"You're not a doctor, put my chart down," she snapped, throwing her pillow at me.

Catching it, I handed it back to her as I read.

"You declined all painkillers?" She was white-knuckling the pain. What the hell was wrong with her? "When did you decline meds? I've been with you since I got here."

"You were in the bathroom. Plus the doctor said it was fine."

"After you probably threatened him. Have you lost your mind? You have two shots in your shoulder and one in your thigh. Not to mention the countless bruises I can see up and down your legs and arm. Take the damn drugs, Melody." I tried not to snap at her, but I was only working on two hours of sleep. This was not the fight I wanted to have with her.

She glared and I glared back.

"No drugs," she hissed.

"You're in pain. You're getting drugs if I have to shoot you up myself." When I reached over to call for the nurse, she grabbed my wrist.

"No drugs, Liam," she whispered. "They increase the chances of miscarriage and stillbirth. I can't lose this one. If I do, I'm done, I can't…"

I stared at her for a moment, not saying anything. I hadn't even thought about the baby; I hadn't had time to process it all.

"Okay. Okay, no drugs."

Once again, we fell into silence. I wasn't sure what was going through her mind. I still couldn't believe she was pregnant. I mean, yes, it was more than possible. We jumped each other whenever we were alone. I was addicted her.

She glared at me and I wanted her, she sneezed and I wanted her. She was everything, and it had been more than a year since we lost…but the science behind how made sense. It was just a lot.

"What do you want to do, Mel?" I asked.

She didn't answer right away.

"Do we have to tell them?"

"No, we can wait." Until we were more comfortable with the idea…until I knew what to do. I had so much to plan and think over.

"Mel," I whispered, walking over and taking her hand. "I love you. I love who you are and what we do, but it has to be different. I can't...you cannot fight this battle. You can't go up against Aviela. Not now. Not like this. I can't lose our child again. You have to step back..."

"Liam."

"Mel, I'm not debating this with you. I swear by all that is holy, I will make Aviela pay. I will make them all pay. But..."

"Let me speak," she snapped as she sat up, only adding to her discomfort. Trying my best to help her, only gave her the chance to push me away with her one good arm.

"Mel..."

"Will you stop interrupting me? It pisses me off and you know it. What the fuck is the point of me telling you shit that ticks me off when you don't fucking listen anyway?" she hissed through her teeth. Her brown eyes narrowed into slits and I tried my best not to smirk. She was sexy when she was pissed at me.

Even with her bruised lips, tangled hair and bandages, my wife still looked hot as fuck.

"Hormones already? Should I just buy the smoothie store?" The look on her face would have scared any man, I on the other hand found it funny by now.

She reached over and grabbed the first thing she could, and threw it at my head. Sadly, it was her own phone. I dodged it as quickly as possible and it broke apart upon impact with the wall.

"You are an ass, Liam Callahan. First, this isn't 'hormones,' it's me. Me with three bullet holes in my body, an asshole of a husband.... and meeting Aviela." She said the last part softly. "The woman who gave birth to me, and also happens to be insane. I've had a rough few days, my reaction is completely normal," she said,

But her reactions weren't normal to me. If this was anyone else, my Melody would have stitched herself back up yelled at me for being late and then demanded that we hunt down who ever the son of a bitch was right then. Her reaction...well, she was hurt. What was worse was the fact that she didn't even realize how much.

"What do you need?" I asked her gently, causing her fist to clench up.

"I need to be looking down at my mother the way she looked down at me," she said as she turned away from me, but I made her face me.

"Mel. I'm never judging you. I don't need you to be strong every moment of forever. I need you to let me in now more than ever."

"She shot me, Liam." Her voice cracked. "With no remorse or hesitation, she shot me with ease. She said that I was nothing more than an unwanted side effect of her job. But I should have known right? Everything we had found out about her said that she was a cold-hearted bitch, but I really didn't think she would shoot. I don't know why. I heard her voice and it sounded like the same woman who used to read to me at night."

I wasn't sure what to say in reply. What could I say? Part of me didn't believe Aviela could pull the trigger either. For God's sake, it was her daughter, her own flesh and blood. Melody and I did not draw lines in the sand, but that was something that I could never dream of doing.

Placing my hand over her stomach, Mel sighed and leaned back into the bed before covering my hand with hers.

"Mel..."

"Fine."

"What?" I whispered.

She looked me in the eyes. "For our child and for your sanity, I will not chase Aviela. But I want you to. From now on, she's your mistress."

"Excuse me?" I tried not to cringe. Maybe she *was* on drugs.

She laughed, pulling me to her until I was once again lying on the small cot they dared to call a bed. It felt like a prison mattress.

"Aviela is your mistress in that I shouldn't know anything about her. Everything involving her will be kept secret from me. Even with the men. If they tell me anything about 'mistress,' you threaten to cut their balls off and make them wear them as earrings," she explained softly.

Only my wife could talk about castration and sound like an angel.

I watched her skeptically. "You're just going to back down and stay out of danger?"

"Depends on your definition of danger," she stated.

"Melody…"

"Don't 'Melody' me. You're not my father. I'm letting you take over the hunt for Aviela; I will help if you need me. But don't need me. I know myself well enough to know that if I get involved, I will want to take over. I will want to hunt her down myself. But I'm not becoming a housewife either. If we've learned anything, it's that Aviela cannot be underestimated. You can't focus on the business and her at the same time—"

"So, you want control of the drugs?" I cut her off. If this were anyone else, I would have snapped their neck.

"Liam…"

"Don't 'Liam' me," I said. "You want me to hunt down your mother while you're off making drug deals with the rest of the country?" *She was definitely on drugs.*

"It's safer and you know it," she whispered.

I could only shake my head at her. Only in our world would selling drugs be safer than dealing with family.

"What would be safer is you spending the day at malls and charity events while I handle this…" She squeezed my hand so tightly I felt my knuckles crack. "Ouch. Damn, baby."

"This is the deal, Liam. Take it or leave it," she demanded.

Always the demanding bitch. She was lucky I fucking loved her. I don't know why, but like a fool, I did.

Grabbing her good arm, I glared down at her.

"You're not in any position to make deals, love. You're pregnant and you're not putting yourself in danger. You are not your mother, and you wouldn't harm our child by letting the same thing happen twice. How would it look, having my pregnant wife dealing smack to junkies and dealers that would put a bullet in their mother's head just to get a line?"

Why couldn't she just spend nine months watching reruns and painting her nails in bed?

She frowned and winced. "Liam, you're hurting me."

"Shit, love. I'm sor—" The moment I let go of her arm, she smacked me over the head.

"I've been pregnant for seven weeks. It didn't affect my ability to handle junkies. I get it, you're nervous, so am I. But we have so much work to do. You cannot do it all alone, nor should you have to," Melody said. "Handle Aviela for me. Focus on that. I can handle everything else. You know I can, and if you tell me not to, I will only ignore you. So why are you fighting me on this? It's a good plan. It's the only plan we have right now. Liam, I'm not asking permission. I own half of our family. I'm doing this, or we deal with both situations."

I hated this.

I didn't want this. I wanted her out of the business. Not forever. Just until…just until I knew they were both safe. Luckily, before I could reply, my phone beeped.

"I have to go," I told her, kissing her quickly before grabbing my jacket from the chair.

"Where are you going?" she asked.

"To find out more about my mistress." The look in her eyes as she sat up told me this would only last about a minute before she was prying the details out of me.

"I'm only taking Fedel, the rest of the men are here to protect you…" I paused looking over once more. I didn't want to leave her. "To protect the both of you."

"And who's going to protect them?" She glared, lying back down.

Shaking my head, I walked toward the door.

"Love you," I said.

She sighed. "I love you too, okay? Happy? I love you. Now leave before you mess with any more of my emotions."

Melody

When he left I stared up at the ceiling rubbing my flat stomach. My flat stomach with a kid inside of it. A kid with really bad timing. Our kid; my and Liam's own kid.

I was going to be a mother…if it made it. If I didn't get it killed again, I was going to be a mother; a mother who wouldn't shoot her child at point blank range.

"I never wanted you. I had orders. I followed them, and you were a side effect. No hard feelings."

I could hear her voice—the voice I so desperately craved as a child—and now I wished she was dead. I felt the pressure building up in the back of my throat, and I tried to push it back down. But I couldn't, and the sob rippled through me before the tears came.

I was not a crier. This was not me. But it hurt. Everything hurt. It hurt so badly and I just wanted to forget everything.

Hearing a knock at the door, I wiped my eyes and nose quickly before taking a deep breath.

"Enter," I called out, and in walked Adriana.

"Mr. Callahan said you would like some herbal green mint tea for the pain," she said, holding the mug tightly as she walked over to me.

She looked me over and I knew my eyes had given me away, but I just nodded and took the tea.

"Liam said to give me herbal green mint tea?" I asked, staring at the cup.

"No." She said. "He said, 'my wife's in pain. Find some natural shit to make her feel better before I get back.'"

"Dartmouth's finest," I whispered, rolling my eyes as I sipped, only to spit the liquid out. "This tastes like shit and mud."

Adriana grabbed a few napkins, cleaning me off.

"I'm fine. But I'm not drinking this." Handing her the cup, I lay back down.

"Is there anything I can get for you, ma'am? I've been trying to get information from the nurses and doctors, but they're a little too afraid to talk." She frowned, eyeing the chart at the end of my bed.

Since when did everyone become a doctor?

"I was shot twice in my shoulder, but it missed the bone, so I'll need a sling but no cast. I have to stay off my leg for a few weeks, plus physical therapy." Thanks, Mom.

"Would you like me to make any calls? I can get the best th—"

"No outsiders. If I need help, I'll come to you."

She stared at me oddly. "Ma'am, I don't have any training in…"

I just stared at her. Today was not the day.

"I'll see what I can do," she whispered.

"You do that," I replied, grabbing the tea again. If it was going to help with the pain, I would bear it. "But before you go, I need information."

"On what, ma'am?"

"Profile Aviela DeRosa."

She froze and stared at me.

"Ma'am, I don't know en—"

"Adriana, I will not ask you again. Profile Aviela DeRosa," I ordered.

She sighed. "From what I can tell, Aviela DeRosa is an extremely narcissistic sociopath. She cares for no one but herself, and has never felt anything for anyone, ever. She appears to be charming, yet she's covertly hostile and domineering, and sees her victims as instruments to be used. She likes to dominate and humiliate her victims. She will never stay in one place for too long. She will most likely spend the rest of her life hopping from one place to another. I would be shocked if she even had a home. I'd also blame it on her childhood, but there have been cases where some people are just born without feelings."

"Then why did she have me?" I sneered. She could have had an abortion and been done with it.

"There could be many reasons. She could have just wanted another person to praise her. Another person to control. She could have—"

"Goodbye Adriana," I cut her off, drinking the rest of the tea.

She nodded before walking out of the room. I just stared at the door. Her words replayed over and over in my mind.

Aviela was a sick, twisted bitch, and I wanted to cut her head off and let it burn. I wanted to hunt her down like a motherfucking dog. But I couldn't do that.

Rubbing my stomach, I remembered how it felt to have steel inside of me—inside of *us*. It was cold and warm at the same time. Saige, in a mere second, had stolen someone from me. From *us*. Liam never blamed me, but it was my fault. I had put my pride above my family. In that moment, I had become somewhat like my mother, and I could never do that again. I was alive—my child and I were alive—because Aviela didn't know. If she had, I would have another bullet wound. Part of me hoped Liam found her and another part of me hoped she hid like a snake in a hole until I knew our child was safe.

For the sake of Liam, for the sake of our child and our family, I would back down from her. I hated it. It wasn't in my nature, but I had to. I had to step down until it was safe…safer.

Hopefully the drugs would be a healthy distraction. We had heroin sitting in the south that we need to move. Not to mention the weed Liam had bought right before the accident. I still didn't know anything about that. I never had a chance to look at the information.

Reaching for the call button, I waited for someone to come. Sadly, it was the bitchy blonde who had eyed Liam when she thought I was sleeping.

"How can I make you feel better today, Mrs. Callahan?" she asked with a fake megawatt smile.

"Tell Declan Callahan I would like to see him." She knew who that was. Everyone knew who the Callahan brothers were.

Her eyes narrowed at me. "Mrs. Callahan, this is a hospital. The nurses aren't here to run personal favors for you."

Not today.

"The nurses are here because we gave a big fat check that spared the board from firing half of its staff. If I wanted to, I could own this damn hospital and have your ass fired and blacklisted so quickly, you'd end up on food stamps until you're ninety. I'm guessing it's really hard to provide for a family, on what is it? Four dollars a day? So if I were you, I would shut my mouth, turn around and run a personal favor for me…wouldn't you?" I snapped, causing her eyes to widen and mouth to drop open.

"You're not moving."

She swallowed and nodded before turning around, all but pulling Declan back into the room.

Declan looked between the retreating girl and myself. "Even in a hospital bed you can still scare the shit out of people."

"It's a gift. What happened with the buy?" If everything went well, we should have been twenty million dollars worth of weed richer.

Declan frowned, moving toward the end of my bed. When he looked at my chart, I felt my eye twitch.

"Touch it and I will make dealing with Coraline look like a cake walk." I was so sick of people looking at me like a victim. I'd gotten shot, it happened. It was time to get back to work, the stupid pricks.

"Mel, you should…"

"Remember the last time you thought I should rest?" Right after I lost our last child.

He sighed. "The deal didn't go as planned. We settled on twenty mil. They wanted thirty mil. Liam was about to, well, be Liam and start cutting them down, he was talking to you, and then the accident. He settled on thirty and we left."

I could feel the headache coming on. My teeth clenched and my fists tightened.

"Liam paid those motherfuckers thirty million dollars? Was this weed laced with cocaine as well?"

The idiot!

"Mel, he wasn't thinking straight. He didn't want—"

"Shut up and get me a phone!"

"You know we will make double that. We were underpaying them anyway. It—"

Pulling the IV from my arm, I slid off the bed, causing him to rush towards me with his eyes wide. Balancing on one foot, I hopped over to him.

"Declan, call them and tell them I want my money back." I glared into his eyes.

"This isn't Bergdorfs, Mel you can't—"

Grabbing his jacket, I pulled him to my face. "Call them back, or you're going to pay me that extra ten."

"How the fuck am I supposed to do that?" He was panicking.

"Not my problem. Get it done or you will never be a father." I smiled, slapping his cheek softly before letting go and hopping back over to the bed.

LIAM

I sat in Fedel's room, eating his Jell-O as he lay in bed. Checking my watch again, I looked at his cut-up face. Glass was a bitch.

"He's late," I told him as I took another bite.

"He's in a wheelchair and my mother is gone. It will take him a moment to get here," Fedel whispered, flipping on the television.

Yes, Gino was in a wheelchair only because my father put him there.

"You do know that I will kill you in front of him if he doesn't tell me what I want to hear?" I told him honestly, watching the game.

From the corner of my eye, I saw no fear in his eyes, and I wasn't sure if that was because he didn't believe me or because he'd already accepted his fate.

"If I'm going to die, can I please have my last meal back?" he asked, glancing at the food I was stealing.

"It's shit," I told him, handing back everything but the Jell-O.

"The Jell-O too," he said.

"Seriously?" I snickered, looking at the cup of half eaten Jell-O.

He nodded.

"You'd better hope it's not your last meal." I handed him the cup as the door opened.

"Gino!" I stood. The blonde nurse wheeled him in. Walking over to her, I grabbed the handles of his chair and pushed him to Fedel's bedside.

"Do you need—" the nurse said.

"No, you may leave," I told her. After she did, the room was silent.

Gino eyed Fedel with anger and worry, but in return, Fedel ignored him, eating his Jell-O as if he didn't even notice he was here.

Gino didn't look old, he looked ancient. Like he had gone to hell and back, and now he was just waiting to go back again. His face was melting, his once long hair was gone and only a few stands of grey hair covered his head. I could see the scars that were marked all over his arms. He was proud of them; they were his battle scars.

"Mr. Morris…"

"Cut the shit, Callahan," he spat out in disgust. "What do you want from me?"

Taking a deep breath, I tried to control myself, but I was done with control. Grabbing him by the neck, I all but lifted the old man out of his seat.

"I was trying to be civil. We were enemies once upon a time, but because of my wife, you became part of the package. It's for that reason that I'm not going to break your arm. You will tell me what you know about Aviela DeRosa. If your loyalty lies with the Giovanni family, then it lies with me, and this is an order."

When his face turned blue, I dropped him in his chair, and took a step back, trying to regain my composure.

Gino coughed and sucked in a breath of air while holding onto his throat like he was trying to expand his airway with his own hands.

"Aviela DeRosa is dead," he said, and I pinched the bridge of my nose.

I was going to kill this man.

"You're lying to me, Gino," I whispered taking out my brass knuckles. "Gino, I don't have the time nor the patience for wasted words. Aviela DeRosa is alive. I know this because she shot my wife three times. Your son, who I am about to kill right in front of you, is in this room because of her. So tell the truth or else your son will die, and you will spend your life as vegetable."

"I...I can't." He shook his head as he stared at Fedel.

Fedel begged him with his eyes. "Pop, we're on the same team. Melody is Orlando's daughter. She's a Giovanni, and we're loyal to Giovannis."

Gino leaned forward, his body now ridged. "That's why I can't. I swore to Orlando I would—"

"I killed Orlando. He's dead, so swear to me and then deal with his shit in heaven or hell, Gino. I doubt he wanted this, so be smart for the first time in your life."

I really wanted this and he was my only lead. Everything else, Aviela was slowly destroying.

"Pop. If not for me, if not for Liam, then for Orlando's baby girl," Fedel said, and I had to hold back an eye roll. Mel was not a baby girl. He knew that. But hey, whatever got the job done.

"Orlando always had a thing for the feisty ones." He sighed, staring at his hands. "We were in southern Italy, and there she was, Aviela Costa, she called herself. She had everyone eating out of the palm of her hands, and Orlando wanted her. She looked like she wanted him too. The whole night, they were in the back of the club, just dancing and talking. The talking became more, and the next thing I know, I'm driving her to and from Orlando's home when we got back to the US. He was so smitten that he just couldn't leave her. I didn't trust her; her eyes held no real emotions. I ran a background check, but everything came out fine. She was Aviela Costa, but I still had this feeling…

"I asked around and no one knew much about her. But her family was dead. So I had the boys double-check for paper trails. They found out almost all of our files—both digital and physical —had been tampered with."

"You told Orlando?" I asked, walking in front of him.

Gino just snickered. "Iron hands was more like an iron head—and not his cock either. The fool was in too deep. He had no idea she was playing him. We were bleeding money, losing connections, and we were about to lose everything else, and she had only been in our lives for three months. He thought it was us. That we were stealing from him. I think he was losing it. Part of him knew, and the other part of him was in love. He set a trap. To this day, I still don't know how he figured out it was her. But I saw him the moment after. He held her neck, ready to snap it and the bitch just said, 'Go ahead, kill your kid too and save me the trouble.'"

Part of me wished he had killed the bitch, but she was still Mel's mother.

"What did he do?" *Mel was here, so he didn't kill her.*

"What any madman would do. He chained her to the bed and hired a nurse. His room became her prison. Aviela fought and cursed, she even tried her charm, but Orlando wouldn't let her go. She slit her wrist. He brought a doctor and had the whole room stripped so she couldn't hurt herself. She tried starving herself, so we gave her soft drugs and fed her through tubes. It was like that for months until finally she caved. Suddenly she began to behave like a wife, and Orlando loved it. But it was only after she gave birth that he unchained her."

"Fuck." I sighed.

Why were our lives so fucking complicated? All I wanted to do was sell drugs, make love to my wife, and rule in peace.

"She ran, didn't she?" I asked.

Gino shook his head. "No, she stayed. I thought it was the kidnap, bound, Stockholm thing you hear about. Or maybe she loved her daughter. But I soon discovered that wasn't the case. Orlando had found Aviela's lover, Leonardo Severino. If there was anyone she cared about, it was him. No one else, just him. Out of spite Orlando had him locked up in the basement, and every time she did something he didn't like, he cut off a limb and gave it to her as a gift.

"Those white gloves she wore, were gifts from her lover, she swore she wouldn't take them off until they were stained with both Melody's and Orlando's blood. She said she wouldn't be satisfied until all the white had turned red. Orlando wanted Mel to have a mother, one who loved her, so he put up with it. Little Melody grew up with her mother cursing her every step. It was only when Mel was six that she started to notice her mother's "love" for her wasn't really love. So Orlando agreed to let her and Leonardo go, as long as they never came near his daughter again."

Things were making sense, but in way, I was still confused. "If this is true, how did Mel get on that plane? Orlando would have never let her go."

Gino frowned. "That's why Aviela stole her. We drove them to the airport, even waited for them to get on the damn plane. We needed to make sure they were gone. We thought we were sure. However, she somehow managed to steal Melody from right under our noses. It went from bad to fucking worse. Orlando didn't realize she had Melody. None of us did. He was the one that brought that plane down. He had the whole thing wired to blow. He hated her that much. There was no way he was going to just let her go. By the time we realized where Melody was, Orlando… Orlando was beside himself with grief. He thought he had killed his own daughter. That's when we found out that Aviela was a DeRosa. We got word from one of our snitches in the Vance household that Vance's men had gone and saved her. The explosives didn't work as planned. It took out the wings but the pilot managed to land on the water. The video was pretty much destroyed but—"

"There was video? On a plane… in the '90s?" Fedel asked him, speaking up for the first time.

Gino stated. "Orlando had it installed, he wanted to see her burn. Because Vance's men didn't know about Melody, and Aviela wasn't awake to kill her, Melody lived. She was left alive because Vance's men just wanted to scare her and left her to freeze. Orlando never thanked God more than he did that night after he had her back. All Melody's childhood memories are basically a lie and he wanted to keep it that way. He made us swear never to tell her and burn anything that would reveal the truth."

Sighing, I sat on the edge of Fedel's bed. "I am a Callahan. I head one of the strongest, if not *the* strongest, organizations in the world. We deal and we sell. Killing is just a side effect of that. I do not have the time nor the patience to deal with your fucked up lives. I do not want to waste my time, money or men in your family shit!"

"Then you married the wrong woman." Gino frowned. "We knew Aviela was a DeRosa because she wasn't a Callahan, and she sure as hell wasn't a Valero. How many other families have enough power to step to us. Back then it was the Callahans led by Sedric, the Valeros led by Vance, the Giovannis led by Orlando, and lastly the DeRosas led by Ivan. All the information Aviela had stolen from us ended up in Ivan DeRosa's hands. I haven't even seen the man—no one has—but that bastard was always been one step ahead of us. The Giovannis and the DeRosas have been at odds since Melody's grandfather murdered Ivan's family. You think Aviela is fucked up? Her father wants every Giovanni erased from existence. This is all just one big battle for revenge."

"Melody is a Callahan. She is my wife." I was getting a headache; I could feel it growing. "There has to be more. What did the DeRosas have on the Callahans? And how the hell did they get Shamus to do what they wanted?"

"Shamus?" Gino questioned, pissing me off. "The old ass who's too busy sucking himself off to give a shit about anyone else?"

"That's my grandfather." I reminded him, not that it mattered.

"Shame," he spat out in disgust. "I don't know anything about Shamus or the Callahans. I told you all I know. Aviela wanted Melody dead before she was even born. After this attack, she's most likely out of the state if not the country. Aviela strikes then leaves. She can't stay in one place for long. Orlando's prison almost drove her crazy… crazier."

"There's more to it than this." I grabbed the Jell-O. "He talked," I said to Fedel. "It isn't your last meal, deal with it."

I walked out. I was so done with this web of lies and clues. Who the hell did I look like, Nancy motherfucking Drew?

The walk to Mel's room was short, and I noticed Declan giving me death stare as he spoke on the phone. I didn't know what his problem was, but if he didn't stop staring at me like I was a low level criminal, I would bust his teeth in. I didn't have the time, nor the energy, and I hated hospitals.

There were too many ass-crack junkies and dead people in one place.

I need a fucking vacation.

I handed the empty Jell-O cup to Monte, who stared at me oddly. Walking into Mel's room, I leaned against the door.

"I want a new mistress," I told her.

"I want a new husband!" she snapped. "You bought the shit for thirty? What the fuck is wrong with you?"

I really need a fucking vacation, and brandy. A lot of brandy.

Twelve

"Till death do us part."

Neal

"Ouch. Babe, I'm fine." I tried pulling away from her, but she wouldn't let go of my face.

Liam had allowed me to come home, and the moment I stepped into the room, the woman all but attacked me, and not in the way a man liked.

"You're *fine*?" she snapped. "You have a black eye, four broken ribs, a busted eardrum! Not to mention—"

"Baby..." I grabbed her hands, forcing her to look me in the eyes. "I'm fine. I'm a little beaten up, but I'm fine. So please, just kiss me."

She glared at me, slapping me on arm before kissing me deeply. I picked her up with one arm and pushed her onto the bed.

"Neal, you're hurt." She moaned as I kissed her neck.

"Olivia," I groaned looking into her eyes. "I had my ass kicked by a woman—a very small woman—and I just want to forget the whole thing. Can we do that? Can you help me forget?"

She brushed my hair back and eased onto her hands. "Get on your back."

Smirking, I rolled over, allowing her to ease onto my waist. Slowly, she began to unbutton her shirt.

"Damn you're beautiful," I whispered as I held her by the waist.

Before she could speak, the door opened and my father walked in.

"For the love of fuck, Pop!" I yelled as Olivia grabbed for the sheet.

"Oh, did I cock block you?" Sedric smirked. "My apologies, I just wanted to check on my first son."

"Get out!" I tried to adjust myself as Olivia held her laughter.

Sedric grinned. "Your mother wants to see you, don't keep her waiting."

I drew in a deep breath. "I will see her in the…"

"Rule Nineteen: Never—"

"Never keep mother waiting," I finished for him. "I know, but I don't want to see her with a hard on! So get out before I decide to move out." This house was huge and yet felt so fucking small all the time.

"Really?" Olivia laughed. I loved hearing her laugh, "Where do you want to go?"

"Doesn't matter. Family stays together. Rule Five: One family, one roof." Sedric winked at her before closing the door. Grabbing a pillow, I threw it at the wood before lying back. I just wanted my wife.

Olivia said to me, as she kissed my lips softly. "Go see your mother. I'll always be here. Always."

Ever since she'd had her first kill, Olivia had changed. Or better yet, healed. She smiled and laughed without caring who saw. She was happy, and seeing her so happy made me happy. It made me grateful to Mel. God only knew how long Olivia would have held onto her anger. We still hadn't found Harvey, but when we did, so help me God, he would pay.

Taking her hand, I kissed it softly before pulling her closer to me.

"My mother can wait," I whispered.

"She's going to kick my ass if I keep you from her," she whispered back, but she never stopped kissing me.

Sedric

"Where is he?" my wife asked as she paced in our bedroom. I continued to flip through my book.

"Most likely enjoying his evening with his wife. Something I wish I could be doing," I told her. If Neal was busy with Olivia, I could be busy with her. However my wife hated when the family was separated.

"How can he be having sex when Mel was gunned down?" she asked. "Not to mention how close he came to losing his life. We should be having a family meeting, or at the very least, we should be at the hospital with them! We could—"

"Sweetheart, Liam didn't want us there…"

"Liam is an emotional wreck. His wife was just shot, why in the hell are you letting him make choices?" she snapped.

It was times like this that proved God chose a special type of woman to drive the men of our family crazy.

Dropping my book on the bedside table, I sighed just watching her.

"Don't look at me like that, Sedric Callahan! Our daughter was shot three times by some stupid bitch pretending to be a mother, and I can't even see her. Not to mention we don't even know how Liam is dealing with this. We should be at the hospital!" She was beautiful, even though she was crazy.

"Sweetheart, lie down next to me," I demanded and she glared. I felt like I was having a staring contest with her, until she finally gave up and climbed into bed next to me.

"Liam is the head of this family, and if he thinks he and his wife need a moment, then we do as he says. I know you want to become the mama bear, but give them a moment," I whispered, holding on to her.

"I'm worried about Mel. It was her mother—I can't call that bitch a mother. Who shoots their kids? What kind of sick, fucking, two bit—"

"Language." I snickered, causing her to flip over and smack me.

"I'm serious, Sedric." She frowned.

"I know, sweetheart. I know." Sighing, I tried my best not to think about it.

Someone had attacked my family; they had harmed my son and my daughter. I wanted to set their blood on fire. I wanted to rip them limb for limb, but it wasn't my place anymore. It was Liam's, and if I thought about it, it made me want to... it made me want to kill.

Liam needed to kill this bitch quickly or I would snap.

Declan

"My boss doesn't like the deal you made," I said into the phone. This was so going to end badly.

"Too fucking bad. Are you people going back on your word? Your boss gave his word…"

"My boss gave his word when we were working at twenty, and you screwed us over for thirty. We're not pleased, and bad things tend to happen when we're not pleased," I hissed into the phone.

"You paid, the deal is done. Go fuck yourselves." And with that, they hung up. Frustrated, I gripped onto the phone, ready to throw it when Coraline appeared before me. She stared at me wide eyed.

"I'm a recovering shopaholic, you can't break your shit. It makes me want to buy new things." She smiled, walking up beside me.

"Sorry. Mel's being unreasonable." I sighed, placing the phone in my pocket.

"So, she's being Mel?" she asked, and I smirked.

"Yeah, which I guess is a good sign." It could be worse. She could be in bed, staring at me with dead eyes as we all tried to get her to function.

Coraline looked over to the wall where Monte, Duncan, and Antonio,—who was sporting a cast on his arm—stood outside of Mel's room. They looked like those British guards who didn't smile, blink, or freaking breathe. They just stood there, waiting for a moment to shoot down any motherfucker who tried to enter that room.

"What does she want you to do?" Coraline whispered. I just stared at her and she rolled her eyes. "You know guys tell their wives shit like this."

"Yeah, but that's usually after the wife's tricked it out of them with sex." I hadn't even thought about that when I said it.

I expected her to snap at me, but she just grinned. "Noted. Too bad you're on the clock. All these beds. Neal's at home having his way with Olivia. Liam and Mel will be at it the moment she's better. It seems as though you like having blue balls, Declan."

I watched as she winked at me, then walked away.

Mel and Liam were going to kill me, but if I had a chance of having Coraline one last time before I died, I had to take it.

I followed like a puppy, watching her ass as she walked towards a back room. Grabbing her arm, I pulled her in quickly before pushing her up against the door.

"Don't fuck with me, woman. I'm at my wit's end." I gasped when she pulled back and allowed her coat to fall.

"But I want to fuck with you, Declan," she moaned, and I almost came in my pants. There my tiny wife stood, naked and waiting for me.

"Jesus Christ, Coraline," I said before grabbing hold of her.

Pushing me back, I thanked God for this moment. I would book my room in hell for this.

Thirteen

"Mrder—all I need is u."
—Jarod Kintz

LIAM

"You've gotta be fucking kidding me," I said to them as I stared at the stacks upon stacks of boxes rising to the ceiling of my library.

"Your grandfather never liked computers." Sedric snickered as the men brought more of the shit in. At this rate, we were going to be buried alive.

"He did this to fuck with me. The bastard knew that I was going to come after his shit eventually." I could hear the old fuck laughing beyond the grave. I would have thrown him in the river, but mother thought it would be best to at least show some sort of respect to our dearly departed grandfather. His body would be buried in the local cemetery, forever separated from his beloved Ireland.

Neal, the giant that he was, dropped the last five boxes around my desk. "That's all of it."

"Out," I snapped. Everyone but my father left quickly. They hated any paper that wasn't cash.

"So you're going to read through all of this alone?" Sedric asked, looking around at what was once a very beautiful green and gold study.

Grabbing one of the brown boxes, I made my way over to a chair.

"Until our favorite snake Aviela slithers out from whatever rock she's hiding under, this is all I can do. Hopefully, this will lead to a shortcut in beheading her." Aviela's head rolling off her neck would be worth the oncoming paper-cuts.

"How's Melody?" he asked, grabbing a box.

"I don't—"

"Yes, you do." He cut me off. I hated when people cut me off. "You need help and you're getting help. Now, how is your wife?"

Pinching the bridge of my nose, I sighed. "You mean the crazy homicidal woman you arranged for me to marry?"

The bastard snickered. "Yes, that woman, whom you're madly in love with and overly protective of."

"There is no such thing as an overly protective husband in the mafia," I replied. "And the woman is driving me insane! She doesn't listen to me at all."

"My poor, poor son. Have you not learned? Women don't listen, they talk. Listening is *our* job. In return, we get sex, children and food." He laughed, making light of how chaotic up everything was.

"I'm listening! She's just talking crazy! I swear sometimes I want to ring her pretty little neck." Other times I just wanted to kiss her down to her…

Concentrate.

"Yes, they do that as well…she may be Bloody Melody, but she's still a female, a pregnant female," he stated.

I froze, staring at him. It had been three weeks since the accident and Mel still wasn't showing. She was great, seeing as how neither of us were ready to tell the family. But apparently we weren't careful enough. Mel was going to be pissed.

Maybe there was hope?

"Does mother know?"

"Everyone knows."

Fuck me.

"Urgh—"

"Honestly, Liam, it's been three weeks since she's drank anything but tea and water? She demanded Neal wear new cologne last night at dinner. We aren't brain dead, we can all connect the dots," he said simply, as he pulled out a brown file.

"Great, you can all connect the bullet holes when she finds out," I muttered under my breath; I didn't even know why we had bothered to try and keep it from them.

"Liam," he said seriously, "you're going to keep her safe—both of them safe—but if you don't relax, at this rate you're to get gray hair or worse, lose it."

I snorted. "When was the last time you saw a bald Callahan?"

"Liam…"

"I heard you, dad. I just need to believe you. None of this makes sense. Aviela makes no sense. If she wanted Mel dead, she would have killed her, but she didn't. I don't buy for a second that the woman has any type of maternal anything." I paused, releasing a sigh. "Natasha's family is gone. They took her body and left. These papers and the Briar are all we have and I just want to set fire to them both. Meanwhile, the very woman I'm killing myself for is yelling at drug runners and selling dope." *Brandy.* My mind begged for it.

Rising to my feet and maneuvering around boxes, I grabbed the bottle at the far end of the room.

"What were you expecting her to do?"

"What would you expect a pregnant woman to do?" I snapped, drinking from the bottle. "I swear, she gets pregnant at the worst possible times. Just to kill me slowly."

"Yep. She planned to get pregnant all on her own…"

"Whose side are you on?" I hissed, causing him to laugh. These were our "father-son" moments. He always knew how to get under my skin.

"And this is why the men call you the Mad Hatter."

What the bloody fuck?

"They call me what?" I do not get a nickname. It's Liam to family, Boss, Sir, and Ceann Na Conairte to every other motherfucker.

"You know, the Disney—"

"I know who the fuck it is!"

He laughed, making me want to rip his tongue from his month and staple it to the paper covered table.

He simply pointed at my face before flipping through some papers. "That, right there, and whatever you are thinking is the reason. Calm yourself down, I think I found something."

Breathing through my nose, I grabbed the sheet of paper he was staring at. But I didn't see anything worth the effort.

"It's just a contract stating you and Natasha's mother were to get married." Thankfully, God's sense of humor wasn't that cruel. If that woman were my mother, I would have lost it a long time ago.

Sedric grabbed the bottle from me and pointed to the witness signature right next to my grandfather's.

Jesus why?

Melody

"Liam is going to kill me," Declan stated for hundredth time as he drove.

"Say that one more time and he won't have to." He was such a little bitch sometimes.

Luckily, he didn't say anything else or I would have had to hurt him. Leaning into the seat, I ate my chocolate slowly as he drove us deeper into the cloud-covered city. I had to admit, there was something about downtown Chicago at night that made me grin. I enjoyed how beautiful it looked from afar, but close up, as you drove through the streets, you saw the thugs and suspicious alleys. At that, I couldn't help but grin. Chicago was our city. Everyone walking the streets was our guest. They lived because of us and they died because of us.

I got a kick out of watching one runner check the street before dashing over to an awaiting car. Whether they knew it or not, they worked for us. They were working our streets. After all, this was our playground.

"This is it," Declan said, as he pulled up in front of the club. There was no line or even a sign for that matter. Just one man dressed in black, smoking what was most likely my weed. He eyed our car carefully, and with envy; Morris' Bentleys tended to have that effect on people.

Opening the glove compartment, I placed my chocolate inside before grabbing my gun with my right hand. My right hand was still a little stiff, but I sure as hell couldn't work much with my left. Thankfully, I could still shoot a gun. Probably not as well as I could before, but well enough to get my point across.

"Melody, are you …"

"Shut up, Declan and stay in the car," I told him, putting the gun behind my back before grabbing my cane and opening the door.

The moment I stepped out, the guard stood straighter and smiled at me. After all, what could go wrong with a little woman using a cane?

"You on the wrong street, lady," he said. "This place ain't for your kind."

I fought the urge to roll my eyes, but managed to smile kindly instead. "I'm here to see Chuck."

His eyes widened before they narrowed. "You ain't here to see Chuck, cuz Chuck ain't seeing nobody today."

"Oh?" Idiot. "Not even Mrs. Callahan?"

"You're Mrs. Callahan? Wife of Liam Callahan?" he stammered. I would have enjoyed it if he hadn't said "wife" as if I was some sort of accessory.

He didn't even give me a chance to reply before opening the door.

"Mel—"

"Sit, Declan. The grown-ups are working," I said before walking—limping—in. My leg burned, but there was a bully in my playground and I hated bullies. I knew what type of club I was walking into, and it wasn't the first time I had entered one. However, the smell of sex, sweat, and other miscellaneous fragrances, made me want to hurl. The place was so dim I was surprised the people could see the very ropes they were using to tie each other up; or that they could even concentrate over the music. But I preferred it loud. Maybe for the same reason they did. The louder it was, the harder it was to hear someone scream.

"You looking for a good time, bunny?" A man grinned at me, eyeing me from head to toe. His cock looked as though it wanted to rip out of his leather pants and attack me.

"Bunny?" I asked without emotion.

He grinned, stepping closer to me. "You know, cute, sweet," he looked at my cane, "injured. You came here to explore your inner lioness, didn't you? Don't worry…"

I simply walked around him, but he grabbed my arm. Before I could smack the shit out of him, Declan beat me to it.

"Touch her again, and I'll kill you," he hissed, and for the first time, I could actually see how he and Liam were related. His green eyes glared into him.

"My bad, man…"

Ignoring them both, I continued on my way, not bothering to make any eye contact with any of the other horny men…and women, who may have been looking for a new partner. However, I doubted most of them were paying any attention to me.

"Mrs. Callahan for Chuck," I told the man in front of the door that stood at the back of the club; he didn't even hesitate. He simply opened the door.

The room, covered in nothing but cheap fur rugs and lava lamps, looked as if I had stepped back in time and into an Austin Powers-esque porno. And there sat Chuck, getting the blowjob of his life, from some very tiny redhead. He was so carried away with himself that he didn't even seem to notice me or the five men "guarding" him for that matter.

They stood against the wall of bear fur, looking at the man in disgust.

"Ugh, seriously!" Declan snapped when he walked in, causing Chuck's eyes to pop open.

His eyes narrowed in on Declan, but he didn't stop thrusting into the girl's mouth…poor girl. How he could find his penis with all that fat rolling off of him, was beyond me. And when he came, he looked like a dying boar. He grunted before grinning and pulling out of her mouth.

"What the hell do you want, Callahan? Ran through all the drugs I sold you already? You people adding it to your tea and biscuits or some shit? " The man snapped out between breaths.

He didn't even spare me a glance. Declan, on the other hand, turned to me as if to ask *what next?*

"You should leave," I told the girl on the floor.

The tiny red head on her knees rose, wiped her mouth and stared at Chuck, unsure of what she should do.

"The bitch stays," he snapped.

Sighing, I nodded, pulling my gun quickly before shooting him in the knee cap. No one ever listened to me until I started shooting, and they said *I* was trigger-happy.

The moment he dropped to the floor screaming, I handed Declan my gun before taking my cane to the side of his face. I didn't stop until the fucking thing broke and I lost my balance. However, once again, Declan grabbed hold of me, helping he regain my balance.

"You thought you could screw me! My family? Have you lost you motherfucking mind?" I hissed at him.

Shaken, he tried to reach for his gun, but one of his men grabbed it before stepping into the background.

"What are you doing? Kill her!" he screamed as he coughed up his teeth and blood. The redhead ran to his side, but he just pushed her away.

None of his men moved.

"Three weeks ago, a stash for thirty was bought after we agreed on twenty. But suddenly, we aren't selling because someone has a cheaper product. Would you happen to know who that is?" I asked, pushing Declan away to stand on my on my own. It felt as though blades were running across my skin, but I ignored it.

Chuck didn't answer, he was too busy trying to stop the blood from flowing down his face while holding his knee. He looked around, but none of his men bothered to help.

"You." I snapped my fingers at one of his men. The smallest of them all, but also most nicely dressed, stepped forward. Which meant two things: he wanted his boss' job and he was sick enough to do anything to get it.

"Help Chuck find his tongue," I told him and he didn't even hesitate. He grabbed the fat boar, pulling him up from the ground before beating the shit into his face. Idiot.

"Jesus, honestly?" I sighed.

Declan snickered before walking over and pulling the man away. Latching onto Chuck's hand, he placed it on the desk before grabbing a pen and ramming through it.

"Lesson one," Declan yelled over Chuck's screams. "You don't punch a man in the head while he's being questioned. How can he answer any questions if his brain is rolling around in his skull?"

"Whatever this bitch is paying you, I'll double it!" Chuck screamed.

Poor, stupid Chuck.

"You mean after you give them their share of the product you've been selling? We've made a lot of money Chuck, and yet no one else seems to be making anything. You've been stealing from the pack." I smirked, taking a seat in one of his fur chairs. The man had a fetish, it seemed.

He stared at the pen in his hand, doing his best to reach for it, but the way in which Declan had him pinned, he couldn't.

A sob broke through his fat lips.

"I was going to share the take with you, I swear! I wanted to make sure it was possible…AHHH!" He screamed as Declan pulled out the pen with as much force as possible before picking a new spot to ram it through.

Strong pen.

Declan grinned. "Lesson two: cheaters and thieves lie. Cause bodily harm the second time and they will tell the truth. Right, Chuck?"

Poor Chuck was going into shock, but nodded anyway.

"I will pay you back! Please…"

Declan grabbed a new pen and once again made a new hole for Chuck.

"Lesson three?" I questioned, smiling, trying to ignore the horrible smell radiating off the chair.

Declan shrugged before smiling back. "He hung up on me after I called for our money."

"Say it ain't so, Chuck." I frowned at him before turning back to the rest of his men. "If he were to die, who takes over?"

They looked confused.

"We ain't got a system," one of them said. "Whoever got the most power—"

"I take over," the very same nicely dressed man said, just as I thought. He was young…older than me, but young. He wasn't muscle, but he had brains and those with brains hated to be second.

"Take a good look at Chuck," I said, turning back to the man whose blood was now running across the table like spilled wine. "This is me being nice. In fact, this is me in a good mood. Chuck thought he was untouchable. Chuck thought he fucked us over, not only once, but twice. But Chuck was wrong."

To prove my point, Declan reached for the cup of pens, but it was empty. Smirking, he pulled a knife and slammed it down, right in Chuck's thumb.

"Lesson four?" I asked him.

"Motherfucker was getting his cock sucked in a lady's presence," he snapped angrily, staring at the girl who sat frozen in shock on the ground. Her blue eyes were wide as she just stared, taking in the screams. *She should have left when I told her to.*

"What's your name?" I asked the man.

"Roy, ma'am," he said quickly.

"Roy, Declan is the man who will be setting up all of our business. We will now be buying at fifteen. You should know, at some point, you will care for someone or something deeply. If you ever stand against the family again, I will take that thing and destroy it in front of you." I nodded at Declan, who, picked up the redhead and pushed her over to one of Chuck's former, men.

"Take care of both of them." Declan told them.

Roy's eyes widened slightly but nodded. We didn't kill in front of others unless they also would lose their lives.

"Anyone have a problem with that?" I asked around the room, but no one answered. Nodding, I rose, stumbling just a bit, but Declan walked over to my side and took my arm. We left Chuck pinned to the table, sobbing like a child.

"I think we've made our point. Good evening, gentlemen." I started walking towards the door when Declan turned and handed one of them a gun. When one of them shot Chuck through the eyes he spoke again.

"Lesson five; never piss off a Callahan. It's a hazard to your health."

"I hope my presence here is enough to haunt you for a lifetime, because I will not be back at this shithole anytime in the foreseeable future. And none of you have any ever met me." I stated as we walked out.

I was only a few steps away from the exit when one of the strobe lights illuminated the corner of a man's face.

"Declan, do you see who I see?" I asked him when we were back with the rest of the sexually frustrated lovers of rope and chains.

He scanned the dimly lit club, and once again I saw that darkness creep into his eyes.

"Call everyone," I told him, making my way over to the bar. I couldn't drink anything, but my leg was killing me, and by the time Declan got off the phone, all of the family would be on their way. Even Evelyn.

It made me laugh and cringe at the thought of Evelyn at a bondage club. But what could I do? Vermin liked to hide in the dark.

"So we wait?" he asked.

I simply nodded.

He was a silent for a moment before whispering; "Why didn't you tell me you had flipped his men?"

"Because I shouldn't have to, Declan. I'm not sure why you keep underestimating me. Or why you seem to think I'm some silly little girl trying to play mafia. I'm neither an idiot, nor would I willingly put the family, the business or myself in danger. If you weren't family, you wouldn't be here." In fact the second time he doubted me, I would have cut off his hands.

"My apologies, I'm still not used to all of this," he replied.

"Your wife seems to be getting there." Despite the fact that I hadn't really had time to spend with the woman.

He simply snickered. "Coraline has changed, but she's still my Coraline. No matter how much she trains, no matter how badass she becomes, she's still my sweet Coraline. She's the sun and you're Pluto."

"A cold, dead, floating rock?" My eyes narrowed at him. "Is that what you say to all the girls at bondage clubs?"

His eyes went wide as he tried to figure out what to say, however, he wisely realized it was just best to keep his mouth shut.

Facing the crowd again, I fought the urge to rub my stomach. It was like I was checking to see if it was still there. But under my loose fitting shirt, I could feel the bump. The kid was fucking with my emotions, and not in the way I would like. I was either happy, horny or hungry. Sometimes all three at the same time! It was driving me insane and making it hard to concentrate.

"They're here," Declan said, looking towards the door.

And sure enough, there was my husband, dressed in all black, and though he didn't look pleased, he still looked sexy.

His green eyes scanned the club before they landed on me.

He looked at me as though he wanted to wring my neck. And if he did, he was in the right place to do it.

"He's going to kill me." Declan sighed.

"Possibly." I said, watching the way everyone seemed to hover around Liam as he walked toward me. I could feel my lust for him grow with each step he took. By the time he got to me, I just wanted to jump him.

"Wife," he hissed at me.

"Come here often, husband?" I smirked.

"I'm going to find Neal before he loses it," Declan said, leaving us quickly.

Liam pinched the bridge of his nose before turning to the bartender.

"Your best Scotch," he demanded.

"Scotch? Someone's uptight."

"Maybe because my wife is in a bondage club in downtown Chicago, with only one man beside her. Melody…"

"I may be carrying your child, but I am not one. Breathe and celebrate. Not only are we now buying at fifteen, but Chuck's dead, and we just spotted Harvey King. Today is a good day. Drink and be Irish, Liam." I turned to watch as Fedel and Dylan pulled a very drunk Harvey away from the women who surrounded him.

Liam stepped in front of my face. "You and I, wife, are going to have a chat later."

"Code for you fucking me angrily?" I smiled and he took a deep breath before kissing me hard, pulling me off the chair.

"Shut up and let me be pissed at you," he said when he broke away.

Liam

How could one woman drive me so insane? There she was, sitting at the bar as men got whipped, and women were chained to walls. She looked completely out of place, but she wasn't even bothered, she just sat there sipping on what I hopped was cranberry juice.

"Stop being pissed at me so we can handle this and go home," she added before smiling.

She was doing that a lot. Smiling and laughing…in public. I knew it was the hormones; it was beautiful, but I didn't want to get used it. With all the shit going on, I was happy that she was happy. I could never be pissed with her for longer than a few seconds before she completely disarmed me with that smile. In my mind, I knew this was God's doing. It had to be. She got pregnant at the worst possible times.

However, from what I had learned, this went far deeper than just Aviela's hatred for the Giovannis. And I now knew that we seriously needed to go to Ireland.

"What's going on?" She frowned, looking over my face as if she were reading something.

"Later?" I said, kissing her lips. "Olivia wants to handle this at the Manor. We can talk after that."

Her eyes narrowed, but she nodded.

We would go home, we would watch Olivia kill Harvey, and then I'd have to explain to my wife why my "mistress" was part of a much bigger puzzle.

Fourteen

"Silence is never the answer; unless the equation is murder."
—Silent Assassin

LIAM

"Jesus Christ, Mel." I sighed, falling beside her.

"Tired already?" she whispered, kissing down my sweaty chest. She was trying to kill me.

"Mel, we need to…" I started to say, but the moment her mouth wrapped around my cock, I couldn't open my eyes, let alone speak.

What number was this? Fifth? Sixth?

I didn't know, or care. Her mouth was heaven, and her stamina was hell.

"We need to what, husband?" she said, as she licked the tip of my cock and watched me lose my mind and my will. At her lips, hands and eyes, I was powerless.

"Well?" she asked, squeezing me once more, and before I could speak, her mouth surrounded me again.

She moved so fucking slow it was painful. I was dying.

"Fuck!" I snapped, pulling her hair and forcing her onto her back. My wife wanted more than just sex, she wanted control, she wanted to fight me here and now, and a part of me knew she wanted me to dominate her.

Her red nails scratched my chest as she pushed, trying her best to get me to lie back so I could be her bitch.

"NO!" I yelled in her face, pinning her hands above her head.

Her nostrils flared, but I could see the amusement in her eyes. I didn't want amusement.

I grabbed a hold of my cock, but the bitch closed her legs.

"Have it your way, then," I told her, as I released my grip on her and flipped her onto her stomach. Before she could even move, I grabbed her ass and thrust forward.

"Ahh…" she moaned, gripping onto the sheets.

"My sweet wife…" I called to her, as I kissed her shoulder and made my way up the side of her neck. I pulled out, only to slam deeper within her.

"Liam…"

"You've pushed the wrong man, wife. You can't keep tempting me like this," I told her, grabbing hold of her ass as I fucked her hard.

She tried to speak, but she was now in the same position I was in: speechless, on the edge. Gripping onto the edge of our bed, she held on tightly, causing the bed to rock with us.

"Oh no, wife…" I murmured, pulling her back. I held her breasts, letting her ride me. Her hands flew back in search of my hair, pulling roughly when they found it.

"Liam…fuck…" she moaned, and I couldn't help but grin.

"That's what I'm doing, love," I grunted, as I kissed her spine before I couldn't hold back anymore.

"Liam…"

"Hold on…" I moaned, trying my best to fight it, but I couldn't. Not with her. Not like this.

"Mel!" I gasped as I came with her, before falling into a heap of tangled limbs.

Pulling out, I lay next her, breathing in the scent of our sex.

"Damn you," she whispered, brushing the hair off her face. She looked so fucking wild, so beautifully fucked that I wanted her again. My cock was going to fall off.

"Damn *you*. This is your fault anyway." I uttered, wanting nothing more than to kiss her.

She smirked, sitting up and allowing me to see not only her perfect breasts, but the small bump that was her stomach. Getting up, I pulled her to me.

"Urgh, you're sweaty." She laughed.

"So are you!" I replied, rolling my eyes. "And neither of us would be sweaty right now had you not jumped me in the car."

"I did not jump you. I simply touched you," she stated, relaxing in my arms.

I loved when she was this way with me.

"You grabbed my cock. You may as well have jumped me."

The plan was get home, kill Harvey, have a talk. But did my wife ever listen to my plans? No. Instead, she grabbed my cock and because I'm addicted to her, there was no going back. We fucked in the car. We were all over each other in the hall and then we ended up fucking against the wall of our room before we ended up on the bed.

She brushed back my hair, staring into my eyes. "I was hungry for you and now that I've fed that hunger, I hunger for some real food."

"Chocolate is not food, love." I smirked, causing her to glare at me.

"Food is anything I say it is, Liam. Now go get me some s'mores," she demanded, doing her best to push me off the bed.

I loved her.

Rolling off the bed, I watched as she stretched out before wrapping the sheets around herself. "I'm going, jeez. But you better eat something healthier…"

But before I could finish, she smacked my ass. Turning to her quickly, I found her smirking. "You put it in my face, what else was I supposed to do?" The innocent way she said it was criminal.

Leaning down, I kissed her deeply before breaking away. "Those are the kind of touches that will get you fucked mercilessly again."

"Feed me and we can talk about it," she said before leaning up to kiss me once more.

I never wanted this to end, but it had to, at least for the moment.

"I'll get the s'mores. But get cleaned up, we need to at least figure out what's going on with Olivia." And then she needed to pack.

Brushing her hand across my face, she sat up. "Or you can call someone to bring it to us while we get cleaned up together. I could hold off eating for a shower."

The moment she kissed me, biting my bottom lip, I knew I was a goner.

Damn her. Damn her.

Melody

"Ma'am," Monte said, handing me a plate of s'mores along with a glass of milk as I sat in the basement.

Apparently, Liam and I hadn't missed anything, even with the extra long shower we took.

Olivia was supposed to handle this on her own, but she refused to see Harvey. She wasn't ready to face the monster yet. You would think she'd be dying to slit the motherfucker's throat, but no. She was bloody hiding.

Liam had gone to get her—i.e. knock some fucking sense into her—leaving me alone with the rapist. That sounded horrible…for him. He was still gagged and bound to the wall. His was shirt ripped, his leather pants were almost to his ankles; he looked as if he just came out of a bondage club alright; it was overall a pitiful sight. His hair was greasy, his mustache seemed as if it were drawn on with a sharpie and his eyes were cold.

This was the piece of shit she didn't want to face? I was expecting more.

"I don't understand females, Monte," I told him as I stared at Harvey, and ate my s'more.

"If you don't, ma'am, there's no hope for the rest of us."

"How would you kill him?" I asked, causing Harvey's eyes to widen as he stared at us. "If it was your lover he had raped, what would you do him?"

Monte glared at the man.

"I would take a page out of the Passion of fucking Christ, chain him to the wall and take his skin off with whips…and for the heck of it, I'd roll him in salt." He spat at his feet.

"You can do better, Monte." I smiled, drinking my milk.

"Crucify him upside down?" He grinned, looking down at me.

"I see someone's been going back to church." Monte wasn't a very religious person, but every once in awhile, he would spend weeks at church. I wasn't sure why, but hey, whatever worked for him.

The rapist mumbled, fighting against his chains as if that was going to help him. I wanted to watch him suffer slowly.

"I'm sorry, you have balls in your mouth. I can't hear you," I told him before taking a bite. He glared, barking out something I didn't understand.

"I think he is insulting you, ma'am. May I demonstrate?" He seemed eager.

"Sadly no, it's Olivia's kill and she's going to kill him, even if takes her all night." I frowned. "But we can suggest it as an option. I've never seen a man crucified before."

LIAM

I do not have time for this shit.
"Olivia Callahan, get your ass out here and kill this motherfucker, I have shit to do," I yelled at the oak door. I could still hear her sobbing.

"You're not helping!" Neal yelled at me, but the moment his eyes met mine, he backed down, as he should.

Staring at the two hundred year old oak door with the hand-carved family crest that my mother had imported from Ireland, I thought about how easy it would be for me to just blow a hole through it and drag her out. Pinching the bridge of my nose, I could feel my father's eyes on me. He wanted to see how well I could handle the family. He was always watching me and it pissed me off sometimes.

Sighing, I took a deep breath and stepped forward. "Olivia, I don't understand your pain, nor will I ever. Nothing I can say will reverse the shit you went through. However, right now you have been given a chance at justice very few people in this life get. You are a Callahan. We don't cry, we don't get even, we bend the scale in our favor and leave it there. I have too much to do to sit here and listen to you disgrace this family. If you're not out of there in five seconds, Neal will divorce you. He won't want to, but he will do it because I will make him. And his next wife won't be such a fucking wuss."

"You're an asshole, Liam Callahan," she yelled, bursting out of the room before storming down the marble hallway. Neal shook his head at me, his jaw clenched, before he followed after her.

Declan and my father just stared at me. "Is there a reason why you bitches are staring?"

"Nope, I will go…make myself useful." Declan said and under his breath. I could have sworn the motherfucker muttered, *"The mad hatter strikes again."*

Melody

Hearing the door open, Monte and I turned to find Olivia, her face puffy and red, her eyes focused only on Harvey.

"I want to be alone with him," she demanded.

Nodding, I looked to Monte, who walked right past her.

"That means you as well," she snapped at me. Obviously, she forgot who had pushed her to this point.

"You're funny," I told her. "Now, hurry up and kill him, I'm running low on snacks."

"Mel."

"Olivia." My voice dropped no longer joking.

Sighing, she didn't say anything. Instead she took a chair allowing it to drag against the floor—metal on concrete—before she stopped and took a seat near me.

"I don't know how to kill him. I want him to suffer. I just don't know…" she added as she stared at Harvey, who only stared back like he was begging with his eyes.

"Easiest problem you could ever have." I said, giving her a s'more. She stared at me like I was insane. "When a pregnant woman offers you food, you take it and smile."

I knew they knew. The way Declan was treating me in the car, he had to have known, which meant Coraline knew, and if Coraline knew, they all knew.

Taking it, she took a bite and smiled. It was fake, but whatever, I was being nice, the least she could do was accept it.

"Monte said you should crucify him," I told her.

She thought about it, sniffling slightly before shaking her head. "Too much effort and people. I want to be the one to kill him. It's not a group project."

It took me a second, but I smiled like the Grinch after he stole Christmas.

"Olivia, have you ever drilled through a man's flesh?" I asked.

"What?" she coughed

"Neal, maybe you can show her," I called out, knowing full well they could hear us, before standing up.

A moment later, Neal came with not one, but two drills. The emotion in his eyes—or better yet, the *lack* of any emotion in his eyes—was beautiful.

"She kills him," was all I said, grabbing my plate and glass to leave. I wanted to stay, but drills always became so damn messy.

Liam stood outside the door, shaking his head at me.

"What?" I asked, turning to watch from the safety of the window.

Coming up behind me, he wrapped his hands around my waist. We were in public and it was odd to me that I wasn't pushing him away. But for some reason, whenever he was near, I felt calm. I felt relaxed.

"You're ruthless, wife," he muttered.

"Someone has to be, why not me?" I replied, leaning into him as I watched Neal hold Olivia's hand. She went for the bitch's belly button. That was going to hurt.

"What had you so stressed earlier?" I murmured, but he didn't answer. He just rubbed my stomach slowly. "Liam…"

"Everyone out," he declared and I hadn't even noticed everyone, but in a flash they were gone.

Turning me to him, he kissed me and I reacted by dropping my plate and glass before I regained my senses and pushed him away, slapping him across the face.

"Fuck, Mel!" he snapped, grabbing his face. "You need to check that shit before our kid comes."

"You need to stop distracting me when I'm talking about work, damn it. What the hell is going on?" I yelled back.

He sighed, rolling his eyes. "Firstly, your mood swings are driving me insane. Secondly, it's about your grandfather."

I froze. "Orlando's father died years ago."

"Not him. Ivan, Aviela's father. He signed as witness on the marriage contract between my father and Natasha's mother. For some reason, he wanted them married." He frowned, staring at Olivia and Neal. He looked jealous, like he would rather be drilling into a man's spine than dealing with this.

Standing beside him, I watched silently. "Why? What does he gain from your father marrying Natasha's mother?"

"I'm not sure." He shrugged. "But the only way we will find out anything is to see the Briars. We have to go to Ireland."

I couldn't help but groan. "You do know they will most likely retaliate for everything that happened to Shamus."

He turned to me, leaning against the window just as blood splattered upon it. "They will. But we have no other choice. We need to find out what's happening."

"Fine." I sighed. "But Olivia and Neal will have to stay. We still have Senator Colemen to deal with. He needs to become the President. Now that Chuck is dead, we won't have to worry about the market for a while. Roy is going to have his work cut out for him as he tries to prove his worth."

"Who the hell is Roy?" He glared, and I just rolled my eyes.

"Our new mule. Breathe, I was just sucking you off wasn't I?"

He grinned like the pervert he was as he eyed me. The moment he took a step toward me, I stepped back. "Slow down. When are we leaving?"

He didn't listen. Instead, he pushed me against the window. I felt someone slam over and over again on it. Frowning, Liam glared at the blood stained window, where Harvey was screaming for help. Reaching to the intercom, Liam snapped, "Will you keep the motherfucker off the glass? Jeez. I swear people don't know how to kill correctly."

"They're having fun. They could use it. Maybe Olivia will finally stop being a pain in the ass." I smirked.

They'd let him out of his chains just so they could watch him beg for his life, and they called us fucked up.

"Where were we?" He turned to me.

"You were about to kiss me against the bloody glass," I replied, and he nodded before lifting me up and pressing me against said glass.

"So, Ireland?" he sighed, staring at me.

"Will you wear one of those 'Kiss Me I'm Irish' shirts?"

He rolled his eyes. "No."

I kissed him.

"Maybe," he whispered when I broke away.

I kissed him again. Deeper.

"Maybe."

"You're cheating, Liam." I glared at him.

"Yes I am." He smirked, kissing me again.

Fifteen

*"Handsome And Brilliantly rich;
their fatal flaw is murder."*
—*Abigail Gibbs*

Neal

If you had told me a year ago that I would be watching my wife drill into a man's spine, I would have laughed in your face. Olivia was not a killer. Olivia didn't want to kill, but apparently she was into torture.

"You laughed." She sneered over the buzz of her drill. The pig screamed loudly, and as he tried to crawl away from her, his voice, like his bones, was cracking. "I told you to stop! I begged you to stop, and you laughed!"

The blood that splattered all over her face made me grateful that I had thought to get her a mask and goggles. She looked like a wild butcher. She looked liked a monster. She looked fucking sexy.

She snapped up, staring at me. "Why did you stop?"

Why did I stop? I thought, looking at the blood that dripped from the head of my drill.

"It's your kill, babe," I told her, taking a seat against the wall. I felt the blood lust; that Callahan blood lust that begged for me to finish him off, to cut his head off and drill into his eyes. It was that blood lust that drove my father and Liam. It was in our DNA. Callahans and blood went hand in hand. If we weren't in the mafia, we would all probably be serial killers.

Olivia stared at me, pulling her drill from his spine causing a sickening pop to echo around the room. Placing it on the ground, she walked over to me, and took a seat by my side, where she belonged.

"Is it always like this?" she asked, as she rested her head on my shoulder. Harvey wasn't moving. He may have been dead. From what I could tell he had seventy-nine drill holes starting from his ankle to his shoulder blades. I did my best to keep her from his neck and head; he shouldn't die that quickly.

"Like what?"

She sighed, pulling the mask from her face. "I don't know. Is it always this easy? This simple. Just kill and not regret it? There he is, the man who caused me so much pain and enjoyed every moment. It was easy. It was so easy to kill him. But I hated him. Is it always this easy?"

I thought about it and nodded. "Yes. After your first kill it becomes easier and easier until it's second nature. There is a line in the world. There are those who can be fucked with, and there are those who cannot be. If people knew their place, then the world would be safer. I just think of it as regulating."

She didn't say anything and I wasn't sure how to take that. This was the part of me that I did my best to hide from her. The Callahan blood, the part of me that thought it was okay to cut out men's tongues if they spoke badly about our family. Yet here we were, watching her rapist bleed out. Liam would want this room cleaned and re-cemented to hide all the blood.

OLIVIA

I felt nothing but relief and that was so odd to me. I expected anger, pain, guilt—any emotion at all, but nothing else came. Was it really so easy to kill people? Or was it because I knew they were evil. With them gone, I felt no need to ever walk down this road again...so what kept Melody and Liam going?

"Can we go?" I asked Neal. "He's dead. Can we go? I just want a shower."

He nodded, reaching behind his back before handing me a gun. "He's going to die anyway if he hasn't already, but just add the final nail."

Taking the handgun, I turned back to Harvey—my rapist. My monster. Standing, I walked over to his body, looking down at his head when he moved.

A dry sob broke through his lips, his whole body shook like mine shook after that night. He looked up at me covered in his own blood.

"I'm sorry. I'm so sorry." He sobbed softly.

"No, you're not," I told him before firing into his skull.

Taking a deep breath, I almost jumped when Mel walked into the room clapping slowly.

On her face was a wicked smile. It was worse than how she used to glare at everyone. Her smiles were mocking smiles; like she knew something you didn't and she was going to use it against you.

"Welcome to the family." She smiled as Liam appeared behind her, placing his hand on her waist.

He glanced around the room and shook his head before staring at Neal, who stood up under his brother's gaze.

"We're going to Ireland," Liam stated. "You and Olivia will be staying here. Can I trust you to keep an eye on this while we're gone?"

I turned to Neal. He loved Ireland. He wanted us to go there this summer, but King Liam would not allow it. Now the ass was taking his wife. However, Neal didn't look bothered, he looked at his brother with pride. I would never understand their relationship.

"Yes. I will look over everything. Declan told me something about the new prices and our new contact. I will watch over that and Senator Colemen," he replied.

Mel's eyes narrowed in on him. "We will be coming back so don't get used to siting on our throne."

"Of course not."

Here I was, standing in a room full of killers and I was one of them. I was a Callahan. God help whoever stood in this family's way.

Sixteen

"I'll kill you in a few minutes. It'll be good for you."
—Frederick Weisel

Liam

"Are we staying in the castle?" Coraline asked, grinning out the plane window. "I haven't been back there since we got married."

I turned to stare at my brother, who smiled so widely I was surprised his teeth didn't fall out as he watched Coraline in her own personal wonderland.

Apparently they were doing well.

"I'm not sure. Boss?" He turned to me.

Rolling my eyes, I shook my head, knowing they would not be happy with where we were going to be staying.

There was silence throughout our large cabin. We were only three hours into an eight-hour flight to Dublin, and I knew I was going to lose my mind.

I should have gotten a larger plane.

After Colemen was president, I was taking Air Force One, damn it.

"Liam," my mother said slowly, breaking away from her private conversation with my father to address me.

"Don't tell me..." Sedric trailed off, straightening his tie as he glared into the side of my skull. I could feel the rage he was trying to bottle up.

"Don't tell him what?" Coraline glanced between us, as if she was seeing two very different outcomes of my answer.

Declan glared, his eyes narrowing, body stiffening, but he nodded.

"Liam…"

"We're staying at Shamus' house in the village," I snapped, pinching the bridge of my nose. For the love of Christ, why couldn't they shut up?

"Shamus' house?" Coraline repeated softly. "As in, Shamus, who's everyone believes was murdered in our house, the man who lives in the hills of Ireland with his men…his very loyal men."

I glared at her. "No, Coraline. I mean Shamus, the ghost of mafia past. What the fuck?"

She frowned, leaning back into her seat, causing Declan's eyebrow to twitch as he stared at me.

However, there was a small snicker from the woman in front of me. Glancing at her, I noticed she hadn't been sleeping like I thought.

"I didn't know you were awake." I sat up, grabbing her hand.

She rolled her eyes at me. "Who could sleep with all the noise you people are making."

"My pregnant wife could." I replied, causing her to pinch my wrist. Taking her other hand, I kissed them before sitting back.

"So, Shamus' house…" She smiled, leaning back as well. "A bit morbid, don't you think?"

I couldn't help but groan, hearing a few '*thank-yous*' from the peanut gallery that was my family.

"Not you too, wife."

"Morbid, but not bad. After all, the Romans killed and made it their own home—"

"Yes and the Roman Empire fell," my father cut her off sharply, causing the smiles on both of our faces to drop as we turned to him.

My mother shook her head at him, flipping through her magazine as if there wasn't a possibility that I would take a dagger to the side of my own father's face.

"Yes," Mel stated, her eyes cold. "The Roman Empire did fall, and yet we Italians still have all the glory. The very suits you wear, the shoes on your feet, are made from where?" she trailed off. "You are not powerful unless you have something Italian."

I rolled my eyes. "Your ego right now—"

"What was the name of that car you were trying to buy?"

"Ferrari En…" Declan trailed off when my father smacked him in the back of his head for me before returning to his book, not saying a word.

"It's not ego when you state the truth."

Mel smiled as she lay back in her chair. She rubbed her temples and closed her eyes once more. The headaches were becoming more and more frequent with each passing day.

It had taken us another week after Harvey's death to finally get everything ready to leave. It would have taken only three days had I not forced my wife to see a doctor. I was damn near ready to give her a CAT scan myself. I needed to know she was okay. That this was just a phase. It was only after I had brought the doctor to our house that she finally agreed.

She and the baby were fine, he had said. I shouldn't worry according to him. But how could I not when the woman I barely ever saw grimace couldn't even hold her head up after a few hours?

"Stop looking at me like that. I'm fine, I saw your damn doctor. Your kid is just fucking with my mind before it's born," she said with her eyes closed.

I snorted. "How did he become mine all of a sudden?"

Her eyes snapped open. "He? I'm sorry, did you and God have a private conversation without me?"

"There was no need. God knows there is no way in hell I could mentally handle a girl right now. Nor does he want to watch the chaos that would unfold when I'm unable to tell a small girl *no*," I replied as my father and brother laughed.

"You're a narcissistic asshole," she snapped at me.

"You knew that when you married me." I winked at her.

"Well, aren't you both cute?" Declan snickered under his breath, causing both Mel and myself to freeze, however, for two completely different reasons.

She stared at me and I could feel her blood boiling.

"Your cousin just called me 'cute.'"

Here we go.

Grabbing her water bottle, she threw it across the aisle at his face.

"I'm going to go lie down before I kill you and drop you somewhere over the Atlantic Ocean." she barked in his face, trying to stand quickly only to stumble forward.

Both my father and I stood at the same time, reaching to grab hold of her. But she pushed us both of away.

"URGH! This kid is trying to kill me! I can't walk straight. I can't think straight. I have no control of my own damn body! And now I have people calling me *cute*. Like I'm a fucking puppy!" she sneered at me, pushing me aside in order to continue on her way. "I am Melody Giovanni Callahan, *cute* is not the adjective used to describe me!"

And with that, she slammed the door to the room. Leaving everyone else but my mother and I a little confused.

"This is why we can't fly commercial," my mother whispered, shaking her head at us.

"What did I say?" Declan asked, making me want to smack the fucking shit out of him.

"You called one of the leaders of the Irish and Italian mob *cute*," my mother informed the stupid fucking idiot that was supposed to be my older cousin. "While she's pregnant. Mel doesn't want to be treated differently, nor does she want to lose the respect just because she's sharing her body. She's going to torture you for this."

Not only him.

Part of me was enjoying my soft wife. Melody seemed relaxed and the fact that she was almost always in the mood for sex, which wasn't really different from when she was cold, was a plus. We even cuddled. She told me she loved me before going to sleep. She was being sweet to me, and the family. To the rest of the men, Mel was kind of a raging hormonal bitch though. They never knew if she was smiling because she was happy or because she was planning to cut off a man's thumb.

"Should I check on her since Adriana isn't here?" Coraline asked, looking at the door.

"Yes, because my wife would love to be 'checked up' on." She liked Coraline, but she may shoot her one day.

Shaking my head at her, I looked towards the man who stood slightly in the corner in front of the mini bar. He didn't seem shocked at the insanity that was our family. Mel had told me his name, but I kept forgetting he was even around…I didn't trust that.

"Your name," I demanded, drawing everyone's attention to the small server. Apparently I wasn't the only one who forgot he was on board.

He took a step forward. "Nelson Reed."

"You're on my plane because…?"

He tried to remain calm, but I could see the nervousness building. "I've flown with Mrs. Callahan before, and Ms. Angelia…"

Before he could finish, Mel stomped out, not bothering to look at any of us. Instead, she turned to Reed, who quickly turned and prepared her tea within seconds. Handing it to her, he spoke, "I'm scared shitless of you, ma'am."

She nodded, glaring at me. "Leave my people alone, yours tick me off."

I'm not going to make it. Throw me out of the plane now.

I groaned, pinching the bridge of my nose as I stood. Then, I followed her into the room.

Before entering, I stopped in front of the worm. "Kiss up to my wife again, and I will rip your lips from your face."

His eyes widened and he nodded quickly as I stepped in.

There, sitting in middle of the bed with her pinky sticking out as she drank her tea like the damn queen of England, was my wife. The room was small of course. It was only meant for short naps; the bed took up the whole fucking room. However, as she sat there, she glanced at me while sipping away, and I wasn't sure what to do with her. She was driving me insane! If I argued with her, I would lose and only piss her off. I wasn't sure if she was rational enough not to shoot me thirty thousand feet in the air. I couldn't calmly speak to her without her thinking I was speaking down to her.

"Mel..."

"I'm going to be a horrible mother," she said out of nowhere. "I feel it. I'm angry and annoyed with it all the time. I keep wishing I wasn't pregnant because then I could think straight, and my head wouldn't hurt. My skin itches, and the nosebleeds..."

"Itchy skin and nosebleeds? What the fuck, when did this happen?" I asked, taking a seat at the side of the bed.

She rolled her eyes, put her cup on the side table. "It's not uncommon, I talked to the doctor about it. He said it should ease in a few weeks. And I quote, 'your body is adjusting. The baby is fine.' I'm not. What if I'm like her? What if I did this to her and that's why…"

"Stop," I snapped. "Women long before you or your mother have had difficult pregnancies. None of them turned out like your mother. She is…"

"She is my mother and we share DNA. I could be—"

"You are NOT like her!" I yelled, causing her to pull away from me to roll onto her side and stare at the wall.

God, this is Liam Callahan. I've sinned but do not punish me like this, I prayed.

Flipping onto the bed, I grabbed hold of her, pulling her towards me. She, being my wife, fought of course, but I would not let up.

"Liam let—"

"I did not chain you up to a bed. You do not have a lover I'm amputating body parts from in the basement…but if you ever did…"

"Liam," she smiled.

I continued. "We both chose this. We are probably the most truthful couple on the face of the planet. Whatever caused your mother to be what she is has nothing to do with your fate. You love me."

"Narcissistic asshole," she muttered.

Smirking again, I kissed her shoulder. "And I love you… our kid is going to be happy because despite it all, we're happy."

"Your sappiness is killing me slowly," she replied, as she rubbed her stomach and placed her head on my chest.

She's back.

"It's part of my charm, and I will need you to find your charm when we land," I reminded her. The bed creaked and rocked as though we were on a ship and not in the sky. Propping her head up, she sighed.

"Figured," she said. "How many of those loyal men did Shamus have?"

Too many.

"The Callahans are from the Irish hillside, and for decades our family has taken care of all the people within our town. From my great grandfather, to Shamus…"

"But not Sedric."

"Not Sedric." I nodded. "The people there are loyal to our family, but they feel as though he betrayed them by leaving and never coming back. I sent a few of the men ahead of us, but if we want to find out anything, we cannot go as aggressors. They most likely hate us for the death of Shamus, but can't do anything because we are still Callahans. We find out what we need to know, we don't kill anyone, and we leave."

"Says the man with anger management issues."

"I do not have—" I stopped when she grinned. "If people didn't always make me angry, there would be no reason for management."

"Anyway," she said as she rolled her eyes, "we go to your homeland, be nice to the locals and what, they just hand over the Briars?"

"Yes."

"That is going to last about ten minutes before one of us snaps."

Melody

The moment we stepped out of the plane I felt Liam's body stiffen at the sight of not one, but five beat up old mystery-machine buses parked in front of our Range Rovers. We had taken a smaller plane from Dublin to the hills in order to cut our time on the road and keep our location a secret until we arrived. The private pasture we landed in wasn't so private.

Dylan, Antonio, Monte and Fedel looked like they were standing on coils and trying to pretend as though they weren't.

Somebody was going to get killed if they stayed this tense.

Why did that only make me want to smile? We didn't want to start a war, but shooting the Irish was what we Italians did...or at least what the Giovannis did. Orlando used to say it was like putting down a wild dog.

"Old Man Doyle," Liam called out as we approached the hairy man who stood leaned against the bus smoking his pipe.

Old Man Doyle didn't look much older than Sedric. He was so young in fact, that he looked like he had just now started to get grey hairs, which were entwined with the reddish brown ones. His beard was thick though, and I wanted nothing more than to hold him down and shave it off his face.

He didn't reply, he just smoked, blowing it out as though we had all the time in the world for his foolishness. One of his men—I guessed—stepped forward, blocking my view of the chain-smoking idiot.

He glared at me before turning to Liam. "Welcome to Ireland, you cocktrough bellgeg caffler." He spat at our feet. "Now take your foucking Italian cunt, and your foucking family, and get the fouck out of our country."

I just broke out in laughter, startling all of them. Turning to Liam, who had to be biting his tongue, I shook my head.

"When I said 'that's going to last ten minutes', I apparently meant five," I said, as I turned to face the dead man walking.

I always wore heels because it made it easier to threaten people when you didn't have to look up, however, seeing as how I could no longer walk, I was going to have to look up this man's nose hairs.

"Call me a cunt again, I dare you. And I will pull your tongue from your ass…or is it *arse*? So take your *foucking* face and bad breath and bugger off, because we both know you can't do shit," I told him.

"Looks like the Italian cunt…"

Before Doyle's man could finish, a bullet went through his foot and Liam took a step forward, pulling me to his side as the man screamed. Guns went up, and out of the corner of my eye, I watched as Declan and Sedric put Evelyn and Coraline in the car.

"She warned you." Liam sighed. I knew he didn't want this, but we sure as hell couldn't allow this to fly either. It was better to put a stop to it now.

"Enough," Old Man Doyle said, pushing off the bus. "Aren't you tired of putting bullets in your own kind, Callahan?"

"Shamus killed himself like a coward." I said.

An amused Declan added, "It was a bullet though."

None of them found it funny. Old Man Doyle blew the smoke through his nose as his jaw tensed.

"Is that the lie you're all telling? Shamus offed himself? You must think us the king of fools. Shamus was kin," he sneered at Liam, who shrugged.

"My kin. Not yours. The affairs amongst my family do not concern you," Liam said. "As my wife said, as my father said weeks ago; Shamus took his own life. I want to know why, and we think the Briars holds the key to that. That is all. Point me in the right direction, keep your dogs on their leashes, and the Callahan fortune will still flow through the town as it always has. Your wives don't want to bury their husbands and children, so step down and be the lesser but *alive* man."

He spit at the ground in front of us before turning back to his beat-up old bus, which Mr. Foucking was using for support.

"You have a week, Callahan, and then we want you gone. Or else." They got into their cars, leaving us standing there among blood stained grass.

"Have you lost your fucking mind Melody? What happened to charm?" Liam roared.

"*Foucking* Liam. *Foucking* we're in Ireland, try to fit in." I smiled before walking to the car.

Damn my feet hurt.

Liam

I could feel my eyebrow twitching as I watched her walk away from me.

"I enjoy her when she's pregnant. She's absolutely hilarious." My father laughed, stepping up right beside me.

"Would you like a bullet through your foot as well?" I yelled, waving my gun at him. "It's like she's fucking high."

"*Foucking*, brother," Declan said, watching the men as they finished loading all our things. "You have to admit, she was charming. They may not have shown it, but they were all surprised by her, some lusted—"

"Finish that sentence and I will actually have to kill my kinsmen," I hissed, leaving them both laughing. I could see them both drunk off their asses for the rest of this trip.

Ripping the door open, Mel's brown eyes snapped up to me. She stared at me as if she were shocked I came into the car. Noticing the stream of text messages that were buzzing in, I sat down.

"What?"

"The President was just assassinated, and not by us."

Foucking Christ, can't I get a break.

Seventeen

"The truth will set you free, but first it will piss you off."
—*Gloria Steinem*

Neal

Walking into Liam and Mel's office, I tried my best not to groan at the phone call awaiting me. All of Chicago was basically scared shitless while the rest of the damn country was in mourning. Of all the places the President could have been gunned down, why the fuck did it have to be here?

Pulling off my tie, I dropped it onto the desk before I took a seat. It was odd looking at this office—my father's and now Liam's—from this position. I had never noticed how cluttered and dark the study was. Everything here, from the cherry wood desk, to the bookshelves that covered both walls, and even the small bar stocked with Liam's Brandy along with Mel's wine, was vintage. The dark leather chair my ass now graced was brought in from Italy as if my mother knew years ago an Italian would be siting in it.

"Power looks good on you, baby," Olivia called from the doors, pulling me out of my own thoughts.

I leaned back to stare at her. "Really? Do I have my grey hairs yet?"

"Neal, they've only been gone for a week," she replied, walking over to me and seductively playing with the pearls around her neck. She looked dangerous in black; it seemed to bounce up into her blue eyes and brew storms.

"Only a week and the President gets wacked in our city, meaning we can't operate with the feds tearing this city apart for the killer." Which meant moving our products just got harder. The bosses were going to be pissed.

"Babe, President Monroe is not the first President to be assassinated," she supposed, stepping behind me in order to rub my shoulders. "I'm sure the feds already have a suspect. Mel and Liam—"

She was cut off the moment the phone rang and I knew who it was.

"Speak of the devil," she said.

I picked up the phone. "Hell—"

"Neal, could you please explain what you're doing?" Mel's voice rang out softly through the phone. So soft in fact I wasn't sure if I should be worried or rearranging my will again.

"Boss, Chicago is on lock down. There's a massive manhunt going on, and every hour more and more police officers are coming in all throughout the country." I waited for her to speak, but she said nothing.

"It isn't wise to move product right now. The shipment through the dock has been taken care of already, but there is no way we can get them out to the dealers right now…"

"What about Senator Colemen?" she asked. Again, still calm; still freaking me out.

Glancing to Olivia who only shrugged, I told her the truth, "As far as I know, Mina's working on another statement, but he's fine."

"He's fine?" she repeated before taking a deep breath.

Oh shit.

"He's shouldn't be fucking fine!" she snapped. "He is nowhere close to fine! Why? Because as far as I know, people are sympathetic, brainless, parasites who jump from one host to another!"

"Um, what?" What in the hell was she talking about?

"You idiot. Turn on the news!"

Turning on the computer, Olivia went to a live stream of the First Lady.

She looked tired but energized; odd seeing as how her husband was just murdered in front of the whole nation, if not world.

"My fellow Americans, as hard as it is to stand here in front of you, I have no other choice. My husband was a strong man, who would never bend to the will of terrorists and criminals. I believe it is truly because of him that I have found the will to say to the man who pulled that trigger: you will not win. You will not silence the greatest democracy on the planet with a bullet. For in killing my husband, you have awakened the beast in me. I will run for President. I will take my husband's torch to the finish line, and you will not silence America!"

"Oh, Fuck," Olivia and I said together.

"My thoughts exactly," Mel stated. "There you have it. The speech heard around the world! Do you want to know who she looks like? Jackie O. Do you want know which first lady all of American loves so dearly? Jackie fucking O. So how fine are you fucking feeling right now, Neal? Because on the scale of pissed to motherfucking enraged, I'm ready to fucking explode!"

Pulling the phone from my ear, I tried my best not to flinch. "Mel, what do you want me to do?"

"Get off your fat ass and work or so help me—I don't care what you do. I would suggest during Colemen's pretty speech to put two bullets in him and even the fucking playing field again—"

Before I could stop her Olivia grabbed the phone from me.

"Have you lost your fucking mind? That's my father!"

"I'll buy you a new one," I heard Melody say. "Now get the fuck off the phone, you're wasting my bloody minutes."

"Boss," I said, grabbing the phone before Olivia smashed it against the wall. "I'm…"

"Did Liam and I not tell you how important it was for us to secure the presidency, Neal? It could be Mrs. Colemen as President or you could aim for Colemen's legs. All I know is, if you have a better idea, start working on it, because if I have to jump my pregnant ass across the pond to do it myself, I sure as fucking hell will. As for the drugs, make them move. Sell them at half the damn price if you have to. But the longer we sit on it, the weaker we look and the more money we lose. Junkies don't care that the President is dead, they just want their fix and what the customer wants, they get!" And with that she was gone.

"She's a monster!" Olivia screamed as I hung up, grabbing my tie and walking towards the door.

"Neal! What are you going to do?"

I didn't answer her because in all honesty I wasn't even sure. So much for having power.

Eighteen

"Sometimes you have to pick the gun up to put the gun down."
—Malcolm X

Jinx

I don't like people. I don't like being around them, and I don't like walking amongst them. My place has always been in the sky. I was born in the sky, somewhere over Vermont of all places. My mother gave birth to me on a plane, and since then, that's the place I've tried to stay. Being a first generation Italian to a nearly blind mother and a deadbeat alcoholic father, there wasn't much room for me to spread my wings as child. My days were spent trying to stop my father from killing my mother, and my mother from killing herself.

It was only when I turned eighteen that I left. I kissed my mother goodbye, left my father a six-pack and joined the Air Force. Days became weeks, weeks became months, and sooner than I could blink, I was dripping in medals of honor. Time flies when you're having fun, and it flies even faster when you live thirty-six thousand feet high. My job was second nature to me; I would have done it for free.

I got my nickname Jinx because no matter how hard someone tried to outshine me, they would fail. I would steal away their look. At bars the women would leave the other guys to be around me. In the air, no one could get near me in drills without something going wrong. To me it was luck, to them I was Jinx.

Life was good, until I found out the bambolina I was seeing was pregnant, just as I was given another assignment. The last thing I told her was to keep the baby and we would talk about it later.

Drop the package over North Korea, come home, get married, be the father mine failed to be, and live a happy middle class life like everyone else. But, that day never came, because apparently, I died…or at least the government said I did.

Moments after I dropped the package, I was shot out the sky like a duck during hunting season. They pulled me from the mangled, smoldering machine I had once called my baby, and tortured me. But I took that one for my country, thinking they would come and rescue me. They had to. Day in and day out, for four years I was beaten within an inch of my life, always asked the same questions over and over again.

"The guns! Who wants the guns?" I didn't know it then, but the package I had dropped was filled with American weapons to arm Korean rebels. America wasn't coming to my aid. They would deny to their dying breaths that I was even in Korean air space.

They had chosen me not because I was good, but because I looked foreign enough and stupid enough not to ask questions. So for four years I did my time in Hell, only to escape during a small riot. I ran for hours doing my best not to be seen, blending in with those trying to leave the country. In South Korea, it took me four more years and a fake passport to finally make it back to the "land of the free, home of the brave."

I found out that not only had the world moved on, but that I no longer mattered within it. Everything once bearing my name was gone; my identity was wiped clean. Somewhere in Vermont, both my parents were dead, my father killing my mother and then himself. The woman and child I had left behind had moved on without me. They were happy... who was I to take that away from them? So I was alone.

I wandered the streets, doing odd jobs here and there all over the country. I lived under bridges, I ate from dumpsters, and on occasion, I would shower in subway bathrooms. My luck had turned and now I truly felt nothing but jinxed.

Then, one day, as I lay at my spot behind the dumpster, I watched as a white Tahoe sped into my ally. In front of it, some poor Irish mutt looked for a way out. He begged the white Tahoe as if he were speaking to a God, claiming he would get her money back. He swore on his life, but it did him no good. Instead, it drove over him as if he were nothing but a rat. I would never forget the sound of his screams, muffled by the blood in his mouth, nor would I ever forget the look in her eyes as she stepped out of the driver's seat to look at her handy work. Realizing I was now a witness, I was pulled from my makeshift home and made to kneel before her.

She looked at me, not saying a word as she held a gun to my head; I could feel nothing but gratitude. But she didn't pull the trigger. Instead she looked at my dog tags—the meager remnants of my past.

"Why is an Air Force Lieutenant living behind a dumpster?" she asked.

I stared at her seriously and simply said, "Budget cuts."

A few of her men snickered, but not her. She didn't even crack a smile. She stared at me as though she could really see *me*.

"Lieutenant..."

"Jinx."

She glared. "Well Jinx, how would you like to join *my* army?"

"Do I have a choice?" After all, I already had a gun to my head.

"We all have a choice. Yours is simple: spend the rest of your days living in filth or join me and walk on water."

I had nothing left to lose. She saw something in me, and because of that, I had my wings back. Flying for the first time after years of being grounded was its own personal high. She gave me what I needed, and in return she had my loyalty. I would die for her and yet there were times…

Melody

Walking slowly through the wet grass, I came to a stop beside Jinx, staring past the cliffs into the sky, hills and lakes. I had to give it to the Irish: their country was beautiful…and green, very green.

"Thinking of jumping, Jinx?" I asked softly as the wind blew by us with a howl.

He snickered beside me, the wind blowing his dirty, blonde, shoulder length hair. "I'm sure you could find a new pilot, ma'am."

Grabbing his arm, I forced him away from the clouds to meet my gaze. The wind picked up, but we just stared at each other. In that moment, his blue eyes looked just as broken as the day I met him.

"You're in that dark place, Jinx," I stated looking away from him, "Your daughter?"

"Yes. I should be proud, shouldn't I? She doesn't want or need my money."

Smiling, I looked up to the sky. "Feminist then."

"God forbid." He spat over the cliff's edge and I simply laughed, opening my arms and allowing the wind to blow past me again.

For miles, all I could smell was fresh grass and seawater. It made me want to fly…it was like I was flying.

"Careful, ma'am," he whispered, grabbing onto my waist.

"Shh, Jinx," I muttered, pushing his hands away. "I'm on top of the world."

It was peaceful on the edge. My life was even more chaotic than I had ever imagined.

"Wife."

And just like that, my peace was gone.

Turning, there stood my husband, in nothing but jeans and a white button down shirt. The wind blew through his hair, pushing it back, making his eyes look glazed over as he glared at Jinx.

"Go help Fedel. Now." He snapped at him, nostrils flaring.

Jinx looked to me, eyebrow raised, before walking off toward the house. Liam watched him like a lion stalking its prey, cautious of any sudden movements. It wasn't until Jinx was far out of earshot that he gave me his attention again.

"Have you slept with him?" he hissed through clenched teeth.

Seriously? He's jealous? "I haven't slept with him since you entered my life, *husband*."

Brushing the side of my cheek, he hovered over my lips, stealing the air from the small bubble surrounding us. "That's not an answer, wife."

"It is an answer. Just not the one you want to hear," I said before closing the gap between our lips. He pulled me closer to him, grabbing my ass and hair.

"You…"

"Let it go. Liam. My past is my past. Yours is yours. You don't see me giving all the women you've slept with the evil eye." If I did, my face would be stuck in a permanent scowl.

"With the exception of Natasha."

"That wasn't my fault, she came for seconds."

"I don't want you to be alone with him."

And we were back on Jinx.

"Too bad," I replied, breaking free of his arms and walking towards the house.

"I'm serious, Melody," he hollered. He was just going to have to get over it. I could feel him stomping through the grass behind me. I could always feel him, even when I didn't want to. The men of my past were none of his concern. He knew damn well I wasn't a virgin when I met him. *The stupid double-standard-having misogynistic asshole.*

"Trouble in paradise?" Declan asked innocently, leaning on the frame of the cabin door, wiping his hands with an old rag.

"You call this paradise?" I asked, glancing around the home that had once belonged to Shamus. It was nothing but a three bedroom stone cabin parked on top of a grass cliff with a few sheep and chickens. I now knew why Coraline hated it here and wanted the castle. It wasn't by any means glamorous; it was like stepping back into the dark ages, or becoming Amish.

All the furniture was handcrafted and the only light came from candles. This morning, Evelyn had milked a sheep, and I half expected Sedric to go hunting with some form of Irish militia. It was funny, you could always spot a cop or a mobster by where they chose to live. Shamus made sure he could see the town from his front door and nothing but open sky at his back.

"Sometimes, getting away from the city is paradise," Declan whispered, taking a deep breath.

"For the weak maybe." For those like me, the cities were paradise. The only place you could find heaven and hell on the same block.

He shook his head, gazing at his brother. "What have you done to him now?"

"Nothing, but remind him what decade we're from."

"Yes, the one where women fuck their employees and wonder why they don't get any fucking respect," Liam snapped, brushing past his cousin to get inside.

Declan glanced at me before walking away quickly. At least one of them was smart.

Deep breaths, Mel.

"What the fuck is your problem, Liam!" I snapped, following him.

"What the fuck is my problem?" he roared from the kitchen table. "I come outside to find my wife, *MINE*, laughing and smiling with another man like an airheaded teenage girl! Not your fake smiles either, your real ones. The ones you give me and me alone, not some homeless prick you hired years ago! It was disgusting—"

I didn't even try and stop myself. Instead, my fist connected with his nose and I reveled in the pop that sounded after.

"You are walking a fine line!" I screamed, as he held his nose, the blood dripping down his hand. "Nothing you say, and no matter how loud you say it, will change my past, nor do I want it to. Did I sleep with Jinx? Yes. Was in love with him? Did I draw hearts around our names and daydream about marrying him? No. It was sex. It was years ago."

"Have you slept with all of them?" he asked, wiping the blood from his face with his sleeve.

"Fuck you," I hissed as someone knocked. "Go away!"

"Come in!" Liam countered.

We glared at each other before Fedel opened the door.

"Have you ever fucked my wife?" Liam asked.

"Don't answer that and get OUT!"

"STAY!"

"I swear to God Almighty, Fedel, I will cut you up and feed you to the damn chickens if you answer that question!"

He could only stare wide-eyed between us before turning to Liam. "We found the Briars, they're in the foothills just north of here. Monte went ahead to make sure they didn't try to flee."

With that, he left as quickly as possible, leaving only silence between us.

"You want me to be ashamed of myself? You want me to say I'm sorry? No. I won't, because then I would be lying to you."

"If you will excuse me, *wife*, I have to go find out about my mistress, at least with her I can expect to be screwed over," he said before leaving. "And I'm taking Jinx with me!"

Sighing, I ran my hand through my hair. "Aren't I supposed to be the hormonal one?"

"Don't mind him," Sedric laughed, walking down the stairs with Evelyn at his side. "He's cursed with the Callahan jealousy."

"First, the what?" I asked. "And second, where are you both going?" It was the middle of the afternoon and they were both dressed as though they were going to see the queen.

"We're going to the festival tonight in town and the curse is more of an excuse Sedric uses to justify why he always lost his mind when another man touched me when I was pregnant." Evelyn laughed, as she slipped her ruby earrings into their place.

"I did not lose my mind," he huffed, trying to fix his bow tie, "I expressed my displeasure with those who came too close."

"You almost broke the hand of a host who took my coat!" Evelyn chuckled.

"The only reason why a man would take that long to help you out of your coat is if he had a shoulder fetish."

"I was seven months pregnant, Sedric, it took him so long because I could barely move."

Shaking my head, I took a seat at the table. "I'm sorry I asked."

They both turned, as if they had forgotten I was there. They very well could have on their stroll through memory lane.

Gliding over to me, Evelyn kissed my cheek. "What we're trying to say is, Liam is going to get a little more possessive of you with your child on the way. He doesn't mean to be, and he probably has no idea why he's acting this way."

"Can't I just sedate him for the remaining six months?" If not, I might not make it.

Sedric snickered. "And deal with all of that rage at once? You're safer taking it in doses."

"If that fails, marijuana cookies work wonders," she grinned, causing Sedric's face to drop.

"You drugged me?" he yelled.

Standing quickly, Evelyn strode towards the door. "Come, love, we don't want to be late. I'm sure Mel would love some quiet time."

"Evelyn." He stalked forward, but she was gone, running as quickly as she could, laughing all the way. He winked at me before running after her.

"This is one fucked up family," I alleged, rubbing my stomach. I tried to imagine its future with us, but I couldn't. I just couldn't see how this would work...especially if I killed its father.

"You're not allowed to be crazy, you hear me?" I murmured down to it before standing. However, I froze, staring wide-eyed at my stomach.

"Mel?" Declan and Coraline called, stepping in also dressed to impress. What kind of festival was this?

"Are you okay?" Coraline exclaimed, rushing beside me.

"No. Yes. I'm fine, the baby just moved… I think it heard me." No matter how hard I tried, I couldn't stop the large smile from blossoming.

It felt weird, but a good kind of weird.

"Can I feel—"

"No," I snapped, harsher than I meant to. "Liam's already in a prissy mood, he should feel it next. Declan, is the Internet working again?"

"Yeah, so are the phones. The wiring in this house is shit, but it should be more stable now."

"Well then, when you're done dancing in the streets, check up on our friend Roy."

LIAM

I could easily slit his throat from here, I thought as I stared daggers into the back of his skull.

He touched her. He was with her at one point before me, and it made my blood boil. The way he stared at her on that cliff, and the very fact he had touched her waist was enough to make me want to rip his head from his neck.

"This is it." Fedel parked and Jinx stepped out, opening the door for me with no emotion displayed on his face. He stood shoulder to shoulder to me.

"I'm inclined to kill you," I told him, rolling up my selves.

"Yes, sir."

"Give me a reason not to."

"I was so drunk I don't remember a thing," he stated. "And I'm a damn good pilot."

Monte stepped outside the sorry excuse for a house, holding the door for me to enter. "So you say, but this isn't over."

Walking forward, I couldn't help but notice that the Briars had downscaled quite drastically. It had taken us a week to find them because we had thought a family as uptight and aristocratic as the Briars could not bear to spend time in the countryside. And yet, here they were, in a tiny one bedroom, rat infested cabin with a hole in the roof and floor. It was as if they were hiding from Hitler.

Gone were the opulent foyers and gilded frames. Now they had nothing but the clothes on their backs and I needed to know why.

They sat quietly in the living room, facing the door as I walked into the kitchen. Sighing, I grabbed the last beer in the fridge and took a seat before the very stupid family who had tried to run from me.

"Natasha is dead, Mr. Briar," I told him, popping the top of my beer with the edge of his table.

The aging man frowned and simply nodded. "Did you come all this way to tell me that, Liam? A letter would have sufficed."

Before I could speak, Fedel's pistol connected with his jaw, unleashing a small river of blood and a tooth from his lips. I felt his pain. Mel's punch hurt like a bitch and it would look worse in the morning.

"It's Mr. Callahan to you," Fedel sneered, pulling his head back up.

Whoever said good help was hard to find obviously wasn't looking in the right places.

"Let me rephrase my question: *why* is your daughter dead?" Not that the bitch wasn't playing with her luck anyway.

"You killed her." Mr. Briar spit out another tooth and blood at my shoes.

"Sorry, wrong answer." I nodded at Fedel, who took his cue to bash Brair's face in with his fist.

"Let's try this again. *Why is your daughter dead?*"

"I don't know! If you didn't kill her, I don't know! Just leave us be," he begged. Grown men shouldn't beg. Not even for death.

"Fedel."

Fedel drew his gun and fired into the man's stomach. I sat back and sipped my drink impassively; he didn't know anything, and as my wife would say, he was wasting words. His wife and second daughter all stood by the stairs watching in horror as he fell back in to the chair.

"DORAN!"

"DAD!"

They screamed. I'm not sure why though. "He will bleed out and die right here if I don't get answers, ladies."

"You MONSTER!" his wife yelled.

"If I got a dollar for every time someone called me a monster, I could end world hunger."

"Just leave us alone! Whatever you want, take it, just leave us the hell alone!" She sobbed, falling to her knees near her husband's body. His blood soaked her jeans and jacket, while her daughter seemed too shocked to even move, let alone speak. She just sat there, staring at the pool of blood as it crept closer to her.

Rising, I pulled her to her feet by her hair before turning to her mother and father; she was shaking against Jinx's knife so badly, it was cutting into her neck.

"I want answers!" I declared stoically in her face as her daughter struggled against me. "I swear to you, you will not only have to bury your husband, but your remaining children as well, so find your fucking voice!"

I released her daughter, and she fell to the ground, sobbing as she went. Stepping over her, I glared into the withered old eyes of Natasha's mother as tears ran down her cheeks.

"He...he said... he said he would kill us all," she uttered to me.

Putting Jinx's knife away, I wiped her tears. "He won't hurt you like I will if I don't find out what I need to know."

"It's all your father's fault!" She declared wide-eyed. "He was supposed to marry me. Shamus made a deal with Ivan.

Everyone made a deal with Ivan DeRosa because that's what you were supposed to do!"

She began to shake, dropping her head as she wrapped her arms around herself. Fuck, I was losing her.

"Go on," I spoke, grabbing her shoulders and forcing her to meet my gaze. She looked right through me. "What do you mean, that's what you were supposed to do?"

"To keep order. The drug business is a big one. No one man can control it all. There has to be a balance; you can only be so powerful. There is only so much crime the world will ignore before they call for justice. Ivan is the scale. He has the power and allows you to have pieces of that within reason. Shamus was too powerful, too cocky, and the feds caught him. But Ivan made it go away, he can make anything go away, all Shamus had to do was get Sedric to marry me." She whispered to herself as she rocked back and forth.

This made no sense!

"Why? Why you?"

"Because my family knew the game but weren't players. We couldn't make him any more powerful than he already was. But he married Evelyn. Ivan didn't like that but Evelyn's family wasn't anything. He let it go because there was balance. But you Callahans always marry the wrong people!" she yelled, spitting in my face as she did.

Stepping back, I wiped the side of my cheek and allowed myself a moment to think. This was the craziest shit I had ever heard. Both Jinx and Fedel stared at me waiting; they were not really fazed at all by her words. But they should have been. Everything we had been fighting to figure out was because of this.

"Ivan doesn't run a mafia monopoly!" I couldn't help but laugh. Not only was this stupid as fuck, but just unrealistic!

"And not only did you stupidly marry his granddaughter, but you married the head of the Italian mob! Every single cop, lawyer, and judge you pay off around the world, he gets a cut. If you and your stupid wife control everything, you will be placed on everyone's shit list! It's a chain reaction…"

"Jinx. Fedel. Clean up this shit, I'm heading back to my wife. This was a waste of my time." Grabbing my beer, I stepped out just as she yelled.

"Ivan's the game maker, not you!" she said. "You're a player, find a way to meet him halfway."

Turning, I raised my bottle to her. "I'm Liam Fucking Callahan! I don't meet anyone halfway. They bend my way, Mrs. Briar."

Monte stood outside, holding open the door to the Range. Sitting back in my seat, I finished my drink.

"Well, this was anticlimactic," I whispered, staring at the fading brick house among the green hills. I wasn't sure what I expected, but this wasn't it. My "mistress" was a bitch, my wife was driving me insane, and all I really wanted was an aspirin.

Nineteen

"Kings kill for empires, madmen for applause."
—*John Dryden*

Melody

I knew it was him, and he knew I was awake. How could anyone sleep with him slamming the drawers of our dresser so loudly? I wanted to give him a baby update and ask him what had happened to trigger his anger, but I couldn't bring myself to speak. He was just pissing me off!

SLAM!

"We've been here for a week," I said. "There is nothing in the damn dresser! So either chop it up for firewood or leave it alone."

"Of course, your highness! God forbid I make you feel uncomfortable." He slammed the dresser so hard the books on top of it fell over.

Sighing, I bit my tongue, trying my best not to explode again.

SLAM!

"URGH!" I screamed, grabbing the pillow behind my head to throw at his face. He caught it with ease then dropped it as I rose from our bed. But he pretended that he didn't even notice me.

"You men and your stupid fucking double standards. How many maids have you screwed, Liam? How many of them still work in our house? I am not yours—"

"That's where you're wrong!" he barked, finally acknowledging me. "You *are* mine! You are so hell bent on reminding me that you belong to no one but yourself. But that's bullshit. It's my last name attached to yours. *You* belong to *me*! And I belong to you, and the sooner you get that through your thick skull, the less grey hairs I will have!"

"I have a thick skull? You're the one—" I stopped, quickly grabbing onto my stomach as the movement became worse.

"Love?" Liam rushed, grabbing hold of me.

"Oh *now* it's 'love'?" I hissed, pushing him away as I wobbled over to the bed. "Damn it, kid, you can't be on his side already."

"Mel," he called, pulling me closer to him on the bed. "What is it?"

Sighing, I laid back holding my stomach. "The kid moved right after you left. It didn't hurt then, but it does now."

Lying next to me, he rubbed my stomach slowly. "Are you drinking the tea?"

"Ugh, I'm so tired of drinking that crap. But if it will help, then I will drink some in the morning." I was not a tea person, but the last thing I needed was more pain.

"When we get back to the States, we'll try something else," he replied, kissing my shoulder.

"I'm still pissed at you," I said softly, leaning into him.

"But I can't be pissed at you because you're carrying my child, talk about double standard," he replied and I was just going to have to let that slide.

"Liam, I'm not ashamed of my past. Long before you came along, I had sex with…"

Breaking away from me, he rolled onto his back. "Ahh, please don't share! I get it. I don't like it, but please don't share."

Rolling over, I watched his face clench into a grimace as though he had smelled something ghastly.

"Men will never change." I laughed, lying back down as music began to flow through the windows. It was loud, like a thousand drunken Irishmen trying to sing to the moon.

"Is that the festival?"

Tilting his head toward the window, Liam silently listened for a moment before sitting up.

"I forgot it was Féile Na Beatha."

"The Festival of life?" I translated quickly.

Smirking, he nodded. "It originated as a festival for the Gods and Goddesses to mark the change from summer to fall. Praising them with songs while wine is shared, all in the hope that they would harvest enough for the winter. Now it's just an excuse to sing obnoxiously loud while drunk in the streets."

"Celtic Gods and Goddesses?" I was trying my best not laugh, however I couldn't help it. Pulling me into his arms, we wrestled on top of the sheets for only a second before he pinned me down.

"Are you laughing at the ancient Gods of my kinsmen?" he smiled above me, only inches from my face.

"I'm sure they wouldn't have minded, seeing as this is probably the first conversation about them in generations. Your ancient Gods suck." I smiled as he shook his head at me.

"Just because they don't get movie deals doesn't mean they suck."

"That's exactly what it means. We have Jupiter, Apollo, Mars. Greece has Hercules and the Olympians. Shit, most Germanic regions have Thor and the Norse deities, and then there's the Irish. Explains why you all jumped to Christianity so quickly."

"Hercules was a hero, not a god." He frowned, releasing my arms as he kissed down my neck.

"Now you have me intrigued with this 'Féile na Beatha.'" I moaned, trying my best not to give in to him, but damn, he knew where to kiss. "We should go and witness your people in all their glory."

Grabbing my breasts, he stopped and looked me in the eye. "Later."

I knew that look.

"Liam, you better not..."

Rip.

I glared down at my now exposed bra before meeting his gaze.

"You dick."

Smirking, he unbuckled his belt slowly. "As you wish, love."

"Oh no you don't." I laughed, pushing him onto his back before straddling him, "You've pissed me off today."

"Let me make it up to you then," he said. Flipping me over before I could even blink, his hands were already pulling my jeans off with ease.

Using his teeth, he pulled at my underwear slowly until they were around my ankles then began kissing his way up.

"Liam..." I bit back a moan when his finger found itself inside me.

"Yes, love?" he said innocently, only stopping his lips to watch me while I moaned under him.

He moved in and out of me slowly...painfully slow, snickering as I rocked against his fingers and tried to force him to move faster.

"Liam..." He kissed me hard, nibbling on my lips while fucking me with his fingers.

"You pissed me off as well. But you're making up for it." He stopped momentarily. "I like seeing you squirm under me."

"Hmmmm…" I moaned again as his fingers went faster, causing me to clench around them.

"All of this because of three fingers, baby?" He laughed, knowing exactly what he was doing. "I wonder how loudly my tongue will make you scream."

"Liam, just…" He didn't give me the chance to speak. Pulling his fingers from me, he spread my legs wide before attacking my pussy.

"Oh my God!" I moaned, as I wrapped my legs around his head and reached down to grab hold of his hair.

His tongue…Jesus fucking Christ his tongue. Holding on to my waist, his tongue went deeper inside of me, shaking me to my core as I thrust against his mouth. I couldn't control myself. I wanted to ride his tongue. I wanted more of him.

"Liam…Fuck…" I screamed out as I came. I held onto him for a moment, trying to breathe before collapsing next to him.

I heard him suck a breath of much needed air into his lungs before crawling up the rest of my body, leaving short, quick, kisses on my skin.

"You definitely made up for it," I managed to whisper, playing with his soft hair.

He pulled me into his arms before lying back down.

He didn't say anything; he didn't even look at me. Instead, he simply stared at the ceiling, playing with my fingers. The look in his eyes bothered me. Truthfully, whatever was preoccupying his mind, taking his attention away from us, was annoying me greatly.

"Please tell me you're not thinking about Jinx," I hissed, resting my head on his chest.

Finally looking at me, he chuckled, brushing my hair back behind my ear.

"Love…"

"Liam, I was with others before you. I can't take it back. I don't want to take it back, nor should I have to. But there is a distinct difference between you and all others," I declared, taking his hands into mine.

I stared at our wedding rings. It was so odd to me. Here I was, married, pregnant, *in love*. Where had the old Mel gone? I was barely able to tell my own father that I loved him when he was alive. Oftentimes, I wasn't even sure if it was love or just respect. And yet, with him… He made me feel soft. He made it okay for me to be soft.

"And that difference is?" he asked, pulling me out of my thoughts.

Groaning, I leaned up just to bite his nipple.

"Fuck, Mel."

"You know what it is, ass. I didn't love them. I really didn't care about them. They were just men. I love you. I care about you, and you're my husband. None of them mattered."

"See, that wasn't so hard, right?" He laughed. I loved the way he laughed. It was like a chilling wind that always cut right through me.

Trying my best not to smile, I headed towards my clothes.

"Where the hell are you going? We're not done having sex yet!" he yelled behind me.

"You're the one who took a break. Now, I want to see this Féile Na Beatha."

He frowned, his eyes roaming over my skin. "This isn't over."

"I wouldn't dream of it." I winked, grabbing a dress before heading to the bathroom.

"Mel," he whispered, so softly I almost missed it.

"Yes?"

"I love you. I care about you, and you are my wife."

I stood there a moment, just staring at him and him at me.

Who were we?

How did we get here?

When did we become this... *in love?*

And why wasn't I more bothered by it?

It was so odd being so open with someone. Trusting someone completely.

"Good," was all I could manage to say before I locked myself in the bathroom and leaned against the door.

Liam

Navigating through a sea of drunken Irishmen and women was a skill my wife did not possess. The moment we had made it into the rundown brick town that was nicknamed Killeshin, she was forced to bury her nose into my shirt to keep from getting sick. There was enough alcohol in the air to make an elephant drunk, and if that didn't bother you, there was always the scent of roasted lamb mixed with the stench of human sweat.

However, you didn't come here for the food, or even the alcohol. You came for the music; which echoed off every stone, shutter, and living thing.

"We can go back," I uttered, pulling her into my arms as the herd swallowed us whole.

"I'm fine, I just need a second to adjust," she mumbled, taking another deep breath in my shirt.

The way she held onto me made her look sweet and innocent, like a gentle cub. It was scary how well she could hide who she really was.

"Liam?"

"Yes."

"What are your parents doing?" she asked, stopping to stare at my mother and father who stood only a few paces ahead of us, closer to the Celtic band.

Neither of them seemed to notice the idiots around them. They were too busy making love with their eyes. Slowly my father fell to one knee, pulling out a small red box to present to her.

"He's asking for her hand in marriage again," Coraline said behind us as she walked up hand in hand with Declan. She grinned so wide her face looked as though it was going to break in half.

"Uncle, the smooth criminal," Declan winked, wrapping his arms around Coraline.

"He proposed the first time here, right?" asked Coraline.

Why, I'm not sure, for she had to know the answer already.

"Yep, I do believe mom was so pregnant she couldn't even see her toes let alone the ring he had bought her."

"At least he had a ring, Declan."

"You're never going to let me live that down…"

"Well, if it isn't the Callahan Clan?" called out Old Man Doyle, and just like that, the music cut, the sea of drunks parted, and his men stalked around us, like vultures to their prey. Blowing smoke out of his nose, his old eyes glanced over Mel in disgust. "And this Italian cunt too."

His men laughed, and one by one all other bystanders, at least the ones with even the slightest mental capacity, retreated into their homes.

"You should lay off the pipe, old man. You don't have very many brain-cells left," Mel hissed, breaking free of me completely to stand on her own.

Using his cane, he stepped forward once more. "In my day, wenches like you kept their mouths zipped and legs opened. Nothing more, nothing less."

Her hand twitched in the direction of her gun, skillfully hidden at the back of her bra. Stepping forward, I forced myself in between them, my father and Declan were beside me within seconds.

"Nice hat, Doyle." I smirked at the old cloth top hat that sat on his gray head. "What the hell do you want?"

Placing his pipe in his mouth once more, he sucked in deeply and blew the smoke into our faces. "You met the Briars. In fact, it has come to my attention you nearly killed one. Your week is over, and it's best if your family returns to the depths of Hell from which you came."

"Or what?" I asked, grabbing the pipe from his mouth. "What will you do if my family and I decide to spend a few more days, maybe even months, here?"

His nostrils flared and I could almost hear his bones crack and pop as he tried to stand up straight.

"You're playing with fire, young man." He spat at my feet. The moment he did, a crowd of men slowly came around us. Even the stupid fucker that I had shot through the foot held his gun pointedly at our side.

"We're from hell, remember?" Mel replied, her eyes scanning over each black rifle. "When you're born of fire, it can't hurt you."

"So young, so foolish," he said dangerously as he slowly pulled out a photo from his jacket pocket. "You think you can come to our country and walk on water? Think you're untouchable? Folks are gunnin' for you while you're gunnin' folks down. All it takes is one, before others step up against you. Go home. Get your filth out of my country because you won't make it another night here."

Turning towards my father, he simply laughed at me, shaking his head at the fool in front of us. My mother being my mother looked bored and annoyed, clenching her gift in her hand.

Glancing down at my wife, she just nodded. Before he could even blink, my fist collided with the side of Doyle's wrinkled face. His top hat flew from his head, rolling onto my feet. Pulling the gun from its holster, I grasped hold of his collar and stuck the barrel in his eye.

"Cousin, is this fool trying to blackmail me?" I sneered, digging in deeper into his eye.

Declan frowned, the same expression on his face as our mother. "I believe so. I wonder if he knows he has no men to back up his threats."

With his one free eye, he glanced around at the men he thought supported him. The man who I shot earlier limped over, grabbing Doyle's top hat and handed it over to Mel.

"Where's your fucking loyalty?" he yelled, struggling under me.

"Isn't it obvious?" Mel replied, dusting off his hat before placing it on her head. "With us."

Pulling his face closer to mine, I held his throat tightly. "You're shit out of luck."

"One day…" he struggled to speak.

"Spare me the sanctimonious bullshit, Doyle. I've heard it all before. Ireland does not need you. This town does not need you, and when your blood splatters over its streets, it will be the rain and nothing else that washes it away."

"Liam," my mother called, stepping forward. "It's Sunday."

Staring at my watch in anger, I pulled my gun from his eye before smacking his cheeks softly.

"How lucky you are, Old Man Doyle."

Rising from the ground, I fought the urge to kick the living shit out of him; old man or not, he had threatened the wrong family. Pushing himself off the ground, he dusted himself off, glancing around at us all before backing away slowly. The very few men still loyal to him helped him into his truck at the end of the street before taking off.

The only proof that there was ever a festival taking place throughout the streets were the lights that dangled in the winds, the scattered bottles on the sidewalks that were still dripping with rum, and the abandoned instruments that only moments earlier were alive with music.

"All we need is a tumbleweed blowing in the wind," Coraline joked, from within Declan's embrace.

Something was off about those two.

"Somebody play for us before I forget it's Sunday!" I bellowed, forcing what looked like Dylan, Monte, and Jinx to the stage.

Taking my wife's hand in mine, I pulled her towards the music.

"Who did you kill?" she asked as we danced.

"You said you didn't want to know about this."

Her lips tightened into a straight line. I wondered for how much longer she could handle being in the dark. Sighing deeply, she glanced around at the new men—the men who had conveniently jumped sides, the men without loyalty—and it was like I could read her thoughts.

"We don't kill on Sundays," I reminded her.

"We don't," she replied, "but others at our disposal never made such a commitment."

Grabbing the top hat from her head, I placed it on my own. "Poor Old Man Doyle."

"Not just him, all of them. We don't need new people and I sure as hell don't trust men who would so easily betray their own."

Precisely.

"What shall we do?" I asked, twirling her around quickly.

"It's Sunday, Liam. We follow examples from the Bible on Sundays. And I distinctly remember a passage about slaying men in their sleep. All that alcohol should be kicking in soon. Irish or not, you people need sleep." She grinned, wrapping her hands around my neck.

"So it is written, so it shall be done," I said as the music ended. Breaking apart, we stood and applauded in the empty streets of Killeshin.

"Declan," she whispered, leaning over to him. "Gather the men—*our* men—and kill them all, I don't care how. We leave at sunrise; I believe Liam has gotten all he needs."

They would learn, all of them. Here in Ireland, back in the States, and all across the globe.

This wasn't a game. This was our fucking family, and nothing trumped family.

Twenty

"What is a king to a God? What is God to a king?"
—*J.J McAvoy*

Declan

Shoving my knife into my boot, I pulled open our trunk and sifted through Coraline's clothes in order to find my new guns.

"I thought we didn't kill on Sundays?" she asked me, gathering up our things around the room.

"Melody and Liam don't. I'm not sure why. It is as though they really believe God appreciates it," I muttered as I loaded bullets.

Laughing, she came over and wrapped her arms around my neck and kissed my cheek. "You speak for God now?"

Rolling my eyes at her, I grabbed my silencers. "No, but a murder at 11:59 p.m. and one at midnight is still murder."

"It never bothers you?" she whispered into my ear.

I didn't answer; I just loaded.

"Declan."

"No, Coraline, it has never bothered me. It never will bother me. I want us to be safe," I replied, looking into her eyes. "I enjoy knowing that our family is safe, I enjoy being a reason why our family is feared."

She simply nodded. "Can I come?"

"You know the answer to that."

"Declan, I said I *may be* pregnant. I can fire a gun. I'm good. You know it." She groaned, releasing her hold on me. I missed her touch.

Rising to my feet, I kissed her, as I grabbed her thighs to lift her up and press her against the wall.

"We can have this fight after we get you to a doctor, G.I Jane." Dropping her, she scowled but it disappeared when my lips met hers.

"Go cut off someone's finger."

"I'll make you a necklace." I laughed as her face bunched up in horror. Gathering my jacket, I walked out the door to find Monte already waiting for me at the top of the stairs.

"Do they know?" I asked as we descended. It had been no less than four hours since Liam gave the order. We were out numbered, obviously, but that didn't matter if they were too hung-over to fight. Heading out the backdoor, I met Dylan and Fedel, along with Gavin and Kieran; six to thirteen wasn't that bad. Both of them had been with us for years, but worked mostly in the streets, keeping an ear out for any dealers who might be skimming us—or worse, talking—then they came to me. I didn't trust them enough to allow them to spend too much time with either Mel or Liam.

"All they know is that we're hurting some people," Monte replied.

Nodding, I looked them over quickly before pulling out my gun. "The men who pulled out guns on the Bosses, they don't get to see the light of morning. Kill them quietly. If anyone gets in your way, dispose of them as well. Any questions?"

None of them spoke, two pulled out knives, and others guns before leaving. I watched them retreating into the dimming darkness like monsters from the depths of hell.

Breathing in the wet grass and the fresh air, I looked up at Shamus' home to find Coraline staring down at me. She winked before closing the window.

Stalking forward like the monsters before me, I couldn't help but think about what a lucky man I was, how revered our family was, and I couldn't wait to share that greatness with any child we had. Walking forward against the howling winds, I stared at the flame shining through the window of Old Man Doyle's home. It was the only thing that really made his home stand out from the rest of the broken down buildings. When we were kids and Liam, Neal, and I would come visit Shamus, and we would always find him here; smoking and drinking himself into a coma with a deck of cards in front of him.

No matter how hard Liam had tried to sit in that room with us, he couldn't. The smoke hurt his lungs so badly he would have to leave. Shamus would tell him to stop lingering where he didn't belong, and Old Man Doyle laughed each time, telling Neal and I how we needed to teach our brother how to be *a man*.

"Liam is never going to amount to anything, boys. It's a sad fact that sometimes not all men are not created equal, sometimes the weak fight and then die off."

Neither of them knew it, but I saw Liam at only twelve years old, standing at the door. He had gone out just to take a breath and came back to prove himself. With a haunted look in his eyes, I watched a part of him die. Through the fog of smoke, he met my gaze and I knew he would never forget. He walked out the door, pretending he was never there to begin with.

"I was expecting Liam." Old Man Doyle sat across the poker table with a cigar in his mouth and his pistol on the table.

Walking forward, I took a seat at the table. "This is below my brother's pay grade."

"And not yours?" he snickered, dealing out cards for me.

"I'm doing this as a gift to my cousin, no payment required," I replied, grabbing the cards.

Laughing, he shook his head. "Who would have thought that the little mutt would become all this?"

Staring at the Royal Flush in my hands, I simply shook my head.

"I did," I said, showing my hand. He stared at it for a moment before reaching for his gun. But before he lifted his hand, I put a bullet into the side of his face. His body crashed onto the floor and his blood flowed towards me like wine on the surface of marble, forcing me to rest my legs on the card-riddled table. Grabbing his cigar, I smoked the rest just as my phone rang.

"Yes, Neal?"

"Tell me you're having a shittier time than I am." He sighed into the phone.

"No can do. I just won a poker game and I have a pretty good cigar in my hands. Life here is good." I smirked, looking down at the old man.

"Well, fuckiedy-do-da-day, then. Can you please tell me who the hell this Roy bitch is? I just got word that he's got high-end snow-cones for sale."

"High end snow-cones? Where did someone like him get that much smack?"

"I don't really give a fuck. We're still trying to figure out who put a bullet in President Monroe." I had almost forgotten about that.

"Deal with the presidential shit. I'll let Mel and Liam know about Roy. We're heading home in a few hours, then you can hand back the crown."

"Heavy is my head," he replied.

"Neal, was that a Shakespearean reference? When did you learn to read?" I laughed.

"Fuck you!" he said, before hanging up.

"Love you too, cousin," I said to no one. Rising from my chair, I walked towards the window and blew out the lone candle.

"Goodbye, Granduncle. Tell Grandfather I said hello."

Twenty-One

"Being powerful is like being a lady... if you have to tell people you are, you aren't."
—*Margaret Thatcher*

Melody

Drumming my fingers on the table, I scrolled through the polls appearing on my phone.

"I'm going to kill your brother, Liam. I swear it." How hard was it to make people like you?

Taking my phone from me, he tucked it into his front pocket and leaned into his chair before flipping through his book. "Political polls don't mean shit. There's no point in worrying about it. Once we land, we'll fix this, seeing as how my brother can't find his balls."

"He quoted Shakespeare earlier this morning." Declan laughed, buttering his toast in the aisle over.

"Seriously?" Coraline grinned, stealing his breakfast before he had a chance to reap the spoils of his work.

"Can you all stop acting as if my son is brain-dead? Neal's talents are far greater than his flaws." Evelyn frowned, as she drank her coffee. Sedric said nothing as he adjusted his glasses and continued to read through the paper.

"Of course, mother…"

"Anyway!" I snapped, trying to get back on topic. "I told him to even the playing field, and yet, here we are, buried under a mountain of shit. This stupid bitch should be grieving over her husband, not running in his place! No one reacts to assassinations correctly anymore."

Laughing, Liam shook his head at me, but before he could speak, Jinx's voice came through the intercom, "Sir, Ma'am, we will be arriving at Chicago International Airport in ten."

Sighing, I leaned back to buckle my seatbelt. Looking down, I found my stomach hanging over my waist.

When had I gotten so big?

Glancing up, I noticed not only Liam, but Coraline and Evelyn staring at it too.

"Declan, did you contact Roy about the sno-cones?" I asked, trying not to bring any more attention to my stomach.

"Sno-cones?" Sedric asked, folding his paper down to stare at us. "How much?"

"Eight mil," I answered. "It's a lot, but we want to make sure it's pure."

"If it is, where did a low level dealer like Roy get pure cocaine?" Liam asked, staring me in the eye.

I read them for a moment, tensing as I got what he was implying. "You think it's a setup."

"How often do you come across pure smack like he's selling?" He had a point.

Cracking my neck, I thought about that for a moment. "I warned him the night we took out Chuck."

"Sadly, stupidity is a force to be reckoned with."

"Do you trust him?" Coraline asked, almost too innocently.

"I trust no one." Pausing, I stared at Liam. "I trust no one, but the family. What should we do?"

"Declan and I will go," Sedric stated as the plane began its descent.

"And I'll wait nearby to watch." Because if Roy was stupid enough to set us up only weeks after I had warned him, I wanted to kill him myself.

"Too many family members in one place. If this is a setup, the police will be there," Declan added, apparently pissed off already.

"The President was just assassinated," Evelyn reminded us, holding onto her seat as the tires met the strip below us. "Do you really think they would do a sting operation now?"

She also had point. But there were too many criminals in on this plan, and Liam and I needed to think.

"We've arrived," Jinx stated.

Liam simply rolled his eyes as he got out of his seat. "Thank you, Captain…"

"Liam."

"What? He is a captain, correct?" Liam replied, his smile slick, eyes glinting with something darker.

"That wasn't what you were going to say and you know it," I whispered before walking past him.

Sedric held the door open for Evelyn and I. Taking my hand into hers, she walked me down the stairs like an infant needing assistance. Glancing back at Liam, he mouthed, "*Be nice.*" Sighing, I held onto her as we walked.

At the bottom Olivia and Neal stood in front of our cars, dressed in all white. Even Adriana stood in a white pantsuit.

"Welcome back." Olivia smiled, pulling me into a hug. "The city hasn't been the same without you."

She's touching me.

"You can let go now, Olivia. People may start to believe you're genuine," I said, as I freed myself from her bony arms.

Her eyes narrowed and her nostrils flared, but she smiled anyways, proving my point. Neal stepped forward, preparing to give me a hug as well, but I pulled back and allowed Evelyn to accept it in my place. He played it off, kissing Evelyn on the cheek.

"Is there a reason why you're all dressed in white?" I asked them.

Neal nodded. "Senator Colemen is having a memorial and charity dinner this evening for both parties. He asked all those attending to wear white as a call for peace, hope, and perseverance in this dark time," he recited.

I stared at him for a moment before taking Evelyn's arm once again. "A living breathing teleprompter. I can't wait to hear your speech as to why Colemen is so behind in the polls. I think he's been lapped twice."

Adriana held open the door for us, and as Evelyn took a seat inside, I noticed Liam had yet to get off the plane with Jinx.

"Ma'am?" Adriana called my attention.

Taking a seat, I simply shook my head at Liam. Funnily enough, I wasn't mad; it was just my husband being my husband.

"So, how are you?" Evelyn asked, petting my hand.

"Evelyn." I stared at her misplaced appendage.

Sighing, she rolled her eyes and let go of me. "Fine. I want to know about the baby. You and Liam haven't spoken about it and I just want details. When is your next doctor's appointment?"

"Evelyn…"

"Melody, give me a break. This is my first grandchild and I'm dying here. I was this close," she held her thumb and index finger barely apart, "to calling your doctor for your medical records."

Adriana snickered quietly.

"Adriana, my appointment is in two weeks, make sure it's possible for Evelyn and Sedric to sit in." The moment I said it, she pulled me into her arms.

"Again with the hugging."

"Get over it, Melody. I'm a grandmother, it's what I do." She laughed as we pulled apart.

"Adriana, what have we missed?

"Neal and Olivia have kept me at arm's length. However, from what I could gather through Antonio, Olivia fired most of the old staff and hired new personnel, redecorated the halls—"

"She what?" Evelyn sat up harshly, pulling against her seat belt.

"The chariot ball this evening will be held in the manor. From what I understood, it was a political tactic, so she fired all the immigrants."

Pinching the bridge of my nose—a habit I was picking up from Liam—I could only close my eyes and rest my head against the chair.

"What else, Adriana?"

"Neal is working on something big for the night. I knew there was a miniscule probability of you or Liam resting with strangers in the house, so I took the liberty of preparing all of your clothing and belongings along with the rest of the family's. He's also added at least thirty cameras around the property for this evening. They're even in the bedrooms."

"God give me the strength not to kill my own son," Evelyn prayed.

Staring out the window, I watched the trees blur by and I tried to wrap my mind around this without losing my cool. I wanted to wring both of them out, but all I could do now was go to this damn function and watch. Afterwards, I'd deal with Roy.

"Adriana, set up a meeting for me."

LIAM

I waited on the plane for the sole reason of confronting Jinx alone. The whole flight, I stared at my wife in awe, ecstasy, and love before realizing I still didn't know that much about her past. I knew about her *criminal* past, but not her personal. She was more than the gun in her hands, and the blood under her heels, and I wanted to know more. So, I waited just outside the cockpit as he parked our jet.

The moment he opened the door, he came face to face with me and paused, dropping his bag onto the floor.

"Boss?"

"You were lying when you said you were drunk when you slept my wife."

"Boss—"

"Never interrupt me, Jinx. You're just giving me an excuse to kill you," I said.

He nodded, standing straighter with his hands behind his back.

"As I was saying, you weren't drunk. And I would like to believe my wife wouldn't have just jumped into bed with anyone. You two were close, were you not?"

He took a deep breath and nodded.

"Good, then what do I not know about her? The small personal things she would note as so insignificant she wouldn't bother sharing. I know she's afraid of the dark, but tell me more."

He kept his mouth shut.

"I'm done speaking, Jinx."

"She loves to swim, but I believe you knew that."

"I do."

"She also loves the opera. She doesn't treat herself to it often. In fact, she hasn't gone since her father died…"

"And she married me."

He nodded.

"What type of opera?" It wasn't my thing, but I could learn to love it if it was hers.

"Italian, of course. Her favorite being *Bianca e Falliero* by Felice Romani. She would never admit it though. She also enjoys documentaries. It doesn't really matter what it's about, if it's on, she makes a mental note to watch it later. Never leave her in charge of the kitchen unless you want to be unintentionally poisoned. Her father banned her from going in after she set the stove on fire. Her favorite food is stuffed artichokes. That's all I know, sir."

"And yet still, it's more than I knew." It bothered me.

"She was never in love with me, sir. It wasn't some romance. She spent her life locked up in the house. I was just a wounded dog she brought in."

"What about you?"

"Me?"

"Did you—" I paused. "Do you love her?"

"In that way, no. Not then either. I have someone. I had someone. Like I said, I was just a wounded dog."

I said nothing more as I walked off the plane. My father stood at the bottom of the stairs with Neal and Declan at his side. Fixing my suit jacket, I ignored them all with Jinx right behind me.

"Damn it." Declan sighed, handing my father an envelope of what I could only assume was cash.

"Neal, you're riding with me." I told him as our Range Rover pulled up, and Monte opened the door for me.

I didn't even wait for him to close the door before asking, "What the hell have you been doing, and who dipped your outfit in whiteout?"

He smiled before straightening his tie. "In a few hours there is going to be charity function at the manor. Melody told me to even the playing field by any means necessary, this is a part of my plan. Someone has to know more about the President. I've been looking over the case for days. It was no prick with an axe to grind. It was a hired hit; I know it. They fired from at least twelve yards away."

"Neal, I want this over. Prove what you need to prove and get it done because if you don't, I will kill him, father-in-law or not."

We needed the presidency, and if Colemen couldn't get it done, I would personally find someone who could.

"Mel made that clear. I understand, and I would not let you down, brother. I swear it."

"Very well then," I said as his phone rang.

"Father?" Neal answered before handing it to me.

"Yes?"

"Your wife just called Declan and I, demanding we meet Roy near the docks in forty-five minutes. She wants you to meet her in her car, which will be parked a block away."

"What the fuck is she thinking? We haven't checked out the area yet." Neal asked, overhearing.

I couldn't help but grin, knowing exactly what my wife was thinking.

"Why didn't she call me?" I asked.

"The same reason I didn't. Your phone is still off. Rule forty-two—"

"Never turn off your phone. Thank you, father, I know. We'll be there soon." Before he could speak, I hung up.

"Liam, you can't be—"

"You did our job for a week, brother. Melody and I have been doing it much longer, do not think for a second you know more than we do. She scheduled this meeting to give Roy no time to contact the feds incase this was a setup. She also owns a few of the abandoned buildings near the docks where a few of her men—our men—guard. And, dear brother, she has a mole. If the police need to move quickly, they will make noise and he will hear it. So, *yes*, we are serious," I stated quickly. If there was anything my wife was good at, it was thinking on her feet.

Clenching his jaw, he nodded and looked to the driver. "Take us to the docks."

"And is there an Opera radio station?" I asked him.

The older man met my eyes through the mirror for a moment before nodding. "Yes, sir."

Closing my eyes, I rested my head as the music drifted through the speakers. I didn't understand opera; I didn't get what the big deal was. But then again, I never had to care, so maybe it was just a lack of exposure. Worse came to worst, I would invest in earplugs and just watch her reactions.

The more I listened, the more I thought about it. Why did she love it? What did it make her feel? So many questions...so few answers. All too soon, the woman's voice faded and the music shifted into something bleaker. It was like a sudden unexpected darkness had fallen on a bright day, and it had happened so quickly that it took a moment for your senses to adjust. I didn't understand the words the man sang, but something told me it was about death.

"Liam—"

"Shh," I whispered, trying to decode the darkness in his voice. It was more than death, but murder, something he did not regret.

Opening my eyes, I turned to face my eldest sibling. He simply looked at me as though I had lost my mind, and maybe I had.

"We're here," he said, but we weren't at the docks. We were on bridge and there stood my wife, leaning against the rails with a pair of binoculars in her hands, and Adriana at her side.

"Head home, Neal. There's enough family here."

Stepping out of the car, I basked in the essence that was purely Chicago. I couldn't help but grin, I loved this city, I loved the wind as it blew through the streets, pushing everything forward, and making sure nothing stayed in one place for too long. The city of big shoulders to carry big dreams. My city.

"I called you," she said as I leaned against the railing next to her. She didn't look at me, instead she gazed through her binoculars as the wind blew by us once again.

"My phone was off. We did just get off a flight."

"Rule forty-two—"

I couldn't help but grin. "Who taught you all the rules?"

Dropping the binoculars, she grinned back at me. "Your father told me when I called him. How many rules are there? Because I think you people just make it up as you go."

"My father has one hundred and six rules," I told her, taking her binoculars to look out over the docks. "His father had eighty-seven. God knows how many I will keep or add."

Pulling the binoculars down, she forced me to meet her gaze. "Rule five of our rules. Always answer my calls."

"Yes, ma'am."

"Good." She nodded, leaning over the rail. "I called Brooks."

"The mole?"

She nodded once again. "Yes, apparently the Chicago PD are out fetching coffee for the FBI to pull off a sting operation. They need to find the President's murderer and every moment that goes by, they look worse. They don't care about the drugs today."

"So Roy's on the up and up," I said, turning my back to the scenery to focus on her.

"Beau says there is a rumor going around that we had the President killed in order to get Colemen into the White House."

"I wouldn't put it past us," I joked, to which she simply rolled her eyes, but I did see the corners of her mouth rise.

"A drug sting could be a way to get us in cuffs. Then maybe make a deal for information about the President."

That would be genius, however…

"The Chicago PD are a bunch of idiots who are scared of their own shadows. I highly doubt any of them would be able to pull that type of thing off, even with the FBI."

"Sir, Ma'am," Adriana spoke up, looking over the docks. "There's movement."

Turning around, I looked through the binoculars only to find nine men all wheeling iced fish towards the factory. One by one, they rowed in pink salmon and scanned the area.

"Does that look like eight million worth?" I asked

"I guess we're going to find out. If it is, we need to get it off the ice," she said into the wind, pulling out her phone.

She was right. If it was quality cocaine, then dropping the temperature would cause it to become moist, chunky, and lose its strength.

"Sedric, I'm sure you saw?" she said into the phone before going quiet. "All right, Liam and I will watch from here."

Adriana handed me a tablet with a live feed of inside the factory. I watched as my father strode in with Declan beside him. It looked as though they were alone, but we all knew better. Roy and his men couldn't see the guns above them.

"Mr. Callahan, I'm happy you chose a place without pens," Roy said to Declan. He didn't smile, instead walked over to one of the fish, pulled a knife and stabbed it, ripping open its skin. Packages of white powder spilled out.

"Pens?" I asked.

"Brother and sister bonding." She smiled, watching the screen carefully.

My father tasted a bit off of his finger before looking to Declan. Their faces were cold, blank...evil.

Declan glanced over all the fish. "Where did you get this, Roy?"

"Looks like it's real." If it wasn't, I'm sure Declan would have been gutting him.

"I respect eh, Callahans, in fact, I'm scared of eh, however, I can't give up my people. You can understand that, right?"

"No," he replied.

"Sedric," Mel stated, still on the phone, "accept it and make sure he sells it off. If he does, we will let his supplier slip for now."

She glanced at me and I nodded, turning off the feed. "Have a sample brought to us."

She repeated it to my father before hanging up.

"Eight million worth of coke easily turns on the street. He could cheat us," I told her.

"He could and then we'll staple pens into his arm. For now, we go home and deal with the politicians."

"Great. Dinner with more people trying to steal my hard earned money."

Melody

"You've got to be fucking kidding me!" I screamed into the mirror of my closet, causing Liam to walk in like an erotic angel from hell. He wore his white pants, shirt and blazer flawlessly, while I, on the other hand, was ready to flip out.

"What's wrong?" he asked stupidly, pulling a loose thread from his blazer.

"'What's wrong?'" I repeated, nostrils flaring, "What is fucking wrong, is THIS!"

I turned around to show him the zipper that had broken less than halfway up my back. I had never, ever in my life not been able to wear any of my clothes!

He laughed. The Irish asshole just laughed.

"This is not funny!" I cursed him, wiggling in the dress, hoping by some miracle the zipper would repair itself and go all the way up.

Walking up behind me, he grabbed hold of my hips and pulled me towards him. Meeting my gaze in the mirror, that grin was still spread across his face.

"Seeing you—my wife of all people—freak out over clothes is the funniest thing I've seen this week."

"Then you need to get out more," I snapped, glaring at the stupid white dress clinging to my body. "And for the record, I am not freaking out. I shouldn't be battling with my clothing for at least another two to three weeks."

"And you got those statistics how?"

I didn't answer.

"Have you been reading baby books without me?"

"No!" I said a little too quickly, causing his left eyebrow to raise. "I Googled it." I pulled away, as I stripped off the stupid dress with the stupid zipper. I was going to personally call Giorgio Armani later.

His eyes scanned over my body and I hated how sexy he looked right now. It wasn't helping me at all. What made it worse was the fact that I could see his erection as clear as day, pressing against his pants.

"Liam, no! We have God only knows how many people in our house right now and I need a dress. We are not having sex in my closet."

Stalking towards me, he just grinned. I took a step back until I was pressed up against my Jimmy Choos. He went straight for my neck, pressing his body against mine. He squeezed my breast with one hand while his other hand grabbed at my ass.

"Liam, you're going to ruin your clothes." It was all I could think to utter.

"Good, then we can both go naked," he whispered into my ear, as he gripped onto thighs and lifted me up with ease. "Now stop fighting me and scream my name."

I was going to give in. I didn't even want to fight him. Damn him.

"Ma'am, I was able—" Adriana froze mid step with a new dress in her hands.

Thank Jesus.

"Leave it, Adriana and go away," Liam snapped, not bothering to look at her.

"No," I said, doing my best to wiggle free of his hands. "I need to get ready. Go cool off on the balcony, I'll be out in a moment."

He stared at me for a few seconds. Rage, lust, and disappointment were all brewing in his eyes. Lowering me to the ground, he snapped towards Adriana who just waited, head held high and posture strong.

"Next time, knock," he hissed at her before walking out.

"Don't mind him, you have another dress?" I asked.

Nodding, she handed me the bag. "Yes, it's floor length, capped sleeves and draped to keep your baby bump discrete."

"I got it, you may go get ready," I told her. It was simple enough and I wanted a moment to myself.

When she left, I hung the dress on the door, and I turned to the side to stare at my stomach again. It was only going to get larger, the kid was only going to get bigger.

Sighing, I went to get dressed, not really caring about my hair or makeup. I just wanted this over with so I could sleep. I was exhausted.

Stepping into my red heels, I took a deep breath, and cracked my neck before walking out. Liam stood, waiting on the balcony as I had asked, staring at the people in the gardens below. I could hear their cackling laughs, fake compliments and the snapping of cameras.

Placing my hand onto his back, I leaned on the rail next to him.

"They all love her." He frowned, looking down at Mrs. Monroe as people gathered to shake her hand and take her photo as if she were already the president. "We need something, anything to knock her down or we will lose, and I can't wait another four years."

"When was the last time we lost anything, Liam?" I asked. He smirked, turning towards me. Taking a step back, he looked me over. "You're beautiful."

"I know. Now, let's make nice with the government before they try to pin us for tax evasion."

He laughed, kissing the back of my hand. "I'd like to see them try."

Twenty-Two

"Political language… is designed to make lies sound truthful, murder respectable, and to give an appearance of solidity to pure wind."
—*George Orwell*

Melody

"It's as if time had stopped. The earth underneath my feet opened, and the devil himself reached up and pulled me into hell. I screamed, trying to reach for my husband in the midst of the chaos. I wanted to die, because I knew in my heart of hearts that he was gone. There was no undoing what I had seen—what *America* had seen! Only moments earlier, we sat in the back of the limo and my husband, President Franklin Monroe, told me how humbled he was to be a servant of this government, of you, the people. He told me his dreams for this country. Being from Texas, where everything is big, his dreams were even bigger. That is why I cannot stop to cry, to mourn, because all I can do is try to honor his dream until my last breath leaves my body."

One by one I watched as the people around us stood, some with tears glistening in their eyes, others ready to go to war for this woman. They were applauding, celebrating. I didn't want to stand, I didn't want to clap, all I wanted to do was take a steel bat to each one of their faces.

"Smile and stand up, sweetie. Cameras are flashing," my husband whispered, as he pulled me up. He was just as tense as I was.

"How can anyone take this woman seriously? Her hair is in the shape of a beehive," I muttered over to him.

"Her husband was the "people's leader." So now, she's the people's widow, beehive or not. Clap."

Clapping in suppressed anger, I watched the brunette on stage smile and wave at her adoring audience.

We were losing. No amount of money could win the love of the people. And every time the bitch spoke, they loved her even more. She ate it up and kept speaking. She was only supposed to give a quick speech about this event, but now I felt like we were at a campaign rally.

"I would like to thank Senator Colemen," she added. For the first time, the man who we wanted to be president was actually focused on. "Many of you don't know this, but Senator Colemen and my husband were college roommates and good friends. When he found out Colemen was going to be running against him, he turned to me and said, 'He'd better still come over for Christmas when he loses.' I hope you still do, even now."

"Always!" Senator Colemen laughed, rising to take his spot on the podium. "Thank you so much, Madam First Lady."

"I hate it when they're humble." Liam sighed, returning to his seat along with most of the guests.

I followed suit.

Olivia looked over the sea of tables quickly. "Where's Neal?"

"Hopefully fixing this shit," Declan whispered, sipping his brandy as Coraline fought her hardest not to fall asleep. She looked worn out. I wasn't sure why; she hadn't done anything.

"Has Neal told any of you how he plans on fixing this?" Evelyn asked, flipping her white silk shawl over her shoulders.

"No," Olivia hissed. "All I know is her highness here told him to shoot my father."

With the exception of Liam and Sedric, everyone's eyes snapped to me. As if this was so surprising.

"I'm all for it." Mrs. Colemen giggled, pouring herself another glass of wine.

"Mother!" Olivia sneered, grabbing her hand. "You've had enough and we cannot seriously be talking about killing my father right now."

Raising her head off Declan's shoulders, Coraline looked around as well. "Neal wouldn't...would he?"

"Wouldn't be the first time one of us killed our wife's father," Sedric whispered behind his glass. To which Evelyn simply diverted her stare to Senator Colemen as he spoke. Sadly, she was the only one really giving him the time of day.

Slamming her fist onto the table, Olivia moved to the edge of her chair. "My father has done everything you people have asked. He is a human being, not a pawn in your games."

"Sweetheart, relax, people are watching, besides it's not like he's been the best father in the world." Mrs. Colemen laughed before drinking again.

"No!" she snapped. "He's my father. Tell Neal to find another way, because if my father dies, it will be on your hands, Melody Giovanni. He is my family, and if you fuck with my family, you fuck with me, bitch."

"Baby," Declan whispered. "Let's go... somewhere else." He tried to pull Coraline away from the table.

"No way in hell. This just got interesting," she whispered back.

Taking a deep breath, I folded my hands on the table and sat up. "Olivia Colemen, I've been fucking with you the minute I stepped into this house." I shook my head slowly, as if I were truly baffled. "You mistakenly think I give shit about how you feel or what you think. It's as if you really, truly, deep in your heart, think I'd give a fuck if you died. A bullet could go through your brain right now and I wouldn't even blink. However..."

Picking my foot up, I stuck my spiked heel into her leg. Not enough to draw blood, but enough to make her gasp out in pain.

I leveled her with a stoic stare, speaking as eerily calm as I could, just enough to be heard. "If you ever threaten me again, the only thing that will be hanging is your body from my bathroom window." Digging my heel in harder, she cried out. "So shut up, listen to your mother, and thank God you're *family*. Because if you weren't, I'd have killed you the first time you opened that augmented mouth of yours."

Dropping my foot, I clapped as Senator Colemen wrapped up his speech. Mrs. Colemen stood, welcoming her husband into her arms for the cameras. We all stood for the photo, smiling like the Brady Bunch on crack.

"What were you all talking about?" Senator Colemen asked, glancing around the table, perhaps sensing the dissipating tension.

"The baby moved again, and my mother almost knocked over the table to feel," Liam lied with ease.

He smiled. "I can only imagine. Kids are great, but I can't wait for the grandkids."

"Yes, please excuse me," I told him, rising from my seat.

Liam stood, making room for me. "Where're you going?"

"Bathroom, *Dad*. I'll be right back." He was so damn overprotective.

Kissing my cheek, he leaned and whispered into my ear, "You're sexy when you're mean."

"I'm always sexy," I whispered back.

He grinned. "You're always mean."

Shaking my head, I pulled away.

It was interesting to be around so many political figureheads at once. They all seemed to have come not for the good cause, but in hopes of being lobbyists. Each one trying to explain why they needed funding for whatever side of bullshit they were on this week. Why the next president needed to worry about *this* or how America was falling behind on *that*. They all looked so clean in their white, yet they were all dirty.

Walking into the foyer of the house, I couldn't help but wonder: if they were the keepers of the law, the people we elected to keep justice, how anyone could be surprised by the type of people *we* were. We were the 'good' criminals. We took only what was ours, sold to only those who wanted, and killed those deserving...for the most part. We even gave back to our community ten times as much as they did.

As I turned the corner, I watched the First Lady enter the study—mine and Liam's— pulling a woman behind her in haste.

Lesbian affair? I thought, trying my best not to smile. *So soon after her husband's murder?* If something like that leaked to the media, I could knock her straight to the hell she supposedly experienced the day of her husband's demise.

I walked over to *the wall,* as we liked to call it—the wall I had shot through only a year ago and destroyed Evelyn's Pollock. She hadn't been able to find another painting to cover it, so instead she had an indoor wall fountain installed. To get to the room behind it was as simple as pushing in a loose tile.

"What the hell is going on here?" I asked, causing Adriana to jump out of Antonio's arms.

Antonio stood straighter. "Neal told me watch the cameras, ma'am."

"Ma'am..." Adriana started.

"Both of you out, now."

I blinked as they both rushed by. Pulling up the study camera, I saw the First Lady clearly. However, the woman she was with cared more about our books, her features were obstructed due to the camera's angle. One thing was disappointingly clear: I was mistaken, that woman was not her lover. The First Lady looked terrified, shaken, as if she were standing in front the devil herself.

"You shouldn't be here," she snapped feebly.

"Why?" the woman asked, pulling out a book. "I paid a whole lot of money for that plate of fish."

The moment her lilting voice reached my ears, my heart began to race; I felt suffocated, I could hardly breathe. The healed bullet wound in my shoulder burned in recognition of her, Aviela—my mother's voice. She stood there in her white suit and even whiter shoes while flipping through the pages of my book with her deceivingly pure white gloves.

"You know why!" The First Lady desperately wailed. "Someone could see us together and know—"

"And know what?" Aviela asked. "That you hired me to shoot your husband, their beloved President, between the eyes?"

Oh shit.

I wanted to go but my hand went to my stomach. So instead I reached for the phone.

"Callahan," Liam answered monotonically.

"Get to the study now. Aviela's there," I told him before hanging up.

The First Lady grabbed the book from her hands, throwing it across the room. "That's not what happened! I never asked you to kill him. He was going to leave me, he promised to help my political career! I asked you to help me secure my future!"

Grabbing a hold of her neck, Aviela pulled her face closer. "And here we are. You're running, some may even go as far as to say you've already won the race for leader of the free world. That's a pretty secured future in my eyes. Now, pick up that book before I snap your pathetic neck and find a new puppet."

She threw her on to ground as if she were trash.

Gasping for air with her hands around her neck, the most *powerful* woman in the world crawled to the fallen book, and lifted it up above her head. Walking over, Aviela took it before taking a seat in my chair. She adjusted the scattered papers as if she couldn't help herself.

Even though it was less than a few minutes since I placed the call, I couldn't help but wonder what was taking Liam so long.

"What do you want from me?" the First Lady sobbed, not bothering to pick herself up. She continued to babble weakly in defeat, it was a stark difference from the woman who'd stood at the podium less than a half an hour ago. "You have no idea what you've done. What *we've* done. I can't do this, they're going to find out—"

"Oh shut up and take a Xanax. You've been doing great, the people love you and that big hair of yours." Aviela grinned, kicking her feet up.

The moment Aviela spoke of her hair, she sat up, wiping her face and smoothing back the stray stands.

"See? Looking more presidential already."

"When I win this election, I don't want you coming around. So how much will it cost for you to disappear?" she asked resolutely, brushing her dress off, seemingly trying to regain some of her decorum.

Aviela smirked, standing up. "Nothing."

"What?"

"Win and make sure the Callahan's never get into the White House. That is how you pay me," she told her before walking out of the room.

"No. No. No," I hissed, trying to see where she went. Apparently, the bitch had taken down most of our old cameras. If it weren't for the new ones Neal had installed, we wouldn't have even caught her in the study.

"Damn it!" I screamed as Liam, Declan and Sedric entered the study to find it empty. As if he could feel my rage, Liam angrily paced across the room, grabbing the book Aviela had left on the desk.

"Find her," he said through a clenched jaw before leaving the room.

Taking a deep breath, I tried to calm down. When the doors to the control room opened, I instantly threw my knife. Liam stared at the knife lodged in the wall by his head before looking up at me wide eyed.

"What did you find out from the Briars?" I asked, still trying to catch my breath.

Handing me my weapon, he looked at the monitors, putting his gun—which he had drawn before the knife hit the wall—away. "What was she doing?"

"What did you find out from the Briars?" I repeated.

"Mel…'

"She killed the President, Liam. She killed the leader of the free world, just to make sure we didn't get the White House. Right now, I do not care about her. I want to know what's going on, now!"

He looked over the screens, still searching for her. We both knew she was gone. There was no way we could get to her right now. Not like this. She had entered our home without us noticing; she could get out just as easily.

"She or an accomplice somehow found and disabled the old cameras in the study. They weren't aware of the ones Neal just installed," he whispered, clicking through the monitors. "She went down the west hallway but…"

"Liam," I snapped impatiently.

"Your grandfather. He was a monopoly taking over the mafia," he spat. "He's been setting up marriages for decades, all with the single purpose of making sure no one family is too dominant. He's trying to spread the wealth, drugs, and power."

"So, basically he doesn't like the fact that Google and Bing are in bed together," I whispered, trying to figure out what this meant.

"Who's Google and who's Bing in this analogy?"

"Aviela had me at gunpoint. Shit, she shot me. Why didn't she kill me? I doubt that it was her maternal instincts kicking in." I could never even *think* of doing anything remotely harmful to my own child. How could she?

Leaning against the desk, he thought it over. "What happened when Caesar fell?"

"Everyone tried to become Caesar."

"That's why she didn't kill you. Killing you right then and there would spark the need for revenge from those loyal to you. Killing us both would open the door to anarchy and more bloodshed, everyone will be trying to fill the shoes we'd leave behind."

Running my hand through my hair, I tried my best to ignore the stabbing sensation I was feeling. "What does Ivan get out of this?" Why did he care? Where was his link in all this?"

"A kick out of controlling the Mafia without getting his hands dirty?" He frowned.

"There has to be more to this, right?"

He thought for a moment and shrugged. "Who knows, but at least we have something to hang around that woman's neck. I wonder how the people will feel when they find out."

"I think they'll bring out the guillotine. I doubt she knows who Aviela really is. She might not even know her as Aviela. But that woman is just itching to confess, we just have to give her a soapbox to stand on."

"I'd better call Neal and tell him not to bother with whatever half-assed plan he was working on." He sighed, texting his idiotic brother.

"Not that it would have worked anyways. I've seen puppies who are more useful than he's been. Though we have to give him credit for the cameras."

Liam shook his head. "No, we don't."

I tried to smile, but there was that pain again.

"Are you alright?" he asked, reaching for my hand.

"Yeah, I'm fine. Just…damnit, Liam. I want her gone. I want them all gone! I saw her, and for the first time in my life, I was truly scared. If I was who I used to be, I would have stormed in there the moment I heard her voice…but…" I paused to stare down at my protruding stomach.

"Mel…"

"I don't like to be scared. I don't know how to be scared. That isn't my nature and yet, there I was," I whispered.

Taking my hands into his, he kissed the back of them. "You weren't being scared, you were being a mother, love. You put your anger and your need for revenge aside and protected our child. That's your nature."

The smile on his face, despite all the things going on, made me want to smile. But I couldn't. One moment I was sitting up, the next, I was hunched over just enough to see blood—my blood—rapidly staining the white of my dress.

No. Please no. Not again.

"Mel? Mel!"

Liam

I don't know what happened. It was all a blur. One moment I was in awe of her, so proud that she had been open with me. The next, I was surrounded by the press as I carried her into an ambulance. I wasn't sure if I had gone deaf or if my brain had momentarily shut down, allowing me to focus without really breaking.

During to ride to the hospital, everything was moving so quickly. Mel was squeezing my hand so damn hard, and yet, I was frozen, unsure of what was going on, unsure what to say or what to do, so I held her hand, brushed her hair back, and kissed her forehead. She was curled up in the fetal position and there was nothing I could do. I was a phone call away from making a man the next President, and yet, I couldn't help my wife.

The moment we stepped into the hospital, they wheeled her away, cutting her dress off as they went. The nurse was already preparing to put an IV in her arm, but I reached out to stop her.

"We don't want drugs."

"Mr. Callahan." I looked up to find that doctor, Am… something. She looked down at Mel, pressing into her abdomen softly, which only made Mel cry out again.

"Your job is to fix her, not make her worse," I snapped, wanting to pop her ugly little head off her neck.

"Mr. Callahan, I'm sorry but it's going to hurt before it gets better. Either way, she's going to need the fluids, and the painkillers have a dual purpose. She needs to be calm or we run the risk of losing this baby," she snapped right back.

The nurse looked directly at me, waiting for me to release her arm, when I did, she had that needle in Melody's arm before I could blink.

"We're going to need a sonogram," she spoke right past me, still pressing on Mel's stomach. Each time she applied pressure, Mel would squeeze my hand. It was like that for what felt like hours, but in reality, it was probably only a few minutes; push, squeeze, until Mel stopped squeezing and her body relaxed. Looking at her, I found her staring at me, completely relaxed with her eyes wide open. It was scary as shit, and yet I welcomed it all the same.

"You look like shit," she whispered with a smile.

"This how all men with wives who terrorize them look," I whispered back, kneeling at her bedside.

She rolled her eyes at me before looking at the nurse who was currently taking her blood pressure.

"What are you giving me?"

"Acetaminophen." The blonde haired doctor smiled, as she grabbed hold of the ultrasound. "Don't worry, it's safe."

"What's wrong with her, doctor?"

"Dr. Lewis," she corrected. "Dr. Amy Lewis we met last year and I just want to—"

"Question one: what is wrong with me?" Mel asked, cutting straight to the point. "Question two: how is my baby?"

"I'm checking your baby right now, but he or she should be just fine," she said as the nurse closed the door and blinds.

"And question one?" I asked.

"You people waste no time…"

"Because we have no time to waste," Mel and I said at the same time. "And *please* don't make me have to ask again."

I almost wanted to laugh at her attempt to be nice and use 'please.' It just made her sound even more annoyed.

"Mrs. Callahan, from what we can tell, you have pre-eclampsia. It's not life threatening, *yet*. However, your blood pressure is very high. If this doesn't change, there is a high possibility of you developing eclampsia, which can be hazardous to both your health, and that of your unborn child. You're going to need to take it easy in the next coming weeks, alright?" Lifting up her dress and placing a blanket over her legs, Dr. Lewis placed some sort of gel on Mel's stomach.

"Easy? As in bed rest easy?" she asked. The one way to make sure Mel didn't relax was to tell her to do so.

"No, I don't think it's that serious yet, but I would honestly recommend taking some time off from work."

"A Callahan that actually works?" the nurse whispered behind us, unaware that I could hear her and I was about two seconds away from strangling her with Mel's IV. However, before I could comment, a small whoosh echoed through the room. It was like a tiny underwater drum.

"That is your baby's heartbeat."

Mel laughed, reaching for her stomach as the whooshing continued. It was strong and beautiful at the same time. It was like the music I could imagine God enjoying, and I couldn't for the life of me tear my eyes away from the black and white picture on the monitor.

Smiling, Dr. Lewis stared at the screen, moving the wand over Mel's stomach. "Would you like to know the sex?"

"Yes."

"No."

"No?" I stared down at her. We were finding out the sex, now.

"Your parents really wanted to find out with us. Evelyn cornered me in the car. Is she here?"

I had no idea. Everything had happened so quickly and my main concern was getting her here as quickly as possible.

"Can you check if the rest of the Callahan party has arrived?" Dr. Lewis instructed a nurse.

Brushing her brown hair back, I watched as Melody fought the urge to fall sleep. We were working on almost eighteen hours of no sleep. That couldn't have helped her condition. She needed to rest more. "Can't we just find out a second time with them in the room? I'm sure I can fake a surprised face."

With her eyes half open, she shook her head.

"This is the least I can do for your mom. Plus, maybe she'll calm down a little."

"Apparently you don't know my mother."

"Are you bad-mouthing me, son?"

Speak of angels and they appear.

Walking over to us, with my father an inch behind her, she kissed Mel's forehead.

"You gave us quite a scare, young lady," my father told her.

Laughing, she grabbed hold of his hand. "Now Sedric, you and I both know you were itching to escape those political asshats."

He could only grin before kissing her forehead.

"Is the baby alright?" Evelyn asked, mesmerized by the black and white screen.

"Can I tell you the sex now?" Dr. Lewis asked Mel directly.

She didn't say anything, just took a deep breath, grabbed my hand and nodded.

"Well then, your son is going to be fine, as long as mommy here takes it easy."

"A boy?" I whispered with a grin so wide my face felt as though it would break in half.

Nodding, she showed us the tiny boy, who was seemingly exposing himself to the world with pride.

"Just like his father." Mel smiled.

I kissed her forehead, her nose, and her cheeks before kissing her lips. All I could think to say was, "Thank you."

"Another young Master Callahan. I can't wait to help with his nursery!" My mother, almost jumped out of her skin.

"I bet you I can get him to love golf early on," added my father.

To which my mother could only shake her head. "Sedric, dear, you're the only man in this family who thinks that's a real sport!"

"Son, don't listen to her. Now your father wasn't any good, but with your mother's genes, there's hope for you," he spoke to Mel's stomach.

Mel simply looked at me.

"And you thought this was going to calm them down?"

Twenty-Three

*"Actions are the first tragedy in life, words are the second.
Words are perhaps the worst. Words are merciless..."*
—*Oscar Wilde*

Coraline

I used to hate hospitals. Everyone was either dying or dead. Yet, right now I felt like I was going to die from excitement. Or nervousness.

"What has you looking like a megawatt light bulb?" Olivia asked, sitting across from me and calmly checking her phone.

"What?"

"Your face. You look like you're about to break out into a show tune. Which is a little twisted seeing as Mel is losing her baby again."

She was such a bitch.

"Olivia, you don't know that," Neal whispered, sitting up in his plastic chair.

"She was bleeding, and curled up in a ball, I'm sure every news outlet is talking by now…"

"Unless you've magically gone to medical school in the last two hours, shut up, Olivia. You don't know shit," I couldn't help but snap at her.

She drove me insane.

Rolling her blue eyes at me, she frowned. "I forgot, you're her little lackey. I wonder how long that will last when she plans to kill *your* father."

"Olivia, enough." Neal grabbed her arm.

She looked him dead in the eyes. "You were going to kill him, weren't you? From wherever you were hiding, you were going to kill him at the end of the night."

"This is not the time or the place for this," he hissed at her.

"For what? To discuss your loyalty? Because apparently you can't even stand up for me, your wife. Other men would move heaven and earth. You on the other hand, don't give a damn. It's all about twisted fucking Mel, and now karma is biting her in the ass. So let go of me," she yelled, pulling her arm away and forcing him to let go. She went to rise, but before she could leave, Declan made his way over.

He smiled, running his hands through his hair. "She's fine. So is their son."

"A boy?" I jumped up into his arms. "Evelyn must be in overdrive right now."

"Who says God doesn't have favorites?" Olivia sneered before walking off to some random part of the hospital.

"Tell Liam I said congrats," Neal said, shaking Declan's hand before following his wife.

"Olivia is driving me up the wall," I whispered, holding onto him.

Kissing my nose, he just smiled.

"What?"

"Mel is fine. We're in a hospital with all types of devices that can find out whether or not you're pregnant," he whispered.

Biting my lip, I nodded as he led me to the front desk.

"Is there anyway we can get a pregnancy test done now?" He winked at the woman who could only smile and nod.

"If I am, Evelyn is going to have a heart attack if we tell her now." I could just see her face; not able to process the information we were telling her before she jumped me.

"Then we'll tell her later and make it our little secret for now." He grinned, kissing my cheek.

OLIVIA

It's not fair. I was always the one being shit on. I was always the one watching as everyone else moved forward while I was pulled back. Mel was a evil bitch! She broke every law; every commandment under God, yet still, her life was perfect. Her life was just the way she wanted it to be.

"You suck, you know!" I yelled up at the sky. "I'm not sure what you do all day, but it isn't working! Life is shit and you know it."

"Are you yelling at me or God?" Neal called out behind me.

"Go away, Neal!" He disgusted me.

He touched my shoulder softly and I was tempted to lean into him. "Olivia…"

"Were you or were you not going to kill my father tonight?" I turned to stare into his eyes, but he couldn't meet my gaze. "I can't believe you."

"Olivia…" he tried pulling me to him

"NO!" I snapped, pulling out of his arms. "Ever since that woman has come into our lives, shit has gone to hell! What happen to the rules? We killed *for* family, we die *for* family? Yet nobody is safe! God forbid you even blink in their direction. Family used to be important to you and everyone else. But now, fuck it. It's every person for themselves, and you don't even have my back. No one has my back but me.

So fuck you, fuck Melody Giovanni, and fuck everything you pretend to stand for."

I tried to leave, but he grabbed onto my arms, shoving me against the door and leading back into the hospital.

"Let go of me!" I pushed. "Neal—"

"No! You've spoken, now it's my turn!" he yelled, grabbing my hands. "First of all, I've had your back. I've had your back the moment you came into my life. I've had your back even after you couldn't trust me with your secret. Even after the family told me *not* to marry you. I've *always* had your back because for some stupid reason I love you. I wasn't going to kill your father tonight."

"What?"

He frowned. "I sat on top of that roof, my rifle pointed at the First Lady. I spoke to your father, he was supposed to push her out of the way and take a bullet to the arm. I'm always on your side. So fuck you for not trusting me *again*."

Letting go of me, he reached for the door handle at my side.

"Move, Olivia."

"No," I whispered, as I jumped up into his arms, trying to kiss him. "I'm sorry."

DECLAN

"What's taking so long?" Coraline sighed, kicking her legs back and forth on the edge of the bed.

The nurse had left with her blood samples over two hours ago. If I knew it took this long to take a pregnancy test, I'm sure Coraline would've rather we waited and done this in the comfortable privacy of our own home.

"Baby, I'm sure they are going as fast as they can." I tried to hide my skepticism. She was excited. She was trying so hard not to be, but she couldn't help it. Her whole body was shaking and in return, so was mine.

We had come so far in the last year and a half. We hadn't fixed everything, and we still went to therapy, but we were happy. I kept trying to imagine us both as parents. What would I teach him or her? Who would they look like? I was hoping that our girls would look like her; had her smile.

"Stop looking at me like that." She laughed, kicking her feet at me.

"This is how I always look at you," I replied, grabbing hold of her legs and kissing her thighs. "And I was thinking of names for our son, Brendan."

"Brendan Callahan? It sounds so boring and simple."

"Well excuse me, what names do you have in mind?"

"Our first kid is going to be girl." She laughed.

"Sorry, baby. Callahan swimmers seem to only produce males."

Before she could respond, the door opened. I stood up as the doctor walked in.

"Please don't make us wait another second. We're both going crazy here." She smiled up at him, taking my hand.

However something felt odd. The doctor before us didn't smile, he looked as though he was in pain. Like he didn't want to break our hearts. When he frowned, I felt her try to pull her hand away.

"We're not pregnant," she said slowly, trying not cry. "I'm sorry we wasted your time, we were just excited. I think we should just go."

"Mrs. Callahan, can you answer some questions for me?" he said to us. We both froze, staring at one another before looking back at him.

"Why? We aren't pregnant, right?" I asked.

He shook his head. "No, I'm sorry, you're not pregnant. But we did find something else in our tests that raised some questions."

"What?"

"We found that you have abnormally high levels of CA 125. From there, we ran a few other tests…" He paused, and took a deep breath as if readying himself.

"The high levels of this protein suggest that there is a form of antigen that exists. It has symptoms that led you to falsely believe you were pregnant. There is a high chance that the antigen is attacking parts of your reproductive system. You explained earlier to the nurse that you have been feeling tired, experiencing abdominal pains as well lower back pains, these symptoms can be a sign of stress, other physical activities, or—"

"Just spit it out already," I snapped; he was going to make her panic.

He seemed to pause to collect his breath, as if reading himself for another long-winded speech. "I'm so sorry, Mrs. Callahan, but such levels of CA 125 leads us to believe that there is a possibility that you may have a cancerous growth in your body. There are other reasons for such high levels of CA 125, but seeing as you are young and not premenopausal, it's my professional opinion that these markers are evidence of ovarian cancer. There are other tests—" The moment he uttered his damning opinion, she stumbled back as if he had slapped her across the face. She grabbed hold of the bed, trying to catch her breath.

"Mrs. Callahan, there are procedures and tests..."

"GET OUT!" I roared at him, causing him to stumble. He was the cause of her upset, her unhappiness. All rational thought left me as he stumbled feebly to the door. I didn't care that he had the unfortunate job of delivering such news to us, it didn't matter that it *was* his job to do so, all I saw was him talking and as a result, my wife, my purpose for living, seemingly being ripped in two right before my very eyes. He was right to leave. I was feeling the irrational urge to make Coraline smile, as she was ten minutes ago, through any means necessary.

One of those means may have included carving his face from his body.

I stepped towards my wife, holding her tightly and hoping for some way to carry all of this burden. I didn't care that marriage was supposed to be a fifty-fifty deal, when it came to anything that hurt my wife, I'd carry all of the burden without a thought.

"Coraline. Coraline, baby, breathe." I held onto her, but she just kept sobbing, until her knees went out and we were both on the floor.

"I'm so sorry," she cried into my shirt.

Biting on my lips, I fought my own tears; she didn't need that from me, not now.

"You've got nothing to be sorry for, baby. We're going to fight this," I whispered, kissing her head. "We're going to fight this and win."

She only cried harder, and I lost the battle against my tears as they started to stream down my face.

Fifteen minutes ago, we were thinking about baby names, laughing, happy, dying to hear two little words: *you're pregnant*. Now I was trying my best not to think about funerals, or about losing her, my reason for living.

Staring up at the flickering lights, I found myself speaking to God, truly speaking to him for the first time in what felt like forever.

If you think you can take her away from me without a fight, you're fucking mistaken. She will not die from this; I won't let her.

Twenty-Four

"Life, although it may only be an accumulation of anguish, is dear to me, and I will defend it."
—Mary Shelley

LIAM

"*This is breaking and unprecedented news. Only hours after Senator Colemen's all-white charity ball and Melody Callahan's hospitalization, First Lady Julie Monroe was arrested and charged with treason and the murder of her husband, President Monroe. Thus, making her the first woman to ever have a hand in the assassination of a U.S. President. The FBI claims they were given an anonymous tip with undoubtable proof of her involvement. First Lady Julie Monroe only days ago vowed to run in her husband's place for this year's coming election. This is all very confusing and honestly unfathomable. But stay tuned. We hope to keep you updated on..."*

"Are you eating my Jell-O?" Mel whispered, trying to open her eyes.

Staring at the cup in my hands, I frowned. "I thought you hated Jell-O."

"You thought wrong, now hand it over." She reached forward, taking the cup from my hands and eating a spoonful.

"How are you feeling?" I asked.

"Like I've been in bed too long...and hungry," she muttered, scarfing down the little that was left in the small cup.

"Sixteen hours of sleep will do that to you." Reaching over to her bedside, I grabbed the second cup I had conned the nurse out of from her tray. She watched my hand before taking my Jell-O once again. "Sixteen hours? Why in the hell would you let me sleep that long?"

"You haven't had a good sleep in days. Besides, there was nothing for you to do anyway." If I had woken her, she would have killed me.

She stopped mid-bite, glaring at me. "In our line of work there is always something to do. So the real question is, what have you been doing?"

All I could do was roll my eyes at her and turn up the volume of the television.

"People all over the world are still reeling over the arrest of First Lady Julie Monroe. It was only hours ago that the FBI announced that the First Lady was arrested in connection with President Monroe's murder. From what we've been told, it took only one anonymous tip to unravel this national tragedy..."

"You tipped them off?" she asked.

"No, I tipped off your mole. He deserves a raise, don't you think? Catching the President's killer is a huge step up," I replied, dialing Declan for what had to be the ninth time.

"That's all you did today?" She sighed, staring at the now empty Jell-O cup.

"Really?" I smirked, shaking my head. "You're not killing my high today, wife. I'm having a son and about to get the White House."

She laughed, as she rubbed her stomach fondly. "First, I'm sorry, it's the hunger speaking. Second, we're having a son."

Sitting next to her, I kissed her forehead, taking her hands into mine.

"We're having a son," I whispered down to her.

"Are you nervous?" she whispered back.

"I think I will be at some point. But like I said, I'm numb with happiness. Are you nervous?"

"Yeah." Leaning back against the pillow, she took a deep breath.

"You're going to be a great mother. So, what do you want to eat?" I asked, dialing Adriana.

She grinned widely. "French Onion Soup with stuffed Artichokes on the side and a large chocolate milkshake?"

"Is that all?"

She smacked my arm.

"Sir?" Adriana said on the other line.

"I want a bowl of French Onion Soup with stuffed Artichokes and a chocolate milkshake—"

"Large," Mel stated, biting her spoon.

"A large chocolate milkshake."

"I'll have it brought over in half an hour," she replied.

"Hurry, before she bites off my arm for a snack," I said quickly before hanging up. She reached over to smack me again, but I grabbed her hand and kissed the inside of her wrist instead.

"Don't look at me like that," she snapped.

"Like what?"

"Like…" She was interrupted by the second phone in my pocket. "Isn't that my phone?"

"It is," I told her, answering, "Callahan."

"Sir? This is Officer Beau Brooks and I believe we may have a problem."

Rising to my feet, I placed the phone on speaker. "You believe we have a problem or you know we have a problem?"

The smile on Mel's face dropped as she glared at the phone in my hands.

"Sir, there is a maid here who says she overheard the conversation with the First Lady and Aviela when she returned to your home to get her belongings after being terminated. She also claims she's seen a lot more within the

Callahan household. But that's all she says, she isn't speaking in detail until immigration gives her a visa. The FBI is trying to make this a double whammy and pull charges up on you also. She's under twenty-four hour protection"

"Shit. Fucking Olivia," Mel hissed. "Brooks, hold on and make sure she can't talk until we call you back."

"How does this involve Olivia?" I asked her when he was gone.

Shaking her head, she took a deep breath. "She fired all the illegals working for us for the charity shit. Whoever this woman is, she's probably sharpening her axe for us, wanting revenge for what your idiot brother's dumb bitch of a wife did. Damn it. This is the last motherfucking time we leave Olivia or him in charge of anything!"

"Love, relax. The baby."

She froze, placing her hand over her belly before turning to me. "We have to move quickly."

"Beau can't kill her," I thought aloud. "There is just too much focused in and around her right now since she knows enough about us to use it as a bargaining chip. Shouldn't she be more afraid?"

"I don't think the maids were that bright to begin with." She sighed, trying her best to keep calm, but she was raging. I could see it.

"Even an idiot knows when to be afraid."

Fear was human nature. People instinctively knew when to stay away. It's what kept the human race alive.

Mel froze, looking up at me. "Not unless she's more afraid of what will happen if she didn't talk. Her visa, Liam. For whatever reason she needs a visa and she needs it now."

"Relax." I kissed her forehead. "I will bring you up to speed after it's dealt with."

"Liam…"

"Mel, no."

The last thing I needed was her stressing out over this. It wasn't worth it. Thankfully, before she could call me a sexist asshole, Adriana walked in with a tray of her food.

"Feed her, I'll be back soon," I said, already dialing as I walked towards the door.

"I'm not a dog, you chauvinistic asshole, and we aren't done here. Who…"

Closing the door, I yelled a quick, "I love you too!"

Stepping into the hall, I was met with a bunch of nosy nurses all staring at the door. "What are you all looking at? Don't you people have lives to save or something?"

They looked away immediately, pretending to be otherwise occupied.

"Declan, this is my ninth call to you. You better be dead or dying somewhere." This family was starting to tick me the fuck off.

"Liam, is Mel alright?" My mother glided on over to me with an array of bright sunflowers in one hand and Olivia standing by the other. She held her head high and rolled her manicured hand over those stupid fucking pearls she always wore.

I didn't bother answering my mother. Instead, I snatched Olivia's arm and pulled.

"What the hell are you doing? Let go of me this instant!" she screamed like the hideous banshee she was.

Pushing her into the stairwell, I grasped on to her neck, forcing her against the wall. "Do you know what I get to do today? I get to clean up your shit. Do I look like a shit cleaning type of person?"

"I…can't…breathe…" she gasped, clawing at my hands so harshly her fake nails popped off.

"If you can't breathe, you can't speak. I'm seconds away from popping your ugly head off of your shoulders—"

"Get the fuck off my wife!" Neal pulled me back, his fist quickly colliding with my jaw.

Falling to the ground, Olivia gasped for air, her hands around her throat, as Neal hovered over her.

"Have you lost your fucking mind?" he shouted.

Brushing the side of my lip, I stared at the red stain on my sleeve. I could feel the sadistic smile tugging on my lips as I stared at my brother.

"This is your final warning, Neal. Control your wife or I swear to God I will kill her."

"I should control my wife? How about not letting your wife fucking control you? Everything is about her! What has she done? Did she not agree with Mel's shoes?"

"The drama between my wife and yours does not concern me. You of all people should know Mel does not need me to fight those battles for her." I again wiped my bruised lip, staring at the jackass in front of me. "However, the moment your sniveling breallóg of a wife fired the maids in my house without speaking to me or fully explaining to them what would happen if they spoke to the police, your wife became my enemy."

He froze as if he was encased in ice.

"I didn't think any of them would..." she said weakly.

"You didn't think!" I roared at her, causing her to jump back. "The drama you've created in this family I can, and have, overlooked. The drama you create in my work—my way of my life—you're lucky you're still alive! Breathe in the wrong direction and you will not live long enough to regret it."

Stepping towards the door, the sad lump of shit that was my brother called out.

"Liam, she…"

"Don't make excuses!" I roared. I took a deep breath, trying to calm down before I blew his brains out in this hospital. "All I need from you is to find Declan and tell him to pick up his damn phone."

Stepping out into the hall, my mother stood waiting. The bundle of sunflowers that was once in her arms were now replaced with a first aid kit. Her eyes went straight to my lip before falling to the scratches on my arm and hand.

"Excuse me, dear." She pulled a male nurse. "Can we get a private room please?"

"Mother."

"Ma'am, I'm sorry I can't—"

"Let me rephrase this, can you please show me and my bleeding son here to a private room in the hospital he helped fund and damn well near saved from bankruptcy?" Her voice was polite, but the grip she held on the nurse's arm screamed hostile.

Nodding, he pointed over to an empty bed. "I can handle his wounds."

"No thank you, dear." She patted his arm. "Come on, Liam…"

"Mother, I'm fine. Stop being ridiculous."

She stepped forward, and although I had to drop my head to meet her gaze, I knew better than to fight her on this. This…this was code for 'I need to talk to you, so shut the fuck up and listen.'

Pulling out my phone, I dialed, as we walked towards the private bed in the corner with the blue curtains.

"I knew one of you were going to need this." She sighed, pulling out the bandages.

"I'm fine. I would be a lot better if people would answer their fucking phones."

"Language."

I couldn't help but roll my eyes. "Honestly, mother?"

"I'm just trying to help you. Do your really want your son coming out swearing? You should prepare to censor yourself. Now, give me your hand." Obeying her, I tried once again to contact Brooks, but he kept sending me to voicemail. Something was happening.

"Declan?"

"No," I hissed at the alcohol she poured on my cuts. "Work. Work I shouldn't have to do, but your daughter-in-law has become nothing but a growing cancerous pain in my...ah! Damn it, Ma!"

"Stop being a baby." She laughed as she wrapped my hand. "Have you gotten any real sleep since this all started?"

I didn't answer, not because I hadn't slept, but because I knew she would say it wasn't enough. I spent most of the day watching over security tapes, Mel's vitals, and contacts with the police.

"You were born with a short fuse, Liam. It becomes even shorter when you lose sleep."

"Sleep or no sleep, Olivia crossed a line and I was so close to killing her just now."

"But you didn't because deep down you love your brother, despite how much you still want to hate him."

"So this isn't about my actions against Olivia, it's about Neal." I should have known.

"As much as I love your wives, my first priority will always be you and your brothers' happiness. Whatever this is with Olivia will tear you both further apart. Neal has waited years—"

"Mother, I don't care. If he wants to stand with me, a spot is open. But he needs to make sure his wife knows where she stands, and that needs to be far away from me. I no longer trust her."

"If you can't stand her now, as the wife of your brother, how will you stand her as daughter to your President? You're the ones elevating her status. Remember, Frankenstein was not the monster, but the doctor."

I hated when she did this. "You're going to drive me to smoke, Ma."

"Smoke? Not drink?" She laughed.

"Dad did that years ago."

Before she could reply, my phone went off; a blocked call trying to come in. Only one person had this number… Brooks.

"Callahan."

"Sir, I got your calls. I couldn't speak…"

"What's going on?"

"The FBI is drafting up a visa, all they need is for her to say the words. I think she has a son across the border."

"You think?" Why the fuck did everyone think and no one knew? "Brooks, step up and fix this. Find a way to let her know what will happen if she opens her mouth. Our public image will not be tarred by this, do you understand me?"

"I'm on it sir."

Beau

Closing my phone, I looked up at all the badges in front of me. Most of them greeting me as they walked around.

"Way to go, Brooks."

"Brooks, working your way up."

"Congrats, Brooks."

All I could do was nod, take a deep breath, and ingest the scent of sweat and stale coffee, before repeating the same old line: "Just doin' my job." For years, I was nothing but a beat cop, and I never asked to be much more. My real job was to watch the streets. Now, word around the department was that I was on the shortlist to becoming a detective.

I needed to get to that maid as soon as possible, but the FBI had her on lockdown in the back of the precinct. They wanted their names on this since they couldn't get their tags on the President's wife. But collaring the Callahans was as close to first place as they came.

"You think it's true?" my partner asked. "If it is, we need to be on this case." He leaned against my desk.

"You're a pup, Scooter. Stop trying to bite off cases when you don't even have teeth," I told him, eyeing the water bottle on my desk. I had a plan, I just needed more time.

"They say the Callahans are the worst thing that happened to this city since Al Capone. That they murder men, women, and children, no problem. They move drugs in the mist; weed, cocaine, heroin. If it's illegal, they sell it and make millions all over the country, yet they're still…"

"That's because we have nothing!" I yelled, drawing attention towards us. "Has anyone ever spoken to a dealer that pointed a finger at a Callahan?"

"Everybody knows it's 'cause they're scared."

"Who is everybody? Is everybody going to testify at trial? There has never been any evidence to prove that the Callahans are anything but upstanding citizens of this city. We don't even have a parking ticket to pin on them. All I've ever heard were just rumors from one cop to another, told over a cold coffeepot. We got officers trying to make cases out of thin air to try and prove themselves. Prove that they could do what so many others had failed to do. Give me evidence and I'll slap the cuffs on 'em. But until then, save your ghost stories and 'drugs in the mist' for your playmates and get the hell out of my face."

He took a step back, biting his lips before placing his hat back on his blonde head. "Well, we got a maid, their maid."

"No, we got an illegal immigrant who feels jilted after being fired, and is now blackmailing the U.S. government for a visa."

"You know what Brooks? All of us are doing something. We're trying! We're trying to save our city. To bring it back from the mobsters and thugs, the Callahans. Why don't you start supporting the team?"

That stopped me. It took everything not to sock him in the face. "Support my team?" I laughed, pulling on my coat. "Kid, I've been here for seven years. I've been shot at, ran over and almost blown up. I work cases I can get arrests for. This ain't a game, *boy*. My coat says 'Chicago P.D.' not Team Cop. My badge says Officer Brooks. You want to prove your stripes? You want to see the Callahans go down, even though you have no clue *who* they are? Fine, whatever. Just meet me in interrogation in five minutes."

Grabbing a water bottle, I walked out of the pen.

"I ain't no rookie anymore," he yelled from behind me. What else could he say?

"Shut your pie-hole, kid and get us some coffee," someone behind me yelled, but I didn't bother to care or to look back.

You can always tell when the Feds were in town; they snatched any high profile case and made sure to slap their names in Big Bird yellow all over the joint. Walking down the hall, I did not meet anyone's gaze before entering the file room. I didn't have much time left. I was playing with a whole new type of fire here.

This water bottle was my only chance left.

The key to being a liar was that you had to believe your lies. It was as simple as that. Tell lies you can believe, and when you do, the world will believe them right along with you. So when I stepped into the hallway, I knew what I wanted to see. I knew the lie I would believe; the maid was a liar and I was going to make her admit it.

Everything felt sharp; my senses had never been so clear, and I was going play every single card I had. The FBI agents were all waiting, hoping they had something. Next to them was Scooter, who was just short of rubbing his hands together.

Staring at the tan skinned, dark haired woman praying at the table, I tried not to break character. "She said anything yet?"

She couldn't have been a day over thirty maybe?

"She won't talk until she sees a visa. It doesn't make sense though. She has a kid over the border. Why not ask for him to get a free pass? She wants a visa for herself instead?" Scooter asked.

"After she told us about the First Lady, she was all 'Hail Mary full of grace,' over and over. If I were Mary, I would be annoyed," the officer to my right scoffed before turning towards the two-way mirror. "This is a waste of time. They're questioning the First Lady right now. It's your collar you should go watch."

"I'll be over there in a minute. I just want to take a crack at her first."

"We," Scooter said, stepping up, "*We* want to take a crack at her."

"Knock yourselves out. Ask Mother Mary for a prayer for me." He laughed before walking off.

Step one; done.

"So, how are we going to go at her?" Scooter asked, trying to walk in, but I stopped him at the door.

"*You're* not a police officer, remember? You're a cheerleader. You can support the team from behind that glass."

Stepping inside, the first thing I heard were her prayers:

"*Dios te salve, María, llena eres de gracia, el Señor es contigo...*"

"*Antoniodita tú eres entre todas las mujeres, y Antoniodito es el fruto de tu vientre, Jesús. Santa María, Madre de Dios, ruega por nosotros pecadores, ahora y en la hora de nuestra muerte. Amén,*" I finished for her, putting the water bottle on the table before helping her into the chair.

"Mary mother of all mothers," I said pulling out my own chair. "My mother loved her too."

"Do you have my visa?" she asked in a thick accent.

"No."

"Then I have nothing for you."

"I don't think you ever had anything for me to begin with."

"I worked in that house! I saw things! I heard things!" she yelled at me.

"Have some water," I told her, sliding the water bottle over.

She pushed it back. "I'm fine, *lo choto*."

"Really? Because you've been in here a while and the last thing I want is for you be dehydrated. Plus, I hope you do a lot of talking," I stated, pushing the water back to her.

"No visa, *no confesión*," she repeated before bringing the bottle to her lips. The moment she looked down, she froze. Her dark eyes slowly read over the words written on the backs side of the label.

"Are you alright, Ms. Morales?"

She just stared at me, eyes wide, frozen solid.

"It's just water." I said, grabbing the bottle. "Not poison. You're safe here."

To prove my point, I grabbed the water and drank.

"The Callahans…." she whispered, hanging her head down low.

"Ms. Morales, I know this is scary. My partner, he reminded me of the accusations against the Callahans. How some say they killed men, women, and even children. How they have no regard for the law. How they would hunt down anyone who tried to stand in their way. If that is true, I cannot imagine what you must have gone through in that house. What you may have seen. We know about your son across the border."

She tensed, water pooling under her eyelids as her lips and arms trembled.

"My mother, she was an *illegal*, worked her whole life for people like the Callahans. She didn't care though. She just wanted her boys to get the greatest chance in life. She would do anything for the boys—for me. Even take on people like the Callahans. That's why you want a visa, right? So you could bring him over the right way. So he wouldn't be labeled an illegal immigrant. I want to help you, Ms. Morales, but you've got to be honest with me. You're the only one who can bring those murdering bastards down. We will protect you. I will personally protect you."

I made sure that she could read my eyes, and it made the tears roll down her cheeks. Wiping her nose, she nodded.

Sitting up straighter, she admitted, "I lied. I don't know anything. I just wanted my boy."

"You've got nothing on the Callahans?" I stated again, glaring into her eyes.

Again, she nodded.

"I have nothing on the Callahans. I just wanted to get back at them. They fired me for no reason, I have nothing, and they took it all away. They just have so much, you know? I just wanted something for my boy."

Shaking my head at her, I grabbed the water. "Hold tight, Ms. Morales. Hold tight."

"Please, don't deport me. *Por favor!* I'm the only one sending anything back. My son is still young. Just like your mama, I just wanted to give him the best, get myself a good job. I need your help, please! I need the visa."

There was nothing more I could say to her, so I simply walked out. Scooter stood glaring at the woman, who had returned to praying, through the two-way mirror.

"Damn it. She's got to know something. I can feel it. We need to get her to talk. We should charge her; obstruction of justice, filing a false report…"

"Yes, Scooter let's charge the only eye witness we have to the First Lady's deception, because she didn't tell us what we were hoping to hear," I snapped. "If you keep jumping head first into everything, your brain will be splattered all over the sidewalk soon enough."

It was only after I had gotten out of the precinct that I dared to rip the paper off the water bottle. In English it translated to three simple sentences:

Your son made it home from school safely today. Your words right now will determine if he makes it through the night. Do not make us do this.

Pulling out my other phone, I dialed, waiting to be directed.

"Welcome to Melody's Flowers…"

"Two dozen of Autumn crocus for the Boss."

"Please hold."

It took only a second before I heard his voice.

"Callahan."

"It's done. She recanted."

"Good work. Sit on her, make sure she doesn't try again."

"Done."

Melody

"It's been handled," Liam stated, finally bringing his sorry ass into the room. He'd left hours ago with my damn cell phone.

"Well, aren't you feeling yourself," I sneered, not bothering to look at him as I stepped into my shoes. Adriana waited with my jacket.

"Are you still hungry?"

I was prepared to beat the shit out of him, but it looked like someone had already started. "What the fuck happened to your face and hand?"

"Olivia." He sighed, stepping over to me.

"Does she look worse?"

"She feels worse."

"I don't care how she feels, Liam."

"I'll get the car," Adriana stated as she took her exit.

He pulled me closer to him and kissed my lips so hard I could feel the cut on the inside of his cheek and I could taste his blood.

Knock.

"Come back later," Liam yelled.

But they didn't listen. The door snapped open and a person I used to know as Declan stumbled in with the same white clothes, now covered in dirt, messy hair and bags under his red eyes.

"Jesus Christ, Declan." Liam released me, walking to him just as Declan fell to his knees sobbing.

"Declan…"

"Coraline has ovarian cancer. She won't speak to me. She won't even move. I don't know what to do. I don't know how to fight this. I don't want to lose her…I…"

"Breathe, brother. Just breathe," Liam whispered, as he knelt down to hold onto him.

Walking behind them both, I closed the door. This was personal. This was family, and no one else needed to see this.

Liam looked up at me as his brother, not cousin here, they were much closer then that. Declan just sobbed in his arms. His eyes asked me a question with an answer I hated: How do we fight cancer?

I knew all too well that sometimes you couldn't. Cancer was a bitch that didn't know when to die. Placing my hand on Declan's head, I stood there. I wasn't sure what else to do. Why was this all happening now? Why couldn't we just deal with one fucking problem at a time?

Because this was real life.

Twenty-Five

*"My mother protected me from the world and
my father threatened me with it."*
—*Quentin Crisp*

Neal

There were very few things I hated more than meeting my father in his old study. It brought back all my moments of failure, stupidity, and unworthiness. My father's study meant something different to the each of us. For Declan, every time he was brought here, it was because my father needed help wiring something on his computer. For Liam, it was the place they bonded; the place they sipped on brandy, talked business. For me, it was the place my father reminded me of what a giant fuck up I was.

I knew after the shit with Olivia that Liam wasn't done spewing; I just thought he would be man enough to confront me himself instead of calling Sedric. It took all I had not to roll my eyes at the old man sitting behind the even older oak desk, surrounded by the oldest fucking books. It was like I was having a flashback to my youth.

"You wished to see me, father?" I asked, not bothering to sit down. We would be at each other's throats in a moment.

Throwing his pen onto the table, he leaned back, and stared at me before folding his arms. "Do you know who I am?" he asked softly.

"Yes, sir."

"Remind me."

I hated these Yoda moments.

"Remind you of what, sir?"

I could see his teeth clench as he lifted his hands, gesturing to everything around us. "Tell me the story I told you as a boy, Neal. Tell me how I came to sit on this chair, in this house, with this family name."

"You were only twenty-two at the time, studying at the Loyola University of Chicago, when grandfather called, and told you that it was time to take over the family. Your oldest brother had been gunned down, mother was pregnant, and gang affiliated crime was at an all time high.

"Every day, Chicago was bleeding under the hands of five kingpins. They were just waiting for the chance to kill each other. You didn't have the manpower, money or clout to get anything done, but somehow you managed to find all five of them and burn their bodies, but not before decapitating them. At twenty-three, you took over Chicago in one night." I recited like a well-memorized monologue.

He clapped, rising from his chair. "That was the story I told you as a proud father. I spared you the details, and thus this is my fault. I made it sound easy. I didn't tell you about the bullets I took, all the ribs I've broken, or scars I have. And I sure as hell didn't tell you how your mother laid on top of you in the bathtub as one hundred and seventy-two rounds shredded through our apartment. She took a bullet for you. When I got there, I sat you on my lap, pulled your mother to my chest and promised the both of you the world on a golden platter. I swore that neither of you would ever want for anything and that you would always be safe."

"No, you didn't tell me any of that." And I wasn't sure why he was telling me now.

"I didn't think I had to." His face remained emotionless. "After everything I did, not once have I ever gotten tied in with the police. In fact, I prefer my name to never drop off the tongue of a blue blood."

"I know this."

"Do you?" He stepped forward. "You know nothing, boy!"

And so we begin.

"I find out today that your *wife* was the reason behind one of our maids talking to the police."

"It was a mistake."

"It was a mistake?" he roared, grabbing the side of my face. "Marrying her, that was the mistake! I knew this. But I allowed it because I foolishly thought what harm could one dumb wench do to us. I thought my son would be smart enough to control his wife. Our wives are a reflection of ourselves, and *you* are failing me! You are failing your brother, and you are failing this family."

I tried to pull away from him, but he just held on tighter, forcing me to meet his eyes.

"I gave up everything for this life, this family; *everything.* And you stand before me telling me it was a mistake? You are my blood, my first born, and I love you dearly, but I need your wife handled, or so help me God, I will take her head next." He pushed me away, and turned back to his chair.

"You and your wife should go pack. The both of you will now join Senator Colemen's bus tours. You will represent the Callahan family far away for now, until everything blows over."

He couldn't fucking be serious.

"Liam needs me, Declan's a mess—"

"And yet, even as a mess, Declan is still more useful. Liam needed his brother, and once again you chose another side over blood."

"Olivia *is* family!"

"Olivia has a ring on her fucking finger, and a name on a damn sheet of paper; she is *not* blood. If she were to die tomorrow, she would be nothing but old photographs and even older memories."

"You could say the same thing about Coraline or Melody!" He was just a fucking hypocrite.

"Coraline is on the board of six charities, she organizes numerous functions that we have, on occasion, used as a cover. On top of that she runs many small businesses in our name. She was doing that even *before* Melody came to this family. She keeps us looking clean to the public. Melody, among everything she has added and given to this family, is also going to have a son. She's starting the next generation of Callahans. They have worth. Tell me, other than the fact that her father is a senator, what has your wife brought to the table?"

There was nothing else to say as he walked over and poured himself a drink.

"So what, you're splitting us up from the family to teach her a lesson?" I finally snapped.

"No." He drank, stepping towards the window. "This lesson is for you, son. Out there, they don't understand us, they hate us. Behind their smiles, they're vultures, waiting for us to fall just so they can pick up the scraps. Out there, you cannot be yourself. You must filter how you speak, take all the shit they throw at you humbly, and smile for their cameras. Out there, you will be a political puppet; and I know that will drive you mad because you are a *Callahan*. So until you start thinking and acting as such, Liam does not need you. Liam does not *trust* you and neither do I. He can't kill you; for neither your mother nor I would allow it. But when he's ready to see you and your wife again, he will call. Until then, see you later, *son*."

"Goodbye, father."

Before I reached door, he called out again. "Fix this, Neal. I refuse to choose between sons. Even if one almost cost us *everything*."

"Who would you choose?"

I already knew the answer, but I wanted to hear him say it.

Smirking at me, he shook his head. "Declan. He's never given me so much shit. Luckily, he's more of his mother than my brother. You and Liam are too much like me; opposite sides of the same damn coin trying to shoot at each other."

"Olivia and I will leave in morning after visiting Coraline." There was nothing more to say; I should have never walked into that office to begin with.

Twenty-Six

"It was many and many a year ago, in a kingdom by the sea..."
—*Edgar Allan Poe*

Melody

Parking outside my old house, I took a deep breath and enjoyed the cold air. It was only the beginning of fall, but it was still cold enough to see my breath in the air. It was like walking through a warzone. There were broken shards of glass and splintered wood everywhere, and walls that were just standing, no longer connected to anything. This was my home. It *is* my home.

Who would have thought it would be nothing but rubble only a year after my leaving. Liam told me to rebuild, but there didn't seem to be a point. It would be a new house without any memories. Even if it was nothing more than a pile of burned ash in the middle of nowhere, it was still my home and I could remember everything. I could still remember the choices I made here…

⚜ ⚜ ⚜

I frowned, cutting the line of coke once more and rubbing it between my fingers. It was the real deal. Finding high quality shit like this cost a small fortune. Leaning into my father's seat, I glanced at the four guards, each standing at the pillars in the corners. They were all on edge, rats who weren't sure if they were on a sinking ship or just fighting through a hurricane. Rumor had it that we were tapped; bleeding money, some would even say. They were right.

Things were falling apart. The Callahans were buying out half the damn west coast, the Valeros were steamrolling Italy, and the Giovannis, we were dying. Half of them hadn't seen my father in over a month, and figured he was sick. The other half thought I'd slit his throat as he slept.

Part of me wanted to just let it fall. There was no way I could run all of this on my own. I could let it die with my father, and I would be able to work my way through school; I had just gotten my acceptance letter to UCLA this morning. I could walk away from this right here and now. I could leave Chicago. My things were packed; I already had my ticket, and yet, I couldn't tear my eyes from the brick that sat on the desk in front of me. Twenty thousand dollars of smack just sitting there, tempting me.

I glanced up at the greasy, sweat stained, blonde haired man in front of me. For the last three weeks, he had been going around the streets like an idiot, talking about how he knew where to get 'the realist shit.' No one believed him. I mean, why would they? He was wearing clothes he must have stolen off a corpse, his hair was so dirty it dropped flakes all over his shoulders, and his shoes looked so worn out, I wasn't even sure why he bothered. He looked like a homeless junkie.

When word got to me, I asked for him and the smack. I didn't really think he would bring it though.

Pulling out the drawer, I grabbed a stack of hundreds before dropping them on the table.

He rushed to the stack of money like it was bread and he was starving. He might have been. "It's good, right? Like I said, one hundred percent cocaine. The best there is."

"Where did you get this? Mr...?"

"Brooks. Beau Brooks, and I got word of this real big wop back east. People are whispering about how he's got mountains of this shit, just lying in his warehouses; millions of profits just being chewed up by damn rats. I'm telling you, girlie, I got the connections—connections your father and I should speak over. I'm sure he'll like them."

"My father is not here. When he's not here, you speak to me. So let's hear it, I will decide if it's worth it or not." Crossing my legs, I waited as he paced in front of me.

"I'm not sure if I should be telling a kid this," he finally said.

"A kid? Do I look like a kid to you? Besides, this kid is also the one that gave you ten thousand dollars, cash." I tried my best to keep my composure. His eyes went straight to my exposed legs before looking back at me.

"No, I guess not."

"Then where did you get this?" I hated repeating myself.

"An old friend of mine is stationed in South America. He's been bringing in small shipments on the side to make extra cash. But he can't move it all, not without risking his job. For the right price, he would sell only to you..."

"And you're his spokesperson?"

He nodded, allowing small flakes to fall from his head.

"You shouldn't be." I frowned in disgust. "But tell him if he gives up all the product he has with him, we have a deal."

Pulling out the bag of money, I stared at it for a moment. This was supposed to be my backup plan—my way out—and yet here I was, dropping the brown bag right in front of him. His eyes lit up and just as he reached for it, I grabbed his hand, pulling his body towards me.

"This is enough for a quarter of it. My father's men will follow you home. Once you're home you're going to call your friend and have all of the product delivered within the next two hours to an abandoned factory near the riverbanks. Do you understand me?"

It was only when he nodded that I let him go and gave him the bag before gesturing for one of the men to take him away. When they were gone, I fell back, trying to breathe. This was crazy. I was crazy.

Why couldn't I just walk away?

"You do know this is why none of them respect or fear you, right?" Fiorello, my father's right hand walked in with a silver tray of what I could only guess was food.

Fiorello had been with my father forever. His parents were both servants here. He in return, was not only the head butler, but he also saw to all of our food. He was the one who tasted it before we ate. He made sure the villa was a well-oiled machine even though his bones cracked and popped when he walked. He was short for a man, and not as fit as all the rest of the men who came through here, but he always blamed that on old age.

"Maybe I don't give shit. Maybe I'm tired," I replied, rising to my feet. I walked over to my father's brandy cabinet.

"Yes, of course you are. After all, you're but a woman. Not even a woman, a child playing grown up," he stated, his gloved hand brushing off the rest of the coke on the table before placing my dinner down.

"You don't..."

"Oh believe me, I understand, Ma'am," he said. "You've done everything your father has ever asked of you. You trained, you studied, and you agreed to be married. But you were still young. Now you are on the verge of making your own path. You think the world outside this life has much to offer you, but you're mistaken. You're willing to throw away your father's legacy, and when he dies, you will have nothing to remember him by. You will be a useless little girl with no protection, no money, and no future. You are fighting for your life—your right to exist—and you don't even know it. But who cares, you're tired." He lifted the lid to reveal a plate of duck before bowing and turning to leave.

"What if I can't do this, Fiorello? What if I let him down and he dies knowing I'm a complete failure?"

"From what I know of your father, he would be happily surprised if you tried and failed than if you to gave up without starting. I know what you're capable of, who you are. I've seen it. Which is why I'm baffled as to why you're trying to hide your nature."

With that, he was gone and I found myself drinking straight from the bottle, which only made me cough. "Ugh, I hate brandy." I needed to find a new drink. Leaving the bottle on the table, I covered up the food. I didn't want to eat. I honestly just wanted to drink myself into tomorrow.

Everything I had ever done was for the good of my father, for his work. It wasn't my fault he was throwing it all away. He had been able to get through one round of chemo secretly only a few years ago. He had beaten cancer once, and now it was back for round two. The only problem was, he didn't want to fight anymore; he was too tired. I had to beg him to try again. He agreed, but only if he could be treated in the house.

No one was allowed to see him, but I was done waiting for him to call. Grabbing the keys, I headed down the marble halls to the last door on the right. It looked like a misplaced closet when you opened the door. However, if you found the steel door lock hidden behind the mop and opened it, there was another bedroom and there sat my father, shaving his own head in front of the bedroom vanity.

"I told you not to enter here, Melody," he hissed at me, not bothering to look up from what he was doing. He was as pale as ever. His left hand would shake every few moments, but he just went on cutting away. The dark curls that once adorned his head drifted to the ground.

"I wanted to make sure you—"

"Leave," he snapped. "Leave an old man to die."

I couldn't move; I just kept watching his hair fall.

"Melody, Leave!" he barked at me.

"No!" I snapped back, shutting the door behind me. "Have you been getting your chemotherapy?"

Slamming the razor down on the dresser, he stood and glared down at me. "You know stubbornness is not attractive. You, Melody

Nicci Giovanni, are nothing but a child, an ungrateful one at that. You do not question me, and you do not raise your voice to me! I run this household! I may be dying, but I am still ORLANDO GIOVANNI! Neither you nor anyone else will treat me any differently. Have I made myself clear?"

"You are not dying! You are not as sick as you think! Get the chemotherapy, Orlando! I refuse to put you in a grave. Ever since I was a child you have dictated every part of my life. I let you do it out of loyalty and love for you; I have to do it because you are all I have! So no, you don't get to die. You don't get to leave me with this shit and just give up, Oh Great Orlando Giovanni!"

The moment I finished, his right hand grabbed my neck and pulled me closer. "Your loyalty should be to yourself. Your love should be only for yourself! No one will ever protect you but yourself. I have spent years trying to drill that into your pretty little head, but you refuse to get it. You are alone. You never had me. It's time you grow up and find your own damn path instead of clinging onto mine!"

The shaving cream still on his half-shaven head fell onto my hand as I tried to pull away. He let me go, dropping me like a wet rag. I slid onto the cool floor. Holding my neck, I tried to breathe. I tried to control myself, but I was done.

"Grow up, Orlando? GROW UP?" *I screamed, picking myself up from the ground.* "I've been grown up since I was six! It's a miracle I'm not a serial killer with the shit I've been through and the things I've seen! You may have thrown money, and trainers, and tutors my way, but you did not raise me, and you sure as hell were never there for me to cling onto. But hey, if you want to die, go ahead, knock yourself out you big coward! In the meantime, I will run this…this fucking empire all by my fucking self and I won't lower myself to steal the top spot, I'll earn it."

"You think you can sit in my chair?" *He laughed, staggering a little as I reached for the door handle.* "I've seen you try, and it's too big for you. You've tried, sweetheart. But don't worry, I've set away *a small fortune along with a few contacts that the Callahans will be interested in. That should be enough for them to still want to marry you. I wouldn't want my daughter to end up on the streets."*

I watched him stumble over to his new bottles, he grabbed one and drank deeply. He was already drunk. He gulped it all down before reaching for the next one.

"To cancer, the bitch that never dies!" he toasted to himself before drinking again. Sadly, that bottle only lasted a few seconds before he threw it against the wall. It shattered on impact, staining the wallpaper a beautiful blood red.

As though someone had taken out his batteries, he fell onto the chair in front of the mirror. He tried to pick up the razor, but between his shaking hand and his undoubtedly blurry vision, he couldn't.

Sighing, I found myself walking over and taking the blade from him. "I'll do it, you look like you lost a fight with a pair of scissors," was all I could say, as I took the old-school blade to his hair.

Snickering, he nodded but I held onto his neck. "I'm on the poison," he said. "I stopped for a while but I started again this morning. I shouldn't have stopped, but it's just as painful as the last time."

I couldn't bring myself to look into the mirror to see his face. I knew it hurt him. I'd talked to all of his doctors and pain was just a side effect; they could do nothing but give him more meds. But the meds made him angry, and sometimes violent. It was one of the reasons he tried to lock himself away.

"How much was this small fortune anyway?" I asked, trying to change the subject.

"Small fortune?"

"The one you have locked away from the Irish pig and his rat family."

"Mel..."

"Don't 'Mel' me with a razor at your skull, Orlando. I have another use for it and it's not going to be wasted on those people."

"What could you possibly want to do with that money that you can't do now?"

I met his eyes in the mirror and just smiled.

I was going to do what he didn't think I could. I was going to make us a force to be reckoned with again. I was going make sure we had the monopoly on cocaine and heroin. I was going to make sure we didn't need any Callahan and damn well no Valero.

"I don't trust that look in your eyes." He frowned, watching me carefully. Even drunk, he was still trying to read me.

"Why, because it reminds you of the look in your eye?"

"No, because it reminds me of your mother. I always knew a storm was coming when I saw that look." He pointed into the mirror at my brown eyes and I just smiled.

Grabbing the towel he had left on the desk, I wiped the leftover cream from his head and kissed it. "I have to go, Orlando. Get some rest."

Taking the razor with me, I left him sitting there, with the rest of his hair lying on the cold marble. Walking back out into the closet, I locked the door behind me before leaving. It wasn't the only entrance to his room. There was a back door into the gardens where the doctors came and went, but he wanted this door locked, so I obliged him.

"Fiorello, just the man I needed to see." I smiled, stepping out into the hall.

"Is there a reason why you're in the closet, ma'am?" he asked, but he already knew why. The walls had ears and the maids would talk. They always talked.

"Never mind that. My father has money in holding for me."

"Ma'am..."

"Don't lie to me, Fiorello. I need to know how much and where it is. After all, I'm fighting for my life here."

He fought the wrinkled grin trying to creep onto his face. "And how will seven million dollars do that?"

Seven million dollars was not a small fortune; it was a large one and just enough to pay off debts along with procuring a few dozen kilos of cocaine.

"You two." *I pointed to the men just standing in the hall. Walking up to me, they stood straighter.* "Yes, ma'am."

"Names."

"Fedel Morris, Gino Morris's son, you were the one who—"

"Stop talking," *I snapped at him before facing the other one.* "You?"

"Monte..."

"A Beau Brooks. Get me everything you can on him, stalk him if you have to. Find out who his dealer is and then make him mine with whatever force necessary. Are we clear?"

"Yes—"

"Then why are you still standing here?"

They looked at each other for a moment before turning to leave.

"Look at you," *Fiorello said.*

"There's nothing to look at because you have a bank to call. So why aren't you doing that?" *His eyebrow raised before he bowed and left.*

LIAM

She left the hospital so quickly, I swear she left a trail of smoke behind her. I knew Declan's announcement would affect her, but I wasn't sure how. What was going through her mind right now? She couldn't have been thinking clearly; if she was, she wouldn't have left without telling anyone. She'd grabbed the keys to the Range and drove off and I couldn't call her because I still had her damn phone.

She was going to drive me insane, I could feel it. I was just going to lose it and murder her one day. If it weren't for the damn GPS in the car, I would have been fucking ready to call in the National Guard.

It didn't take long for me to notice her when I pulled up to the remains of what used to be the Giovanni Villa; her old home here in Chicago, the place where I first met, and was shot by, her. She sat on a pile of old rusted pipes, just staring, completely oblivious to the world around her. Parking right next to her car, I grabbed the water bottle. The moment I stepped out, a gunshot went off and I dropped to the ground. She just broke out in laughter.

"Have you lost your damn mind?" I yelled at her, looking at the hole in the car door.

"Stop stalking me. I wanted to be alone!"

"Then use your fucking words! You could have killed me!"

"Stop being melodramatic," she said. "I knew I wasn't going to hit you. I'm a better shot than *you* are." She sighed, looking up at the stars.

Fuck that, she can get dehydrated for all I care, I thought, throwing the water bottle back into the car.

"Hey, wasn't that for me?" she asked, watching as I came over to her.

"No, that water was for the wife who doesn't shoot at me," I replied, glaring at the glock in her hand.

She frowned. "How many wives do you have, Mr. Callahan?"

"As much as I love this banter of ours, what are you doing here, Mrs. Callahan?" I didn't understand why she didn't just rebuild it. After the home was burned down, she wouldn't allow anyone to touch it. It was nothing but rusted scrap metal, broken china, and a few walls fighting to stay erect.

"Did you know it was here I decided to fully join—run the family business?"

"No, I wasn't aware you spent much time in Chicago." I wasn't sure how I would know.

"I usually came for two reasons: my father had business to attend to, or he had a doctor's appointment."

"There were no doctors out in California?"

"There were, you ass," she said, rolling her eyes at me. "However, Dr. Anderson was here. I never knew why they had such a bond. But he was the one who helped deliver me, so I'm guessing he never told the police that Orlando made sure Aviela didn't leave. Loyalty was a big thing to him, yet he held none. He told me once, with his hands around my throat, only ever be loyal to myself. To only love myself."

"He put his hands around your neck?" Now I was more than glad I put the needle in his arm.

"Calm down, macho man. My father didn't abuse me, it was the cancer talking. While he was on chemo, he would get so violent, so cold. He was dying, and because of that he didn't want to take it. We would have weekly fights about it. He locked himself away so he wouldn't flip out on me. And when I was seventeen, I was ready to walk away. I was done. I was tired. I had gotten into UCLA, my father was almost near bankruptcy and people were jumping ship faster than we could blink."

"And you turned it around." Everyone in our "world" believed that it had been her father who had breathed life back into the Giovanni name once more. She was amazing.

As she smiled up at me, her eyes glazed over with a look I knew brought only trouble. "You want to know how?"

I wasn't sure.

"Ok?" I replied, taking a seat next to her.

"My father had money stashed away for you." She laughed, running her hands through her dark hair. "He was worried that you wouldn't marry me if I had no money, and worse yet, no power. He kept a black book of every judge, police officer, and politician that were indebted to the family. Not to mention a few stretches of weed fields down south. I was so pissed when I saw it. First off, I am worth way more than seven mil."

"Yeah, *now*," I joked, to which she just lifted her gun at me.

"Seriously?"

I couldn't help but laugh. "So you took my seven million and...?"

"I took *my* seven million and bought product through one of Beau's associates."

"Beau? As in Officer Brooks?"

"Yep, he was just a poor beggar when I met him. I still don't know if he was a junkie or not."

"What is with you and bums? First Jinx, now Brooks?" She sure liked strays. Hopefully that was out of her system.

"I'm not going to ask how you knew about Jinx, because I may shoot you." Her brown eyes narrowed in on mine. It made me want her more when she looked at me like that.

"Anyway, Beau knew a soldier in South America smuggling it in. I offered him a job, he offered me everything he had: connections, workers, smugglers. In return, I gave him a way out. Apparently, he had two kids to feed and he didn't want to be a drug dealer all his life. Seven million was enough; I owned it all, and the moment I did..."

"The Gold Rush," I whispered, grinning. "You were behind the gold rushes. It damn well pissed the shit out of Dad. Every junkie and dealer in the goddamn country wanted only gold rush. You sold it cheaper and stronger than we ever could. We were bleeding money and we had no idea who was behind it."

My father had damn near went mad searching for the source of her shit.

"Seven million became twenty eight million in the first month. By the end of that summer, I had stopped the bleeding, and all those rats who left us came running back."

"I'm sure you had a field day with them." Rats had no loyalty after all.

"Fiorello took care of them." She laughed and shivered, not because of the cold air, but at something I clearly didn't understand.

"Fiorello?" I asked her, placing my jacket over her shoulders.

She stared at it for a moment, then back at me before nodding, stretching out her legs in the rubble. "Our head butler. The day you came, he most likely bowed."

"Ah, the guy from *Downton Abbey*."

"Yes," she rolled her eyes. "To celebrate, I invited all the men for a large banquet at this very villa. A video was played from all the men who left. To prove their loyalty, they were supposed to shoot themselves. None of them did and so I had snipers do it. The rest of them were warned by Fiorello."

"You didn't want Fiorello with you when you moved in?"

She frowned once again and I hated it. "No. He wouldn't have come, and I wouldn't force him. He stayed for my father and after my father died, he went back to Italy. I found out Brooks had applied for the force but was rejected a year before he came to me. Part of me believed he could bring my family down and get the credit if he joined. Still, I used my father's black book, cashed in a few favors, and he was in; my personal mole, working the Chicago police. It took me years, but I did it. Even after the Valero burned down our fields, the Giovannis were still on top. After the gold rush, the feds were on the hunt anyway, so I focused on the crystal and heroin."

"And Coraline's..." I couldn't even bring myself to say it. It was so odd. She was good. She tried her best to be as tough and as bad as us, but she was too good. I liked that about her.

"And Coraline's illness brought it all back. It made me wonder how things would have been if my father never had it. Would I have gone to UCLA? Who would I be?"

"A cute, sweet, college graduate, most positively still married to me. My life sure as hell would have been easier."

"You really want me to shoot you, don't you?"

Laughing, I pulled her to me, wrapping my arms around her. "I can see it. You would actually be as innocent as you look."

"All I see is you walking all over me and bending me over for sex like your personal plaything." She pushed back, clicking the safety on before putting the gun away.

Watching her handle her gun made me want to bend her over now. This wasn't the place. The last thing I needed was for her to get sick again, but the car...

"Why are you looking at me like that?" she asked, to which I just grinned.

Leaning over, I grabbed her legs and picked her up bridal style.

"Liam fucking Callahan, put me down right now!"

"Not until I bend you over in the car. Of which you owe me a new one anyway!" I smiled.

"You stupid, Irish brute!"

Twenty-Seven

*"Everything Dies. That is the law of life-
the bitter unchangeable law"*
—David Clement-Davies

Declan

Up the halls, down the corridors, in circles, I ran. She just upped and left, not bothering to speak to a nurse or even text me. I had no idea where she was or where she was going, and what pissed me off the most was the fact that it was my fault. I never should've left her alone, but I just needed a goddamn second to breathe, to gather the broken pieces of myself. I should have been with her; I should have never left her side.

"Declan?" My father grabbed hold of me in the middle of the lobby, but I couldn't meet his eyes. I just stared at all the faces passing me by, some in snow white coats, others in blue scrubs, but most of them were just visitors wandering about. None of them were Coraline.

Where was she? Damn it, where was she?

"Declan? Son? What's wrong? Speak to me." He shook me like he did when I was child, forcing me to meet his eyes. They looked just as tired as mine. I wouldn't be surprised if I now shared the wrinkles he now wore.

"Coraline. She's gone. I don't know where she went. The nurse said she checked out." She'd checked out without me, without anyone in the family.

"Son, she's at the church down the street. I had Monte follow her...."

I didn't even wait for him to finish speaking before I broke out of his arms, rushing out the automatic double doors and into the blaring streets. I had no idea what street I was on, my mind was coming undone every moment she wasn't next to me.

The church my father spoke of was in sight, farther down the road. Pushing through the crowd, I did my best not to run, to stay calm and to think of what I was going to say to her. With each step that brought me closer to the looming brick cathedral, I felt the words drip out of my brain and disappear into some gutter.

I wasn't sure what to say. I must have been going out of my mind. Like a madman, I'd been running all over the damn hospital, calling her phone over and over again. Now I was standing outside of the intimidating wooden doors of Saint Margaret, unsure of what I could possibly say to her.

Mind went back to the first time I had met her. I was entering Eastside Diner to escape the monsoon that was pouring over the city. The moment I saw her run in, out of breath, dripping wet, and laughing like a madwoman, I found myself unable to look away from her. She had this presence about her and it drew me in.

It felt like a lifetime ago.

Sighing, I grasped the church door and pulled. As the door swung open, I saw her. She stuck out like…well, like a drunk in a church. She sat in the candle lit cathedral with her legs propped up on the pew, and a bottle of vodka in her hand. Not a soul dared to rear their heads. Blessing myself, I walked the aisle, my feet echoing as I hurried to reach her. She didn't even look up. She just drank.

"I called you," I whispered to her.

"A lot of people called me. I threw my phone out the window." Again, she put the bottle to her lips.

That was rational.
"Okay."
"Okay."
I was waiting for something…anything. For her to break down like before, maybe even scream, but instead, she sat comfortably in the second row staring up at the cross hanging over the sea of candles.

"Coraline, talk to me. Please."

"I don't want to talk. I just want to drink."

"Coraline…"

"You want to talk? Talk to God. Ask him why he's such a dick. Why does he give with one hand and then slap you across the face with the other?"

She got up from the bench and stumbled forward. I reached to help, but she simply pushed me away, spilling some of the vodka over her hand and over me. Ignoring it, she continued moving towards the altar.

"Did you know only four percent of women diagnosed with ovarian cancer are my age?" she asked. "Slap one. Thanks, Big Guy!" She laughed, drinking at the foot of the cross. "I have stage two, which means both of my ovaries are shot! Because, why the fuck would I need ovaries, right? Oh, and so is my uterus. It's not like I haven't been dying for a child anyway. *Dying*, funny, *Big Guy*. You're just hilarious!"

"Coraline—"

"Stop Coraline-ing me! Damn it! If I live…"

"You *will* live!" I wanted to grab her, but she kept pacing away from me. Watching her pace like that was driving me crazy.

"Yeah, because you're an almighty Callahan. You see all, know all, *are* all, right? Every one of you walks on water! You all can do as you please and God simply looks away! Olivia is right, he's picking favorites, but what else is new?

We thought we caught it early, well we were wrong! I was wrong…so wrong…I thought I was pregnant. What kind of idiot thinks they're pregnant? How did I not know? I didn't see the signs until I was too far gone! How did I not notice?"

She tried to drink, but her bottle was empty. Rearing her arm back, she prepared to throw it, but I took it from her before she could. Pulling her into my arms, I just held her. I wasn't sure what to say, or how I could make her feel any better.

"You want to know the icing on the cake?" she whispered, leaning into me. "This church—the church down the block from the hospital—is named St. Margaret of Antioch. She was the saint of childbirth, pregnant women, and dying people…"

She drew in a sharp breath and it was as though someone had stabbed us both.

"You aren't in this alone. It's you and me. You and I have cancer. *We* have cancer. And I swear to you I will never leave your side, but I need you to fight this. I need you to come back to the hospital," I whispered, kissing the back of her head.

"I can't. I can't do the chemo. I can't knowingly inject myself with poison, lose all my hair, let my bones become brittle, not to mention…I can't, Declan. I just…"

"You can, because I can't live without you. I can live without a kid—I truly can—but you…you are not up for debate. You stay for as long I stay, and I plan to live for a long, *long* time. So please, for the love of me, come back and let's fight this bitch so we can get back to our lives."

She is the most important thing to me. She is everything.

Twenty-Eight

"Defense is our best attack."
—*Jay Weatherill*

LIAM

"How much is this one boy costing us?" My father sighed, smoking like a steam engine while leaning against my '69 Mustang.

I readjusted my gloves. "$58,378.23. But I paid a flat sixty just to get it over with."

God, I hate the cold. But what could I expect from a winter in Chicago? The past few months had gone by painfully slow, and now, here we were, standing outside and freezing our nuts off for a kid.

"I could think of ten different things to do with sixty grand, and none of them revolved around smuggling a boy over the border."

Sixty grand was like a grain of sand on a beach for us. He was just bored, so bored in fact, that the man had even taken up writing.

"You didn't have to come, Father."

"You are all out of brothers for the time being. I figured we could use the quality time now that you're weeks away from becoming a father yourself."

The biggest shit storm that had fallen upon us in the last couple of months was Coraline, and I could hardly blame her. She'd had a hysterectomy, and each day she looked at an enlarged Mel, she broke down. It was finally too much, and Declan took her back to the castle in Ireland. She still had months of recovery to go through, on top of another round of chemo. I would give them as much time as they needed. Declan wasn't just my cousin, he was my brother, and Coraline was his heart. Neal and Olivia, on the other hand, were one step behind dropping off the face of the planet. After their exile, he and Olivia only spoke to me when they had to while on the campaign trail. I did have to give them credit, they were finally good at something: being sock-puppets. They smiled for the cameras and made us all look good. In a few weeks, they would be home, and I would need to speak with Neal, but for now, I needed to make sure that all the hatches were locked down.

That reason was exactly why we were currently parked right outside the city, waiting under the bridge for my package.

"Are you nervous?" my father asked, handing me his cigar. I waved him off; it wasn't worth the hassle Mel would give me if I came home smelling of smoke. She was more than sensitive to it now.

"Nervous about what?"

"About your son. I understood why you and Mel didn't want to talk about it while there was still a chance she could lose him. Your mother and I have tried to give you both some time to let it sink in, but, we're both kind of shocked you haven't had more worries. Neither of you have even mentioned a nursery, nor did Mel want a baby shower…"

"She didn't want a baby shower because we both knew she would have snapped and killed every last one us." I could just see her now, a baby rattle in her hand, hammering away at some poor schmuck's skull. And that poor schmuck would have probably been me.

Mel and I had spoken about the baby; we spent most of our evenings talking about him. What we would name him, how we would handle our work and parenting. Mel didn't open up well to people. It had taken two years of marriage for her to even truly be open with me. Going to my parents was not something I figured she could do just yet.

"I know you and Mom want to be included more," I said, "but Mel's just not good with being personal, you know this. She's working on it and I can't push her. We're thinking of naming him Ethan Antonio Callahan."

"Ethan?" He grinned, turning to face me.

"Yeah." I grinned in return. "I wanted something Irish, and she told me to fuck off, that his last name was Irish enough. She kept reading off Italian names, I kept asking if it was a name of an appetizer or entrée. We went down a line of 'E' names and Ethan just popped out at us. Feel free to pass it on to Mother so she can start embroidering sweaters and monogramming silverware. Hopefully that will keep her off the baby shower thing."

"About that..." he trailed off.

"*Please* tell me you didn't. Please, for the love of God, don't tell me Mother is going forward with it." Pushing off the car, I turned to him.

He continued to smoke, trying his best to not meet my gaze.

"Are you kidding me? I'm doing all I motherfucking can to just make it through the next couple of weeks. She's going to think this was me."

"Aww, the poor Boss is afraid of his big, pregnant wife?" He laughed, throwing his cigar on the ground.

"Says the man who probably tried to talk his wife out of this and failed. And I'll let her know you called her big." As if he could stand up to his wife either. We were both fucked, and the moment I got the chance, I was throwing him under the bus.

"Your package is here." He nodded towards the van driving through the small creek towards us.

Peering up at the bridge, I spotted the guns waiting as the older van pulled up right in front of us. I hated dealing with human traffickers; they sickened me. The shit we did was of each person's own free will. We didn't hold the needle to their veins or the powder to their noses. It was all on their own accord. Traffickers were sick and they deserved everything that was coming to them, but they still knew how to get a body. And I needed this kid.

The four men pulled the small boy out of the truck. Both his hands were bound, a blindfold over his eyes. The poor kid must have stood at my hip. He fought and struggled against the men, with tears rolling down his face. They held onto the collar of his torn, filth covered shirt.

"I told you he was not to be harmed and that he was to be informed of where you were taking him," I said.

"He alive, ain't he? Lucky too 'cause we got another offer for him. It's gonna cost you another ten. Or we'll take him and walk."

Why people chose to test my patience was beyond me. It was like they wanted me to repeatedly prove I was willing to beat the shit out of them. My father glanced at me with a sickening grin on his face that could have only been matched by mine. I nodded and he knew what this meant.

"Let the boy go and you get the money we settled on, along with your arms," I said.

They smiled at each other before grabbing the boy again.

"No! No! *Déjame ir.* Let go!" The boy cried, trying to fight.

Sighing, I pulled at the stacks in my jacket and threw it at one of their chests.

"That's the half I owe you," I told them before throwing another ten towards him. "And that's the ten. Now hand over my package."

They were all enjoying the fact that they had just stiff-armed a Callahan. They dropped the boy like a sack of potatoes onto the ground. Walking over to him, I took off the blindfold and ropes.

"Who would have thought that the legendary Callahan had a thing for exotic young boys?" one of the men said. "We can make this a continuing business venture."

"Hold on a second," I said before looking down. "You are safe. *Estás a salvo*," I whispered to the boy on the ground. His brown eyes were wide, shaken, and nothing but a reflecting pool of fear. I enjoyed the look on adults—on *men*—but for children who didn't even have all their teeth, it pissed me off.

"I'm taking you to your mother," I said. "I promise, take a seat in my car." He looked at my father then back at me.

"You take me to my mama?"

"I promise."

Nodding slowly, he took my hand and walked the three feet back to my car, my father simply opened the door for him and used his body to shield the window. Our eyes met right before I took off my jacket, throwing it on the hood and allowing them to see the two guns at my back. He simply pulled out another cigar, the man was always packing.

"What the fuck is this, Callahan?" They yelled, unleashing all their guns as two of my cars boxed us in. One by one, my men came out, guns all pointed at them.

"This, my friends, is what happens when you try to cheat me. When you insult me. Each one of my men is just itching to take your heads off. I would suggest you drop your weapons."

Their dark eyes gazed over at the nine barrels pointed at their faces before letting gravity take hold of their guns; they dropped them at their feet, holding their hands up in surrender.

Crossing my arms over my chest, I stared at the last man on the right, still holding my money in his hairy hands. Reaching out, the little man handed me all of it before heading back in line. Strolling over to my jacket, I dropped the money and started to whistle. I pulled out my knife and gun before turning back around.

"Strip," I demanded.

"Fuck y—" Before he could finish, I threw my knife right into his nose. His body fell back as he suffocated on his own blood, desperately gasping for air, crying in pain until he couldn't cry anymore.

The rest of them started to take their clothing off.

"I have no respect for you pigs, but I was willing to let that slide for business. Then you come to me, late, ungrateful, and disrespectful. It hurts me." I sighed, loading six bullets into my revolver slowly. I enjoyed watching them panic while I did this. "And when I hurt, somebody else gotta feel my hurt. It's what makes my world go 'round."

Smiling, I shot at the first man in the groin. He screamed so loud I'm sure he popped a vein in his neck.

"Do you feel the world spinning?" I grinned.

Melody

I feel like an obese Jackie Kennedy.

I sighed, fixing the stupid red hat on my head right before Fedel and Monte opened the door for me.

The moment my foot crossed the line and the door shut behind me, I was in enemy territory, and I stuck out like a middle-aged man on spring break. Every badge turned towards me, some wide-eyed, others standing up straighter and fixing their ties. I felt like I was on display, but that was the point. That's why I'd worn this polka-dot coat with the gloves and hat. I wanted every damn officer in this department to notice me as I stepped into their house.

"Can I help you, Mrs. Callahan?" A young, blonde officer asked, stepping up quickly.

"You know who I am?" I smiled.

"Everyone knows who you are, Ma'am. Your *husband's* name is on just about everything 'round here. May I help you with anything?" I didn't like the way he referred to Liam, there was an edge at the back of his voice, but I wasn't Mel right now. I had to be Melody Callahan, sweet wife to a fat cat Chicago millionaire. It had been a while since we had taken down the First Lady and everything had been quiet. Too fucking quiet. And with the election around the corner, I was making sure that there would be no more surprises this November; we were in the home stretch.

"Yes, Officer…"

"Officer Scooter."

"Well Officer, I'm looking for a Ms. Morales. She was a maid in my house. I haven't been able to reach her for some time and I'm quite worried."

His whole body language changed. His arms went to his waist, and his expression, along with his jaw, hardened. "Well, Ma'am, there ain't any need to be worried. Other than being jobless and without her son, she's just fine. Due to the recent events with the President, we are keeping our witness under protection."

Did this fucker just try to backhand me under-handedly?

"I only recently learned about her losing her job," I said. "If you could please let her know she can have it back once this has all died down, I would be grateful." *And I won't slit your throat.*

He frowned, looking me over carefully before glancing over to Fedel and Monte. "A lot of muscle you have there just to see a maid. I'm sure you people can find a new maid in a jiffy."

"Who, them?" I pointed to Fedel and Monte. "My husband is so paranoid sometimes, and now that I'm pregnant, he's just gone bonkers. Ms. Morales has been working for us for years. She's been trying to bring her son over. When I heard my sister-in-law fired her, I felt horrible. She's not only done so much for us, but now she's stood against injustice, against the most powerful woman in the country. With that type of strength, I wish I could do more for her. I truly want to let her know that the Callahans are in her corner if she needs anything. You can do that, right officer? I'm not breaking some super-secret police code, right?"

"Yeah." He nodded. "I'll have it passed along once she testifies tomorrow."

"Thank you, Officer Scotty—"

"Scooter."

"I'm so sorry. I'm horrible with new names. It's pregnancy brain. Can you believe I'm almost eight months already? Well, I'll be off. Thank you again." Reaching out to take his hand, he smiled as he shook mine.

"You too, Mrs. Callahan. Congrats on the Senator's win."

"He hasn't won yet. The election isn't for another three weeks." Or did he have a crystal ball up his ass?

He shrugged. "Everybody knows now that the First Lady is out of the picture, your man is about to become the leader of the free world. You Callahans always have the best luck. How do you all do it?"

He wants to do this now?

"We're just blessed, I think. Good things happen to good people, right? I still can't believe all that mess with the First Lady."

"You know," he laughed, "there's this crazy rumor going around about how you were all connected in this somehow. That this was all part of your husband's master plan to get his guy in the White House for his own agenda. The First Lady said she had help, but she didn't know the woman's name. What do you think about that?"

He was pushing the wrong hormonal woman right now.

"Should I...call my husband or my lawyer or something?" I asked him, rubbing my stomach.

Before he could speak, Brooks walked up beside him. "Mrs. Callahan? Is there anything I can do for you? I'm so sorry, none of us knew you were coming in today."

"No, Officer...?"

"Brooks, Ma'am. Your family helped pay for my old partner's injuries from that Chicago factory fire last year." He reached out and shook my hand. The moment his rough hands met mine, I squeezed before letting go.

"Please, don't thank us or apologize. I'm the one who came unannounced. I had some information I wanted to pass on to Ms. Morales. But Officer Scatter…"

"Scooter."

"Right." I blushed. "Told me he would handle it. I really should get going before my husband calls searching for me."

Before I could leave, the golden haired fucker had to get the last word.

"I'm glad to see the rumors of you marrying a Callahan for power were all false. You both seem very happy."

Biting my tongue, I forced myself to smile once more. "All these rumors. No wonder you all can't bring down the crime rate. It seems all you do is gossip. Good day."

Monte opened the door to the street as the car pulled up onto the curb. I wobbled slowly down the stairs with Fedel hovering behind me. They all did that, and now that I was showing so much, I couldn't even get out of bed without help. Sliding in, I took off my hat, throwing it against the seat.

"That no good motherfucking cocksucker! I want his head! I want to beat the shit out of him until his neck snaps and then drop him over a damn canyon!" I yelled, breathing through my nose as I rubbed circles on my stomach.

"Ma'am, please. Mr. Callahan—"

"I swear on your head that if you tell me to calm down out of fear of my husband, Fedel, I will remind who I am— baby or no fucking baby. Do you understand me?" Liam had all but drilled into their minds that I was in need of not only a bodyguard, but someone to keep me calm.

He nodded, glancing over at Monte as if to say: *you're up.*

"Would you like me to handle the officer, Ma'am?" Monte looked back at me.

"No." I wanted to be the one to take care of that self-righteous prick. But he couldn't die, not yet. "I want eyes on him at all times. I don't want to deal with another wannabe hero cop. Right now, I'm more worried about making sure this plan works."

"Ma'am, why go through all this trouble for a maid?" Fedel asked. "She hasn't said anything to the police in months." For some reason, his voice was just grating the fuck out of my nerves.

"We can't kill her if the police have her under protection, and killing her would only make us look bad. Aviela went through a lot to prevent us from winning the White House, and in a matter of weeks, we will have eighty-seven percent of the electorate. There has to be backlash for that, and we don't want them using the maid against us. So we have to keep the only leverage we have: her son. She can have a job and her child, that is just as good as buying her off. Aviela can't get to us through her."

"But will he let the maid know?"

Grinning, I nodded and stared out of the window. I waited for the phone call I knew would be next. When Beau had called informing us about his partner's ambition, we'd figured it was best to kill as many birds as possible with one bullet. We would prevent Aviela from taking any action against us through the maid, make sure she couldn't kill the maid, and now we had given Officer Scooter a damn bone.

"Ma'am, Beau's on the line." Monte turned, handing me the phone.

"Put him on speaker," I whispered, rubbing circles into my stomach as I closed my eyes. I really wanted to take a hot bath and unwind; the pains in my ankles were a nuisance.

"You're on," Monte said to him.

"Ma'am, you were right, Scooter wants the maid to go undercover at the house after she's testified. He's running it past the Chief now. Should I—"

"Help them anyway you can, Brooks. Goodbye."

"Oh shit." Fedel stated forcing me to snap open my eyes. They both stared out the windows with their mouths hanging open before Fedel met my eyes in the rear-view mirror.

Looking out, I felt myself starting to hyperventilate. There on the Callahan's giant entryway was a massive blue sign draped in ugly birds, rattles, and cribs.

"Please tell me that doesn't say what I think it says," I hissed, my nostrils flaring as we drove.

I stared at the onslaught of cars swarming like an invasive species in our driveway. All the damn women from Evelyn's monthly charity functions were there with their fake Stepford wife smiles, and big boxes with obnoxiously large bows. It was like they were walking in slow motion with the wind blowing their hair back and their laughs reaching my already frayed nerves. Jesus Christ, it was a whole other level of hell!

"I'm going to bloody kill her. Chop her into little bits and sprinkle her over fucking Lake Michigan." I couldn't believe—well, I could believe she would do this, but damn it all. "Is there any way to get to the garage?"

"No, Ma'am," Monte said. "All these cars are in the way, and she's spotted us." He nodded over at the woman dressed all in blue, waving and smiling at all the other women I knew she hated as she made her way over.

I could handle a lot of things, but a crazed mother-in-law was not one of them. But I couldn't hide out in the car like a bitch. Damn her.

Dear God, give me the strength not to kill anyone.

Stepping out, I was met by one of the plastics with the fakest red hair I'd ever seen.

"Oh my God!" she yelled and it sounded like she had cats trying to claw their way out of her throat. "Melody, you're huge! Are you sure you aren't having twins? My cousin totally, like seriously, thought she was only having one. I kept telling her, 'Sissy, you're huge! There has to be another baby in there somewhere!' And lo and behold, she was having *triplets*. You're just giant, how are you still in those heels of yours? I love Giuseppe Zanotti, but there is no way I could ever wear them while I was pregnant. Not at least with my first child, this is your first child, right? You and Liam must be so excited, a boy…" The moment her hand went to my stomach, I grabbed a hold of it as I stared into her eyes.

I wanted to kill her. She just kept yapping away. I didn't even know who the fuck she was, and she was talking to me as though we were best friends. I wasn't going to make it. Who did she think she was? Who did she think *I* was, that she could just come up to me like this?

"Melody, my arm." She winced, as she fucking should.

"Mel, dear!" Evelyn came over, pulling me into a one armed hug, effectively loosening my hand off the very lucky woman in front of us. "You and that pregnancy grip of yours. I swear she could make men cry without even knowing. Are you alright, Nicole?"

"Of course," cried the hyena, "I'm not some delicate little flower. I'm stronger than…"

"Thank you, Nicole. We will see you inside, we have great *wine*." That shut her up and sent her running like a dog with a fresh scent.

"Now Mel, before you threaten to kill me—" Evelyn said.

"We're beyond that, Evelyn. I'm now trying to figure out where to dump your body."

Sighing, she rolled her eyes before taking my arm in hers. "Mel, I know you hate this type of thing, but it's all I have. You have your empire, well this mine. I handle public image. I'm the reason why, if *God-forbid* you all need character witnesses, we have people to spare. My first grandchild is going to have a goddamned baby-shower and it's gonna be the best one in the state. There will be cake, there will be pictures, and there will be baby games. You will handle it out of pure love for me, Mel, because you have not seen me crazy yet. Once they are drunk enough, you can leave, okay?"

"I want Liam here. None of that all female bullshit," I replied, waving at a few more women as they stepped out of their cars.

"He's already here." She smiled, leading me to the door.

This would be the longest few hours of my life.

LIAM

Everything within the house was dripping in blue and white; blue and white chairs, blue and white crystal chandeliers, paints, gift bags. If you could see it, it was either blue or white. It had taken her six hours to pull this shit off while Mel and I weren't home. Which meant she must have been planning this for weeks, and my father kept his mouth shut until it was too fucking late.

There were more intoxicated housewives in my house than in all of Orange County; and they sat in one massive circle around Mel, in the midst of our living room.

"She's being...unlike herself," my father whispered beside me. We were prisoners, unable to move out of the room, but unable to get close to the damn circle. So all we could do was stand by the door with our tinted blue wine glasses and watch.

Mel laughed, pulling out yet another wool onesie, which would go great with the wool vest she had gotten before, along with the silk scarf, cashmere booties and the red fleece jacket. After all, newborns just love their fleece. Mel smiled and thanked them before looking up at me and showing the ridiculous outfit. All of them snapped their necks as they turned towards me, awaiting my approval; it was only when they weren't looking that Mel's brown eyes glazed over with rage. She was being tortured, but so was I; all I could do was nod and grin as well.

"How much longer must this charade go on? I have plans for us tonight," I whispered. Though now that my mother had sprung this on her, I doubted Melody would want to go.

"Until your mother has enough pictures to fill up half your child's baby book," my father answered. "What are your plans?"

Pulling out the tickets from my coat pocket, I handed them over to him.

"Bianca e Falliero by Felice Romani?" he read. "I wasn't aware you enjoyed opera. It's a beautiful one."

"I don't, she does. And since when do you know opera?" He had never once spoken about that hobby before.

He smirked. "I know all, son."

"Bull—"

"Who is this from?" Mel asked, searching the white box in her hands for a tag or card. No one answered, each of the women looking at each other commenting only on the wrapping.

"Were all the gifts wanded and hand checked by the men?" I asked my father, leaning off the wall when Melody's eyes met mine again.

"All of them were, including that one. I saw to it myself, though we didn't check for cards," he responded.

Each one of the women leaned forward, all of them dying to see what was inside. I, on the other hand, was not taking any chances.

"Can a father-to-be open one of the gifts? Or am I breaking some ancient tradition?" I winked at them, causing Mel and my mother to roll their eyes while the sane women giggled.

"Oh, I don't see why not. Right, ladies?" one of them said.

"Of course!" another answered.

"This is so sweet," someone else said. "You guys should take a picture. Right, Evelyn?"

Coming up to my wife, I kissed her cheek before taking the box slowly out of her hands. The whole thing was padded and soft when I lifted the lid. I mentally prepared myself for everything but what it was…

"Aww!" they cooed as I pulled out the white teddy bear dressed in the finest black suit a bear could have, along with a top hat and a small tommy gun in his hand.

"A little violent, but so cute," said another one of them.

"Liam, sweetheart. There's a note in the jacket pocket." My mother pointed and sure enough, right in front of its tiny red handkerchief was a little card that had only two words and a letter written upon it:

Love Mom

~A

"Thank you all for this," I said. "Honestly, our son is going to want for nothing. I'll escape back into my little corner now." They laughed. At least someone could laugh as I handed the mafia bear back to Mel.

She didn't look at me. Instead, she focused on the women in front of her, asking for the cake.

Stepping into the hall with my father, I did my best not to yell. Someone was going to die. I wasn't sure who, but I knew damn well it wasn't going to be my wife, my child or myself.

"There is a mole in my house. This is the second time she's gotten in. I want them found, *now*."

Twenty-Nine

*"Blood!...Blood!... That's a good thing! A
ghost who bleeds is less dangerous!"*
—*Gaston Leroux*

Melody

Sitting at my vanity, I couldn't tear my eyes away from the idiotic toy. My mother was like the Joker, playing mind games with people all while reminding us that she was always there, lurking. Somehow she had gotten this toy to me without appearing on any cameras and without alerting any of the men on guard. Liam had already taken it apart and stuffed it back together, there were no cameras or wires in it. It was just a toy. I didn't get it. Even with how fucked up I was, every time I looked down at my stomach, I felt my throat close up as I tried to fight back the emotions building their way up. He wasn't even here yet and I knew I would die—that I would do anything—for him. How could my own mother be so hell-bent on destroying me? Even with her issues with Orlando, I'd come from her, I was part of her, and she still wanted to kill me.

"You look stunningly beautiful," Liam said as he stepped up behind me, and met my gaze in the mirror.

I couldn't help but grin as I turned to face him. There he stood, not even a foot away from me, dressed in a full tuxedo, shiny black shoes and he'd even bothered to comb his hair.

"Where are we going?"

He had gotten me a brand new dress; long, blue, draped silk, chiffon, bustier with an internal bodice by Alexander

McQueen. It fit my stomach perfectly, and I knew that he'd had Adriana's help with this, but it was beautiful and a little grand for a normal night.

"The right response is *thank you, sweetheart and you look amazing as well.*" He pouted, trying to fix his bowtie.

Rising, I grabbed a hold of the tie myself. "With the exception of your hair, you look amazing. Now where the fuck are we going?"

"You have no idea how to do this either, do you?" He smirked, looking down at my failing attempt to tie his bowtie.

"Not even a little bit." I laughed, letting go. "But isn't that what good wives do? Fix their husbands' ties?"

"Is it? I think the fact that you can't tie a bowtie is charming." He kissed my forehead before looking into the mirror.

Crossing my arms, I simply stared at him for a moment. "You're laying it on thick, husband. And you haven't told me where we're going yet."

He sighed. "We're going on a date."

"Liam, I've told you—"

"You don't date. I know, but *I* date. And since marriage is about compromise, I'm going to ignore you."

"I'm sorry, asshole, but how is this a compromise?" I was not going to be steamrolled by him only hours after his mother's little stunt. Having a baby shower with women I didn't know and didn't like; I was still a bit ticked about it.

Rolling his eyes, he pulled out two tickets from his jacket and handed them to me.

"Bianca e Falliero." My eyes caressed each word slowly, like they couldn't believe what they were seeing, before I glanced up at him.

How did he know?

I loved this opera. It was the very first one I had ever seen with my father.

I wasn't sure what else to say, except, "You don't like opera."

"No." He leaned against my dresser. "That's why it's a compromise. Tonight, I just want you to enjoy yourself, not as a boss, but as yourself."

"They're one and the same, but thank you," I whispered. He really didn't understand how much this meant to me. I had to fight the urge to cry. What in the hell was wrong me?

"Shit. Ugh, these damn hormones!" I groaned, trying my best to stop my makeup from running.

Placing his hand on my waist, Liam pulled me closer to him, and all I could smell was warm honey and cinnamon. He didn't say anything, he simply held onto me as I held onto him. This wasn't the first time in months I'd cried over the smallest things in front of him. Crying wasn't something I liked to do. It was foreign to me and I preferred it that way. He didn't tell me it was okay, and he didn't bring attention to it. He just held me until I was calm enough, and then he never brought it up again. I was grateful for it. It made me feel more in control of myself, in control of my surroundings. It made me feel safe. *He* made me feel safe when I had never realized I needed to.

"Liam?" I whispered.

"Yeah?"

"We have to go or we'll be late."

Laughing, he let go of me, but before I pulled away from him, I ran my hands through his hair a few times. I wasn't expecting him to moan, and lean into my hands, but he did. It was like petting a lion.

"Don't ever comb your hair. I love it as it is," I whispered to him, pulling slightly and causing him to lick the corner of his lips as he stared at me; his eyes were glazing over with fire and lust. "I love you as is."

His chest expanded quickly before relaxing. It was like he was releasing a deep breath he never knew he was holding. Cupping my cheek, he brushed his thumb over my lips, which most likely smeared my lipstick but I didn't care. I could see the amount of control he was exerting. I could also see his cock throbbing against his black slacks, fighting against his zipper, wanting nothing more than to be freed of its fabric prison and embedded deep within me. His thumb graced my lips before going to my cheek.

"We should go," he repeated in a whisper. "We're going to be late." He pushed himself off of my dresser and stared at his fingers on my skin. He seemed memorized by the trail he was making from my face to the valley of my breasts.

"That only depends on how fast we are," I whispered back, grabbing hold of his hand and kissing his palm before turning around.

"Jesus fucking Christ, Mel." He moaned, lifting my hair with one hand and cupping my breast with the other. Kissing down my neck, he squeezed my breasts, palming them almost reverently.

"Hmmmm…" was the only sound I could form once his hand left my chest, moved to my thighs, and slowly lifted up my dress.

"God, I love you," he whispered, biting my ear.

Reaching behind me, I pulled at his pants. "Liam, I need you right now."

"With pleasure." He gasped, pushing my hands away and quickly undoing his pants.

Bracing myself on the edge of my vanity, he wasted no time grabbing my hips, and rubbing himself against my ass before he buried himself within me with one swift thrust.

"Ahh!" I moaned, my mouth dropping open. The mirror in front of us added to my excitement, making me gush as I watched him dominate me. He also watched, with a wicked grin on his lips as he thrust deeper and deeper, one hand on my hip and the other in my hair. I could feel him throbbing inside me, filling me. It was fucking beautiful and I wanted more. Leaning down, he kissed my back, sucking hard on my skin.

"Fuck," he moaned, releasing my hair and hips, as he grabbed onto the dresser as well. He fucked me so hard that everything, even that damn bear, fell onto the ground.

"Liam…" I moaned, "I'm Ahh…fuck"

"Come with me, love," he whispered. "Ride it with me." He picked up speed. I couldn't even see straight, let alone speak coherently.

"Fuck, Liam!" Through squinted eyes, I watched as he came, his eyes rolled back into his head, his lips parted slightly to release a pleasurable sigh before his muscles relaxed.

"Great sex while pregnant, check." I gasped, totally fucked and happy.

"If this is just the pre-opera sex, I can't wait for the post." He grinned, as he slowly pulled out of me.

LIAM

God, she knew how to make a man crazy. My plan was simple: get her to the opera house, accept my award for husband of the year, spend the night in each other's arms and try to ignore the shit that had gone down at her baby shower. But the moment she said 'I love you', I couldn't control myself. I wanted her, and by God I was going to have her any way I could. Our sex life had been placed on the back burner for the last few weeks, but in one moment, one thrust, it came back with a vengeance and I wondered why we'd slowed down to begin with.

It took her an hour to hide the fact that we had just fucked like wild dogs before we could finally leave for the opera. Those who were lucky enough to get tickets would have to wait until we got there. After all, I was funding this production. The entire car ride over, her hands were squarely tucked into mine, but she wouldn't meet my gaze and I knew it was because she was processing. She was always processing, sometimes overthinking. She was used to being emotionless, cold as ice and yet, her walls were breaking. I could see it. And if I could tell, so could she. She was trying to find a balance between who she had been forced to be, and who she really was. She was forced to be, by all attributes, a ruthless sadist.

But the woman who sat beside me, leaning against the rail like a young girl in a candy store and watching the opera singers below belt out their souls was my real wife. Under her ice, under the screwing, fighting, and bullets, was a woman who held so many different passions. She looked completely amazed by the singers on stage; she smiled effortlessly. Even in the darkness of the booth, I could tell she was completely carefree.

She watched them, and I watched her.

"Love."

"Shh," she hissed at me, not even bothering to look up. "Contarino is offering his daughter, Bianca, in marriage to Capellio, who is from a rival family in hopes to end years of feuding between their houses."

"It sounds like us."

That caught her attention. She glanced up at me, her delicate little brown eyebrow raised.

"Not exactly. Listen to her." She took my hand, leaning against the red chaise lounge in which we both sat up.

Breathing in deeply, I listened to the sorrow in her voice as she wept at her fate. It seemed as though she was begging the audience for help. However, my Italian was not fluent enough to understand a word she was saying.

"Why's she so sad?" I whispered.

"She's in love with Falliero, a military hero. Her song is called *Della Rosa Il Bel Vermiglio*," she replied.

I wasn't sure why she loved this so much. Part of me wondered if she had once loved someone else and was unhappy that she had to marry me.

"Liam, my hand."

I hadn't realized I was squeezing. "Shit, I'm sorry. Are you alright?"

"You think I like this because I can relate to it?" She shook her head. It was odd how she could read my mind.

"No," I lied.

Thank God we had a private booth.

Or else we would actually have to see all the dirty looks I know were directed at us.

"This was one the first plays my father took me to," she said. "I hated it up until he told me this was my, Aviela's, and his story. He told me he was Falliero, the lengths he had to go through to stop my mother from marrying the wrong man. Ever since then, every time I went to see it, I imaged them on stage acting out their lives."

"Do you want to leave?"

She didn't answer; her brown eyes widened as she stared down at the singers on stage.

"Mel? Love, what is it?"

She shook her head and pointed to the red curtain on the side of the stage. She shifted forward in her seat to get a better look. I followed her gaze, watching the small Italian actress dance around the two men pursuing her, but no one was there. Looking over to Mel, she sat back, her eyes void and completely glazed over.

"Mel…"

"I thought I saw her—Aviela—standing in the corner. She was in white and then she was gone. It happened so quickly."

Again I looked, and again I saw nothing. Luckily for us, the lights slowly brightened as we reached intermission and the curtain fell.

"You're leaving." I rose, pulling out my phone. She was here. I would find her, but I couldn't do that with Melody so close to danger.

She rolled her pretty brown eyes at me. "Liam, I'm not even sure I saw her."

"When have you ever doubted your senses? If you saw her, she's here. I trust you."

"Or it could be baby brain. I swear some of my senses have been totally…"

Her phone vibrated loudly in her in purse, cutting off the rest of her sentence. We both looked at each other before she pulled it out and of course the caller's ID was blocked. I reached for it but she simply pushed my hand away, answering herself.

"Mother dearest, was that you hiding behind the curtain?"

"You've made my job so much harder, Mel bear," Aviela's fake sweetened voice travelled through the phone. "You are not going to be safe anywhere."

"You would know, seeing as you're the one apparently stalking my every move." Mel replied.

"Enough of these games Aviela," I hissed into the phone. "Show me your face so I can bash it in." I wanted to do more than make her unidentifiable, but unfortunately, she was still my wife's mother.

"*Correte lungo piccolo bastardino irlandese. Le donne stanno parlando.*" And with that, she was gone.

Run along, little Irish mutt. The women are speaking.

The fact that I knew what she said proved my Italian knowledge was increasing, and so was my temper.

Mel's jaw tightened as the lights dimmed and the voices that carried through the opera house drifted off into gentle whispers and then disappeared altogether. Scanning the seats below the stage, I searched for her phantom of a mother who came with no other purpose than to make our lives hell.

"Damn her for ruining this too," Mel whispered, rising from her seat and grabbing her coat. I held open the mahogany door to find both Antonio and Monte, dressed like they were part of the secret service, waiting on us.

"Ma'am, sir, is everything alright?" they asked, already reaching into their coats.

"Get the car, we're leaving. Be on guard, Aviela is somewhere nearby," Mel commanded before I could even get a word out. Even pregnant, she still demanded respect and radiated authority.

Drawing their weapons, we walked as quickly as Mel's belly would allow through the draped corridors and down the grand blood red carpeted staircase that overlooked the front entrance. Monte walked two paces behind us, Antonio to the right of Mel and I right in front of her. The moment we exited the theatre, the wind blew past us as we stepped into the thunderously loud and frigidly cold Chicago night. Fedel pulled up so fast the tires skidded on the pavement.

Before he could even open the door, one single shot tore through the wind beside me and a spray of warm blood splattered across my face.

In that moment, my heart stopped. I turned and caught a glimpse of her bright brown eyes, widened in absolute shock as she went down. Blood drops seemed to hang in the air, time slowed, and for what felt like hours. I couldn't hear a thing, couldn't even remember how to breathe. All around her was just so much blood, like red wine spilling over a white rug, staining it forever.

It's not hers. It's not hers! My brain screamed, forcing me to move again to see past the blood. Blinking for what felt like forever, Monte and Fedel both shielded Mel as she sat up on her knees, blood soaking her dress and her hands.

The bullet had missed her. She had stumbled because of the weight of Antonio's body as it came down.

Fedel yelled, glancing back as the sirens descended upon us. "The police are on the way, sir. We need to go."

"We aren't leaving him on the fucking street!" Mel hissed, staring into the hole that was now between Antonio's eyes.

"Mel, it's not—"

"I said NO! And that was a motherfucking order," she snapped. "We aren't running, we aren't leaving him, and we are going to make that bitch pay!"

I kneeled beside her, not caring that the rapidly cooling wetness underneath me was blood. It seemed to be flowing out of him like a never-ending river. Neither of us spoke. I was grateful it wasn't her. When I watched her fall, when I thought she'd been hit, it was the worst moment in my sorry excuse of a life.

"Are you okay?" I whispered, and she glared at me as if I had asked her the dumbest question ever to leave a man's lips. I looked at her stomach. Her stomach spattered with stains of blood. It wasn't hers, but she had still fallen.

"He's fine. Monte caught me before I went down," was all she said before she tore her gaze from mine and back to the man I barely knew but owed everything to.

"The cops are here," Monte said, holstering his weapon and finally facing us. In his eyes a storm was brewing harsher than anything even Mother Nature could produce.

"What do you want us to do?" he asked, finally looking at me.

I glanced over my shoulder as four cars with stunning red and blue lights pulled up. The occupants didn't even wait for their vehicles to come to a complete halt before jumping out. I knew these were just the tip of the iceberg, the first of many public servants who I could only imagine were chomping at the bit to get some sort of recognition or in with the Callahans. Whether to try to use it for personal gain or thinking this would be their shot at law enforcement glory, only God knew.

"Give the police a statement," I said. "Then go drink on my dime. We grieve for our loss, and then we find this bitch and burn her alive."

It was all I said before the yelling began as they came to *save* us.

"Sir, Ma'am, come with us! We're clearing the area! Are you hurt? Do you need medical attention?"

All I wanted was a date, not the fucking flood gates of hell to open.

Thirty

"What strange creatures brothers are!"
~ Jane Austen

NEAL

"Another," I hissed, throwing back my shot. The bartender simply raised his eyebrow at me, shaking his head, yet he continued to pour.

What was he going to tell me? To go home—scratch that—to go back to my hotel room? With as much as I was tipping him, he'd better keep his opinions to himself.

"Well lookie here, if it isn't *the* Neal Callahan. Maybe this is my lucky night."

Fuck man. I sighed before turning to look at Archer White, the lead presidential reporter for fucking *TIME* magazine, a.k.a. a fucking pain in my ass.

"What do you want, Archer?" I sneered.

"One Pepsi."

"Pepsi? You pussy." I laughed.

He pulled out his cellphone, ready to start recording. "Can I quote you on that?"

"What the fuck is your problem? I'm not running for motherfucking office! Who gives a shit about what I say?"

"The people of the United States are losing democracy. Your father-in-law is running without any real opponent. He's basically won and that's without answering any real questions: women's rights, gay rights, global warming, war, economic relations, education…"

"I get it! Now go ask Senator Colemen, 'cuz I still don't understand why you're pestering me."

"You're his son-in-law, you've been on his campaign trail for months. You bought your wife a brand new diamond necklace the same day you went to a soup kitchen. You're a fucking prince, and your whole family feeds on greed. Have you ever worked a day in your life? All this money you people just suck down your fat throats—"

Snatching his neck, I pulled him up onto his feet. "Now that we're both standing, say that to my face you fucking—"

"NEAL!" Mina, my least favorite political strategist and leash holder, grabbed my arm, doing her best to pull me back. "Neal, we need to go now. No more drinks."

I let him go, but the asshole couldn't seem to shut his dirty fucking month!

"Do you have an addiction, Mr. Callahan?" he asked, rubbing his neck as he held his phone up.

Snatching it from his hand, Mina left a bill on the table. "Journalists used to be respected. They didn't stalk citizens, wait for them to drop then poke at them. You can quote me on that. Good night, Mr. White."

I felt like a child the way she dragged me from the bar. Her tiny olive toned hand wouldn't let go of my shirt until we crossed the ivory floors into the damned elevator. Of course my *master* suite would be on the 67th floor.

"Have you lost your fucking mind?" she hissed at me, her dark eyes burning with rage. "You could have killed him."

"No, I *should* have killed him. He didn't have any right to speak to me like that. I'm a fucking Callahan!"

"So what?"

"So what? Being a Callahan…"

"Being a Callahan doesn't mean shit here! It's about being a Colemen, being President. I get it, you're used to breaking the fingers of people who even look at you funny. But, like I said when you first joined the trail, you have to take the mud thrown at you, and you have to take it humbly. The big picture, remember? We're on the home stretch. Just keep doing everything you've been doing up until tonight."

"Yeah, you mean keep being a bitch. Thanks for reminding me, Mina. I'll just go iron my money suit now." I stepped onto my floor.

"That's all I ask." She shook her head as the door closed and all I could do was flip her off.

I wanted to flip the damn world off. Moving from the suite's living room, covered in pastel colors and generic paintings of flowers, I found myself at the mini bar.

"Don't you think you've had enough?" Olivia whispered, stepping out of the living room in her red silk robe.

"I'm not supposed to think, remember? I'm just the funny, supporting husband with the big wallet," I told her, popping open the champagne that was recently delivered.

"Why is this so hard for you? I don't get it. For weeks you've been brooding like a kicked dog!"

Of course she didn't get it; she never got it! "Because, I *am* a fucking kicked dog! My family exiled me to this damn position because I didn't know my place."

"Exile? You're in a fucking master suite in a five-star hotel! For once you're out on your own and you can't even handle that! You're a grown man, Neal. Act like one."

"Shut the fuck up! For the love of God, Olivia, shut up! It's my mistake to think you would get it, but you just can't. Family is everything! You have no brothers, no sisters and your parents hate each other. Of course you have no idea. You've never trusted anyone, you depend solely on yourself and it's why you're dying inside. You're dying for validation and love from people who really don't give a shit about you, who don't know you. But you prefer it like that."

"You're drunk, I'm going to bed before you damage our relationship any further."

"You do that." Was all I could say before falling onto the couch. Rolling around, I tried to make myself comfortable, but of course, the great five-star hotel couldn't get a couch that fit all fucking sizes. I found myself staring at the chandelier above, unsure whether or not I should go to her. I didn't have to wait long before a pillow landed on my face.

"Fuck you for making me too angry to sleep," she snapped before punching my arm.

"Aye! Stop it."

She didn't and I grabbed her hands, pulling her over the couch and forcing us both onto the ground.

"Olivia, Jesus, control yourself!" I yelled, pinning her arms across her chest.

"Get off of me, you son of a bitch! I'm dying for validation? How about you? You're dying for your little brother to love you, your father to respect you, for some meaning to your life. Well guess what? If you didn't give up your title as Ceann Na Conairte you would've had all of that and more."

I wanted to strangle her, but someone had to fucking knock on the door. Our eyes met before we both got up, fixed our clothes and rushed to the door. She gripped my arm, pulling me to her side before opening the door.

"Hi," she said so fake I fought the urge to roll my eyes.

The butler smiled back before handing her a letter. "From the Senator. Mrs. Callahan, Mr. Callahan."

"Thank you, and good night," Olivia said, closing the door before opening the letter.

"Your father does know we were only a floor beneath him, right?" And I was the spoiled rich kid?

"He's inviting everyone for breakfast before we head back to Chicago. Apparently we're done. Maybe now you can learn to smile again," she said before throwing the card at my face.

Grabbing it to make sure I wasn't dreaming, I wanted to do a little happy dance. I was finally going the fuck home.

Declan

I held it right next to the side of her face, waiting for her to look away from her copy of *Pride & Prejudice*. She was so immersed in the words of Ms. Austen that she didn't even look. It made me want to laugh. Instead, with one finger, I pulled the book down.

"Declan! Mr. Darcy was just about—" She froze when she saw the joint in front of her face.

"As you were saying?"

She smiled, taking the joint from my hand. "You spoil me."

"Someone has to." I laughed, sitting up on the bed and lighting it for her. Her hands shook slightly as she reached up to grab it. Taking a long drag, she laughed through a cough.

"Slow down or you're going to finish my entire stash."

"Ooooh boo-hoo. I'm legally allowed to smoke." She relaxed into the pillows behind her.

"Not in Ireland."

"Stop, you're killing my buzz."

Taking the book from her lap, I flipped to the page she was on. "Were you gushing about Mr. Darcy again?"

"Jealous?"

"Please, Darcy can't hold a candle to me. Look at this smile, these eyes." I posed for her. She stared at me through the smoky haze before laughing outright. "There goes my ego."

"You have a great head of hair too," she whispered, leaving the joint on the side table to run her hands through my hair. "I'm glad you didn't cut it for me."

The smile on my face fell when I met her eyes. Collapsing against the pillows, I reached up to the blue scarf that she donned on her head.

"You know I would have, right? I would have shaved off my eyebrows too."

Even though she grinned, I was serious. The last couple of weeks had been hard. Her mood swings, her pain, losing her hair. I wanted to do anything to help carry that burden. All I could do was just be here...I prayed that was enough for now.

"I'm sorry I was such a bitch yesterday," she whispered, curling up against me.

Wrapping my arms around her, I tried not to think about it. "You weren't."

"I was. I don't know what came over me. Just because I have cancer doesn't mean I get to throw my food at you. It hurt to eat and I wanted you to hurt—I don't know why—but I'm sorry. I love you."

Biting my bottom lip, I blinked a few times before brushing it off. "You're fine, baby. Those carrots were overdone anyway. Now can you explain to me why you insist on rereading this again?"

"It's a classic."

"There are many other classics."

"Listen Callahan, *Pride & Prejudice* is a timeless romantic classic that makes my toes curl. So no hating."

Pouting, I lifted the book with my free hand. "And I thought I was the only one that made your toes curl."

"Nope, you and Jane, but for different reason." I loved how she felt when she laughed against me. "Now read."

"Yes, ma'am." Flipping to my favorite part in the novel, I read: "There are few people whom I really love, and still fewer of whom I think well. The more I see of the world, the more am I dissatisfied with it; and every day confirms my belief of the inconsistency of all human characters, and of the little dependence that can be placed on the appearance of merit or sense."

Before I could blink, she was up and running toward the bathroom. I had learned the hard way that she hated when I followed her into the bathroom. We had screamed at each other way too much over it, so I forced myself to simply let it go. I waited on the bed, my feet restless against the floor, just wanting to leap forward if she needed me. It was a long ten minutes. But then she finally stumbled out.

"Do you need help?" I asked. Rising, she shook her head, and reached for the end of the bed. Hugging the bedpost, she took a deep breath but it didn't help. Her legs gave out from under her, but before she could fall, I caught her.

"Damn it," she whispered.

"You got farther this time. Baby steps, remember? You just got off the chemo," I whispered, hugging her to me as I sat back on the bed.

"I just want to be better already."

"You will. Just don't push yourself too much." I knew she wouldn't listen, but I would be here. Each and every time I would be right here reading whatever repetitive classic she needed me to. And if it meant having her by my side just a minute longer, I'd do it forever.

Thirty-One

*"Nothing thicker than a knife's blade
separates happiness from melancholy."*
~ *Virginia Woolf*

Melody

"Mrs. Callahan, are you sure you don't need a doctor?" Scooter, the know-it-all cop, asked me as I rested against our Range Rover.

The whole opera house had been cleared just a few moments ago, but none of the guests had left. The only thing more tragic than an opera was our real lives. With dogs, the pigs were there with their flashing lights, silver badges and yellow tape; all of them taking pictures of Antonio's body as he lay there, cold and lifeless. He wasn't supposed to die. My men died when I fucking said they died...at least if the world worked as it should.

"Mrs. Callahan?"

"We're fine, officer," Liam said. "I think it's time I took my wife home." He came to stand beside me.

"Mr. Callahan, if you have anything to add to this investigation—"

"Like I said before, we were leaving the opera when our bodyguard was shot," Liam hissed, opening the car door for me.

"That's what we're trying to get at. There is no reason for anyone to kill your bodyguard. That bullet may have been for you, Mrs. Callahan. This type of shot was the same used on the President." Scooter stood up straighter, as he grabbed hold of my car door.

"On the news they said that was the First Lady…" I started when he cut me off.

"It was, but she has an accomplice we have no information about. If you could just come down to the station, maybe help to find the connection—"

"You're a cop, not a detective, if you have any more questions for us, please contact our lawyer. Goodnight, Officer," Liam stated, helping me into the car before slamming the door closed. "Drive."

Fedel didn't need to be told twice. It felt odd leaving a man behind. Antonio had been with me for years—with Fedel for years. Antonio was a mentor to both Fedel and Adriana. I knew Monte must have called her. It wasn't the type of news you broke over the phone, but Adriana would want time to separate herself from us.

Next to me, Liam was so tense he felt frozen, and all I could do was stare into the darkness of the night sky. Chicago was used to death. I was used to death. Neither was I grief stricken nor was I in shock; I was just fucking angry. I felt powerless, and it was a feeling I wasn't familiar with. This was bad. We need to retaliate quickly or we would have anarchy. The reason our men trusted us and were loyal to us was for the simple reason that we were the biggest and baddest animals. Aviela was making us look weak. This has to end, I just wasn't sure how. How could she be so fucking good? How could she kill, get into our house, know where we were going? Who knew that much?

I sighed as we pulled to a stop in front of the house. When Fedel opened the door for me, I didn't even wait for Liam, or anyone else for that matter, to help me. Seeing Evelyn and Sedric along with Olivia and Neal all huddled in the middle of the foyer made me want to scream. I didn't want to deal with this shit right now.

"Thank God you're alright." Evelyn sighed, making beeline for my stomach as I took off my coat and handed it to the maid.

"That depends on your definition of alright, Mother," Liam stated, walking in and standing beside me. "May I ask what you two are doing back here?"

"We live here," Olivia snapped.

"Olivia…"

"Liam, I'm sorry, it's a force of habit. My father is done campaigning and is back in Chicago so we…"

Neal grabbed her hand, stepping forward in the hopes of shutting her up. "Declan and Coraline will be back in the morning. I figured you would want the family together before we get even with this bitch. Tell me what…"

I couldn't listen to them for another goddamn second. They were just so fucking idiotic, why waste my energy on the waste of space. Walking past them, I pretended they weren't even there while walking up the stairs. The bottom of my feet hurt like a bitch's ass at a BDSM club. All I wanted was my bed, but sadly I knew I couldn't go there just yet. I didn't usually go to Adriana's room. It was sort of beyond decorum, but what hell, I made the fucking rules. Pushing into her room, I knew wouldn't see her.

Her bed was made, every book she surrounded herself with was stacked around the room like erected monuments, and her curtains were closed. Breathing deeply, I walked over to her bed and grabbed every one of her pillows and threw them to the ground, creating a makeshift bed for me to lie on. I felt like a damn penguin, but it was the only way I could see her. The moment I was on my side, I saw her curled up under the bed, her eyes spilling tears she couldn't control.

This was Adriana. After everything she had been through, the only place she ever really felt safe was under the bed. It was a habit she couldn't shake after being taken.

"He asked me to marry him," she whispered, moving her hand so I could see the ring. Even in the darkness, I could tell it was small and forged into the shape of a teardrop. It was very much Adriana. "I told him I wanted to think about it. I told him I wanted to talk to you. But the truth was, I was scared. He told me to keep the ring, that it would help me think. I should have just said yes."

"We all know you would have. So did he." I smiled at her. Like me, she just wanted to be difficult.

She rolled her eyes, hoping to stop her tears but it didn't work. "I can't move. If I move, life continues on and I can't…I loved him so much."

"Then don't move," I whispered to her. The problem with loving someone that much was the fact that it hurt ten times more to lose them. Great love only equaled great pain eventually…that's why Liam was going to have to die after I did.

LIAM

"What number are you on?" Neal asked, stepping into my office.

Staring at the glass in my hand, I downed it quickly before pulling out another bottle from my bottom drawer.

"I'm not counting. What do you want?"

Sitting across from me, he sighed and pulled out two cigars. "I want to help you. I want to be your brother again. I've spent weeks on a campaign, being asked how it feels to be a Callahan, what we're like, what do I think about families on food stamps right after I bought Olivia another diamond necklace. Father told me that I would hate it; being without the family and having to actually pretend I give fuck almost drove me mad. Olivia ate it up. She loved it. We were like string puppets on stage dancing for everyone else; going where we were told, keeping our comments rehearsed, being the better fucking person to people whose necks I could snap off if I wanted to. Part of me had a hard time dealing with you as my boss, but I'd rather dance under your strings than anyone else's."

Staring at him for a moment, I handed Neal a glass and took the cigar. "Do you have a light?"

"As long as you don't tell my wife." He laughed, holding the flame at the end of it.

"At least you can lie to yours. Mel can sense smoke like a bloodhound. Truthfully, she knows me well enough that she just lets me slide on some lies for the sake of my pride." We both sucked in smoke.

"You've both come a long way from trying to kill each other." He had no idea how wrong and right he was. She still tried to kill me, except now it usually had us both naked. "What are we going to do about this Aviela bitch?"

"She's one step ahead of everything. We make a play, she makes one better. Any thoughts?" Because I was all out of motherfucking ideas.

He sat back, leaning against his chair and scratching the back of his head. "None. I don't get it. That shot… it was a fucking good one. It's the type of shot I aim to take."

"Get to your point."

"My point is, she could have easily killed Mel. Just like she could have after the accident. She had Mel in her crosshairs, so why didn't she?"

"That I understand." I wish I didn't, but I did. "She gets off on the physical torture. She poisoned Orlando for years. Now she's making sure her daughter lives in fear. I want to know her end game. There is a bigger picture here. What's going to happen when Colemen wins office? We both know it's going to happen, that's why you're home early. He has a ninety-one percent likelihood to win. That's higher than any test you've ever taken."

"Fuck *you*."

I grinned, downing the rest of my brandy.

"So? What do you want us to do?" he asked seriously.

Smoking, I thought about that for a moment before pulling out the phone in my pocket.

"Aviela called Mel right before she took the shot. I'm sure it's a burned phone, but still, look into it for me."

Dropping it on the table in front of him, I put out my cigar and stood.

"Yes, boss."

I didn't trust him as much I as I wished I could. Moreover, I didn't trust his wife. There was a rift between us that went beyond just our childhood. However, if there was anyone in the world able to gain my trust, it was him. After all, he was blood.

"Don't finish all my brandy," I directed before leaving. I hadn't seen Mel in over an hour and my hands were starting to twitch. Every damn lock had been changed for a second time, we had added at least twenty different cameras and now had men checking the grounds every hour. None of that extra security really gave me any peace of mind when it came to her.

"Mel," I called out when I entered our room. Our bed was still made. I had figured she would be asleep.

"In here," she yelled from the bathroom. Following the scent of vanilla and the soft glow of candlelight, I noticed her dress and shoes in a pile next to the door. The sight of her soaking in our bathtub—the mounds of her breasts covered with suds, her hair in a messy bun, strands sticking to her neck and her eyes closed—was almost enough to bring me to my knees.

"Stop staring. I would invite you in, but it's a little warm for you," she said softly, not bothering to open her eyes.

"Yeah, sure. You and I both know you want that tub to yourself." Rolling up my sleeves, I took a seat on the marble right next to the pearlescent tub, and rubbed circles onto her stomach. She took a deep breath, her breasts rising, before she relaxed into my hand.

"Antonio asked Adriana to marry him," she whispered. "I'm not sure how she's going to handle this, and I don't have time to help her...I don't know how."

"We can't. The only thing we can do is cut off the witch's head."

She smiled, her eyes only opening slightly. "Who gets what part? I want more than a pound of her flesh. One for me and one for my father."

"You've been reading *The Merchant of Venice* to him again, haven't you?" The kid was going to come out speaking old English.

"It beats you reading *Atlas Shrugged* any day."

"That novel is—"

"A vision of what the world could be, blah, blah, blah. Thank God you read it while I'm sleeping."

"Obviously you weren't in a deep enough sleep..."

Before I could finish, she splashed the water with her hands, soaking my face.

"Couldn't help myself." She laughed.

"You're lucky you're pregnant."

"Correction: *you're* lucky I'm pregnant because I would so easily kick your ass. Again."

"You beat me once."

"Once is all you need." She waved her hand over her stomach as if to prove her point.

I was too tired to even argue. Resting my head against the tub, we both sat in the calmness trying to unwind. But my wife didn't believe in rest. She was always thinking about work.

"How much did Roy pay us?"

Sighing, I didn't move. "We made just over 312 million, most of the money is going offshore, remember? Are you planning on taking the money and running?"

She shook her head and sat up straighter. "Nope, just thinking maybe we should go away when the baby is born."

"We have a few weeks."

"Actually, I think my water just broke."

"What!" I yelled, jumping up. "Are you sure? How can you fucking tell? You're in water!"

"Ahh…" she hissed, grabbing the sides of the tub. "I'm fucking sure, so stop panicking and help me out of this damn thing!"

Dropping a few towels on the floor, I grasped her arm and her waist, holding her to me as I pulled her out. I wanted to just lift her, but I doubted that I would be able to. Slowly, I walked her back into our room, and helped her onto the bed.

"Adriana packed a bag."

"Got it," I stated, running to her clothes. "Ahh shit, I just stepped on one of your fucking heels!"

"Liam, I need clothes, my soft sweats."

Glancing around the rows upon rows of clothing, I had no idea where the hell any of her shit was.

Grabbing the black pair, I rushed over to see her breathing quickly. Looking up at me, she stared at the sweats in my hands. "That's not the one."

"Does it really mat—"

"Your son is trying to push his way through my motherfucking vagina! I want my bloody grey sweatsuit!" she screamed, before taking a deep breath, and rubbing my hand onto her stomach.

I felt myself freeze. *She's in labor. Holy shit, my wife is in fucking labor.*

"Oh, please, please don't do this, Liam! Don't be that guy who faints! I need my clothes!"

Nodding, I ran back into her closet, avoiding her damn shoes, and pulling the suit off the hanger before rushing back to her. Kneeling before her, I pulled her pants up around her legs.

"Ah, this really fucking hurts," she hissed, grabbing hold of my shoulders as another contraction started.

"Just breathe, baby." Holding the sides of her stomach, we stared at each other, breathing until it passed.

Sighing and cracking her neck, she put on her jacket.

"Thank God for baby books."

"Dad," I said into the phone. "Listen, Mel's water just broke..."

"What?" he screamed before yelling for my mother. "Evelyn! Mel's in labor..."

"Pop, listen to me! I need a barrier around us as we get to the hospital. We're heading down now." I think he got me, but I couldn't tell with all the shuffling around the room.

"Of course you were going to come early and when I was exhausted," Mel whispered to her stomach. "As if I wasn't nervous already."

Taking her hands, I kissed the palms of each of them. "We're going to be okay. All of us are going to be okay, I swear."

She nodded, her eyes drooping slightly; the clock on the dresser beside us seemed to taunt us, as it flashed, *2:04 a.m.*

"I'm not ready for this. He's early, Liam. He can't be early because I'm not fucking ready. I can only do this when I'm ready," she whispered through deep breaths, as who could only be my mother, knocked against our door repeatedly.

"Liam? Mel? Are you okay? Can we come in? How far apart are your contractions?" My mother knocked like she was fucking SWAT.

"If there is any woman on this planet that can do this, it's you." I waited for her to nod before calling out to my mother. "We're good, come in."

"Oh thank Jesus!" she yelled, running in with curlers still in her hair, while wearing a pair of sweatpants I didn't even know she owned.

"ARGH!" Mel screeched through her teeth. "Can someone please get me to a damn hospital? No way in hell I'm having this baby here."

MELODY

"These endorphins better kick in hard when he gets here!" I screamed through another contraction before falling back onto the pillows. "It's been nine hours. I just want sleep, damn it."

"Shh, baby, I know," Liam whispered, dabbing the sweat off my skin.

Finally, I smacked his hands away. "Your fucking hands were what got me in this shit. The moment this is over, I'm cutting your dick off and buying pit bulls just so they can eat it!"

"Mrs. Callahan, we need you to relax—" said a nurse.

"Have you ever tried to relax with a head trying spilt your vagina? I have a nice vagina. A cute, tight, great vagina! Ask him, that's the reason why I'm like this. I'm trying to calm down, but again, there's a head coming through my fucking awesome vagina! Now, you people leave me alone, I want everyone out!"

I'd tried everything and the damn meds they were giving me weren't working. This was what you got when you spent years experimenting with different drugs. My body could eat epidurals for damn breakfast. They wouldn't give me more for the baby's safety and what I could say to that? Fuck it, I want meds. The doctors and nurses wouldn't leave, they just wrote me off as though I was just another bitching pregnant woman.

"Liam, I want them out. I need a second, please," I whined, covering my face with the blanket.

"Okay." He kissed my head before snapping at the doctor,

He ushered them out of our birthing suite. Our usual doctor wasn't here, so we were stuck with some random woman who kept probing me like we were on a damn date. I didn't look up. I just wanted the pain to stop.

He brushed my hair back as he spoke. "I know this is a dumb question, but how do you feel?"

"Scared. Tired. Frustrated, and so fucking tired," I whispered, leaning into him as he held me in his arms.

"You're doing great, love. It's almost over."

"How do you know?" I'd overheard the damn nurses say this could be another long one and that was only after hour eight. "I'm so done being pregnant, Liam. I swear to God!"

Before he could tell me some other placating bullshit, I clutched his hand as another wave of aching rushed through me. I clenched my teeth together so hard I thought they would break; I couldn't even hear myself scream.

"Mrs. Callahan? What are you feeling?" The doctor yelled, rushing back in with a new pair of gloves in her hands.

Staring at her for a moment fighting the urge to rip her head off. What the hell? I was feeling pain! What kind of motherfucking question was that?

"Pain. I want to push," was all I could bring myself to say.

She checked my dilation with one hand as she used her other hand to push against my stomach "I'm sorry, Mrs. Callahan. You can't."

Fuck.

"How are her vital signs?" she asked, turning to the male nurse next me.

"Her blood pressure is elevating with each contraction, but not going down."

"What the hell does that mean?" Liam snapped, pulling away from me for the first time since we had come into the suite.

She looked at the number on the monitor as she listened to my stomach for a moment, then the doctor shook her head. "We're going to have to do a cesarean, Mr. and Mrs. Callahan."

"You want to cut her open." Liam shook his head, as he pinched the bridge of his nose. He glanced at me helplessly, and I could see the worry in his eyes.

"Your baby isn't positioning himself right, and your blood pressure is rising. This is the safest way for you and your child—"

"Then do it," I demanded, taking Liam's hand. "If it's the safest way."

Nodding at her, Liam kissed the back of my hand as he sat beside me. "You're going to be fine."

"Okay, we're going to prep you..."

I just tuned her out, and focused on the lights above me. I relaxed slightly at the feeling of the cold towel Liam was using to blot my skin. Everything just had to be so fucking complicated, damn it.

"Mrs. Callahan, I'm the anesthesiologist, Dr. Meroe. I'm going to give you something to make sure you feel nothing, but you'll still be aware enough to greet your bundle."

I wanted to speak but I couldn't. I was too tried, and all I could do was nod and fight back the nervousness building at the base of my throat.

"Can you feel that?" Liam whispered, staring down at my stomach, his eyes glistening with...something...as he watched me.

"Believe me, if I felt it, you would know," I said, trying to readjust myself.

"Okay, Mr. and Mrs. Callahan. Your son is going to be here in a few seconds..."

"Seconds!" My head snapped to the side, but I couldn't see anything. Hands gripped me and loosened just slightly. There was a tug, and a lot of pressure, then nothing.

"Here we are," the doctor cooed from behind her mask as a soft cry—my son's cry—rang throughout the room.

I felt myself take in a deep breath just as Liam did, biting his lips and trying his best not to let the water building under his eyes to fall. There he was, a bundle of blood and fluid, wailing.

"Would you like to..."

"Yes," Liam answered, cutting her off and taking the pair of scissors. I didn't realize I was crying until I had to wipe my face, as I watched Liam cut the cord.

Our son's little hands were waving everywhere.

I held my arms out for him, and the moment he was in them, I knew I never wanted to let him go.

"Hello..." I cried, kissing his head, "I'm your m...mo..."

"She's your mommy." Liam finished for me as he kissed my shoulder. He stood beside me before brushing our son's little red checks.

Nodding, I cooed to him softly. "I'm your mommy, Ethan."

"Thank you," Liam whispered before kissing me once again. "Thank you so much for this...for him."

Thirty-Two

*"The value of marriage is not that adults produce
children, but that children produce adults."*
~Peter De Vries

LIAM

I watched him. I couldn't help it. He was just so tiny. I could hold him with just one hand. I hadn't slept in hours... days? Who gave a shit, I had a son. He was here in my arms, drooling. He'd been in the world for only six hours, yet still I couldn't imagine a moment without him.

"Liam, please, stop hogging him," My father huffed, moving to stand behind me. "The old folks would like to hold him before we die."

"Be careful," I hissed, slowly transferring him into Sedric's arms.

"Hello, little one," he said to him, and once again, my son just waved his arms around in his sleep, as if he wasn't used to all the space around him. "Your father says I have to be careful, but forgets that I once held him and his brothers like this. Thankfully you got your looks, and hopefully your smarts from your mother."

"I'm right here." I rolled my eyes at him as he walked over to the couch next to Mel's bed. She was only partially asleep, watching my father and me through barely opened eyes. She had only taken short naps; surely she needed more sleep.

"Love," I murmured, brushing her hair back before kissing her head. "Sleep. You not only need it, but deserve it."

She smiled, her eyes closing as she reached for my hands, which rested on the side of her face. "I know, and I want to, but I'm afraid. What if I miss something or he needs something? He'll be hungry again soon. It's been a few hours since I fed him."

That was probably the most awe-inspiring thing I had ever seen in my life. Before I could say anything, there was a short and soft knock on the door right before my mother wheeled in a very excited Coraline. She had a yellow scarf around her head, and shopping bags in her lap. Behind her came Declan, Neal and Olivia, each of them holding balloons, flowers and cards.

"Oh my God, he's so cute!" Coraline squealed, trying her best to keep her voice down while bouncing out of her seat. "Cancer survivor calls dibs after grandpapa!"

"Coraline! I called it already, I'm his first uncle." Neal scowled at her as a faint smile played on his lips.

"Cancer beats uncle." Coraline stuck her tongue out at him. "Doesn't it, Mel?"

Mel giggled—actually giggled, nodding for her to go next.

"Only six hours old and he's the most mature person in the room," my mother stated, kissing his little feet before coming over to us. I wasn't sure if I liked the fact that all of them were here, hovering over my son. In all honesty, I just wanted it to be my wife, my son and myself for now. Guessing what I must have been thinking, Mel took my hand, and squeezed tightly before letting go.

"Congrats, brother, he already looks like a hell raiser." Declan laughed, pulling me into a quick hug.

"If he's anything like how we used to be, I may end up with more gray hairs than Mom and Dad."

"I don't have gray hair, Liam."

"Of course, Mother," Declan and I said at the same time, which only made us both laugh and grip hands again.

Yeah, I was going to be in for it, but I had no doubt that it would be worth it.

"May I say Mel, you look beautiful." Neal smiled, handing her a bundle of yellow roses.

"You may, even though I know you're lying," she replied, taking the flowers from him. "Thank you, Neal. They smell great."

"Look at this, I turn my back for one moment, and he's charming my wife immediately after she gave birth to my child," I joked as he reached out to shake my hand. I pulled him in, giving him the same hug I gave Declan.

"He's just trying to charm her so that he can hold Ethan before anyone else." Olivia smiled, her gaze fixated on the little man now in Coraline's arms.

Evelyn was close by, showing her how to hold him.

"So it's official, right? Ethan Antonio Callahan?" Coraline asked and when he took a deep breath, she, my mother and Olivia practically melted where they stood.

The sight of his little chest going up and down was the most beautiful thing in the world.

"Actually, it's Ethan Antonio Giovanni Callahan," Mel spoke up, reminding me of our earlier conversation.

"Antonio?" Olivia frowned. "You mean after the guard who died?"

"Yes, the guard who took a bullet for me…for us both. It was the least I could do for a man who was in many ways my friend as well." No one could argue with that. No one dared.

Ethan hadn't been in Neal's arms for more than a few minutes before he started to wail. Mel sat up, immediately reaching for him. Swaying back and forth, Neal placed him in her arms. I had no idea how she knew what to do or when those instincts kicked in, but she knew exactly what he needed.

"Now, why are you crying?" she whispered to him. He reached up, smacking her face a few times and putting his hand into her mouth before relaxing. It was like he knew who she was, and just by knowing she was his mother, he was at ease. Part of me felt a twinge of jealously at how close they were already, but it was overwhelmed by the amount of joy and excitement I felt. He was finally relaxed when a flash went off, causing him to stir again.

"Mom!" I snapped, as she held her phone to her chest.

"Oh hush before you make him cry. Let me enjoy this. I need to send this to the rest of the family, and you can't expect me not have his picture." She grinned, flipping through her phone.

"You already took a hundred pictures from the second you saw him." She was going crazy with glee, and not just her, my father was just as giddy. They were…well, they were happy. We were all happy. Reaching out, my son grabbed hold of my finger, squeezing as tightly as he could, as though he was trying to prove something. Like he was trying to say 'Look dad, look how strong I am'.

"What color eyes do you think he'll have?" Mel asked me. Right now they were the standard blue that apparently most babies were born with.

Before I could answer, everyone else took it upon themselves to do it for me: "Green."

"Can the father get a word in please?" I mocked them, turning to my wife and child once more. I stared in awe at the new person that was half of me; my heart stuttered at the thought. Brushing his hair back, I answered my wife. "Before the peanut gallery can interrupt again, I think…I really don't care, as long as he's healthy."

"That's why I'm here." An overly preppy red-headed doctor walked in with a single nurse at her side. "Hello, everyone. I'm Dr. Yang and I just need to run a few more tests on him, and if—"

"Don't say *if*." Mel frowned, her eyes glaring into her. "He's fine, and you're just making sure he's still fine, got it?"

My father laughed at how wide the woman's eyes opened. "Of course, Mrs. Callahan. We're going to take him for an hour or two and then we will be right back with him. I'm sure he's fine."

Mel's body tensed and I knew she was going to ask to accompany him, but she really needed to rest.

"I'll go with him," I said. "I'll feel better if you get at least two hours of sleep."

Sighing, she kissed his forehead before slowly handing him over to me. He smelled like fresh flowers, and rain, and just baby, an indescribable scent that seemed to permeate his skin. Kissing her quickly, I walked over to the doctor.

Don't drop him. Keep his head up. Don't hold him too tightly. Is he breathing? Don't wake him! Those were some of the thoughts that ran through my mind; it was like my whole being was now wrapped around him.

Holy shit, I was a father.

Melody

"Don't worry, you're going to close your eyes and before you even know it, they will both be back demanding your attention." Evelyn laughed, kissing my forehead. It was odd. I wasn't used to anyone other than Liam doing that, and even so, it had taken me a while to adjust to him. But I guess seeing me with a baby tucked into my arms made her forget who I was.

"We're going to head out and let you have some space." Sedric smiled at me. He looked as if he were holding back a hug or something. The best I could do right now was squeeze his hand.

I was pleased that I still felt like myself, only now I had a greater priority and that was my son. He was the person I now lived, and would die, for and I would do everything in my power to make sure he was safe. Which meant I had to be stronger, maybe even harsher with those around me. I would be anything, do anything, to protect him.

"Bye, Mel. Oh, I got Ethan some cute new clothes for him to come home in." Coraline grinned, leaving the baby blue bag on the chair Sedric had previously occupied.

"That reminds me, the press will be tripping over themselves for pictures..." Olivia started, but I cut her off quickly.

"Neal, make sure any and all press around our house is taken care of immediately. Also, I want a new car, something that isn't too flashy, with tinted windows. A Volvo, maybe?" I'd heard all this shit about them being safe, so I might as well.

"I'll get right on it, boss." He grinned, but I still didn't trust him. He made way too many fucking mistakes, and if he weren't family, I would have already killed him. Olivia bit her tongue—as she should—before taking a deep breath and playing with the pearls at her neck.

"Declan, stay a moment?" I turned to him. None of them waited or even looked back. Evelyn wheeled Coraline out, giving us the privacy my statement insinuated.

"What do you need?" he asked, rolling up his sleeves.

"The house swept, I want every last one of our security cameras firewalled and impossible to be hacked. Then get a profile of all of our employees. Make sure they know their lives depend on what they don't see or hear, and who they let into my house. We brought a little boy over the border to keep his mother quiet. The police want to use her as an informant. Focus more on her." Saying it all out loud made me relax, just a little bit.

"I'll get working on everything, but Neal told me that Liam is having the house swept again as we speak. He has fifteen men walking the property here and roaming the surrounding areas." Of course he was. He and I were too much alike; sometimes it was crazy.

"I'll leave you to get some res—"

"How's Coraline?"

He frowned. "She's doing better, but I don't think she's up to do anything right now."

"I'm not asking as your boss."

"Oh." He nodded slowly. This was one of the hassles when dealing with family. "She has her dark days, but she's been doing better. It's a slow process but she's getting there.

It's been a few weeks since she's been off the chemo, and she starts therapy soon."

"Good. I'm glad." I yawned. My entire body felt so heavy.

He said something before stepping out the door, leaving only silence and the muted whirring of the machines in his wake. Finally, I could rest and allow my eyes to close.

"Hi, sweetheart," someone whispered over me.

I felt like I had only just closed my eyes, but now they felt harder to open. "Wh…I…wha…" I couldn't form words. What the hell was going on?

"Don't worry, this will be over very soon." I knew that voice. With all the might I had, I forced my eyelids open, blinking quickly at the stream of light pouring into my eyes.

"Avi..Avi…" I hissed through my teeth.

"Not here." She grinned, looking at the name on her lab coat. "Here, I'm Doctor Yang."

She was pushing my bed down the hall. I tried to move, but my body felt like it was encased in lead. Nurses, doctors, patients, and walls passed me by without my control. All I could see were her damn blue scrubs and bad red wig hovering over me. Clenching my teeth, I tried my best to speak but the muscles in my jaw were useless. Whatever she fucking drugged me with, I wasn't used to it.

"Liam…kill…"

"My doctor friend will keep him and little Ethan so busy he won't notice until it's too late. Now sleep, sweetheart." I didn't have time to brace myself before she stabbed me in the fucking neck. I no longer had any control over my body. That's when the tears started to fall. I refused to believe that I may never see my family again.

Fuck her. If she thought she could end me like this, she didn't know who she was fucking with.

LIAM

Something was wrong. I could fucking feel it in the pit of my stomach. The fucking doctor was taking her sweet time looking him over, but that wasn't my problem. Something was off and I couldn't put my finger on it.

"Liam." Declan stepped in next to me, staring at Ethan through the window. He was blissful as he gurgled in his little incubator.

Declan was stiff, his jaw was clenched so tightly that it looked like stone, he breathed through his nose slowly, watching the doctor's hands carefully. Hearing the door slide open, I watched as my father walked in without even bothering to look at me. He stepped up to my son, blocking my view of the doctor.

"You have five seconds to start speaking, Declan." My hands twitched, more than ready to bash someone's head in.

"Don't make a scen—"

"I asked you a motherfucking question, you work for me, now answer. What fuck is going on Declan?"

He was silent.

"If I have to ask you again…"

"Mel." He paused. "She's gone."

Taking a deep breath, I tried to ignore how quickly my heart was pounding. "Did you check with the—"

"She's gone. Evelyn went back to check on her and noticed. No one has seen her in the last two hours. I hacked the hospital cameras..." He handed me his cell phone, but I didn't need to fucking see it.

"Aviela."

The bitch! I'm going to fucking kill her!

"Liam, breathe."

"I want this whole fucking hospital on lockdown! Every fucking exit, shut! How the hell did she get to my wife?" Right under my nose.

Every head in the vicinity turned towards me, but I didn't give a fuck. I would slit each one of their fucking throats.

"She got in using Dr. Yang's badge and a wig. Liam, don't..."

I started towards the door before he could even finish, but he jumped in front of me, halting my steps. "We have eyes everywhere. There are cops all over this place."

"Bring me Dr. Yang! Take her out back. Block out the damn cameras."

"Okay. I know you're panicking, but brother, breathe," he replied.

Running my hands through my hair, I took a step back, and breathed through my nose before nodding.

"Get her the fuck away from my son. I want men around him at all times."

When he left me, I tried not to think about her. I couldn't think about her not being in her room waiting for me. I just couldn't handle that. Fuck. How did she fucking get her? Fuck.

"Let go of me!" The bitch hissed as Declan all but dragged her out of the Ethan's room by the arm, lifting her tiny frame towards me.

"You better speak before I get down there or so help me God, your definition of pain will be obsolete by the time I'm through with you." That's all I said before walking into my son's room. Seeing Ethan in my father's arms burned deep down into my soul. She wasn't just my fucking wife, she was his mother. He had a mother that loved him and I had to bring her back. He wasn't even a fucking day old and he already had to deal with this shit. Kissing him, I stepped away, and watched him rest in my father's arms.

"Dad..."

"Go. No one is getting near him. Your mother will be here in a few."

I nodded. I couldn't even breathe correctly anymore. I felt like Atlas, struggling to balance the weight of the world.

"Liam, if there is a man who can get her back, it's you."

I had no fucking choice. How could I live without her? I couldn't even think. Rolling my sleeves up, I walked away. I told myself over and over again that I couldn't kill the doctor. But the line between the living and the dead was a very thin one. I would see how far I could take it before she broke; I had no doubt that she would.

Neal was already waiting for me when I stepped out into the sterile hallway. His body was as rigid as mine. No words were needed, so we didn't waste them. Aviela came after the family. She *stole* our family; my fucking wife. Someone was going to die, that went without being said.

Pushing open the door to the staircase, Neal handed me a gun, but I shook it off. Aviela chose this woman as a decoy; I doubted a gun was enough to scare her. I was going to beat it out of her.

My Mel is gone. How the fuck? She took my fucking wife. She took my motherfucking wife! My mind was in a loop as we went down the stairs.

I didn't want to think, for when I did, I felt like a failure; I felt pain and anger.

Pushing open the door, I was hit with a harsh blast of cold dry air and snow. There, begging, as she was held against the wall next to the dumpster with rats at her feet was Dr. Yang. Her lips were busted and her eyes held tears. Declan shook his head, stepping back to let me through.

I didn't have time for this. Marching forward, I grabbed a fist full of her fake red hair. I pulled her off the wall before slamming her face repeatedly into the dumpster before throwing her body aside. I was tempted to keep going, but surely if I continued I would permanently incapacitate her.

"AHH!" She groaned, spitting out what looked to be at least three of her teeth onto the white canvas of snow. It was sort of beautiful, the contrast of her red blood on the untainted ground. I relished in causing her distress, making her feel a fraction of the pain that was radiating through my entire being. Kneeling next to her, I pulled a switchblade out of my sock and held it to her hairline.

"I will scalp you alive and then let the rats eat your fucking face, do you understand? Now, tell me everything you fucking know!"

"Ahh..." She groaned.

"Do you think I'm fucking joking? MY WIFE IS GONE!" I slid the razor across the skin of her hairline. She tried to fight, but I pulled her hair back, exposing her newly torn flesh, as blood streamed down her face and stained the snow around us.

"Please! I'll tell you everything," she wailed.

"Start talking before I remove your entire face," I snapped. Either way, I was going kill her.

"All she told me was that she wanted her daughter back. I gave her my badge; she was going to save her daughter. She said that if she stayed with you, she and her son were going to die—"

"Where are they?" I roared, slicing the blade behind her ear, almost detaching it. Her blood flowed, rolling down her face and neck. I doubted her ability to see as she opened her eyes, the normal whites were saturated with red.

"I don't know, I swear all she said is that they were going home! That's all I know, I swear. I'm so sorry, she told me I was saving her…"

"Police!" Fedel alerted, forcing me to momentarily let her go. Dr. Yang crawled into a little ball, sobbing in the dirt and snow as the rats sniffed her blood. Looking at her broken form, I still wasn't satisfied. She wasn't writhing in pain and that was unacceptable.

Sure enough, down the alleyway a cop car slowed, stepping out with a flashlight. Each one of them pulled out their guns. These fools wouldn't be the first Chicago officers gunned down in a back alleyway, and I didn't have time for this shit.

"Is there problem here?"

"Please! Help me!" Dr. Yang suddenly yelled from behind me. Their eyes went wide, running towards her until they saw my face clearly.

"Mr. Callahan."

"Get in your car. Drive away. You didn't see anything. You have two seconds."

"NO!" Doctor Yang said from behind me. "PLEASE! PLEASE HELP!"

"One," I stated and they both nodded, ignoring her.

"Sorry for bothering you, sir," the older of the two men said before turning around and retreating; the doctor gave a defeated cry when his car drove off.

"Kill her, and I want a list of all the properties the Giovannis held." Wiping the blood off my blade, I headed back to my son.

Mel, I will find you. By God, I will find you.

Thirty-Three

"The marks humans leave are too often scars."
~John Green

Sedric

He was twelve hours old. Smaller than the distance between elbow and my wrist, and here he was, motherless. He was suffering like Liam suffered as an infant. It had taken Evelyn over a decade to finally hold him...to love him. And every second Mel that was gone, Ethan was forced to travel the same path his father had. Right now, he was oblivious to it all, as he slept in his bassinet, lost in his own little world.

"Sedric." Evelyn burst into the hospital nursery. "A nurse went to look for Mel so she could feed Ethan."

"Shit." It was only a matter of time before the police would be brought in. With the police came the media, investigations, and people digging deeper into our lives.

"Does Liam know?" I asked, pulling out my phone.

"The nurse already went to his superiors. It's only a matter of time." No sooner had the words left her lips, a silent red siren went off around the room. We blinked at the brightly flashing lights that were supposed to catch a nurse's attention without waking the children.

"What do we do?" she whispered, walking over to Ethan.

The only thing we could. "We tell the truth. We left Mel to get some rest and when we came back, she was gone."

"The timeline won't match up, Sedric. I went to check on her hours ago. Either we tell them we knew she was missing for hours or someone has to screw with the camera footage." It was a lose-lose situation because in the end, it would kick up more questions than any of us were ready to handle.

I couldn't leave her or Ethan alone to prep Liam for the questions that would most likely be hurled his way. All I could do was stand in the middle of Ethan's personal nursery as the red lights above us flashed non-stop.

"He knows." She sighed, allowing him to grab her finger. "He knows his mother is gone. Just like Liam did."

"Evelyn…"

"Liam and I aren't close. It's my fault. I left him alone for years, and when I finally woke up, he wasn't a baby anymore and he avoided me. Not once has he come to me for advice. I know he loves me, but it's always been you. His anger, his pain, his loneliness, are all because I wasn't there." She trembled in my arms as her tears soaked my shirt.

"Liam loves you, and this is completely different. Mel didn't…Mel was taken, but she'll be back. We're talking about the first woman to take over the Italian Mafia. The moment she can, she will get back to us and leave nothing but a wake of blood behind her. This will be over soon." I hoped my words would be true. Every moment she wasn't here, Liam would spiral. I knew this about my son; he couldn't handle being abandoned again.

Declan

Nothing but a sea of blue was flooding the walls, drowning out the white coats that normally infested the hallways. Cops made me sick. They were nothing but self-persevering, opportunistic leeches hiding behind shiny badges. The nurse had set us back and now the hospital was on its own lockdown, forcing us to stay in a private wing instead of searching for Mel. Liam hadn't said a word since we took out the doctor. He sat like a man made out of marble, his head permanently attached to his hands.

"Mr. Callahan," a short balding man said. He was dripping in medals, which he undoubtedly wore for the cameras outside.

"May I ask who you are?" I asked. "My brother is both tired and devastated, as you can imagine." I stepped beside my brother. He looked up at me, eyebrow raised.

"Mr. Callahan, I am Superintendent Wendell Homer. I wanted to personally come down and tell you that we will do everything in our power—"

"Let me stop you here. We're Callahans, we are used to people kissing our asses for personal benefit. So, save your words for the press hounds outside and find my sister-in-law." As if they could. The Chicago PD were a running joke across the country.

His back straightened from his ass-kissing position before he placed his hat on.

"Has anyone received any ransom demands?" he asked and I had to fight my initial reaction to roll my eyes.

"No. We haven't."

"Okay, but expect one. These types of low lives always hunt for a fast paycheck. We're going to need a list of anyone who may have a grudge against you..." He stopped as Liam laughed.

He laughed hysterically, leaning in his chair and running his hands through his hair. "Do you know how much we are worth?" he asked him. "32.7 billion dollars. That puts us between Wal-Mart and Michael Bloomberg on Forbes' richest people list. You want a list of people who have grudges against us? Start with the whole fucking state and work outward!"

"Mr. Callahan, I know this is difficult, but please trust us. We will not stop until we find her. Until we find who did this. We know that your guard was murdered only a day ago. This is obviously connected. Give us time. We will do everything," he said, almost begged, but Liam was done with them. Instead, his green eyes glazed over as he stared emptily at the wall. Neither of us had anything more to say.

"Would you like to make a statement? Plead to the kidnappers to return your wife?" he questioned, making me want to punch his tiny Teletubby self in the face.

"In all your time as an officer, has that shit ever worked? Do you really think they give a shit?" I really couldn't comprehend why he thought that that was even an option.

"It doesn't hurt to try. Please excuse me," he said, waddling down the hall, as more police officers arrived on the scene.

Sighing, I took a seat next to my brother.

"We've got a list of twelve properties," I said. "Five are out of the country. I've called Anna and told her to call in every favor she had in Interpol for flight records."

He took a deep breath, pinching the bridge of his nose. "Good. I can't move, not with these fuckers crawling up my ass. Get all the men we have on the outside to start searching. I want Neal to go with them. He's been in the public eye, traveling the country."

"Neal? I'll go, Liam."

"No, Declan. I need you here. I need you going through every fucking camera in the damn state. These fuckers have red tape to go through, you don't. I'm not wasting another bloody second just because they want a photo-op. If Aviela wanted her dead, she could have killed her months ago. She wants Mel alive. And I know my wife, as long as she's alive she will be trying to contact us." What if she couldn't? What if...

"Liam?"

"Do not motherfucking 'Liam' me, Declan. She's my wife. She's a fucking fighter, a leader. I have full faith that she's going to beat the shit out of her mother and come home with her head on a stake. She didn't become who she is by being weak. She's strong. I'm going to be strong. And our son will know that. So don't you dare 'Liam' me, and do your fucking job."

With that, he got up and walked away. I wasn't even sure if he knew where he was going. I couldn't even begin to understand his pain. The only person on the face of the earth that he could be honest with was gone.

"Declan." Coraline wheeled up out of fucking nowhere with her hands pulling at the rubber band on her wrist—something she had taken to doing during her treatment.

"A..."

"What can I do? What should I be doing? I need to do something. Evelyn told me and I—"

"Coraline." I dropped to my knees, taking her hand in mine. "Just watch Ethan, I don't want you getting hurt."

"But Jas..."

"No! I need to concrete on Liam. This family and I cannot do that if you're in the middle of this. I'm begging you. Just watch Ethan, avoid the police, and focus on your health, okay?"

She sighed and nodded, but she didn't meet my gaze. Kissing her forehead, I held her to me for a long second. "I love you, baby. Just keep your head above this and we will get through it."

"We always do," she whispered. "I'm going to see Ethan, and before you ask, don't worry about me. I can push myself."

"Of course you can." I looked up to see Adriana; she was standing in the middle of the hospital wing, taking in the chaos around her. Her hair was drenched, sticking to her face. It seemed as if she was trying to hold it together, wrapping her arms around herself. She looked like a wet, dying puppy without a home.

She was Mel's right hand. There had to be more properties that Mel hid from us. I wouldn't put it past her to have tricks and funds up her sleeve that no one knew of.

"Be safe," I told Coraline before leaving her and walking over to Adriana. The halls were crawling with badges but I wasn't sure where else to take her.

"I don't understand," she whispered, her hands shaking. "She was with me hours ago. I don't...No...She doesn't get kidnapped. She's not the type. She's *Melody*."

Great, she's losing her shit too.

"Adriana, I know this is hard, but I need you to think. Okay? I need you to tell me all the properties Mel has, everything."

"I can't do that, Mel would—"

"Mel is not fucking here, Adriana, and you work for us, for this family," I hissed through clenched teeth, trying not to draw too much attention. "Now, I need you to tell me anything that Mel has failed to inform us about."

"She has fifteen million, and a loft in Cagliari, and a private house in Varna, Bulgaria. And… she has private homes no one even knows about all around Italy. I don't know them all; it's her safety net. The only record of that shit is in her head. Those are the only two—"

"It's fine. We will keep looking, okay, Adriana? But right now, I need you to keep calm and breathe. You need to get out of here. You look like you just shanked an old woman. Go home." First Antonio, now Mel. I was surprised she wasn't rocking back and forth in the corner.

"I'm supposed to watch her back, especially when she can't. That's my job. That's my only real job. Everything I do and everything I've done is because I wanted to help her. I would do anything to help her."

I knew that. I doubted anyone would say differently. "Go home, Adriana," I repeated as I pulled out my phone. I hoped to God Liam was right and that Mel was trying to contact us.

Thirty-Four

"You can tell whether a man is clever by his answers.
You can tell whether a man is wise by his questions."
~ Naguib Mahfouz

LIAM

As I watched them I could feel my blood boil, but what else could I do? Olivia held Ethan, and fed him some shit in a bottle, that only disgusted me more. But he had to eat, and his mother wasn't here. Pinching my nose, I tried to balance myself. I couldn't even close my eyes, that only made me think of her. How tired she must have been. How well could she fight if she was hungry and tired?

Aviela does not want to kill her.

I tried to convince myself of that fact.

"Mr. Callahan." I turned to find The Little Engine That Could, standing in the midst of the chaos that was now the NICU, watching me and my family through the glass.

"Officer Scooter."

"Mr. Callahan, I gotta ask you a few questions. In cases like this..."

"They send a rookie cop to find my wife?" And they wondered why I didn't trust them.

He sighed, taking a step forward. "You know, I was handpicked to join the FBI right outta the academy! I may not look like much, but I'm damn good at my job. In forty-eight hours, your bodyguard was shot. The same type of shot, with the same type of the round used to assassinate the president. Now your wife was kidnapped out of one of the most highly protected hospitals in the country. There is a connection here, I can feel it. So help me, sir. Help me find your wife. Now everything you say is important."

There was no getting rid of the man. He reminded me of an annoying superintendent I used to know.

"Why didn't you join the FBI?"

"Because this is my city. I'm not abandoning it or the people." Exactly like a superintendent I used to know.

He was going to be a problem. "Before all of this happened, my wife told me she had a strange encounter with you at the station, Officer. So take your morality and get me a real officer. Not one trying to blame my family."

"Mr. Callahan…"

"No. Don't bother. Tell the superintendent I only want the real FBI looking for my wife, nothing less. So respectfully, get the hell out of my face." Grabbing the door handle, I left the blond-headed idiot alone.

Stepping into the NICU, I didn't even bother to speak to my father or mother. Taking Ethan out Olivia's arms, she stood up, hand still on the bottle, waiting for me to sit down in the white rocking chair.

"Liam." My father sighed and I knew that he had seen the officer and me speaking, but I couldn't deal with him right now. I just needed to hold my son. He gave me the hope I needed at the moment.

"I don't understand. How did she know when to get her?" Evelyn whispered, kneeling right in front of me.

The same way she knew everything else…her mole. The only way I would find her was to find that rat. But the only person who could have given her so much inside information had to be close. The only people who were that close were family. So as they huddled around me, my father, my mother, Olivia…I pulled back. Who the fuck was betraying me? The only person I could fully trust was the little person in my hands.

Once I knew who it was, I wouldn't hold back.

Melody

I hated being drugged. It always left a bad taste in my mouth. My father used to drug me in an attempt to make me stronger, immune. Now I felt as though he knew my mother was a sicko bitch and had been trying to prepare me for her. But I doubted anything could have prepared me for being pulled from my hospital bed, while recovering from major surgery, to now being chained to the seat of a private fucking jet. She sat in her seat, her auburn hair tucked behind her small ears with a wrinkled copy of *Wicked* in her hands and dark framed glasses on her face.

"Would you like wine, Ma'am?"

I should have fucking known.

I glanced up at the pale, familiar hand of Nelson something or the other… my fucking flight attendant. He poured my favorite red wine into a glass for the woman before me. She said nothing as she held up her wine glass for him.

"You're the rat on my ship."

"Really, Mel Bear? You think I couldn't get closer than your flight attendant?" The woman who gave birth to me sighed before flipping the page.

"Do not call me 'Mel Bear,' you insane bitch. As for you, rat, I will skin you while you beg for my forgiveness, but not before I make you watch me kill your meth-head sister in the most painful way possible." I pulled against the chain, but all it did was cause me pain. I could feel the stitches pull at my skin, and even though it was painful, it made me think of Ethan.

"Nelson, get her something to eat."

"Give me anything and I will embed it in your skull," I hissed. My skin was hot, my emotions were raw, and all I wanted was to be free.

"Suit yourself then, you were always temperamental as a child." She said snidely, again flipping the damn page.

"Maybe it was because I knew my mother was a weak, conniving whore that would one day shoot me like a dog after poisoning my father. In the end, he didn't suffer and I was there. He was happy so you fucking…" the heat that radiated off the back of her hand when it connected with the side of my face only made me smile.

Her glasses were off, her hair falling out of place and her back was bone straight as she glared into me, nostrils flaring and eyes wide.

"Did you slap me because I called you a whore? Or because you didn't get to kill Orlando?"

"Leave us," she hissed and every one of the men on her plane went towards the back. It wasn't that far; I couldn't even see why she bothered.

"Are you gonna tell me a secret, Mommy? Are you going—"

"Enough," she said. "You don't understand the shit I've done for you. How hard it was to leave you with that fucking monster, to protect you from Satan himself. You know nothing."

"You poisoned my father for years. You shot me down. You killed my guard and now you've separated me from my husband and child. So fuck you and your life story, bitch. I know enough to say at the end of this, you will die, and I will feel *nothing*." I wanted to kill her now. I just kept eyeing the wine on the table wishing for two more inches of chain so I could smash it against her skull.

She took a deep breath, and placed her hand on her book. "Have you read this?"

"No, but don't worry, I'll read the spark notes." God, my breasts hurt. Everything hurt, but knowing that my son didn't have me made my heart burn.

"God, you're so much like me it hurts. I've always been so proud of you. I've watched you grow, and become the fighter I knew you were when I first held you in my arms. I swore I would always do what was best for you."

"This," I pulled on the chains, "is not good for me. But, if you're not full of shit, unchain me, hand me a gun, and I'll believe you."

She frowned, taking the wine to her lips. "You don't want to hear this. This layer of anger and sarcasm, it's just you trying to block me out."

"No, it's me, still hormonal and in a shitload of pain because of you. But please go on and tell me how I'm so fucking wrong, Aviela. Tell me your entire sad, pathetic life story. I will try to hold back my disgust. But while you speak, know that I'm going to be thinking of ways to kill you." *While I try to deny how badly I wanted to know the truth.*

"You've always liked to test me. Whatever Orlando told you were lies, Mel bear."

"Were you poisoning him for years?"

She said nothing, staring out at the dark seas thousands of feet below us.

"Point one for Dad."

"Orlando…all the damn Giovannis are monsters. He killed my uncle, my brother, my fucking mother."

Point two for Dad.

"Women like us, Mel bear, serve the men above us to survive because we are warriors, and until we get our own army, we do as we are told." She spoke in a hushed tone, her eyes glazed over. "If Orlando told to you to kill Liam slowly and painfully, you would have done it. I regret nothing. The Giovannis, they are the reason why my father was the way he was. I couldn't wait to kill him for the suffering he made me go through; kill Orlando, then get out. But you came and I didn't want you to come into this life. But Orlando just didn't know when to die and forced you into this trap."

"So what you're saying is that you've always wanted me dead." I wished Orlando had taken her out the moment I was born.

"NO!" she snapped, slamming her hand on the table, spilling her wine across it.

Good ole Nelson was there in a flash, cleaning. She didn't even look fazed.

"I've always tried to save you, Mel bear. I knew he would take you and form you into a monster just like him. Just like my father had done to me. But then I had you, and I never wanted to leave you. For years, I stayed in hell for you. To watch you, until one day, I couldn't take anymore. I took my chance. I got you and I planned on leaving, disappearing to where Orlando and Ivan couldn't find us. We were going to be happy and free. But Orlando came looking for you, and my father for me. I knew Orlando would turn you into a monster but Ivan—his granddaughter, a Giovanni?—he would have thrown you with snakes then sent your body to Orlando. I chose the lesser of two evils."

"So you're telling me that Ivan didn't know I was alive all this time? I doubt that. From what I can tell, he knows everything about all the families. So why now, mother dearest?"

"He let you be because I took my punishment and he figured you wouldn't be able to make it once Orlando died." She smiled, reaching over the table to take my hand. "But you did. You overcame it all and you fucking showed him how stupid he was to underestimate my daughter."

"You're not my mother. I'm not your daughter. Let go of me and finish your fairytale. What was your punishment?" I pulled my hand back.

Her hands clenched together as she readjusted herself. Unbuttoning her shirt slowly, she opened it, and everywhere were scars and dozens of small brown circular wounds that looked to be cigar burns. They littered her pale shoulders, stomach and I knew it reached her back. The distance between knife scars and burns was short. Luckily for her, none of them looked new. If I wasn't chained to this seat, I may have felt bad…maybe.

"When he was done and satisfied, he let you go, not caring what you did. Orlando was destroying his himself and his "empire" was beyond repair. But I watched you. Your first kill was Atticus Flanagan, an Irish mutt who stalked you down at the seaport. You surprised him and he ended up face down in the lake. You were, fourteen?"

"Thirteen."

"You sold your first kilo at—"

"I was there. I know, Aviela. Why are you fucking with my life now?"

"Because you stupidly laid down with the mutt and his dirty little family. Ivan wanted you dead instantly, but I convinced him that he couldn't take out the head of the Italian mafia. Imagine all the chaos. All the wars as people tried to replace you. He thought I cared about you, that's why I shot you. I needed him to believe that I could kill you if I wanted to. Ivan is all about balance, about keeping the underground *under* ground. But you are my daughter. You had to reach higher, you had to control the president of the United States. You reached a little too close to home for him."

"Ivan is in the White House?" Shit.

She didn't answer. "I told him you wouldn't win and street wars weren't worth killing you. I made sure to kill the President just to secure his wife. She would have the pity vote, yet you still out-played me. So like I said, you've made my life so much harder than it needed to be. This is the only way I know how to protect you now. We're going to have a do-over. We're finally going home."

"I have a family, Aviela. A son who he needs me! I won't fucking run from a fight and I sure as hell won't run from him. "

"You're not in a fight. You never even got in the damn ring. Ivan has you. He's the only untouchable one in this game. In an instant he can take your son and burn you like he burned me. He would kill Liam. But this is a win-win. He gets his balance, the Italians will break away, leaving Liam less powerful. Liam will be devastated, but live for your son. He won't even be able to control President Colemen. Once that man gets power, he will block out your husband. Your son will live, and because you're like me, you can watch from afar and learn to be okay. Your child will be okay, Mel bear. He's alive because you loved him enough to stay away."

She's ri—

I pushed that thought out of my mind, and leaned against the chain so she could see my eyes.

"I will get out of this. I will kill you, and I will protect my family the same way I always have. I'm Melody Nicci Giovanni Callahan, I don't run away. I destroy everything in my path, which includes you."

She smiled as she lifted her red stained book. "That's why I brought the chains. You will learn, and when you have, I'll let you see him. Pictures, videos, maybe a few of his old toys over time."

I felt my heart stop. I didn't want her anywhere near Ethan, *my* Ethan. How would she be able to get videos and pictures? The mole. But who would Liam let close enough to our child for that?

"Olivia. Olivia is the fucking mole." She hated me enough. She wanted me gone…

"Try again." She flipped her page, but I couldn't see who else. It couldn't be Coraline, she was just too sick, Evelyn… hell no. Neal? No, he craved Liam's love. None of the family would betray us like this. But, who the hell would be that close, Fedel, Monte, Antonio… the only other person would be…

"You know, don't you?"

"Adriana." I hit my head against the seat. *Fuck.*

"To her credit, she's willing to do anything for you. All I had to do was tell her the truth and she realized what you cannot. You're not safe. She was starting to withhold information, so I reminded her who she worked for. So sad her love had to die because she got cold feet."

This was my fault. How could I trust her? Orlando had always told me humans were liars by nature, that friends were foes in disguise and to never make it personal.

How dare she?

"You're hurt."

"No, I'm enraged and looking forward to putting a slug through her ungrateful little heart." Leaning back, I knew I wouldn't be able to relax, but my body couldn't take any more right now. All I could do was close my eyes and plan. Nothing she said had changed how I felt about her. The moment this plane landed, I would have to act. Fast.

Thirty-Five

*"Imagine trying to live without air.
Now imagine something worse."*
~Amy Reed

Melody

"*Five days ago, my wife Melody Giovanni Callahan was kidnapped only hours after giving birth to our son. I want her back. My son and I need her. My family and I are offering one hundred million dollars for her safe return. Mel, if you're watching, I'm not giving up. I won't ever give up until I have you back. Our son and I miss you and love you so much…*"

"I think that's enough for now." Aviela's voice grated on every nerve in my body.

My hatred for her continued to fester each moment spent in her presence. She turned off the television, and rushed from the kitchen to place a plate in front of me. "Giant meatballs and spaghetti. Your favorite, right?"

I just stared at her, doing nothing to hide my hatred and disgust for the woman who gave birth to me.

"A hundred million? You should be insulted." She took a seat at the other end of the luxurious dining room table before spreading her napkin and dropping it on her lap. She had chained me to every fucking chair until we reached this place, which, from what I could tell, was on the edge of a beach. Then, I was upgraded to a wheelchair. The last two days had been more of the same rhetoric about how she was trying to save me, how she only did this to protect me.

I didn't know who she was trying to convince.

All this time I thought she was some cold-hearted mastermind, always plotting, always one step ahead of us because she was just that good. But I was wrong. She was delusional; I wasn't even sure if she really understood what she was doing. Part of her still saw me as that little girl she left in the middle of the ocean, while another part of her understood I was grown.

I thought she was strong; I'd admired her tenacity and her tactics in getting what she wanted done efficiently and effectively, but the moment she spoke of her father, Ivan, she became weak. Whatever he had done to her had broken her. She was at his beck and call—his lap dog—and it disgusted me. She was no better than the low-level sycophants that worked for me.

Every day she washed and combed my hair and even dressed me, all while keeping me chained. She treated me like I was her own personal doll. The second day I tried playing nice, today I tried not speaking. There was something seriously wrong with this woman.

Despite my tactics to evoke a reaction from her, she acted as if nothing fazed her. The only time I got a response from her was when I "misbehaved." Other than that, she gave no indication that she was here in this space other than physically. I needed to get out of here but I didn't even know what country I was in.

"Do you need me to get someone to help you, sweetheart?" she asked, cutting into her food with her finely polished silverware. She nodded over at the soon-to-be dead rat's rail thin frame at the door. Nelson came over, and like a robot, he cut into my food before bringing it to my lips.

I guess even sycophants can have sycophants.

Opening my mouth, I took the food into it and chewed it briefly before I spat it into his face.

"MELODY!"

He took a step back as Aviela walked forward. Nelson wiped his face slowly before glaring at me.

Aviela grabbed my face, forcing me to meet her eyes. "I am trying here, Melody. I want you to be happy with me, okay? I love you, but you have to let go of him and that child. They are your past, a past you would never have had if we could've been together. I love you, so please behave, because I don't want to hurt you."

"The only thing stopping me from snapping your fucking neck right now are these damn cuffs. So fuck y—"

She slapped me so hard my teeth cut the bottom of my lip. Licking the blood off, I looked up to her, smiling. "You're a horrible mother, always have been... always will be."

She slapped me twice, then a third time before she pulled back.

"Stop making me hurt you!"

My face burned and I knew without looking that my cheek would have an imprint of her hand on it.

I laughed without humor, and wondered briefly if her brand of crazy was infectious or hereditary. Banishing the thought from my mind, I focused on the woman breathing harshly before me.

"Is that what dear old grandpa used to say to you?"

"You know nothing."

"I know enough. This isn't helping. You think you are, but you aren't. Let me go, tell me who Ivan is and we can all be free of him."

She shook her head, running her hands through her short hair. "No, no. You don't know him. You don't know anything. Just let me protect you, sweetheart. You can't beat him, no one beats him. It's okay…"

"You, me, and Liam, we can take—"

"NO! I said no! I'm going to protect you, okay? *Me*, your mommy. Not Liam, not anyone else. You're gone now. Ivan won't bother your family. Just be good, Melody. Be good for me, okay?"

It was like trying to reason with a child having a tantrum. "Ivan is just a man."

"ENOUGH!" Taking a deep breath, she smoothed out her expression. "You've ruined a perfectly enjoyable dinner. You were so well behaved when I was raising you."

"You never raised me, Aviela."

She looked me in the eyes then and they seemed flat; there was no depth to her, just a hollow shell of the woman that was once my mother. Standing up straighter, she walked over to the fireplace that was situated under a painting of a younger version of herself. Pulling a syringe off the mantle, she sighed before turning to me.

"Aviela," I hissed, knowing what was coming. I tried to back away from her but she just kept coming.

She brushed the side of my face, and if it weren't for what she was about to do, I'd think she was attempting to be tender. "This will help your pain."

"AVIELA, DON'T!" She pushed my sleeve up my arm and I tried to fight her off but the robot came to her aid, grabbing my shoulders.

"No," I said as the needle found my vein.

"You know what's ironic?" Aviela asked. "I bought this batch from your dealer."

"Mom," I whispered as everything spun in colors.

"Shh, sweetheart. We will try again tomorrow, okay? You will be good for me later. Everything will look and feel so much better. I promise, okay baby? I promise."

I felt like I was floating, drifting towards Ethan and Liam. No one could hurt us here. No one could find us; we were all drifting. We were happy, I was happy.

LIAM

"Our son and I miss you and love you so much, Mel. Thank you." As I pulled away from the microphones, the reporters began shouting their questions as their camera flashes blinded me.

"Sir, the car is ready," Monte said, leading us into the hospital.

We were supposed to be checking out today. The cars were already waiting around back for us. Part of me wanted to stay. I came with my wife; I should be leaving with my wife. But I couldn't stay, the faster I got home, the faster I could get out and work.

My mother stepped forward with my son—my and Mel's son—who was fast asleep wrapped in a small blanket and wool hat. He was a good sleeper. Mel had talked to him in her womb, demanding that he get used to her sleep patterns when he was still in her. It was a tad bit crazy, but mostly beautiful. She claimed she wouldn't be a good mother, but I saw it everyday, and now she didn't even have the chance to prove it to herself.

Before I could walk to him, officer pain-in-my-ass was already on my tail. "Mr. Callahan, we asked you not to do the ransom."

"And I ignored you."

"Mr. Callahan, with a record like that, we are going to get thousands upon thousands of calls distracting us from the real leads, making it harder—"

"Then get more people on the damn phones," I roared. "You want me to do nothing? My wife is out there and I plan on getting her back, even if I have to give away all my money, seeing as how the Chicago PD can't do their jobs."

"You said you wanted a real FBI agent. Well, I called in a favor, Mr. Callahan and we will find your wife. Avian Doers, *the director* of the FBI has now commissioned a team. Just give us—"

He was cut off as Ethan began to whimper in my mother's arms.

"All I hear are words, Officer. Now if you'll excuse me, my family and I would like to get home."

"Mr. Callahan, is there something you're hi—"

"Officer Scooter," Declan said. "My brother has just asked you to leave us alone. Please do so before we refuse to speak with any more of your kind." He was wheeling in Coraline, who hung her head low as she stared at her thin hands.

The officer shook his head. "I wouldn't advise that, sir. That would only make us think you have something to hide. You don't have anything to hide, correct?"

"Goodbye, Officer," Declan said as I took my son. He smelled like air-dried laundry and flowers.

No one had really spoken to me within our family; it was hard to do so when so many people were listening in. Neal and Olivia were at the house, waiting for our return, and doing a sweep of the house...or at least Neal was. I had no idea what his wife did other than spit poison.

"Oh no you don't," I whispered to the little man. He yawned, his face scrunching up like a prune. "Get some real sleep."

"Liam, I also got a car seat for him. I gave it to Monte, so it should be in the car," my mother said once we reached the alleyway. The same alleyway the doctor had died in. The fresh snowfall had covered all traces of her.

"Thank you, Mother," I replied, pulling Ethan's hat down to cover his ears. He was more than ready for the weather with all the clothes on him; I was worried he was going to be too warm, but the nurses told me to keep him as warm as possible.

"Liam, we need to go." My father held the door open for me. I looked at the baby seat and realized this would be his first car ride.

Mel would have wanted to put him in herself.

He yawned once again when I put him inside, smacking his own face a little as he tried to get his thumb into his mouth before drifting off.

Declan came up to me with a phone in his hands as I took a seat inside the car. "Neal says the house is clear. He's ready to fly anywhere you needed him to."

"Have him check it again," I said, rolling up the window. Without another word Monte drove, leaving the rest of them to get into the fourth car. The car before us and behind us pulled in tightly. Through the rear mirror I could see our men.

"Sir," Monte said. "I have to tell you something."

"Are you betraying us, Monte?" Because somebody was…someone close and he was as close as they came.

His eyes met mine through the mirror before he shook his head. "No, Sir. Never."

As if the guilty ever admitted it.

"Then speak."

"There is this rumor spreading among the Italians that you had the boss taken and killed."

My blood felt as though it was boiling right under my skin. I didn't have time for this shit!

"How bad?"

"The old five families are meeting tonight. They want your head."

"How did you come by this information, Monte?"

He smiled. "The boss, Sir. Fedel handled the men in the house, and I handle the moles outside. When Melody took over, she made sure to have a mole within all the old families. It's how she stayed ahead. Only I know who they are, but they are completely loyal to her."

Apparently my wife had more secrets than I knew. "They reported to you?"

"They aren't aware of Aviela or Ivan. That's how the boss wanted it. They knew nothing about her or her family, and she knew everything about them. Now they don't know what to believe," he said, obviously picking his words very carefully. "What do you want me to do?"

My phone rang before I could answer.

"Declan."

"That burn phone Aviela used didn't tell us where—"

"Declan. Why was he wasting my time?"

"Liam, I was able to get a record of all the calls she made on a payphone near the train station. I got the camera feed, and you will never believe who was there to pick up her call. They finally fucked up."

"Declan."

"Adriana, Liam. Adriana is the mole. I'll send the video to your phone."

Melody

"Agh…" I moaned. I still felt like I was spinning, and there was a horrible taste in the back of my throat. Nelson sat on the other end of the tea table, which had nothing but sweets on it. The rest of the room was about the size of my closet back home; it didn't make sense, it was designed for adults but covered in small dolls.

"Where's Aviela?"

"Most likely calling your right-hand woman. Adriana, right? Did you know she was the reason I got a position on your jet?" He leaned back in his chair. "No, you wouldn't have known that. Your mother outsmarted you in every way, and you can't even be a nice little girl for her."

This motherfucker.

"Look who found his balls."

"I never lost them! Do you remember this?" he asked, lifting the stained white jacket I had given him the very first time we met.

But I wouldn't waste my breath on him.

"When you threw this at my face like I was less than human, it took all of my control not to put a bullet in you right then and there." He pulled a gun out from behind him, placing it on the tea table. "You told me to give it to my sister not knowing it was your drugs that killed her!"

"People die everyday, I don't force them to take the things they do."

"Don't play coy with me!" he yelled. "You don't know how long I've waited for this day. You destroyed my family. She was doing so well, and then you had to tempt her with your new shit. They were so fucking strong, she lost it. You fucking killed her!"

"Your family destroyed itself. Don't blame me because your sister lacked self-control! Would you threaten McDonald's because you ate their food and got high blood pressure? Now please, get out of my fucking face, you little prick." My head felt as though it was going to explode.

"I thought you'd say that. You have no fucking shame," he hissed, pulling out the same syringe Aviela had used. "I wonder how much fucking self-control you'll have left. By the time I'm done, you'll be begging for it."

Again I pulled on the cuffs; they were weaker. Five days of pulling had started to wear them out. But before I could do anything, he held my arm down.

"Think wisely, Nelson," I said. "I will break free and—"

"Shut up!" His fist connected with my cheek. "You're full of nothing but hot fucking air."

"Don't."

But he didn't listen. Once again, the needle found its way into my vein, and once again I felt euphoria. Biting my lip, I tried to ignore the colors in my eyes, the pleasure flowing through my body.

He pulled my hair back, smiling only an inch from my face. "What was it that you called my sister, a crack-whore?"

He stroked the side of my face with his gun as if I were his pet, and even brushed back my hair with his other hand. "How do you feel?"

Throwing my head forward, I smashed it against his nose.

"FUCK!" he screamed, holding onto his nose. The best thing about being so fucking high was that nothing hurt and I felt invincible. So even when I should have stopped as the cuff dug into my skin, I pulled hard against them and for the first time in five days I managed to free my wrist. I wish I could have said the same for my ankles.

He turned as blood dripped down his nose, but before he could point his gun in my direction, I grabbed the fork on the table and stabbed him as hard as I could. I thrust the fork so hard into his arm that the only reason it stopped was because it hit bone. He dropped the gun, reached over and clawed at my hands trying in vain to pull the fork out; a feat I was sure his scrawny ass would never accomplish.

"You little bitch!" He reached for my hair again, but I pulled the fork from his arm, causing him to scream before I stabbed him in the shoulder. This time, I didn't linger in one place too long. I stabbed him over and over, and his blood splattered across my face until his knees buckled, forcing him to kneel before me. He held onto his neck, trying to stop the river of blood that was soaking his shirt.

"You should have walked away!" Pulling the fork out one last time, I drove it into his throat. "You should have never fucking crossed me, bitch. Scream and you'll bleed out faster."

Pushing him out of my face, he fell onto the floor. He looked like a fish out of water, trying to breathe, yet drowning in his own blood. I had no idea how much time I had. Aviela came to me every night to read, smack, or insult me, depending on how she was feeling.

"Keys," I hissed, pointing down at my ankles. He wasn't dead yet, the least he could do was be helpful. But he didn't move; his eyes slowly began to turn into his skull.

Well he's useless.

I had no other choice but to use the bloody fork. Bending to the chains at my feet, I tried to focus, all too aware of the clock ticking behind me.

"Focus, Mel. Focus." It didn't help. The drugs burned in my veins. What was worse was the voice in the back of my mind. I wanted to give into the false sense of peace they provided. I wanted to be on a different plane with Liam and Ethan again. I was fucked in every sense of the word, but I couldn't focus on that now.

"Finally." Pulling off the chains around my feet, I tried to stand, but my legs buckled under my own weight. Grabbing hold of the end of the table, I wobbled over to Nelson. I took the gun right next to his head and kneeled next to him, pressing it into his eye.

"Where is she?"

He didn't get a chance to reply before the door opened. "Shit, Cod—"

Before he could even get the words out, I fired, signaling a parade of alarms to sound throughout the house.

"You…re…ne…ver…get…ting…out…" Nelson sneered as the blood poured from his ears.

"Tell your sister I said hello." I thrust the gun into his eye before pulling the trigger.

Step one: Call Liam.
Step two: Kill Aviela.

Liam

We fucked up. Mel and I had come to trust the people that surrounded us. We'd gotten used to them, and in a way, we *cared* for them as though they were our own family. But they weren't. The truth was, they were broken China that we'd found, hot glued together, and still tried to use. No matter how hard we tried, and no matter how much glue we used, it would never change the fact that they were cracked; broken plates would never be reliable. A broken cup still leaked.

We had trusted Adriana. *I* had trusted Adriana. Yet here I was, standing on platform B of the Ogilvie transportation center, waiting for Judas. My hand trembled with rage, wanting nothing more than to rip her apart. For five days she had watched us, watched me and my son suffer in agony; she probably laughed her ugly fucking head off.

"Boss, she's coming your way," Monte spoke in my ear. When I turned towards the stairs there she was, blonde wig, giant glasses and all.

When she saw me, she tried to turn, but Monte was already waiting behind her. Pulling off her wig, she turned to me, sighing deeply as she made her final free walk towards me.

"I've been waiting for you to find out," she whispered, keeping her head down.

"Where is she?"

"I don't know."

"What does Aviela want?"

"To save her from Ivan. Lia—"

Grabbing her arm, I pulled her closer to me. "Do not say my name. I want to snap your fucking neck right now. Was Antonio betraying us too, or were you lying to everyone?"

"No. Antonio would have never—"

"And yet you did." She winced as I squeezed. "Who is Ivan?"

"He's demented, a psychopath."

"So are we! The only reason you're still alive is because Melody would want to kill you herself."

"I've suffered," she whispered. "I did this to protect her. Aviela may be insane but she knows how to protect her! She's been doing it for years. She loves—"

"Do you hear yourself?" How had we been so blind to who she really was? "Make contact now."

The moment I let go, she wiped the tears falling from her eyes. It only served to anger me even more. How dare she cry!

"Adriana, do not test my patience."

"After taking Melody, Aviela sent me this." She threw her phone at me.

If she had this, why did she bother coming?

"She calls every Thursday at 12:01am. Answer only on the third ring. Tell Mel I'm so sorry."

I didn't even have time to blink. She threw herself off the platform, and her body disappeared as the train swept it down the tunnel, screeching as it tried to stop.

"Fuck."

Thirty-Six

"Look like the innocent flower, but be the serpent under it."
~ William Shakespeare

Olivia

There were certain guidelines that all politicians and their families followed. It only had three basic rules:

First: at some point there will be a chance to get ahead. Take it and never look back.

Second: people will talk, make sure you control what they talk about.

Third: always be willing to cut off the head of your enemies, especially when they're on their knees.

"Neal," I whispered, walking up behind him.

He didn't look at me, he didn't even speak. He just drank, as he stared at the sun as it set over the tree line in his brother's office.

"Adriana committed suicide. Liam went to see her, and she just jumped. No one knows who she is though, so she only got a few minutes of air time before they went back to covering Saint Melody—"

"Olivia, our sister-in-law was kidnapped," Neal said. "You can hold your vitriol for when she comes back."

"Neal, the shit has already hit the fan and Liam is too blind to see it." When would he start being the man I knew he was? "They are calling in the fucking FBI. In a few hours, some of the baddest Italian bosses are meeting to bring down this family. What were you saying about Roy? He's not paying full price anymore? Neal, step up. If not for me, then for Liam. He needs you to have his back. We don't know who to trust, but we're family, and until Mel gets back, we can't just wait to be moved around like chess pieces. Get in the chair and lead, or we will be pushed off the cliff."

I could see it in his eyes: that willingness to die for his brother. But there was also that hunger to lead, to be the Ceann Na Conairte.

"How did you know about the meeting?"

"Nobody pays any attention to Malibu Barbie," I said, sitting on the desk. "The question is, what are you going to do?"

He eyed me carefully.

"Neal."

"I'll let him deal with that. The very first thing we need to worry about is keeping Roy and the rest of the small fish in line. The election is in a few days. How's your father doing in the polls?"

And just like that, he was a whole different person.

"His win will cast a small shadow on Melody. We're thinking if she isn't found by then, we will make an announcement."

"Hopefully, she'll be back by then. This much attention on the family isn't good."

"Hopefully." Or not. "Do you have a distraction in mind?"

He sat down, relaxing into *his* chair. "No. But I'm forming one."

"Well," I jumped off the desk, "I'll leave you to your thoughts. If you need me, I'm going to go spend time with Ethan."

"How is he?"

"Perfect in every way. He doesn't know anything is wrong, and I'm going to make sure he doesn't miss any maternal love."

He kissed my palm. "Don't get too attached, baby. Liam's going to keep him all to himself, and when Mel gets back, I wouldn't be surprised if they took off for a while after all this shit."

No. No one was taking Ethan from me. He was happy and I was going to make sure he stayed that way.

"Of course. Now get to work. I'm serious. I'm sure we're bleeding money. At least this is one thing Liam will be happy to get off his plate." Kissing his cheek, I left him. Stepping out of the office, I called the only person I knew would take the bait…after all, he'd taken it once before.

"Hello, Officer Scooter speaking."

"Liam Callahan killed his wife."

"I'm sorry, what? Hello? How did you know? Hello? Please, repeat that?"

Hanging up, I pulled the sim card out of the phone before snapping it in half. I walked into the blue and green nursery, and there he was, in his little white crib reaching up for the star mobile.

"There's my boy. Who woke you up, huh?"

He spit up bubbles, as he looked up at me. It was amazing how much love was in his tiny body. Lifting him into my arms, I found myself drifting towards the window. Liam had been so paranoid he had placed bars on it.

"Your daddy is crazy. But don't worry, he's going to go away for a while, I promise."

Neal was going to be Ceann Na Conairte.

My father was going to be president.

And I would take care of him.

Of all of them.

Thirty-Seven

"Deserves it! I daresay he does. Many that live deserve death. And some that die deserve life."
~J.R.R. Tolkien

Scooter

I didn't understand why everyone was so damn scared. We got him. We fuck'en got him. I knew something wasn't right. The man was hiding something and now I knew what it was. He was a bigger monster than I thought. I knew he was behind countless murders, but to kill his own fucking wife?

"It's not enough," The Captain said. I threw the folder on his desk, the document I had spent hours building.

"Sir—"

"It ain't enough, Scooter."

"Bullshit!"

"Officer…"

"No! I'm tired of this shit. Everyone is so fucking scared of these assholes that they turn a blind eye." Pulling off my badge, I threw it onto his desk. "Take it. Are you in their pockets too? Or are you like the rest of these moral-lacking pieces of shit scattered in this city?"

He rose from his chair so quickly it crashed into the blinds behind him. "Have you lost your damn mind? Do you hear yourself? I have half a mind to kick you off this force anyway."

"Go ahead! It ain't like we do shit. I just told you two of his previous girlfriends ended up dead. Natasha Briar's body was found naked in a ditch. Now his wife is missing and the man has been hiding something from day one! We got a call, a recorded call saying Liam Callahan killed his wife."

"Scooter, all you have is circumstantial evidence."

"Since when did we fucking need more? We've been trying for years to get this fucker and now here's our chance. Be the man this city needs. Step up, for the love of God. Make those bastards pay!" He looked at me before looking at the folder on his desk. Folding his arms over his chest, he shook his head and turned back to the window.

"Sir."

"Get some rest, Scooter. We go after him in the morning. I'll get the warrant. It's going to take a while to find a judge that will willingly get in on this."

I wanted to go now, but I knew he was right. The last judge that spoke out against the Callahans ended up hanging from a bridge. Although, once again, no one could pin it on them.

"This is right, Captain. We're doin' the right thing. I know it."

He didn't look at me. "Be here by 7:00 a.m. Go home, kiss your wife, and prepare yourself."

He made it seem as if we were going to a war, an all-out battle. But I had studied the Callahans for years. They were all about their public image; they wouldn't do anything that would cause them to look anything less than perfect. They worked in the shadows and now they were about to meet the sun. Walking out of his office, I didn't bother making eye contact with anyone.

That didn't stop my partner from coming up to me. "What was that about?" Beau asked, grabbing the file off his desk.

I wanted to trust him, but I didn't know if I could. "Nothing, the boss man was just laying one into me again for talking to the Callahans."

"I told you." He sighed. "Just keep your head up, okay? Don't let it get to you."

"Yea, thanks. I'm going to head out." I didn't wait. Grabbing my keys, I left the station as more officers came in. Everyone had been working around the clock to find Mrs. Callahan. It felt like there were more people searching for her than there were looking for the President's killer. If she had only listened to me. I had thought she was in on it, in whatever operation they had going. But she was nothing but another victim. So many casualties, all so they could make money—blood money. The moment I sat in my pickup, my phone rang and I already knew who it was.

"Scooter."

"Hey," she whispered, "are you coming home soon?"

Sighing, I brushed my hair back, staring at the phone in my hand. "I'm sorry, the Captain's making us work late on the Callahan case. I'm going to sleep at the station if I get a chance. It's crazy here."

"Yeah, of course. I'm just heading to bed. I just wanted to make sure. I love you."

"Yeah, goodnight. Lock the door," I replied before hanging up. I sat there for a moment then threw the phone against the dashboard.

"Fuck!" Even knowing I was wrong, I couldn't stop myself. I still drove to Englewood to see her.

The city was bad, but there was no place that was worse than Englewood. The moment I crossed the bridge, all I could see were run-down apartments with boarded windows and stripped cars. If you left your car for too long, you wouldn't be able to find it when you needed to. I parked in front the liquor store before walking down to her apartment with my head held high. The men sitting on the stoops didn't bother with me. They knew I was a cop, but they also knew I had grown up here.

Apartment B-24. My childhood home, and even though my mother was gone, I couldn't just let it go.

"Coming, baby!" a voice yelled through the door after I knocked.

When she opened it, her red hair was dripping from the shower she must have just taken. She smiled at me. "Well, look who it is."

"Do you have a client tonight?"

"I thought you got me the place so I ain't have to work so much."

"Good, cuz I feel like celebrating. I'm finally taking those fuckers down."

Her eyes widened as she opened the door from me. "Then let's celebrate, baby."

Part of me felt bad, but that was eclipsed by the thought of getting Callahan.

Finally.

Thirty-Eight

"Freedom for the wolves has often meant death to the sheep."
~Isaiah Berlin

Liam

I needed to see my son. I hated being away from him for so long. It had only been two hours, but a lot can happen in that short amount of time…like your wife could be kidnapped from her hospital room. I had to make it fucking clear that this was not the time for people to be plotting against me in Italian restaurants. In fact, there was never a fucking time for that shit. Declan opened the door for me and the wind blew harshly around us. I knew he was ready to back me up, but I neither needed nor wanted him to.

"Declan, wait out back in case someone decides to run," I told him before walking in.

Just as I thought; the place was packed, and when I entered the hostess froze. She must have been the one who answered the phone earlier. Without a word, she pointed to the double doors that led to the kitchen.

"Clear this place out, now," I said. She gave a quick nod as she followed me.

Some of them seemed to get it, and abandoned their meals and threw their bills onto their tables before exiting.

"Excuse me, you can't be in here, Sir," a young boy yelled, lifting his hands from the dishwater. The chef came over quickly, smacking him over the head and nodding towards the last pair of double doors. On the ground was a man choking for air, spitting up blood. The three men dressed in black suits and shiny shoes jumped at my entrance, guns pointed and ready in my direction.

Lifting my wrist, I glanced at my watch.

"Go ahead," I said. "Pull the trigger."

I could see it in their eyes that they really wanted to kill me but were physically incapable of doing so. The guns fell from their hands and I simply walked over to the empty chair the now dead man had knocked over. Stepping over him and lifting his cards, I leaned back.

"It's a pity," I said. "I was hoping the pancuronium bromide wouldn't have kicked in so soon. I told her to put it in your drinks after an hour, she seemed a bit eager." Throwing a pair of threes into the center of the poker table, I looked into all of their dark eyes. "It's getting harder to find good help these day. Your friend here might have had a bad reaction."

"You poisoned us," one of them said.

"No, I *paralyzed* you so that we can all have this conversation. Who the fuck do you think I am?" Taking a gun from the table, I shot the fucker in the gut. I watched as the blood pooled into his shirt and bled onto his tie before he rolled to the ground.

"I don't fucking understand," I said. "The point of my and Melody's marriage was to stop the bloodshed between my people and yours. Yet, here I am."

The oldest man with his hair slicked back grimaced as much as the drug would allow.

"Stop acting," he said. "We know you killed her. You fucking Irish can't ever be trusted."

Something in me snapped, and before he took a breath, I stood. Taking the chair I had just been sitting in, I broke it against his face. It collapsed as I hammered the broken pieces into his body as he lay helplessly on the floor, screaming but incapable of doing anything else.

"You don't fucking know shit!" I roared down at him, as my blood boiled over. My hands were shaking with so much rage that what was left of the chair slipped out of my grasp. But I didn't stop; I lifted my foot and slammed it into his head.

"You aren't shit," I said. "You are the scum on the bottom of my feet. Not fucking worthy to wipe my ass. How fucking dare you accuse me!"

CRACK.

His face tore open and I could see bits of his brain pouring out. Wiping the blood off my face, I turned to the two sitting at the table. The man I shot was still taking deep breaths while the other stared wide-eyed at the old man, trying his best take in what just happened.

"You all disgust me. You came to my wedding, promised loyalty to my wife, and by relation to me as well. Yet, here you are, like roaches in a dark room plotting against me. You all hurt me, and when I hurt, so does everyone else."

"Callahan, what were we supposed to think?" one of them asked.

"You aren't supposed to think!" Grabbing him by his neck, I glared into his eyes. "*I* fucking think. *Melody* fucking thinks, you don't."

"I—"

"You're lucky I've already shot this one." I pointed to the bleeding man in his chair. "Which means you get to live. You are going to be my little messenger. After the drugs wear off, you're going to tell every last fucking man, woman and child what happened here. Until I am dead—and only when I'm dead—am I out of this game. Until then, I fucking *own* you. Are we clear?"

His face was void of all emotion, but he nodded. Taking the gun, I held it at his kneecap before pulling the trigger.

He wouldn't feel it that much, but it would hurt like a bitch in a few hours.

"I said, *am I clear?*"

"Yes!" he hissed.

"Good." Patting his head, I walked over to the bleeding man and I thought about ending him quickly but decided against it. Pushing his chair back, I stared at him as he lay on his back gasping for air but the holes in his lungs kept them from inflating.

"New shoes," I said to him before putting a hole in both of them and dropping the gun by his face. "Never mind."

Fixing my tie and suit, I walked out the back door where Declan was leaning in the alleyway smoking while the snow fell around him. He looked me up and down slowly before shaking his head.

"Clean up crew?" he asked.

Nodding, I pulled out my phone. "Is the camera up in Ethan's room?"

"Yea. Just put in the code."

Seeing him made me relax. Not much, but enough that I felt as though I could breathe. All I wanted was to be with him now. Seeing Olivia rock him back and forth didn't sit right with me. Mel would be pissed if she saw any other woman—especially Olivia—holding Ethan for so long.

Mel, where the fuck are you?

"Liam, it's 11:30 p.m."

Which meant thirty-one minutes until Aviela called, and that was the last fucking time I was doing anything on that bitch's time.

Staring as Olivia kissed Ethan's head, I pushed hard against my temples and sat back into the seat.

"Take me home."

Melody

Holding my breath, I waited until I heard the wooden floors creek louder and louder as he came towards the bed. All I could see were his feet. I cradled the gun to my chest knowing that I had to move fast. The second he looked out the barred window, I slid out slowly, shooting him in right through the heart. He buckled and I didn't waste any time. I grabbed his neck and twisted.

Stripping him of his guns, two grenades, and knife, I placed them into my jeans before rushing towards the phone.

"That bitch," I whispered. She had cut all the lines.

I couldn't wait. Running into the hallway, I didn't bother hiding. I knew she had cameras everywhere. She already knew where I was, and the only chance I had was to keep moving, the only problem was I had no clue where the fuck I was going.

"There! *Ecco! Eccola*," was all I heard before bullets came flying towards me, shattering a flower vase, art and furniture.

Damn it.

"I give up!" I yelled as I dropping my gun. "*Mi arrendo!*"

"*Vieni fuori*. Come out!"

Doing as they asked, I came out and showed them my hands. Their eyes widened at the grenades in my left.

"*Arrivederci,* motherfuckers!" I yelled as I threw them both as far as I could. One of them got stuck in the chandelier and I dove for cover. As my body hit the ground and rolled, I managed to grab my gun and hide behind the wall.

Smoke flooded the halls as though a volcano had erupted. Flickers of flames ignited throughout the house as I picked myself up off the ground. I coughed as my nose and lungs burned. Spitting out the blood in my mouth, I walked towards the moans.

"Ahh…" a cry came from my left. I walked over to him. If he was coherent enough to moan in pain, he was cognizant enough to answer me.

"Tell me where is she and I end your pain now." I held the gun directly over his only good eye.

"*Si cazzo cagna.*"

"Wrong answer," I said before putting him down like the dog he had so beautifully called me.

Walking down the hall, I held my stomach only to feel the heat of my own blood.

Damn it. My stitches were torn.

I knew it was only a matter of time before it happened, but I was at least hoping that I would see Aviela first. Taking a piece of the wood, I held it over the small flickers of flames in the rubble until it lit up like a torch. As I walked, I ran it over the walls, igniting the wallpaper as I moved further down the hall. This place was going to burn.

I soon found myself in the grand entrance, the large oak double doors that led outside the mansion loomed before me. I dropped the torch. The door slammed shut, trapping me inside as the flames continued to spread. I had never been to hell, but as I watched the fire creep over paintings and up the walls, I was sure that this was pretty close.

"Mel bear, where do you think you're going?" I could hear her voice, but I could barely see her as she walked into the foyer.

With a gun in one hand, and a knife in the other, I stalked down the grand staircase, carefully and slowly, as the broken marble floors rubbed against my bare feet.

"AVIELA!"

I searched, but she was like a ghost moving from one side to another before I could focus in on her. It was like she wasn't bothered by the fire, or anything at all, she was just toying with me. I didn't stop walking until I stood in the middle of the foyer.

"AVIELA!"

I wasn't going to stop screaming. I was going to keep yelling until I woke the fucking dead. I hoped her house burned; I hoped she burned with it. I wouldn't stop until one of us was in the ground.

"Mother!"

Hearing something behind me, I turned, and there she stood, dressed in a white, but covered in smoke and ash, her hair and eyes just as wild as mine. She held a gun to my face.

"You really know how to piss a mother off," she said throwing her gun to the ground.

Pulling back the safety, I raised the gun and tried to ignore the spotting in my vision. She stared at me emotionlessly, almost as though she was unsure of where she was. It was borderline insane how dead she already looked.

"Really, a gun? That's how you're going to do this? Where's your spine, sweetheart? Did your father make you fear a fight? He was always such a pussy—"

I pulled the trigger. I didn't want to stop pulling, but one bullet in her arm was more than enough to prove my point. She stumbled back and grabbed on to her arm.

"I was going to shoot you in the head but I still need to figure out who Ivan is," I told her, walking closer.

She turned, throwing a pieces of broken marble, dust, and glass into my face before sweeping me off my feet.

"You ungrateful little bitch. *Io sono tua madre!*" she roared kicking, me over and over again. "*Tua madre!*"

Her fist connected with my face as the gun was ripped from my hands. Grabbing her foot, I twisted and brought her down, fighting until I was on top of her. "How many times do I have to tell you? Just because you carried me in your womb does not mean you are my mother!"

With the little space between us, she pulled her fist back and punched me square in the nose before kicking me off of her. Rolling closer to the flames, I spit out the fresh blood in my mouth before trying to get up. My eyes locked onto the gun as I stood.

"I didn't want to kill you, Mel. I really didn't."

"Cut your bullshit, Aviela. You want to fight me, then do it."

Circling the gun and each other, she just shook her head. I jumped at her, but she grabbed my arm and flipped me onto the ground.

"Ah…" I held back a scream, trying in vain to push down the pain.

I got back on my feet and kicked the back of her legs, bringing her to her knees. She retaliated by kicking and punching, even with her blood flowing from her arm to stain her once pure white dress. With each hit I felt myself stumbling backwards, trying to block her until my body was pressed up against one of burning walls. Its heat seared into my back.

She raised her fist and brought it to my face, this time I ducked and her hand got stuck into the wall of the green. Using that to my advantage, I punched her in her stomach, knocking the wind out of her and driving her backwards.

"Who is Ivan, Aviela?"

Wiping her lips didn't stop the blood, it only stained her other sleeve.

"Someone you and I can't touch! I'm trying to save you! You cannot go back!"

"You thought I couldn't touch you, and yet, here we are."

"I never thought that."

She grabbed my fallen knife, and thrust it towards my head. Dropping down, she came towards me and kicked me once in stomach before taking a fistful of my hair.

"You strong-headed little fool. You can burn down my house, you can kill my men, but you cannot take down my father. No one can take down my father because everyone works for him, sweetheart."

"Who is *everyone*?"

"You never give up, do you?" she asked with the knife at my neck. "When will you get it? You are me. We fight the same, we bleed the same. I know Father, and I know you. I've been watching you for years. He will destroy everything, and this is your chance to escape. I'm saving you. So run Melody, and never look back."

"Would you still love me if I did, Mommy?" The moment I said that, her arm dropped and I grabbed her, twisting around and pulling her arm back with me. I kept applying pressure until I heard it pop.

She screamed, and grabbed her dislocated arm while fighting against my grip. But I only took hold of her neck and squeezed.

"Well do it," she didn't struggle against my hands. "You don't love me, right? You think I'm crazy, but killing me won't save your son *or* your husband."

"No, but it's a start," I whispered through my own tears as I gripped on tighter and tighter.

Tears poured down the side of her face as I looked down at her.

"Lo...ve...yo...u" Was the last thing she said to me, but I couldn't let go of her neck.

I strangled my mother.

Finally, when my eyes began to burn, and my lungs cried out for air I let go, to see my own hand marks around her neck. Rising, I limped and hobbled towards the doors almost falling outside of them. I managed to make it only feet away from the house before I fell onto gravel walkway outside. I felt so sick, my body shook. Rolling over on to my back, I pulled out the syringe I had saved, wrapped like a jewel in my pocket. Staring at it for a moment, I wished I didn't have to take it again. My motor functions were failing badly; I needed to keep going. I needed to slowly ease off it or I could die outright.

Fighting back the tears, I clenched my fist before I injected half of the syringe's contents into my arm. Then in disgust, I threw the syringe back at the mansion. Finally, when I could move again, I sat up as burnt pieces of papers fluttered outside of the house. But before I could move closer...

BOOM.

An explosion blasted through the mansion and I was thrown back again. With my remaining strength, I grabbed onto one of the papers. The edges were charged, but its contents were still readable enough for me to discern that it was a birth certificate. *Aviela's birth certificate.*

I stared at his name. I knew this name. I had seen it or heard it somewhere…

Shit.

It's just the drugs, I told myself as the tears fell, but I knew that was a lie. Ivan was much higher than I ever thought. We were all just puppets. I needed help. Physically, mentally, I needed fucking help, and I knew that there was only one person I could really trust for that.

Lying there, I wished for Liam.

LIAM

I wanted nothing more than to throw the phone against the wall, but I didn't want to wake Ethan as he slept in my arms. It was 8:30 a.m., and Aviela had never called. I was at my wit's end, but I didn't want him to feel so much anger from me.

"Liam, I can—"

"Olivia, if you come in here one more time, I will bust your face in," I snapped at the woman peeking in from the door. "I don't need sleep. Goodnight." She had been like a hawk ever since I came home.

Her eyes narrowed in on me. "I was trying to help, Liam. I didn't want you to be too overwhelmed. Goodnight."

"Goodnight, Olivia" Standing up, I placed Ethan back in his crib. My phone rang.

Shit.

Looking through my pockets, I grabbed it quickly, trying to silence it. The number was blocked. Who the fuck was calling me so early? If I had to kill one more person this week I was going to lose my shit.

"Callahan," I whispered, brushing Ethan's head.

There was no reply, just a deep intake of breath, and for some reason my heart jumped. I fucking dared to hope. I opened my mouth but I couldn't even form a fucking sentence.

"Wife?"

There was a dry sob on the other end before I heard her voice. "Hello, husband."

I felt my knees go weak at the sound of her voice. From head to toe my body shook.

"Love, where are you? Are you alright? Aviela—"

"Liam, I'm fine."

"You're lying. What is going on?"

"Liam, I can't come home," she cried, almost sobbed into the phone.

"Aviela..."

"Is dead. I checked. She's dead, Liam. Adriana..."

"Killed herself."

Running my hands through my hair, I backed away from Ethan's crib and walked over to the window. "Melody, what the fuck is going on? Tell me where you are. I'm coming—"

"I can't. I'm not right. I need to fix myself. I can't...I just can't..."

"I'll fix you! You'll fix me. That's how this works! What have they done to you? Melody, please, just talk to me. Tell me what's going on. Tell me where to find you."

"Liam..."

"If you think for a bloody second that I would ever let you go through any of this alone, you've lost your mind. I will find you, I will bring you home, and I will fix you, do you hear me? Because I need you to fix me too."

She didn't speak. There was nothing but her breath.

"Fuck, Melody! Answer me. Listen to me."

"Can I hear him? I need to hear him again."

"No," I snapped, pinching the bridge of my nose. "You can hear him when I bring you back home."

"Liam, I swear to you, I will always come back to you. I love you. I need you. You are home to me. Ethan and you are my only family, the only people I would die for. You are it. You are everything. I need a moment. I can't come back like this, please don't make me come back like this. I need to hear him, I'm begging you."

She sounded like she was in serious in pain…dying almost.

"I will come after you," I told her, pulled the phone away from my ear in order to breathe. I walked over to Ethan and placed the phone right next to his ear.

If she honestly thought I was just going to let her go, she was fucking crazy. Her mother had truly fucked with her mind. Listening to her coo at Ethan, my heart burned through my chest. What could make her not want to come home? What was going on?

"Mommy will never ever abandon you, I swear. I love you, my sweet baby. I love you so much."

I pulled the phone from his ear and spoke into the receiver. "If you truly love us, come home. Let me bring you home."

"If I came home, I would only hurt you and him. I need to fix me," she whispered. "I love you so much."

"I love you t—" My voice broke. "Melody, don't do this."

"I…" she tried to say. "Liam, Ivan is a code name for someone in the government. I saw his name on the guest list for Senator Colemen. I think it is Avian Doers."

That was all I heard before silence rang out on the other end.

"Melody?"
Silence.
"Mel?"
Silence.
"Wife, answer me!"

I didn't want her to be gone. I couldn't handle her being gone. It felt as though my body was too heavy to stay upright on its own, like the world was crushing my lungs. The phone, like everything I held dear to me, slipped out of my hands. When had everything gone so wrong? When had I failed? How could she just leave? What had happen to her?

"Liam."

"WHAT!" I yelled so loudly that Ethan jumped before letting out cries, and part of me wanted to join him. Taking him into my arms, I wrapped myself around his tiny body. "I'm sorry, kiddo," I whispered into his ear.

"Son," My father stepped in, "The police have a warrant out for your arrest. They will be here in thirty minutes. We need—"

"Make sure all our rooms are secured and I'll be out in twenty-five minutes. Send Mother in."

"Liam, you can't be—"

"Goodbye, Father," I said to him, taking a seat in the rocking chair. Staring at the big eyes looking back at me, I tried to think of what I was going to say to my son.

"Your mother and I are starting this parenting thing badly," I told him when the door closed. "But we'll make it up to you, I swear. I hope when you're my age you look back and all you see is us, that we didn't miss anything. Rule number six: sometimes in order to win, you have to lose."

He smiled and for a moment, and it was like he could read my mind. He reached out for me and I kissed his hands as I cradled his little head.

"Don't worry, you'll never learn them all. I think my father made them up as he went." I rocked him until his eyes drifted closed.

He was another thing I didn't want to let go of. Placing him back in his crib, I fixed my suit and brushed my hair just as my mother walked in, fire burning in her eyes.

"Your father says you've lost your mind."

I kissed her cheek. "I don't want Olivia to touch him. Neal either, for that matter. Please, keep him safe until this is over, or I get out, whichever happens first."

She slapped me. "So you *have* lost your mind. Liam, we can call the lawyer, make bail. Just because they arrest you doesn't mean this is over. They still have to prove you're guilty. That's democracy."

"Mom, no judge will give me bail. I will be gone for a while until I prove my innocence. But if it makes you feel better, call the lawyer."

Looking back at Ethan once more, I walked out to find my whole family lining the hall, each of them just as angry as my mother.

"Make sure nothing derails Senator Colemen from becoming President, am I understood?"

"Fuck that!" Neal snapped. "What about you? You can't just walk out there. Have you lost your fucking mind?"

"I second that." Declan walked up, trying to read me. Leaning in, he whispered, "Is there a plan here? You have an endgame, right?"

"Just to proclaim my innocence to whoever will listen," I said. "Don't break anything while I'm gone."

Walking down the hall, every servant came out to watch as well. They poked out of rooms, and even froze on the grand stairs as I walked towards the door. Among them, the little boy I smuggled over was holding onto his mother's dress.

"It wasn't me. I swear, sir. I swear," she cried, holding him closer to her.

BOOM.
BOOM.
BOOM.

"Mr. Liam Callahan, this is the Chicago Police Department, we have a warrant for your arrest in the murder of Melody Nicci Giovanni Callahan."

Opening the door, I walked out into the sea of flashing lights.

Epilogue

"To betray you must first belong."
~ Harold Kim Philby

OLIVIA

The cheers made the stage we stood upon rumble with such force that I had to hold onto Neal. I squinted against the flashing lights in order to see straight.

"Thank you, America!" my father yelled, riling them up even more. "I am proud, honored, and so blessed to be your President. It's been a long and strange journey, but together we will change America for the better. We will make this country—that city on the hill—great once again."

"How much longer is this going to take?" Neal whispered as he leaned into me. I wanted to roll my eyes.

Where did he have to go?

"Neal, the judge denied bail. Your brother is going to spend the next five months in jail before the trial. Right now, this is a win. A bloody good win when we so badly need one, so smile for the damn cameras." Leaning away for him, I took a small step forward, waving and smiling at all the people who came to see us. The Colemens, the first daughter of the fucking President of the United States, we did it.

How big is my crown now?

"I am smiling, dear. But I will not just forget about my brother. That judge needs to go—"

"Can we talk about this later?" Why couldn't he just let it go? Liam wouldn't give two shits if he were arrested. The judge was a hard ass and I loved her for it. She wanted Liam behind bars as much as I did. Now if Evelyn would just let go of Ethan, everything would be perfect.

I would handle that later.

When my father took a step back, I applauded even louder, wrapping my arm around Neal's as we were led backstage where Mina stood, suited up with her head set and clapping like a seal. Everyone around her stopped to take pictures of my father.

"Mr. President."

"POTUS."

My father is the President.

"Olivia, I've got to go," Neal said, pulling away as everyone focused in on my father.

Grabbing him by the arm, I pulled him into the hall, but it was just as full of people as inside. He didn't even blink as he broke free of me before heading over to the elevator.

"Neal," I hissed, stomping over to him.

He shook his head as he waited for the golden doors to open. It was the only place we were going to get a damn moment, so I just bit my lip tapping my heels on the marble until we stepped in.

"I don't want to hear it, Olivia."

"Neal, my father just won the election! And you want to go back into your basement with Declan and Sedric trying to figure out how to save that idiot!"

"OLIVIA!" His hand hovered over my neck as he breathed through his nose and tried to hold himself back.

"Neal, he's not even trying! It's like he *wants* to be in that cell. Tell me when are you going to stop wasting your time, and mine, on a brother who doesn't give a shit!"

He shook his head, and pulled off his red tie before he stepped out of the metal box on the ground floor where his black Mercedes was already waiting for him.

"Neal, please stay, or at least bring Ethan so we can all take photos."

"I'll see you at home, Olivia," he said as Fedel held open the door for him. "But don't forget it was my idiot brother who took your useless father and made him President."

The door shut. Fedel's eyes burned into mine before he got into the driver's seat.

"UGH!" I screamed as his tail lights faded out of the garage. It made me want to take off my Prada pumps and throw them after him.

Just as I was turning around, a black Lincoln came up slowly. Stepping forward, I waited until I could see my reflection in the tinted glass. The door opened, waiting for me to take a seat. Taking a deep breath, I slid in. "So I finally get to meet the face behind the voice."

He turned to me. His graying hair, deep brown eyes and crisp suit all looked so familiar to me. He sat there drinking from his crystal cup, completely relaxed and amused.

"Olivia Colemen Callahan. It's a pleasure to finally meet you." He gave me his hand, but I didn't shake. I just waited.

"The moment Liam was arrested, you popped up. And I think you're the one who got the judge to sign off declining his bail. So, who are you? I've seen your face before...are you a rival boss?"

He smiled, shaking his head and staring out the window. "No, I'm not a rival boss. Or at least not a boss of the Mafia."

"Then who are you?"

Reaching in his pocket, he pulled out a small card and handed it to me.

Avian Doers, director of the FBI.

Shit.

"I want a deal."

"Flip it over, my dear," he said, leaning back.

It felt like it had taken me longer than it should have to flip the business card over with my red nails. But when I did, I froze. He had written his true name on it.

"You're Ivan," I whispered.

"Now, let's talk about a *different* type of deal."

About the Author

J.J. McAvoy was born in Montreal, Canada, and currently studies humanities at Carleton University. As a child, she wrote poetry, where some of her works were published in local newsletters. J.J.'s life passion with literature has always been the role of tragic and anti-hero characters. In her series, *Ruthless People*, she aims to push the boundaries not only with her characters, but with also readers. She is currently working on the final Ruthless People novel, *American Savages*, and hopes the closer to the series will leave everyone jaws on the floor.

http://iamjjmcavoy.com/

Acknowledgements

To the army of people who helped make this book possible: Natanya, my agent, Amber and Nicolette, my editors, and the Ruthless People fans who have been with me from the very beginning and have supported me through hell and high water, thank you all so much. When I say this book could not have been written without you all, I truly mean it. It has been an absolute roller coaster of emotions since I started this journey with you all, I would not trade it for the world.

Printed in Great Britain
by Amazon